FERGUS LAMONT

Robin Jenkins was born in Cambuslang in 1912 and spent his childhood in Lanarkshire. He was educated at Hamilton Academy and Glasgow University, graduating in 1935 with an honours degree in English. He married in 1937 and worked as a school teacher in Glasgow and Dunoon for a number of years. He has three children. His first novel, *So Gaily Sings the Lark*, was published in 1950 and more than twenty other books of fiction have followed, including a collection of short stories, *A Far Cry from Bowmore* (1973). *The Cone Gatherers* (1955) received the Frederick Niven Award in 1956, and *Guests of War* (1956), and *The Changeling* (1958), were highly praised by many critics.

Robin Jenkins left Scotland for Afghanistan in 1957, teaching for three years in Kabul. From then until his retirement in 1968 he lived abroad, working for the British Institute in Barcelona and teaching in Sabah (North Borneo), in what was once part of colonial Malaysia. Afghanistan and then Malaysia became the settings for six further novels, most notably *Dust on the Paw* (1961), and *The Holy Tree* (1969). Robin Jenkins now lives in Argyll and recent novels, such as the Arts Council Award-winning *Fergus Lamont* (1979), have returned to Scottish settings.

Robin Jenkins

FERGUS LAMONT

Introduced by Bob Tait

CANONGATE
CLASSICS
32

First published in 1954 by Eyre and Spottis-
woode. This edition published as a Canongate
Classic in 1990 by Canongate Publishing Ltd, 16
Frederick Street, Edinburgh EH2 2HB.
Copyright the estate of J. D. Scott. Introduction
copyright Christopher Harvie.

The publishers gratefully acknowledge general subsidy from the Scottish Arts Council
towards the Canongate Classics series and a spe-
cific grant towards the publication of this title.

Set in 10pt Plantin by Hewer Text Composi-
tion Services, Edinburgh. Printed and bound in
Denmark by Nørhaven Rotation.

Canongate Classics
Series Editor: Roderick Watson
Editorial Board: Tom Crawford, J. B. Pick

British Library Cataloguing in Publication Data
is available on request.

ISBN 0-86241-311-7

Introduction

In *Fergus Lamont* Robin Jenkins is at his sharpest on themes that have long absorbed him: ambition, delusion, mission, fraudulence, snobbery, goodness and cruelty. His great creative stroke in this novel, first published in 1979, is to filter these themes through the vision of a central character and narrator who is generally preposterous, often repellent and probably crazed. The cruelties, divisions and absurdities of the wider social and moral landscape are ironically heightened by being seen through Fergus Lamont's reflections and his mad redemptive mission. The result is an extraordinary novel, comic and serious, teasing and painful.

Since the narrator is, to an extent, an unreliable oddball, it would be as well to bear in mind one of Robin Jenkins's central purposes as a writer. In 1955 Jenkins wrote an essay called 'Novelist in Scotland' in which he said this about the Scots and the writer's task: 'We have been a long time in acquiring our peculiarities: in spite of ourselves, they are profound, vigorous, and important; and it is the duty of the Scottish novelist to portray them.'

There is a strong, even stern sense of that duty to be clear-eyed throughout Jenkins's work. It is all the more striking, therefore, that Jenkins chooses to register so many of our 'peculiarities' by way of Fergus's squint gaze: a very odd viewpoint indeed. But that central purpose which Jenkins declared in 1955 has remained constant. Indeed, he achieves it to a masterful degree in *Fergus Lamont* by drawing on other qualities which he called for in that same essay. We should, he said, admit the superficial greyness of Scotland and put it boldly in the picture. We should then bring to that setting 'comic bravado', 'bursts of devastating self-criticism', 'sardonic' and 'irreverent' humour, and 'a resolute sadness that harks back to our old incomparable ballads'. Fergus Lamont's strange, futile life and reflections provide us with these qualities abundantly.

Readers familiar with Jenkins's work will recognise some settings and characters akin to others which have featured in his novels before and since *Fergus Lamont*. But perhaps never before had he hit upon such a startling and comprehensive permutation of these elements.

The principal settings of the novel contrast with each other most strikingly. They highlight the worlds of difference which separate a people forced to share Scotland's none too generous space. These are the working-class districts of Gantock, a town near Glasgow. Within these districts there are keenly appreciated gradations from the squalid to the precariously respectable. A great social gulf separates the poor areas from the douce homes of the burghers of the West End. It is a gulf bridged only shakily, and in the end unsuccessfully, by Fergus's socialist teacher, Limpy Calderwood, and by his protégée, Mary Holmscroft. She is Fergus's early schoolmate whose political crusade on behalf of the people haunts him as he pursues his quest for his own and the people's spiritual salvation.

The working-class and middle-class worlds defy rapprochement, but at least they are locked together by the force of mutual mistrust. The world of the gentry, to which Fergus aspires, seems by comparison almost an extra-planetary zone from which rarefied representatives occasionally condescend to make inspirational appearances on earth. The lands and houses of the gentry, not very distant geographically from the Gantocks of this world, conceal lives more mysterious and remote from the rest of Scotland than the Outer Hebrides.

It is exactly appropriate that the deeply fraudulent Betty T. Shields, whom Fergus marries for status rather than money, should have conned her way into upper-class circles as a hugely popular writer of inspirational fiction for the masses. In this way she is a great asset to the ruling class, especially in wartime, just as she serves individual members of it in bed.

Even Betty's repeated infidelities fail to disabuse Fergus of his pathetic, idealised vision of a patrician class released from material concerns into a kind of state of grace: free to dispense angelic goodwill and benevolence. Jenkins deploys the noted Scottish art of reduction here, for Fergus's imagined noble spirits are at best dimly good-natured and craven, and callous at worst. But Fergus's messianic fever demands that there must be some higher plane on to which he can be elevated and from which he can dispense effortless peace and wisdom for the benefit of the working-class people from whom he has risen. Other-worldliness in some form or other is to Fergus an essential guarantee of both superiority and purity. So, to complete his transformation into a spiritual luminary, Fergus turns to a second kind of remote realm, Oronsay in the Hebrides, there to purge himself like a prophet of old. By the end of a ten-year exile there he fondly imagines that he has cleansed himself of selfishness and learned to love his child-like Kirstie, who dies having failed in every attempt to get through to him that she wants to have his child.

Much of the success of the novel lies in its power to make us wonder how this strange creature, Fergus, will make out in his succession of environments: working-class Gantock, fee-paying school, the trenches and officers' mess during the First World War, the country house, the croft.

He is strange precisely in the sense that from the age of seven he has set out to re-create himself by developing a dual persona: the aristocratic gentleman poet, and the redeeming example of courage low-born but triumphant over poverty, trial by battle, female treachery and the struggle for humility. If there is something in him akin to the 'holy fool', it is oddly dressed up in an officer's tunic or tweeds. His concept of his quest is in itself comically incongruous and in his own account of how it unfolds he reveals, unconsciously as it were, many an absurdity. That is part of the delight of the book.

But the story is driven along by other factors as well which condition Fergus's life and our view of him. Two of these are arrestingly bleak. The first is the death of Fergus's mother when he is seven years old and the last-ing significance of that death. The second develops more gradually. As Fergus the narrator, in his seventies, looks back over a period spanning two world wars, he partially comes to recognise his failure to inspire hope, courage and reconciliation. Indeed he begins to see that his quest has separated him from others. More, it has led to him reject-ing others as much as his mother was once rejected. Yet he is still a snob (repelled by the sight of a once beautiful girlfriend), and his reported attempt to reconcile himself with Gantock is deeply equivocal. This failure to come to terms with himself is poignant.

Fergus's fate, and the flawed self-consciousness which goes with it, turns on the nature of his mother's death. Only twenty-six when she drowned herself, she was beautiful and wayward, having lived with a sick old man for four years before returning briefly to John Lamont. After her death Fergus discovers that he may be the bastard son of an earl's son. John Lamont had been willing enough to accept her back as he has been happy to treat Fergus as his own. But these two key reconciliations are not to be. Fergus's mother finds it hard to be caged in Gantock. When her judgmental father rejects a gesture of reconciliation from her, she makes her conclusive escape.

The bewildered and appalled little boy pledges himself to fulfil the destiny which his mother has dared to leave him as his inheritance. He adopts as his dress the only other thing she bequeaths him: a kilt, agonisingly out of place in Lomond Street. It declares his distinctiveness defiantly: he begins to set himself apart, just like his mother before him.

With Isobel Murray, I have argued elsewhere that the story can be compared fairly with Dickens's *Great Expectations*. A complementary Scottish comparison can be made with recurring stories on the theme of the 'lad o' pairts': in which some brilliant boy from an impoverished background is encouraged by his teachers and others to rise to some kind of eminence. Variations on this theme are to be found elsewhere in Jenkins's own work, including the relatively early *Happy For The Child* (1953) in which we already find that the price of such intellectually powered ambition is liable to be alienation from family and friends. Another not uncommon feature of this theme is that the 'lad o' pairts' should fulfil quasi-religiously an obligation to do good in the world: as befitting one marked out by grace to be one of the Elect. This serves to account in part for Fergus's almost religious espousal of his mission.

But Jenkins's surpassing ploy here, surely, is to enliven the old theme with such a rich set of twists. Fergus has the apparent grace, i.e. the sheer good luck, to have an aristocratic father as well as brains. Or, at least, and this is enough, he supposes this to be so. The combination inspires him to try to elevate himself and then others by the dazzling power of his example, his reflected glory and noble sentiments. As to proof of his superiority, his modest but sufficiently respected talents as a poet are suitable signs of great worth; but they are not essential. Any mark of distinction, however acquired, will do the trick. For a person so convinced of inner merit, it doesn't matter if he is unscrupulous in achieving heights for the sake of the common good.

So it is that in his efforts to transcend the confines of working-class and middle-class life in Gantock, Fergus Lamont achieves a heartlessness equivalent to the small-mindedness and dogmatism which brought about his mother's death. In one of those moments of partial recognition, right at the beginning, he says: 'Puritanic and parochial Scots, you murdered my young and beautiful mother. As one of you, I must share the blame.' Quite. He transforms but fails to transcend the puritanism and parochialism of the tribe. It infects what he imagines is the antidote.

Jenkins has created a subtly powerful portrait of a man dedicated to potty, ill-conceived objectives. In *A Would-Be Saint* (1978), the central character, Gavin Hamilton, is dedicated to the conversion of others by an exemplary Christian life and by being as little beholden to others as possible. Jenkins pursues the logic of Gavin Hamilton's mission relentlessly, leaving room for little else to fill the character out. In *Fergus Lamont*, by contrast, what we are able to see, beyond the complex and cracked figure of Fergus himself, is an even more intricately flawed culture. Look hard. Enjoy.

Bob Tait

Part One

ONE

Half Scotland sniggered, and the other half scowled, when in letters to the *Scotsman* and the *Glasgow Herald*, I put forward my suggestion that prisoners in Scottish jails be allowed to wear kilts, as their national birthright, if such was their wish. Those sniggerers and scowlers may well snigger more moronically and scowl more impatiently when I now confess that I donned my own first kilt, at the age of seven and a half, not with pride and joy, but with reluctance and anguish; and also that for the rest of my life I never buckled one on without feeling something of the grief and shame with which James IV, unhappy parricide, must have put on his penitential shirt of iron.

Puritanic and parochial Scots, you murdered my young and beautiful mother. As one of you, I must share the blame.

My mother bought the kilt from a second-hand clothes dealer called Lumhat Broon. It had once belonged to a boy whose father was a director of Stewart's of Gantock, the shipbuilding company for which my 'father' (the honourable good-hearted champion quoiter John Lamont, whose name is on my birth certificate) worked as a joiner, and my maternal grandfather, Donald McGilvray, as chief pay-clerk. The tartan was the dress McLeod.

She had seen the kilt in the window, beside the tile hat; but she had not gone into the shop to buy it, she had gone in to avoid Mrs Maitland and Mrs Blanie who were coming along the street. She had been so agitated when asking Lumhat to show us the kilt that I was too worried to object.

In the house, with this yellow and black kilt spread out over her lilac lap, my mother, twenty-six years old, pale-cheeked and red-haired, urged me, with a passion I thought extravagant and unfair, to put it on.

I

I kept muttering dourly: 'They'd a' ca' me a jessie.'

I had seen boys in kilts before, toffs from the villa'd West
End, as remote from us in tenemented Lomond Street as
the whites in South Africa are from the blacks.

Her delicate hand gripped the cameo brooch at her breast,
so tightly that I could see her knuckles turn white.

More than sixty years later that brooch lies before me on
the table, yellowish with age. I think of the peaty water of
Puddock Loch, and shudder.

'You'd look like a prince, Fergie,' she whispered. 'As
you should.'

I considered the consequences of obliging her. My eyes
went skelly with apprehension.

'Jock Dempster wad lift it up,' I groaned.

Suddenly she was in tears again. I could do or say nothing
to comfort her. I didn't know her well. She had been away
too long; and, as I had tried to hint, ever so tactfully, she
was a bit too beautiful, too perfumed, and too haughty for
Lomond Street, and for me.

She had come too unexpectedly. I needed longer than
three days to fit her into my life.

'And if he did you would give him a right good kick
on the shin, wouldn't you? Have you got my red hair for
nothing?'

Too embarrassed to compare our hair, I studied my
boots. As weapons they were formidable, with their tackets.
I had the courage too to use them. But it wouldn't do any
good. Anybody I kicked for laughing would howl with pain
all right, but then everybody else would laugh all the more.
Fergie Lamont in a kilt would be funny, Fergie Lamont in
a kilt in a fury would be funnier still.

The trouble was, though I found her contempt for other
people's opinions of her exciting, I also found it alarming.
That walk with her had been a pleasure and an agony.

Through in the kitchen our canary Rob Roy burst into
song, but only very briefly.

It was my mother who had bought him years ago, and
when she had gone away he had missed her. So my
father had told me; but when I had mentioned it to
Miss Montgomery, my penny-buff teacher, she had been
shocked. 'No, Fergus. Canaries only miss other canaries. If
that. Besides.' She too disapproved of what my mother had

done, and like all the rest wasn't going to tell what it was.

My mother's tears frightened me. I had seen women weeping before, but for reasons easily understood; when someone had died, if the rent couldn't be paid, if a husband had been brutal. These tears of my mother's had some cause more terrible and desolating than death or poverty or cruelty.

'Whit was it you did?' I whispered, once again. 'Why did you go away? Why is everybody so angry?'

Her scent reminded me of the roses in my grandfather's garden. Other boys' mothers smelled of pipeclay, scrubbing brushes, baby's milk, parozone, and black lead. She spoke too in a more ladylike way than any of my teachers. I would have liked very much to be able to brag about her to my friends, but I couldn't, there were too many things to be settled first; and I just couldn't see who was going to settle them.

'Oh, something terrible,' she murmured.

I wasn't sure whether or not she was joking.

'But whit?'

'Some day they'll tell you. But do you know what I want you to do now? I want you to put on this braw kilt and go up the brae with me to see your grandfather.'

I blew out my cheeks in the loudest, most incredulous gasp I could manage.

Once, seated on his knee, I had boldly asked my grandfather where she was and when she was coming back. A tall stern man with a black beard, he had replied in the same calm voice he always used, whether reading bits out of the Bible or discussing his roses. 'She is in hell, Fergus, and no one ever comes back from there.'

I had had a hard job not to grin, because just a few days before one of my best friends, Smout McTavish, had shouted to Miss Cochrane to go to hell. She had already given him two of the tawse for getting his sums wrong, and he had thought that was enough. She had dragged him to the headmaster who had given him two more for swearing. The joke was, Smout was one of the few boys in our district who seldom swore.

Inside his beard my grandfather's mouth had gone as hard as railway lines. 'When he's no' pleased,' Jim Blanie had once whispered, 'your grandfather looks like Goad.'

'I don't think he wants to see you,' I said, cautiously.

'But if you come with me, Fergus, and ask him for me, maybe he will.'

I was sure he wouldn't, but I felt I ought to oblige her.

'Whit will I wear under it?' I asked.

Few of us in Lomond Street wore underpants.

'Soldiers don't wear anything under their kilts.'

I wondered how she knew. But even if it was true, soldiers just had Boers shooting at them, they didn't have Jock Dempster or Rab McIntyre come whooping out of a close to snatch up their kilts and show their bums to lassies.

'I could take my barrow and gether dung.'

She laughed.

'Weel, he said I should. He needs it for his roses.'

'I'm sorry, Fergie. You gether dung if you want to.'

'It's my grandfather wants it, no' me. I've got nae roses.'

She hugged me then, laughing and weeping at the same time.

'Whatever happens, Fergie, wherever I go, I'll always remember my wee kiltie gathering dung for his grandfather's roses.'

'You said you wouldnae go away again.'

'Ah, but you see, Fergie, I thought I could stand it here, as long as I had you. It's only you I've missed. But I don't think I can stand it.'

I knew it was really my father she couldn't stand. (Let me in the meantime call John Lamont that.) Since she had come back, three days ago, she had hardly spoken to him. He had been very quiet too, though once he had shouted at her. In our room-and-kitchen with the lavatory outside on the stairs privacy was never easy. She had slept with me in the room. My father had stood outside the door for a long time, sighing. She had sighed too.

No neighbours had called to say they were glad she was back, not even the Strathglasses or the Kerrs who lived on our landing. Everybody seemed sorry for me, instead of being pleased. My Aunt Bella had seized me by the jersey in the street and demanded that I go and stay with her. I had indignantly refused, though I liked my Uncle Tam and his pigeons. Aunt Bella was the one who, after my grandfather, hated my mother the most.

'If you go away again,' I said, 'take me wi' you.'

She considered it for half a minute, a long time.

'We'll see, Fergie. Let's try on the kilt, shall we?'

'Oh, a' right.'

With a groan I took off my breeks. I placed them where they would be quickly available if I lost my nerve.

Eagerly she wrapt the kilt round me.

To my relief it was too long.

'Kneel,' she said.

'Hae I to pray?'

'I doubt if that would help much, Fergie. Soldiers kneel, you see, to find out what's the right length. The edge should just touch the ground.'

When I knelt the kilt lay in folds on the floor.

'That's easy mended.' She tugged the waist up to my neck almost.

'I can hardly breathe.'

She buckled it there.

'Your jersey will cover it. Look. What a pity you've not got a tweed jacket and a sporran and green stockings.'

'I'm glad I havenae.'

'Don't be silly. You look braw.'

I thought I looked a terrible jessie. They were sure to laugh at me. Except Smout, maybe. He would be too ashamed of the holes in his breeks. To hide them he stood against walls or lampposts or dustbins or even big dogs.

Looking in the mirror, my mother put on her feathered hat, lilac in colour to match her costume. She dabbed scent behind her ears. I liked its smell, but I suspected it was one of the things about her that angered the women of our street. I wished she hadn't put it on, but I would have died rather than beg her not to.

She noticed my anxiety. 'Well, if we're going to be gathering dung we'll need something nice to drown the smell.'

Where had she been, I wondered, miserably, that she hadn't learned there was nothing nasty about the smell of horses' dung, even when it was fresh?

TWO

Because I was nervous and my pintle felt chilly and unharboured, I was no sooner out of the door than I needed to pee. I tried to find out if I could hang on till I reached my grandfather's cottage where there was an inside toilet and it could be done in comfort and safety. I decided that if the circumstances had been ordinary I could have waited, but not if I was likely to be given frights and shocks, because of the kilt and because too of the animosity of neighbours towards my mother.

'No sense in being uncomfortable,' she said coolly. 'We've got plenty of time.'

My grandfather didn't get home from his work till nearly six. It was just past four now.

Because I was myself wearing a garment too bright and splendid for those dark brown walls and grey stone stairs it struck me more forcibly than ever how out of place my mother was. The idea of someone so beautiful and delicate having to use our lavatory seemed to me awful. Twelve people used it. Sometimes the seat was wet.

There is a magic in courage. My mother went down those stairs as if they were of white marble, and stopped outside the lavatory door as if inside was a magnificent room with carpets and chandeliers.

It was snibbed. I sniffed. There was the smell of tobacco smoke. Old Mr Strathglass was inside. He never hurried. I heard him farting.

Shame made my need more urgent. I began to groan.

'We'll try the one below,' said my mother.

I was aghast. Did she not know that in our street, in our tenement, as in all the streets and tenements round about, no trespass was condemned more vociferously than using another landing's lavatory? The one below ours too was Mrs Grier's, the woman I feared most among all our neighbours.

It was open and empty. It stank of piss. The cistern roared. The small window was broken. There was shitty paper on the floor.

'Delightful,' said my mother. 'But in you go. Hold up your kilt.'

She closed the door on me and stood guard outside.

I was in such a panic-stricken hurry I wet the tail of the kilt. When I came out I had another need even more desperate: this was to get away before Mrs Grier or one of her spies discovered what I had done.

Luckily we met no one on the stairs, but when we went through the close to the backcourt there, near our coal cellar door, in the sunshine, among the washing, with their feet in dusty dandelions, were Mrs Grier herself and two of her most frightening cronies, Mrs Leitch and Mrs Lorimer.

Rather than pass that fearsome trio I would gladly have given up the dung-gathering, but my mother took me by the shoulder and marched me right past them.

These were women I had never got to know. I had not been inside their houses. Their children were all grown up. They couldn't have been more than fifty, but to me and my friends they were sinisterly old.

Mrs Leitch was hump-backed, with a twisted nose that made her speech snuffy. Her nickname was Mrs Sneuch-Sneuch.

'Michty-me, Fergie,' she cried, with a snuffly giggle, 'is that the bumbee tartan?'

I nodded politely. I was busy trying to open the coal cellar door.

The second of Mrs Grier's companions was fat Mrs Lorimer. By herself she was amiable and harmless enough, but when showing off to Mrs Grier she could be horrible. Once she had thrown a handful of clothes pegs at Mrs McGuire, and called her a Papish cunt, just for using Mrs Grier's clothes pole.

Now she waddled up to us and spat in my mother's face.

Later in my life I was to see men's guts spilled about their feet and their heads blown off, but those sights did not dismay me, with a sense of unconquerable evil, as much as that big spittle sliding down my mother's cheek.

With a proud smile my mother wiped it off with her handkerchief, which she then flung to the ground. A sparrow, thinking it might be bread, hopped up to take a look at it.

In my misery I wished I was a sparrow, with sparrows for my mother and father and grandfather and neighbours.

At last I had the coal cellar door open. I dragged my barrow out. I was very proud of it, but that afternoon I didn't care if its red and white paint got covered in coal dust. Into it I flung the rusty shovel I used for dung-gathering.

What I was waiting for, in dread, then happened. Slow

and splay-footed, Mrs Grier approached us. She was big-headed and thick-throated, with a hairy mole on her chin: my friends and I called it her devil's spot. She had shaggy grey hair. She wore a red blouse with a hole at the left oxter: grey hairs could be seen.

'Whaur are you gaun wi' the barrow, Fergie son?' she asked. 'The braw barrow your faither made wi' his ain guid honest hands.'

As always, I distrusted her kindness. She was the wolf dressed up as grandmama.

'I'm going to gether dung,' I replied, 'for my grand-faither's roses.'

'Are they rid, your grandfaither's roses?'

'Some are rid. Some are white and yellow.'

'I'm thinking nane are as rid as a face no' a spittle's cast awa' should be wi burning shame.'

At first I thought she meant my own face. Certainly it felt hot and red.

'Bring us some dung, Fergie,' said Mrs Lorimer, 'and we'll chuck it at this shameless whure, your mither.'

'Whure' was a word heard often enough in our district, applied to rainy weather, a marble that stopped short of the hole, a quoit that fell in the wrong place, a horse that hadn't won. Sometimes, with 'wee' in front of it, it was used to denote exasperated affection. But mostly it was a term of abuse. I objected strongly to its being applied to my mother, by a stupid fattie like Mrs Lorimer.

'It's you that's an auld whure,' I yelled, 'a fat auld whure.'

I rushed off with my barrow and almost crashed into a clothes pole.

My mother overtook me in the close. She was panting. It was me she was angry at.

'Don't ever let me hear you say a word like that again. Do you hear?'

'But she spat on you!'

I was to be tormented in nightmares by that spit.

'They're dirt, not worth bothering about.'

I didn't understand. I was more than willing to hate them for what they had done to her, but I couldn't see how they could be dirt if they lived in Lomond Street, in our building in fact. If they had lived, say, in Davidson's Vennel, where the houses were slums, then of course they would be dirt. On Sundays Mrs Grier wore a hat, not such a fancy one as my mother's, but fancy enough. The women of the Vennel wore shawls even on Sundays.

'You shouldn't be living in this horrible place,' said my mother. 'You should be living in a castle.'

I liked the idea of living in a castle, but I couldn't agree that the close was a horrible place. It was washed twice a week. Mrs McNair who lived on the ground floor was very particular. She decorated the stone floor with pipeclayed squiggles. On rainy days I had played happily at marbles or ludo in this close. Mrs McNair didn't allow football.

Through the close lay the street. I could hear the cries of girls playing. Jessie McFadyen was sure to be among them. She was daft enough, and fond enough, to want to feel my kilt. I hoped Peggy Maitland, my cousin, was there too. She would restrain Jessie.

'Well, what are we waiting for?' asked my mother. 'Forward march.'

Her voice was so hoarse it frightened me. So did her eyes. They were like blue glassies. They reminded me of my grandfather's. His went like this when he was talking about boys that swore, men that got drunk, women that had babies but weren't married (like Katie Murdoch up the close next to ours) and, especially, Roman Catholics.

Spitting on my palms, as I had seen workmen do, I grabbed the shafts of my barrow and wheeled it through the close on to the street.

The girls were playing peaver on beds chalked on the pavement right in front of the closemouth. Jessie McFadyen was among them.

They let her play out of kindness. She spoiled every game she took part in. If it was peaver, she hopped on all the wrong squares; if it was skipping ropes she got them fankled round her neck. She was soft in the head. Everybody said it was a pity, for with her long fair hair and big blue eyes she was the prettiest girl in the street. Usually, though, as now, she had a snotter at her nose. She was in my class at school. When Miss Cochrane took us out into the playground to play games, like ring-a-roses, Jessie would take nobody's hand but mine.

First to notice me, she screamed and clapped her hands.

The other girls, including Peggy, were pleased too. They gathered round me.

'Oh, Fergie, you're a real braw wee kiltie!'

'Whaur's your sporran but?'

'And your Glengarry, wi' a feather in it?'

'Are you going to learn to play the bagpipes, Fergie?'

But it was really my mother they were interested in. They kept glancing up at her: Peggy Maitland, especially.

I knew Peggy well. My father paid her a sixpence a week to take me to school in the mornings, and after school to escort me to my Aunt Bella's, where I stayed till my father came home from work. She was saving up to buy a new dress: she had showed it to me in a shop window in Main Street. She was thin, with pimples on her face.

She bent down and hugged me.

'I don't look a jessie, do I?' I muttered in her ear.

'You look like a wee gentleman, Fergie.'

That was far from reassuring.

'Will onybody laugh?'

'Onybody that laughs will get a keeker from me.'

Nor was I reassured by that threat of black eyes.

Since it was summer and sunny and warm, the street was crowded. People liked to come out of their small dull houses. There were women with bare arms at every closemouth and at many window-sills. The usual group of men without jobs chatted at the corner outside Boag's shop, perhaps joking about the notice 'No Credit' in the window. In the roadway some boys were playing football. Among them were Jock Dempster, Smout McTavish, and Rab McIntyre. The ball was a bundle of rags bound with twine. At one end the goalposts were mounds of dung, at the other caps and jackets.

This scene of community at other times would have contented me. Now it filled me with foreboding.

Rab was the first to notice me. 'Oh Christ,' he cried, clapping his hands across his eyes, 'look at wee Fergie.'

It seemed to me he had a cheek to be shocked: his breeks, his father's old ones cut down, were wider than my kilt.

The game stopped. Jock had his bare foot on the ball. He looked round to see what Rab was shouting about. Thirteen years of age, like Peggy he was a pupil of Kidd Street Advanced Division School, where he got the tawse

every day, not just for being stupid at lessons but because
he wasn't ashamed of being stupid. Always in rags himself,
he was inclined to look on neat clean clothes as affectation.
Often, round corners, we rubbed dirt on our jerseys and
rumpled them before asking him to let us join in.

Except for Smout, the others yelled and danced in derision. They waited for Jock to express loud blasphemous
disgust.

I waited too, but at the same time I dourly wheeled my
barrow over to the goalposts of dung and shovelled them in.
Smout, the goalie, was too fascinated by my kilt to try and
stop me. The holes in his breeks hadn't been mended. He
had learned though how to stand, in a twisted cross-legged
way, so that his bare behind wouldn't be seen.

My mother watched from the pavement. Peggy Maitland
stood close beside her. She would have put her arm through
my mother's if my mother had let her. With part of my
mind I heard from down the street a woman's voice shriek-
ing at Peggy. It was her mother ordering her to come away
from mine.

Jock picked up the ball. With it under his oxter, like
an ambassador's hat, he came running up to me. As he
passed he gave Rab a kick in the backside to stop him
chanting 'Kiltie Cauldbum'. When he reached me he did
a very strange thing: he faced my mother and bowed.
Then, blushing, he helped me shovel the dung into my
barrow.

My mother came over. She smiled at Jock.

'You're Jock Dempster, aren't you?' she asked.

He nodded eagerly. I had never seen him so eager.

'Well, Jock, thank you for being kind to Fergus.'

He was so shy and yet so pleased that he picked up a
dollop of dung as if it was a rose. I thought he was going
to offer it to her.

When we moved on, he gazed after us heedless of the
gibes cast at him from every closemouth and window-sill.
He had done what among a graceless people always pro-
vokes angry derision: dressed in rags, he had dared to be
chivalrous.

'The young are more generous,' said my mother. 'There's
still hope for Scotland.'

I wasn't sure what she meant. Besides, I was trying hard

not to hear the terrible things that women were shouting at her.

In time to come Jock was to wear a kilt himself and be killed in it. So were Rab and Smout. Their names are on the Gantock War Memorial.

THREE

At last we came into less familiar streets. Here there was laughter at the expense of my kilt, but it was reasonably good-natured and could be endured. We had, however, still another ordeal to undergo. We had to pass the Catholic chapel.

From the outside it looked almost like a Protestant church. It partly hid itself behind some yew trees. It seemed to know it wasn't wanted. The Catholics had to wait a long time before anybody would sell them land to build it on. My grandfather was one of those who tried to prevent them.

As we passed it I did not this time spit—I had acquired a horror of spitting—but I did mutter aloud the rhyme which was my own secret way of nullifying the Papish magic:

Hail Mary, fu' o' grace,
Stole a penny frae the brace,
Put a ha'penny in its place,
Hail Mary, fu' o' grace.

Rather proud of this incantation, for it had always worked in the past, in that no priest black as a crow had ever kidnapped me, I glanced up to see if my mother was impressed. To my astonishment, I caught her in the act of crossing herself. I was so shocked I stumbled and spilled some dung.

'What's the matter?' she asked.

'Whit did you dae that for?'

'Do what?'

I did it myself, very quickly. I almost expected the dung to turn into roses.

'That,' I muttered.

'Maybe I thought it would help.'

At last I thought I understood. The mystery was solved. She had become a Catholic. That would explain why my grandfather didn't want to see her again, and why Mrs Lorimer spat in her face. Mr Lorimer was an Orangeman. He marched in parades wearing a yellow sash.

I felt hopeful. It seemed to me it couldn't be very hard to change back.

'Are you a Pape?' I asked.

'What a nasty word. If you mean Catholic, say Catholic.'

'Are you a Catholic then?'

'What difference would it make?'

It was hard to be patient with such wilful stupidity. Surely she knew my grandfather didn't like Catholics. In case she had forgotten I explained how when I visited him I had to make sure there were no Catholics, such as Pat McGuire, with me.

She murmured something. It sounded like 'nonsense'. But surely it couldn't have been. Everybody knew that if they were given a chance the Catholics would overrun the whole country, and then, as my grandfather had told me often, no man's soul would be free.

'Your grandfather has no right to set you against Catholics or anybody else.'

She seemed to have forgotten that my grandfather was an important man. As well as running the Sunday school and the Band of Hope, he was an elder of the Auld Kirk, and a town councillor. He knew the Provost, and the Chief Constable, and even the Sheriff.

'You're far too young,' she said.

She halted and put a hand to her side. We were now climbing the long steep brae up to my grandfather's cottage. Behind a barrier of sleepers was the railway line. I put my eye to a hole in a sleeper. The lines glittered in the sun. They were as hard as my grandfather's mouth. I remembered putting a ha'penny on the line in the hope the train would flatten it into a penny; it had been ruined.

Suddenly I noticed three boys. They were trying to catch butterflies. One of them was Jim Blanie. He moved awkwardly. This wasn't because the bank was steep and the grass long and the wild-rose bushes thorny. It was because he had a boil high up on his leg. He always had boils.

I watched him as, cautiously, he crept forward to some gowans. There must have been a butterfly resting on one of them. In my imagination I smelled the grass, felt my wrists and knees smarting from scratches, and was deliciously afraid lest a train or a policeman should come. I admired the butterfly's yellowish wings with the black dots. For a few moments I was a butterfly myself, about to be seized between enormous fingers.

I was both disappointed and relieved when Jim made his pounce and the butterfly rose just in time to escape. I was very happily aware that it was more beautiful twinkling away in the sunshine than it would have been lying crumpled on Jim's sweaty palm.

My mother moved on. I wanted to grumble that I was tired, that I had the barrow to push, that the kilt made my legs feel funny and weak, and that it was no good hurrying for my grandfather wouldn't be home yet and the cottage would be shut up. But I knew that if everybody else was against her, except Jock and Peggy, I would be for her, whatever happened.

Besides, it was now much more pleasant than among the tenements. Sheep bleated at us from one field, cows mooed at us from another, and larks sang down to us from the sky. On the firth a ship sounded its horn. These were all friendly, reassuring sounds. If I turned my head I could see, beyond the blue firth, the hills of Dunbartonshire and Argyll. They cheered me up, perhaps because on Sundays and holidays, when there was not so much smoke, I could see them from the window of the room where I slept.

My grandfather's cottage, called 'Siloam', was one of a row at the side of the road. It had roses in the front garden, but it was the garden at the back I liked best; this looked on to a large green field with whin bushes scattered about like golden sheep. The gate was made of iron and opened with a noise like a corncrake. I hoped my mother realised I should need help to get the barrow up the stone steps. When I turned to look at her she was shaking her head, although I hadn't asked her yet. She was paler than ever: there was sweat on her brow. Slowly I understood that what she was denying or rejecting had nothing to do with helping me with my barrow.

She knew this cottage better than I did. I had been told she used to visit it with me when I was a baby in my pram. My grandfather must have helped her up the steps with the pram.

'Are you coming in?' I asked, after a polite interval.

'Do you think I should, Fergie? I haven't got permission, you see.'

When I brought my friends here, I gave them permission; but this was different. I felt baffled.

A bumble-bee hummed near. Perhaps taking my kilt for a bed of flowers, it seemed to be thinking of landing on it. I knew now why girls were always afraid of things like bees and mice going up their skirts. I shuddered as I thought how painful it would be if my pintle was stung.

'It'll be a' right,' I muttered.

'Will it, Fergie?'

'Aye. You can sit in the gairden at the back. There's a seat there.' I decided not to mention it was made by John Lamont. But perhaps she knew. She was not a stranger. She was somebody returned.

'There'd be no harm in me doing that, would there?'

She came in the gate, and helped me lift the barrow up the steps. I approved of the careful way she did it. No dung was spilled.

I led the way round the house. To my relief the garden looked the same as always. I seemed to have been dreading some ominous change in it. I pointed out the seat to her. Then I couped the dung on to the compost heap. I smacked my hands together, as workmen did when the job was done.

There was, though, ahead of me, another job, a lot harder. I had to persuade my grandfather not to send my mother away. I didn't know yet how I was going to do it, but at least I could tell him she was not a Catholic. It seemed to me no two people had less in common than my grandfather and Mrs Grier. What then could my mother have done to have made them both hate her?

Often, when I couldn't be bothered doing something I didn't want to do or was afraid I couldn't do, I pleaded, with a whimper in my voice, that I was too wee, too young. Now this excuse was no good: there was no one to offer it to. As I flicked a fly off a rose-petal, I felt very sorry for myself.

I was whistling a sad tune as I went over to where my mother was seated, on the seat my father made.

She had taken off her shoes and hat. 'You're a rare wee whistler. What tune's that?'

I could not tell her it was Aunt Bella's favourite. She might have thought I was being disloyal.

(It was Burns's 'Aye waukin' o,' that beautiful, haunting love-song. When Aunt Bella sang it, or 'soothed' it rather, she was not thinking of Uncle Tam, who should have been her 'dearie'; she was thinking of her two dead children.)

On the back of the seat were carved roses. I sat beside her. I followed her example and shut my eyes.

Another ship sounded its horn. The echoes were sonorous and exciting. It was saying goodbye. I felt, obscurely, that it represented trust and interdependence.

'Where's she bound for, do you think?' asked my mother.

'America, maybe.'

'Do you know what I wish, Fergie? I wish you and me were on that ship, sailing away.'

I decided not to mention that I was once on a ship that sailed to Rothesay and back. We ought not to have been talking about ships. We should have been talking about what we were going to say to my grandfather.

But she seemed to want to sleep. Her eyes were still shut. She made little sleepy grunts. Her head kept falling forward. A lock of her hair was loosened.

I kept very still and quiet.

A butterfly twinkled past. I wondered if it was the one Jim Blanie tried to catch. I made a vow never to catch butterflies again. I knew I would not keep it.

I tried hard not to feel impatient or restless or itchy. Pretending I was in school, I folded my arms and pressed my lips tightly together. I scarcely breathed.

After a long time—it was only three minutes really—I decided to go round to the front of the house to see if my grandfather was coming. I slid off the seat, and tiptoed away, as best I could, for the path was made of white chuckies.

I sat on the doorstep, in the shade, with my kilt tucked under in the way I'd seen girls do. The stone was cold on my legs. There was no sign of my grandfather coming up the road. He would be easy to see, for he always dressed in black, except for his collar.

Old Mrs Pollock came slowly down the road, carrying a shopping-bag. She was a neighbour of my grandfather's. She talked to her feet as if they were a dog; they must have been painful or something. I kept very still, for I didn't want her to see me. She would have been sure to

ask me to go down to the shop for her. I felt that I must
be here when my grandfather came.

At last I got tired of watching. When I got back to
my mother she was still sleeping. I felt it was a little bit
unfair.

I had another four spells of sitting on the doorstep, on
the look-out.

Then I saw him. I was not surprised he had his bowler
hat on his head, though the sun was still warm. He did
not approve of men walking in the street bareheaded. The
number of things he did not approve of was very impressive. I counted some of them on my fingers: Catholics,
comics, pubs, theatres, high-heeled shoes, cigarettes; and
on Sundays everything except going to church and Sunday
school. I didn't know what his attitude was to kilts, but I
suspected he disapproved of them, though he was born in
the Hebrides and could speak Gaelic.

I prayed that my mother would not appear before I had
a chance to plead with him on her behalf. I still didn't know
what I was going to say.

Deep in thought, he had his hand on the latch of the gate
before he noticed me. I was now standing up, with my legs
apart, in the way quoiters do to give them good balance.
I felt I needed good balance, even if I was not going to
throw a quoit.

He smiled and frowned at the same time: the smile was
for me, the frown for my kilt.

'Well, Fergus, it's yourself. This is a pleasant surprise.'

Unlike all of us born and brought up in Gantock he spoke
pure English. He said 'well' instead of 'weel' and 'yourself'
instead of 'yoursel'.

I barred his way.

'I brought you some dung.'

'That was very kind of you, Fergus. My leeks will be the
better of it.'

'Look, I've got on a kilt.'

'I've been admiring it. It's not the Lamont tartan, though,
or the McGilvray.'

I took a deep breath. 'My mither bought it for me. She's
back, you ken. Oot o' Lumhat Broon's. She's roon' the
back in the gairden. I think she's asleep.'

I had cast a spell. For the next twenty seconds nothing

in the whole world moved: I had brought everything to a standstill. My grandfather was at the centre of this terrifying immobility. Even his beard did not move in the breeze.

I began to feel I was shrinking. In a minute I'd be smaller than a bee.

'She's come to see you,' I whispered, in a voice suitable to my tininess. 'She's sorry. I think she's come to say she's sorry. If you think she's a Catholic, weel, she's no'.'

He looked gigantic. His face covered the sky. His bowler hat was as big as a tar boiler. His voice was like thunder.

'Come by yourself, Fergus, and you'll always be welcome.'

Gently but irresistibly, he pushed me aside. He unlocked the front door while I gazed on indignantly. I couldn't believe he would go in and shut me out. But he did. When I crept forward and tried the door I found it locked. I listened with my ear to the keyhole, but I heard nothing. I imagined him on his knees on the blue carpet in the living-room, praying. My grandmother in the photograph on the wall smiled down at him. I had been told she too had red hair, like my mother and me.

I had myself knelt on that carpet beside him, pretending to pray. He would be explaining to God why he refused to forgive my mother and welcome her back. I wished he would explain to me.

I was aware that there was something terribly wrong in his rejection of my mother, who was also his daughter. It was a great burden on me. I felt I hadn't enough strength left to go and tell my mother the bad news.

Late that night, while I lay asleep and all the lavatories in the building were empty, with their pans leaking and their cisterns sighing, my mother went down the stairs again, by herself.

In the kitchen John Lamont, hearing her go out so quietly, lay on for another hour or so, telling himself he had no right to follow her. But he became so anxious that he had to go through to see if she had taken her suitcase with her.

She had not. Relieved a little, he thought she must have gone out to walk in the dark empty streets, trying to make up her mind whether she should stay or go away again, this

time for good. Again he felt he had no right to interfere. So
he went back to bed and without meaning to fell asleep. He
had been at work that day and was tired. It was six o'clock
when he awoke. She had not returned.

It was I who found the envelope she had left. Needing
comfort I suppose, he awoke me. Still half-asleep, I heard
something crackle under my pillow. He took it from me,
but not before I had seen my name, Fergus, written on it in
pencil. Inside there was no letter, just a small photograph.
John Lamont stared at this, sadly and desperately. Once
he even glanced at me with what looked like anger or
accusation. I was still only half-awake, and not altogether
sure that my mother really had been there. I felt confused
therefore, and frightened. Having no one else to blame, I
blamed him: just as he seemed to be blaming me.

Usually so indulgent, he absolutely refused to let me see
the photograph. He shoved it into the pocket of his working
jacket, as if it was like the one Jock Dempster had, of a
woman with no clothes on. I knew it couldn't be that.

When I whimpered that it was really mine, my mother
had meant it for me, he told me harshly not to be a baby.
When I swithered whether to wear the kilt or breeks I
lost patience and decided for me; that was why, on that
most difficult day of my life, I wore breeks.

He left the key in the lock, in case my mother should
come back. Going down the stairs, I reminded him that we
hadn't cleaned out Rob Roy's cage and put fresh seed in.
He snapped that the bird wouldn't starve. I was amazed.
Usually he liked cleaning out the cage. He and Rob Roy
whistled together, making me jealous. Both of them were
better whistlers than I.

On our way to Aunt Bella's he looked back a dozen times,
as if he hoped my mother was behind us.

Aunt Bella and Uncle Tam lived up a close in Kirn Street.
Their tenement was older and more dilapidated than ours.
The people who lived here thought themselves superior to
those who lived in Davidson's Vennel, and in their hearts
admitted that they in their turn were inferior to those who
lived in Lomond Street; while the inhabitants of Lomond
Street accepted that they were not quite on the same level
as the inhabitants of Nelson Street, where the closes were
tiled and the lavatories inside.

I had once overheard a man at the street corner remark to his mates after Aunt Bella, or Mrs Pringle as she was to them, had passed, that when she was a young girl, Bella Lamont, she had had the finest pair of diddies in the town. Another had said she still had, if you took a good look. Still another had said it was a pity she was so unbonny. A fourth had suggested she would be bonny enough if she would just smile. And a fifth had ended the conversation by reminding them she hadn't much to smile at, two weans that hadn't lived longer than a week.

She answered the door in a thin nightgown. Her bosoms, which I couldn't help looking at, were big and round like balloons, but heavy too, as if filled with water, or milk. She had her black hair in cloth curlers. Her face was screwed up in its usual scowl.

Putting on a coat, she took command of the situation. She was very capable. Her neighbours wondered how she could keep her house so well furnished, and herself so well dressed, and twenty pigeons so well fed, on the pay of a bricklayer's labourer.

As she talked, she set the table for breakfast.

'Of course you'll go to your work,' she said, to her brother. 'Nae sense in losing a day's pay, or running the risk o' losing your job. She's gone for good this time.'

'She's left her case.'

'She'll send for it. Did you think madam was going to cairry her ain case? You forget she's used to servants.'

'Carefu', Bella. Fergie's here.'

I was seated on a stool in a corner. Though I had more urgent questions to ask than any of them, I had to keep quiet, otherwise I'd be banished through to the room.

She turned to me. 'Whit happened at your grandfaither's yesterday?'

'Nothing.'

'John Lamont, are you going to let him talk to me like that?'

'He doesnae want to talk aboot it. I don't blame him. Some Christian, turning his back on his ain daughter.'

'So you're taking her side against Mr McGilvray?'

'Why shouldn't I? He's the one maistly to blame.'

'Mair to blame than her? Is that whit you're saying?'

'You ken whit I mean.'

'I ken this, you were the one eager to mairry her. You became a Christian yoursel', if you remember.'

Then, with glances at me, they decided to say no more, until I was out of the way. It wasn't the first time a conversation like this had been cut short to keep me from learning something about my mother.

A child's cunning is not entirely instinctive. Even if he has been only three years in the world he is bound to know some of its ways. I was seven. I knew the value of persistence as a tactic, if one's cause was good.

'I want to see the photie,' I muttered. 'It's mine. It was under my pillow. It's got my name on it.'

Knowing she was in the wrong, Aunt Bella tried bluster. 'Did you hear that? *His* pillow. *His* name. John Lamont, I'm sorry to tell you that fellow's going to cause you mony a sair hert. Impudence is in his bluid.'

My Uncle Tam always kept out of the way and let others do the talking. Even if the conversation was about pigeons, he wouldn't say much. He had tousled fair hair and a cheerful grin: too cheerful, in some people's opinion, for I had once heard Mrs Grier say he was only ninepence to the shilling, by which she meant some of his wits were missing.

'Naebody can help the way he's born,' he said.

'That must be so, Tam Pringle,' said his wife. 'Otherwise you'd shairly be a lot smarter than you are.'

He grinned happily at the insult, and winked at me.

'Why shouldnae he see the photie?' muttered John Lamont. 'He'll hae to be told one day. I promised.'

I piped up: 'What hae I to be told?'

Aunt Bella answered in a flash. 'That as soon as the shop's open you've to go and get me a quarter stone of tatties.'

I was baffled. It was another triumph for adult cunning.

Like a commander, Aunt Bella issued us our orders for the day. At the shipyard my father was to make it clear to his workmates he wanted no inquiries, especially from those who professed sympathy: he must therefore show on his face a lot more dourness and pride than he usually did. Uncle Tam was told to remember he got paid for humphing bricks, not for talking about Nancy McGilvray. As for me, first I was to do her shopping, then I was to go out and play with my friends as usual. If they, or their nosy mothers, did any speiring I was to pretend I was too wee to know anything: I was very good at that.

FOUR

All that day I had a funny feeling I had something missing, not an eye or an ear or a leg, but something just as necessary and conspicuous. Girls and women, and even my pals, would stare at me and look shocked, as if my nose was eaten away by disease, like the woman's who lived in Cowglen Street. Most of them were too sorry for me to ask about my mother. When any did I followed Aunt Bella's instructions and looked as stupid as a seven-year-old is expected to be. They all assumed my mother had gone away again.

I went up to the house four times. Once I let Smout McTavish come with me. Of all my friends he was the one least likely to pester me with curiosity about my mother. It wasn't that Smout wasn't curious about her, he was obsessively curious about everything, but the difference between him and everybody else was that he never asked, he just waited till he found out. He was like the small birds that see the bone first but don't come to peck at it until all the bigger birds are finished with it.

Though six months older, he was smaller than I, hence his nickname. His hair was always cropped so close you could see his skull. He had big brown solemn eyes, and he seldom laughed, at least not outwardly. I often wondered if he was chuckling inside.

He lived in a single-end, with his parents and three sisters. There were two set-in beds. Smout himself slept on the floor on an old mattress: mice trotted over him. If he was sorry for himself, no one ever heard him say so. That he was embarrassed by the holes in his breeks was shown by the way he tried to hide them, but still he didn't complain. He was very fond of his family, especially his mother. Other women said Mrs McTavish should be ashamed of herself, going to every whist drive in the town, instead of staying at home and looking after her children. But Smout was pleased that his mother was a good whist player and won prizes.

The McTavishes were considered out of their class in

Lomond Street. Single-ends there were meant for married couples, not families of six. That was the way slums developed. The Vennel was the proper place for them.

Smout was the perfect guest. When I made pieces they were thick and uneven, for I wasn't good at cutting bread, and all I could find to spread on them was condensed milk. He ate them with solemn relish, and when some of the condensed milk dripped on to his knee he licked it off as neatly as a cat. When we played with my glassies on the carpet he raised my self-esteem by plunking like a lassie: I plunked like a boy. When I needed to pee and said I would stand on a chair and do it in the jawbox, because the lavatory outside would be sure to be occupied, he just nodded: lots of others would have made rude jokes. He uttered polite little coughs when I showed him some family photographs: Aunt Bella and Uncle Tam at their wedding, my McGilvray grandparents in the garden at Siloam, an unknown uncle and a cow beside some hills, my father about to throw a quoit, my mother with me as a baby in her arms, me as a baby sitting on a cushion, and my father's father and mother just sitting on chairs. This last interested Smout most, to my surprise. He put his finger on Mr Lamont, senior.

I wondered if it was the moustache like the Kaiser's that he found interesting, or the watch chain, or the big ring.

'He doesnae look like a lord,' said Smout.

I did not know what a lord was. I wondered if it was an official in the Masons or the Orange Lodge. Mr Lamont had died of fever before I was born. He had been a storekeeper in Stewart's.

'My mither telt me,' said Smout, 'as a secret, that your faither's faither was a lord.'

Thus casually, out of the mouth of my most reticent friend, came the first hint of my aristocratic birth, at any rate the first hint to take root in my mind. Perhaps there had been previous hints when I was genuinely too wee to understand.

'Is it true?' asked Smout.

'I don't ken. He worked in Stewart's.'

Smout nodded, letting me know he thought he had talked about it enough.

If he had asked to see my mother's case with her clothes in it I would have adamantly refused. He didn't ask, so I insisted on showing them to him.

He gazed at the beautiful clothes without comment. When I asked him to touch a red blouse to feel how silky it was he touched it and said it felt silky. When I asked him to smell how scented it was he sniffed it and nodded. If he had asked where she was I was ready to answer that she had gone to Glasgow for the day and would soon be back. He didn't ask, and therefore, as I held her blouse in my hand, I felt the loss of her very sharply, and was afraid.

Smout had his eye on my kilt lying on the bed.

'Dae you need galluses to keep it up?' he asked.

'It's got buckles. Look.'

'Sodgers wear kilts.'

I nodded.

'There's a difference between a kilt and a lassie's skirt.'

I wasn't so sure about that.

'I like the colours.'

'They're a' right.'

'You couldnae wear troosers that were yellow and black. You'd look daft.'

'Maybe you'd look daft in this.'

'Could I try it on?'

I was wary. If it had been anyone else I'd have been sure he was kidding. Smout never kidded. I remembered that he hadn't laughed at me yesterday when I was wearing the kilt.

'If you like,' I said.

As if they were of silk, he took off his ragged trousers and laid them on the floor, with great care. His pintle was longer than mine. His behind was so skinny it reminded me of rabbits hung up on a hook in the butcher's.

Ignoring my inspection of his private parts, he wrapt the kilt round him and buckled it on. It came well below his knees, but he didn't seem to mind. Its splendour made his dark blue jersey with the holes at the elbows, and his filthy sandshoes, look more poverty-stricken than ever; but he didn't seem to mind that either. He admired himself in the mirror. He smiled.

'Yin day I'll hae a kilt,' he murmured.

FIVE

Puddock Loch has long since been filled in: today council houses stand on its site. When I was a child it was a place of adventure and danger. Parents warned their children not to go near it, for its banks were precipitous and its water deep enough to drown in. A path passed close to it, leading to McSherry's Wood, a lovers' haunt. It was a pair of lovers who saw, in the moonlight, first my mother's handbag on the path, at a place where the fence was broken, and then down below, in the water, under some alder bushes, my mother herself.

Two policemen came knocking on our door at two in the morning. I heard nothing, being sound asleep. My father got up in an eager hurry, thinking it was my mother come back at last. One of them was Sergeant McCormick. He knew my grandfather. There was no mistake, he said: he had seen Nancy McGilvray, as she used to be, too often not to recognise her. There weren't two women in Gantock with such bonny red hair.

Even my father's shock and anguish had to be expressed in whispers, so as not to waken me. It was an unsuitable time to knock on a neighbour's door, and anyway it was better to leave neighbours out of it in the meantime: so the young policeman was ordered to stay with me until my father came back from the mortuary.

It was half-past six before I awoke. The first thing I did was to look to see if my mother was there. I was whimpering with disappointment when I heard, coming from the kitchen, what sounded like a man weeping. I listened harder. It was a man weeping. It was my father weeping. In my shirt tail I crept through, ready to weep myself.

My father was sitting with his face pressed against the table, amongst teacups. Usually the sight of cups on the table was reassuring, since it meant people had been drinking tea, and the world was the safe companionable place every child liked it to be. But not that morning. Aunt Bella, who should have been in her own house, was seated by the hearth, with her face hidden behind her hands. Wearing his Sunday suit, Uncle Tam stood on the hearth rug. He was smoking a cigarette.

'Whit's up?' I asked.

I felt a painful need to pee. I should have done it in my chamber-pot, but I had forgotten.

Aunt Bella keeked at me through her fingers. She saw me squeezing my knees together.

'Go and make yoursel' comfortable,' she said, in a voice harsh with kindness.

I wondered if my father had toothache or something.

The wink Uncle Tam gave me was curiously crippled.

Peeved a little, for I didn't like everybody to know I still used a chamber-pot, I went through to the room. Nervousness made my fingers shaky and my aim bad.

I had to cover myself somehow. It was either the kilt or my breeks. I chose the kilt. It was like choosing my mother. From that day on I never wore trousers.

This time, when I returned to the kitchen, my father was at the sink splashing cold water over his face. Above him Rob Roy's cage was still covered. Uncle Tam's cap was on the sideboard, beside the cup my father had won for quoiting. Aunt Bella's face looked strangely bare. It wasn't just because she had taken away her hands. There was another reason. She had given herself the task of telling me.

'Whaur's my mither?' I asked.

'Would you like some tea?' she asked.

I shook my head, scornfully. I had asked for my mother, they were offering me tea.

'There's been an accident,' she said.

My father let out a great groan. Then he covered his face with the towel.

Uncle Tam beckoned with his finger. I went over to him, making sure I didn't pass close enough to Aunt Bella so that she could grab me. He was sitting opposite her. He tried to lift me up on to his knees, but I resisted. I wasn't a baby to be nursed, and besides, I knew they had terrible news for me. I preferred to be standing when I heard it.

'Your mither—' her voice trembled, for she often said she was a better mother to me than my mother ever was— 'is deid.'

'Does he ken whit deid means,' whispered Uncle Tam.

'He kens.'

She was right, of course. I had seen all sorts of creatures dead: flies, bees, minnows, butterflies, beetles, earwigs, spiders, mice, cats, dogs, and even people: when Morag McFadyen, Jessie's wee sister, had died two or three months before I had let myself be lifted up to see her in her coffin.

My father suddenly rushed out of the kitchen, with a wail. I felt deserted.

'She was found drooned in Puddock Loch,' said Aunt Bella.

I had once been frightened by a dragon-fly there. I thought of it now. What I had just been told was so terrible I knew I had better think as little about it as possible, and instead think hard about other things, things not important, such as that dragon-fly, and the tea caddy on the mantelpiece with the scenes of Rothesay painted on it, and the tap dripping in the sink.

'She must have gone for a walk,' murmured Uncle Tam, 'and fell in. It's slippy there.'

It wasn't slippy on dry days. There hadn't been any rain for a week. But if she hadn't fallen in, did it mean she must have jumped in? My heart gave a great leap in sympathy. Just in time, I thought of baggy-minnows and frogs' spawn.

'Dae you understaun'?' asked Aunt Bella, hoarsely.

She could not see, not having enough imagination, that I was deliberately warding off understanding, because I was afraid that when I did understand I would be more stricken than I could bear.

Then she said something that she later regretted, though she never apologised to me for it.

'You're like her. You've got nae affection.'

'For Christ's sake, Bella,' said Uncle Tam, 'he's only seven.'

SIX

My father insisted that the coffin be brought home and placed on trestles in the room. I slept beside him in the kitchen. It was me who discovered that Rob Roy was dead too: he lay in the cage with his legs in the air. Uncle Tam said he had died of old age, but I was sure my mother's death had something to do with it. When I shut my eyes

I felt that everybody and everything would be dead when
I opened them again. My relief was tremendous when,
opening them, I saw a fly or, if I was at the window,
people below in the street.

The coffin was left unscrewed, not because neighbours
might call to see my mother in it—my father refused to let
any of them in—but because he hoped her own father might
come to say, if only to her corpse, that he had forgiven her,
and was praying she was safely in heaven.

I didn't go out unless with my father or Aunt Bella or
Uncle Tam. I needed them to keep my friends at bay. Once,
seeing Smout McTavish by himself, with his back against a
lamppost, I stopped beside him. Aunt Bella waited to let
me speak to him. But I didn't speak, nor did he. We didn't
even nod or shake our heads or blink our eyes.

Aunt Bella must have been confirmed in her opinion that
I lacked affection. Certainly I took care not to let her or
anyone else see me weep.

The night before the funeral she and I were in the house
alone. My father and Uncle Tam had gone out. They didn't
tell me where they were going.

Aunt Bella played with me at ludo. Every now and then
she asked if I was ready for bed. I kept saying no and
shaking my head. Then I foolishly yawned. Immediately
she gathered up the pieces and closed the board. In less
than ten minutes I was in bed, with my face washed and
my supper eaten. I pretended to go to sleep at once. She
drew the curtains across the bed and turned the gas down.
I lay looking at her through the gap between the curtains.

She sat down at the fire with 'Peg's Paper' in her hand,
but she couldn't settle to read. She got up and stood at the
sink, but the dishes were washed and there was nothing to
do there. She opened a drawer in the sideboard but seemed
to forget what she was looking for, because she closed it
again without taking anything out. She went through to
the room where the coffin was. I heard her talking, but it
must have been to herself, for there was no one there except
my mother, who wasn't really there. She was wearing a long
black dress.

I was beginning to think I might as well let sleep have
me when there was a knock on the outside door. Aunt Bella
hurried to see who it was. Stupidly, for a few seconds, I

thought it might be my mother come home again: it was so easy to forget she was dead.

There were two or three voices. One sounded like Mrs Grier's. Had she come, I wondered in horror, to shout angry things at my dead mother? Surely Aunt Bella would keep her out.

Then into the kitchen came not only Mrs Grier, but fat Mrs Lorimer too: the first carried a bottle wrapped in tissue paper, and the other a bunch of flowers. They had black shawls over their heads.

Aunt Bella invited them to sit down. They thanked her politely, but before sitting down Mrs Grier, still with the bottle in her hand, came over to the bed and looked in at me. There was a smell of whisky off her breath. I pretended to be sound asleep. It was lucky it was her, because if it had been somebody I wasn't afraid of I might have burst out laughing.

'Puir wean,' she said, as she turned away. 'Does he ken yet, Bella?'

Aunt Bella was taking glasses out of the sideboard. 'Ken whit, Maggie?'

I was astonished at her calling Mrs Grier Maggie. I had not known they were friends. I hadn't known either that Aunt Bella drank whisky.

'Aboot his mither, I mean. And aboot his real faither.'

'As faur as I'm concerned, Maggie, my brither's his real faither.'

This was unintelligible. I put it away in the part of my mind where I kept things to be considered when I was older. I suspected many of them would turn out to be lies.

'I understaun' your feelings, Bella,' said Mrs Grier. 'Say when.'

Mrs Grier poured whisky into the glasses. Aunt Bella and Mrs Lorimer said when. Mrs Lorimer said it with a sad giggle.

'We hope you don't mind us coming up to keep you company, Bella,' said Mrs Grier. 'When we heard your brither and your man were in the "Auld Hoose" droonin' their sorrows, Teenie and I thought it a shame you should be left on your ain. Weel, here's to John Lamont, a decent and unlucky man.'

They drank. Mrs Lorimer smacked her lips.

'Maybe his bad luck's ended,' she said. 'D'you think, Bella, noo he's free, he'll mairry Bessie Armstrong? He's been sweet on her for years.'

I had seen Miss Armstrong with my father two or three times. She was cheerier than Aunt Bella. She worked in a draper's in the Main Street, and lived up a tiled close in Nelson Street.

'She'll want better than this, will Bessie Armstrong,' said Mrs Grier, looking round the little kitchen. 'Lomond Street will no' be guid enough for her.'

'John Lamont's a first-class tradesman,' said Aunt Bella. 'He'll no' stay here a' his life.'

'Still, Bella, even first-class tradesmen lose their jobs,' said Mrs Lorimer.

I understood this part of the conversation very well. Smout McTavish's father had been idle for months. Some men were always idle. My grandfather had said it was mostly their own fault, there was always work for those willing to do it.

'Wad Bessie want to take on a stepbairn seven-years-auld?' asked Mrs Lorimer.

'If she didnae,' said Aunt Bella, 'I'd be glad to tak him.'

They meant me. I thought I'd prefer Bessie; in any case I didn't want to be parted from my father.

'I'd think twice before I did that, Bella, if I was you,' said Mrs Lorimer. 'Whit's going to happen? In the future, whit's going to happen? Tell me that.'

Mrs Grier laughed. 'This is whisky we're drinking, Teenie, no' tea.'

'Dinnae laugh, Maggie. Is he going to be claimed? Yin day, will there be a cairrage in the street, sent for him?'

'Let's talk aboot something else,' said Aunt Bella. 'He micht waken.'

'He's sound asleep, Bella,' said Mrs Grier.

I almost smiled.

'Is it true her faither's no gaun to the funeral?' asked Mrs Lorimer.

To my alarm I was slipping into sleep. It was like falling down the bank into Puddock Loch. I tried to hold on to a bush, but it was no use. I fell asleep thinking how could my grandfather go to my mother's funeral when he thought she was in hell.

SEVEN

My grandfather did not allow my mother to be buried in her own mother's grave; nor did he go to her funeral. He displayed atrocious callousness; yet, by the sheer effrontery of faith, he compelled most people to think of him as a Christian of formidable and magnificent staunchness.

About a month after the funeral, feeling helpless, with that utter lack of authority children have, not to be confused with innocence, I resumed my Saturday afternoon visits to 'Siloam', but I nearly always went alone. When he asked me why I no longer brought my friends I made excuses: their mothers needed them to go messages, or they wanted to play football themselves or watch Gantock Rovers play, or they grumbled that the brae up to his house was too steep, or they were too shy. I did not tell him the real reason was that I did not want them to come, not even Smout who would have been as discreet as a mouse. I did not know it myself then, but I was profoundly ashamed of him.

Never once did he mention my mother. Nor did I. After we had worked in the garden we would sit on the seat, in the sunshine, and he would ask me questions, about school, about my friends, and about Bessie, who was going to marry my father and become my stepmother. As soon as I told him she never went to church, and refused to get married by a minister, he immediately lost interest in her. I realised then that he was never interested in people who didn't go to church. It puzzled me all the more therefore why he disliked Catholics so much. Even Mick Flynn and Pat McGuire, the worst swearers in our district, went to chapel regularly.

If it was rainy or cold we would sit in the parlour. Across the hearth from me he would read, stroke his beard, occasionally nod, and now and then look up and give me a smile. I was to fall heir to those books, turgid priggish self-satisfied accounts of missionary work among the heathen.

Anyone looking in would have been touched by the scene, the small silent kilted boy and the tall, bearded godly man, in such rapport apparently that they did not

have to say a word to each other for half an hour at a
stretch. The truth was, I felt more and more oppressed.
In desperation I would try to count the ticks of the big
clock with the wooden eagle on top. I felt relieved when
I had to slide off my chair and go outside to the cellar to
fetch more coal. I took longer than I needed to.

Without knowing clearly what I was doing, I put him to
tests. A family called Frame had been thrown out of their
room-and-kitchen in Laverock Street, near the Vennel, for
not paying their rent. Their furniture had been dumped on
the street. Mrs Frame had a baby in her arms; she had five
other children, all young: one of them, Jean, was in my class
at school. Mr Frame hadn't worked for years: he said he
had hurt his back. Some people thought he was, to use the
local word, 'scheming', that was, keeping up a deliberate,
cunning pretence. My friends and I once followed him to
see if he would, when he thought no one was looking,
straighten up and walk normally. He hadn't. Either his
pain was genuine, or he was a very good 'schemer'.

The eviction itself had not shocked me: it had been too
exciting. What had shocked me, though, was the anger
shown by neighbours of the Frames against the factor's
men and the police. Women had screamed and shaken their
fists. It had struck me as strange that so much misery, and
so much hatred, could be caused just by a lack of money.

I was curious to know what my grandfather thought.

'The Frames were put oot o' their hoose on Tuesday,' I
said. 'I saw it.'

He paused in his reading. His mouth went hard.

'The polis were there. Women were yelling at them.'

'I don't think you should have been there, Fergus.'

'Mrs Frame had six weans. They were taken to the
poorhoose.'

'They will be well looked after there.'

'She didnae think so. She bawled it was a disgrace.'

'Not paying what you lawfully owe is a much greater
disgrace.'

I pondered over that. It was too deep for me.

'Couldn't somebody hae gi'en them the money to pay the
rent?' I asked.

There were lots of people in Gantock who could. I saw
dozens of them every Sunday in the Auld Kirk. Some came

in carriages from the villas in the West End. My grandfather himself had money in the bank: so, anyway, Aunt Bella maintained.

'It isn't helping people to give them money like that, Fergus. If money isn't honestly worked for it does more harm than good.'

'But Mr Frame cannae work. He's got a sair back.'

Somebody had once said it couldn't be all that sore, considering he had six weans. I could see no connection. Perhaps my grandfather could.

'His back is not so sore as to prevent him from frequenting public-houses.'

'You mean, going into pubs?'

'That is what I mean, Fergus.'

I pondered again. Nothing was easier than going into a pub: you just pushed the door and walked in. Even Mr Chalmers who had only one leg found no difficulty.

'I believe he also gambles.'

I had never seen Mr Frame put a bet on with a street bookie, but it was likely he did, like lots of other men. I couldn't see what his sore back had to do with it.

'You may be sure, Fergus, that if people are deserving of His help the Lord will not withhold it.'

He spoke with not even the merest tremble of doubt or indeed of pity. Young though I was, it seemed to me that it was really my grandfather himself who decided whether or not people deserved Jesus's help. Hadn't he decided that my mother did not deserve it?

Then there was the case of Jack Burnett.

While Miss Cochrane was writing on the blackboard Jack picked up his inkwell and, with his left hand, for he was corry-fisted, hurled it at her. Luckily he missed, though some of the ink splashed over her face, like black blood. Jack was always in the front row because he never got his sums or spelling right. Miss Cochrane was never done taunting him. This was easy to do, for he always wore clothes too big for him, and his ears too were very big. Usually he endured, with only a scowl. Therefore we were all amazed when he suddenly lost his temper and threw the inkwell.

Mr McGill, the headmaster, was sent for. He arrived with his slippers on and his tawse in his hand. Jack refused to say he was sorry: he knew it wouldn't have lessened his punishment. He was given, in front of us, six on each hand, as hard as the headmaster could manage. After the fourth he broke and went down on his knees, howling for mercy. Girls wept. Smout, sitting beside me, with his arms folded like the rest of us, shut his eyes and licked his lips; like mine they had gone dry.

Afterwards, when Jack showed us his hands, they put me in mind of lumps of mince.

I had told Bessie. She had gasped with anger. If she was Jack's mother, she said, she'd go straight to the school and teach Mr McGill and Miss Cochrane something they evidently didn't know: the difference between cruelty and proper punishment. She didn't say how she would teach them, but I felt reassured. As long as there were grown-ups like Bessie, children didn't have to feel their cause was hopeless.

Telling my grandfather, I took care not to show my own feelings, or to mention Bessie's anger.

'So he got twelve. He was howling. He went doon on his knees.'

'So he should have, Fergus, in repentance.'

'He just wanted them to stop hurting him.'

'Surely he deserved his punishment, Fergus? It was a very wicked thing he did. He could have killed Miss Cochrane.'

'She said she could get her cat to coont better than him.'

'Sometimes stupidity is wilful, Fergus.'

'Does that mean he could be clever if he tried?'

'Not clever, perhaps, but certainly less stupid. People are often stupid because they are lazy, inattentive and disobedient.'

I had seen Jack baring his teeth like a dog in an effort to concentrate.

'You mustn't be alarmed, Fergus. You may be sure his punishment will have done him good.'

It had made Jack plunk school the very next day.

Why, I wondered, had Bessie, who never went to church, reassured me, while my grandfather, who carried round the plate, frightened me? She was always on the side of people, he on the side of God. Bessie might have said it was the same thing, but I felt sure he would not. There were some people with whom God, in my grandfather's opinion, was displeased: like the Frames, like Jack Burnett, and like my mother.

EIGHT

In those days not all teachers were physically brutal, but too many of them were spiritually dull. It was no compensation that they were conscientious and diligent: the harder they worked at quelling originality and instilling conformity the less they deserved praise. After forty years they looked back in retirement with benign satisfaction upon careers more heinous than Herod's: he extinguished life only, they had extinguished the spirit.

My friends and I in Gantock did not suffer our spirits to be extinguished. Outside school we had our own games and pursuits. These taught us to be enterprising, inventive, quick-witted, courageous, and persevering. It is true they did not improve our parsing.

I have already mentioned the stalking of butterflies. This induced in us patience, stillness, quickness, and pity. We learned that once the powder was off the wings they lost their power of flight. Remorseful at having robbed such beautiful creatures of so wonderful a gift as flying, we would feel, in the sunshine, shame dark as night, and we would vow never to do it again. That vow would be broken, perhaps on the same day, but, feeling guiltier than ever, we would make it again, and again. In our moral predicament, we used to put the blame on God for not giving butterflies stings or teeth.

Bumble-bees had stings. Catching them took more nerve. I can still remember, as if it had happened yesterday and not sixty years ago, how, having snatched from a purple-headed knapweed and squeezed to unconsciousness (as I thought) in my handkerchief, a 'sodger', so-called because it was khaki in colour, I laid it gallously on my left palm, for Smout McTavish, Jim Blanie, and Jack Burnett to inspect. With its last flicker of life it stung me, painfully. I threw it to the ground and squashed it under my shoe; but even as I took that furious revenge, and as I licked my smarting palm, I knew, without needing Smout to tell me, that it had just been trying to defend itself, and I was the one in the wrong.

We knew not to take hawthorn blossom into our houses. It was supposed to bring bad luck. Our other name for it was bad man's flourish. We believed it had been used by the Romans to make the crown of thorns for Christ. Yet I loved its strong sweet scent, and its creamy abundance, and its association with mysteries long ago.

We learned to distinguish mushrooms from toadstools, and whelks from mussels. We made peashooters out of the stalks of cow parsley, effective for a while if you could stand the smell and taste. Haws were used for pellets: baked in the oven they became hard as iron. We threw up sticks to knock down chestnuts, in a quest for a glossy Goliath that would become a 'bully of a hundred'. We sought out birds' nests, and had a pact never to harry them or steal eggs. We fished for minnows, but never in the Puddock Loch: after my mother's death I never went there, and my closest friends, Smout and Jim, agreed not to go there either. At Hallowe'en we carved turnips lifted from local fields. We were alchemists, with our mysterious sugar-olly water, made of water, sugar, licorice, and any other ingredient that might give it a strange flavour. After being vigorously shaken, it was kept in a dark secret place for a certain number of days. Then we would chant:

Sugar-olly water, black as the lum,
Gether up peens and you'll get some.

We were close to our pagan past. The pins asked for were those used by witches to stick into the clay effigies of people they wished to put a spell on or make die.

All those, and others, were the ploys of spring, summer, and autumn, carried on in the fields and moors above the town, and on the seashore below it. In gaslit winter we kept to the streets, closes, and backcourts. There we played Bethlehem, run-sheep-run, hunch-cuddy-hunch, foot-and-a-half, hop-step-and-a-jump, bubbly-jock, kick-the-knacket, moshie, cat-and-bat, and others I forget, as well as of course rounders and football. As I grew older and stronger, I became a leader. 'Dockies' was my favourite game. In it the leader performed various athletic and daring acts, which his followers had to do after him, otherwise they dropped out. I was the most dare-devil dockies-leader in the district.

I would hang upside-down like a bat from a lamppost,

with my legs twisted round the bar at the top: a feat easier
for those wearing trousers. I would jump from the top of
the coal-cellars over three dustbins. I would walk across the
street on my hands. I would climb up a drain-pipe to the
roof, touch the gutter, and climb down again: this too was
easier for those whose legs were covered. Trying to emulate
me, my friends sustained jarred ankles, scraped knees,
bruised fingers, and split skulls. Smout hated 'dockies'.
He said it was a stupid game, and anyway his bones were
too delicate; but we knew he was afraid. Mrs Blanie once
gave me a row because Jim came home with his mouth full
of blood, because he had put his teeth through his lip.

Being poor, we had to make our own toys: bogies out of
old boxes and pram-wheels; kites or 'dragons' out of crossed
sticks, brown paper, paste, string, and a clod to give weight
to the tail; sledges out of bits of wood, with the metal round
barrels for runners; lassoes out of clothes ropes; aeroplanes
out of paper; whips out of string or leather laces, to keep
spinning the peeries we bought in the shop, but which we
coloured with red, white, and blue chalks; and girrs out of
iron hoops, and cleeks out of stiff wire bent at the end.

If there had been any suggestion that our games should
be organised or supervised by teachers or youth club leaders
or any adults however well-disposed, we would have felt
insulted. Our independence was what we valued most.
We were nobody's prisoners or protégés. We belonged to
ourselves.

For myself, though, as officer and poet, it was a marvellous seed-time.

NINE

After passing the qualifying examination, we left Primary
and went on to Advanced Division. This meant for us
a building in Kidd Street that looked like a prison or
poorhouse. Its corridors were tiled like public lavatories.
The playground was divided into areas for boys and girls by
a high spiked fence. It was patrolled by a black-whiskered
janitor, nicknamed Kruger. He lined up the boys and
marched them in as if they were the Scots Guards.

I had heard of 'Limpy' Calderwood long before I met
him. Older boys told stories about him. Lame in the right
leg, he lurched across the classroom floor as if it was the

deck of a ship in a storm. To the headmaster's horror, he refused to give religious lessons. There was often a smell of pepperminted whisky off his breath. Other teachers had pictures of the king in their rooms, Limpy had one of a glum-looking man in a bonnet. I was to learn this was Keir Hardie, for Limpy called himself a socialist. He had visited the homes of outstandingly clever boys and girls to try and persuade their parents to send them to the Academy and perhaps afterwards to the University. Nobody knew of any parents who had been persuaded.

What had puzzled me was that no one ever boasted of having been strapped by him. He was that rarity, that penny black, a dominie without a tawse.

A University graduate with honours in history, qualified therefore to teach in the Academy itself, where his sister Cathie was a teacher of French and German, Limpy had chosen to come and educate the aborigines of the East End. It was to the credit of the school board, reactionaries to a man, that they let him teach at all, since he called himself an atheist as well as a socialist. But then his father and grandfather had been highly respected well-to-do Gantock doctors, and he and his sister lived in a fine big house in the West End, looking out on to the Firth.

That first morning we newcomers entered his room apprehensively. Because he had no belt it was feared he must use some other more sinister methods of discipline. If the teacher was soft, the choosing of seats in a classroom could become a competitive scramble, since no one wanted to be at the front, and some liked to be near the warm pipes, and others wanted to be near their friends or sweethearts.

Whatever Limpy was, it wasn't soft. He glowered at us with what he imagined was ironical sympathy (as I later learned) but which struck us as magisterial malevolence. It was certainly more effective than irate bawling would have been. Most of us sat in the nearest empty seat, and folded arms. I deliberately chose one in the front row. I was wearing my Sunday jacket and kilt.

My fearless grin must have been conspicuous among the submissive frowns and nervous winces. Glancing round boldly, I saw more than one close their eyes in prayer, or lick their lips or press their knees close together. I winked at Smout McTavish and Jim Blanie, but neither winked back.

'Well, Teuchter, what do you find funny?' asked Limpy.

Behind me the slaves giggled sycophantically, though many of them had names as Highland as mine. He had used the most contemptuous name a Lowlander can call a Highlander: it implies, among other things, heathery ears and sheep-like wits. It had often been shouted at me in the streets by fools.

'Do you mean me?' I asked.

Behind me they gasped at my impudence. Locked in a cage with a bear, a wounded one at that, they hated me for poking it with a stick.

Limpy had a thin, sallow, clever face, with a little black moustache and long sideburns. It wasn't designed for expressing the love of humanity that his principles bade him possess. The scowl with which he looked at me was indistinguishable from that of any other teacher confronted by what he took to be impertinence.

'Stand up while you're talking to me,' he snapped.

I stood up.

'What's your name?'

'Fergus Lamont.'

'That extraordinary garment you're wearing, do you always wear it or is it for special occasions?'

'I always wear a kilt.' By not saying 'sir' I was hitting back hard.

'Really? I can't believe it. You, there.' He pointed to a girl beside me. 'Is it true? Does he always wear a kilt?'

She blushed. I didn't know her. She had been at a different primary school.

'Yes, sir. They ca' him Kilty Lamont, sir.'

'Do they indeed. Well, that's interesting. Where do you live, Lamont?'

'Lomond Street.'

I was too proud to mention that it was at the better-off end, opposite the bowling-green, in a two-room-and-kitchen, with an inside toilet. We had moved there three years ago.

'Lomond Street? I wasn't aware there were any shooting-lodges or baronial castles in Lomond Street. You know, Lamont, I once visited a cattle show in the Hebrides. The only persons there wearing kilts were the laird and his son. They lived in the big house and talked like upper-class Englishmen. All the crofters wore shaggy trousers.'

Before I could speak there came from behind me a voice, a girl's voice, shaky a little, but clear and resolute. 'It's no' fair to try and get us to laugh at him. He's got as guid a right to wear a kilt as ony laird, if he wants to.'

Limpy was as astonished as I. Moments later he seemed delighted too, which I certainly wasn't. I needed no girl to stand up for me.

Especially one so undersized and pale and shabbily dressed. If it had been the girl beside her, with red cheeks and long silky black locks, who was defending me I might have felt pleased and flattered.

'Who are you?' cried Limpy, laughing.

'My name's Mary Holmscroft, sir.'

'Is he your sweetheart?'

'I've never spoken to him.'

'Ah, so it's simply fair play and justice you're interested in?'

'That's right, sir.'

'Well, well. Do you come from Lomond Street too?'

'I come from the Vennel.'

She said it just a little too promptly, too coolly, and too proudly.

When I turned round the red-cheeked beauty pointed at her swelling breast and shook her head vigorously. This was to let me know she didn't come from the Vennel.

Limpy stood up. He held on to his desk. He seemed excited.

'Well done, Mary from the Vennel,' he said.

Then he addressed the class.

'You've just had your first lesson in this room. You'll never get a better. Be grateful to this girl. Be proud of her. Feel honoured she is your classmate.'

Most of them looked puzzled and anxious. He had spoken fervently, as if he had meant it. Yet surely it was nonsense? How could they be grateful to a girl from the Vennel, and proud of her? Their parents had warned them to keep clear of Vennel scruff.

When we were going out at the end of the period Limpy asked her to wait behind. Some showed resentment at this show of favouritism on the very first day, but I felt curious and envious. I wanted to know what those two were saying to each other, and to be a part of it.

Meanwhile, the other boys were envious of me. This was because the red-cheeked girl attached herself to me as we walked along the corridor and introduced herself as Meg Jeffries. She was the best-looking girl I had ever seen, but it was really small, plain, flat-chested Mary Holmscroft I was thinking about.

After four, when the school was skailing, I waited in a closemouth not far from the girls' gate. The rain had gone off, but it was still cool and windy. Meg Jeffries came out, wearing a warm red coat and a hat to match. I withdrew into the close so that she would not see me. It was Mary Holmscroft I wanted to escort home.

I could not have said, with complete honesty, that part of my reason wasn't a desire to see in what slummy part of the Vennel she lived. All day my jealousy, and my admiration, had increased. She had shown herself brilliant at every subject. She could do parsing and analysis with ease.

She wasn't alone as she came out of the gate. Judging from the shabbiness of their dress, her two companions were from the Vennel too. When I stepped out of the close, they gave me a startled look and then raced on ahead, chanting: 'Mary's got a beau, Mary's got a beau.'

She was quite unembarrassed. 'Did you miss Meg?' she said.

I walked beside her. I thought I caught a whiff of under-clothes too long unchanged. In her house in the Vennel it wouldn't be easy to keep clean.

'What did you think of Limpy?' I asked.

'Mr Calderwood, you mean.'

'All right, Mr Calderwood. What did he say to you when he kept you behind?'

'That's our business, no' yours.'

'Have you lived in the Vennel all your life?'

'Yes.'

'I've never heard of you.'

'Why should you? Are you often in the Vennel?'

'No fear.'

'I'd heard of you.'

'Because of my kilt?'

'And because of your mither.'

I was taken aback. This was a subject I would not talk to any stranger about.

My mother's disgrace and death were still mysteries to me. My father refused to talk about them, and I had vowed never to ask my grandfather. Since taking to drink Aunt Bella had become milder but not any more communicative. Uncle Tam always said he knew nothing. Bessie, my best hope, kept saying I must wait till I was older: I had been a bit childish for seven, I was still a bit childish for twelve, perhaps I would be mature enough at fourteen, or twenty-one, or forty.

People outside my family, like Smout's mother and Mrs Grier, probably knew, but I took great care never to give them a chance to tell me. My mother would not have wished me to discuss her with them.

'I'd raither not talk about my mither,' I said.

'Please yoursel'.'

We were now entering the Vennel. Really a street, the name had been given to the whole district of narrow lanes and ruinous tenements. It was the oldest and slummiest part of Gantock. The women of Lomond Street knew, and were always warning their children, that, perched as they were on the outermost edge of civilisation, very little was needed to make them topple off. The Vennel was where those went who toppled off.

Scruffy women at closemouths gave my companion fairly friendly nods, and me astounded glowers. Their raucous hilarity followed us.

'Weel, you've seen whaur I live,' said Mary, stopping at her close.

'That's no' why I came.'

The protestation, half-hearted because it was only half-true, wasn't heard by her. She had gone into the close and up the stairs.

In any case, I had to look to myself. I had been sighted by a pack of Vennel wolves, or rather my kilt had. They came yelping down the street towards me. I could have stood my ground and fought them off, for though there were six of them they were all under ten, but in the affray my legs might have got bitten and my kilt torn. So I raced away. They pursued. One, the swiftest and boldest, got close enough to grab the tail of my kilt. I had to turn and cuff his ear to make him let go. Swearing vilely, he tried to break my leg with a swing of his boot; but he missed and fell. His mates gathered round him, howling with glee. It was their way of eating the wounded.

TEN

One wet dreºry winter afternoon, with the lights on at two o'clock, and the air so stuffy and foul that when Alec Munro farted the smell was hardly noticed, we had a history lesson from Limpy that was to haunt me for the rest of my life.

Though the curriculum stated that we should study the kings of England Limpy insisted on teaching us instead the history of our own country. His method was to take some ordinary Scotsman or Scotswoman of the past and imagine what his or her life must have been like. We were encouraged to ask questions and offer suggestions.

That afternoon, though, I had a headache and wanted to get out into the fresh air. Even Meg Jeffries looked ill in the gaslight.

Limpy sat at his table. There were some books on it.

'Today I'd like to tell you about a Scotsman who lived less than a hundred years ago. Some of you may have grandparents who were born while Donald was still alive.'

Alec Munro, the simpleton of the class, put up his hand. 'Please, sir, my great-grannie's eighty-two.'

'When she was born, Alec, our friend Donald would be about twenty-six.'

'Whit was his ither name, sir?' asked Meg.

She asked questions not to please the teacher but to impress me.

'It could have been Munro or Lamont or McTavish or McDonald or McLellan or Gillies or Jeffries.'

We noticed he had used our own names.

'Donald was a soldier in the Sutherland Highlanders. He was born in Farr, a village in Sutherland. One day his chieftain, the Countess of Sutherland, was asked by the government in London to form a regiment of soldiers. Donald was selected to be one, because he was big and strong and young. He didn't grumble because he thought it was his duty to obey his chieftain, and the Countess had promised all the soldiers that their parents would be well looked after while they were away.'

Our eyes glittered with pride. This system of loyalty on the part of the clansmen and paternal care on the part of the chieftain seemed to us noble. It made patriotism the finest thing on earth.

Only Mary Holmscroft was scowling.

'Before he left, Donald was presented with a Bible by his parish minister.'

My eyes became moist. I imagined Donald, in a kilt, outside a small thatched church, being handed a Bible with gilt edges by a white-haired minister.

Suddenly Sammy Jackson, who sat nearest the door, put up his hand. His job, to which he had appointed himself, was to let us all know whenever Mr Maybole, the headmaster, was spying outside.

'He's there, sir,' he called, hoarsely.

Limpy never bothered to lower his voice.

'In 1805 Donald went with his regiment to Cape Town.'

I wished old Maybole would go away. He was spoiling the story. Most of my classmates, though, were hoping he would come in, still crouching, for he sometimes forgot to straighten up.

'Mary, would you come and point to Cape Town for us,' said Limpy.

Out she went and without hesitation pointed to it on the map of the world on the wall.

It was a wonder to us all how she knew so much. It was rumoured Limpy had lent her an encyclopaedia.

'At that time,' went on Limpy, 'the Dutch possessed the Cape of Good Hope. The Sutherland Highlanders were ordered to attack them and seize it. Some of them were drowned before they reached the shore, but Donald fought bravely in the battle. He was commended by his commanding officer.'

'It's a' richt, sir,' hissed Sammy. 'He's gone.'

'He remained with his regiment at the Cape for the next eight years. His pay was very low, but he still sent money home regularly. He also contributed a penny or two to Missionary Societies.'

'Did he write letters hame, sir?' asked Smout.

'He couldn't write, Willie, and his parents couldn't read.'

'Couldn't the minister that gave him the Bible have written letters to him?' asked Mary. 'Somebody could have read them oot to him.'

'That's just what happened, Mary. The ministers wrote letters to all the soldiers. They told them everything was fine at home.'

'So the Countess was keeping her promise?' asked Mary, sceptically.

'The Countess herself lived in London, but her factor, a gentleman called Mr Sellars, was looking after them on her behalf.'

We were all pleased, except Mary.

'He's back again, sir,' called Sammy.

'After serving abroad for thirteen years, Donald returned to Britain and took his discharge. He was eager to go home. It was a long difficult journey in those days. He had to walk most of the way. He didn't mind. He was alive and well, and he was going home, to see his parents again and his brothers and sisters, and the house where he was born.'

'Good,' said Meg.

We all agreed. If ever a man deserved a joyful home-coming it was our Donald.

'When he entered Strathnaver, his native glen, he got a shock. The villages were empty. The houses were all roofless. Their walls were blackened with soot. It was the same at his own village. There was no one there, except one man, a stranger, who seemed to be looking after the big flock of sheep grazing in what used to be the village's corn field. He wasn't a Highlander. He explained that all the people were gone either to Canada, across the Atlantic, or to the seashore twenty miles away. It had nothing to do with him: he was paid to look after sheep, that was all.'

He paused.

We asked questions.

'What had happened?'

'Had there been a war or something?'

'Was it an earthquake?'

'Or a fire?'

'No. What had happened was that somebody had discovered there would be a lot more money for the landowner, the Countess, if the people were cleared out and sheep brought in in their place. Those that weren't willing to go were dragged out by force and their houses set on fire, sometimes with people still in them.'

'Didnae the polis stop it?' asked Archie Paterson, whom the police had once stopped playing football in a farmer's field.

'The police were there, but not to stop it: their job was to see that the people gave no trouble. Not only the police. Soldiers were sent to Strathnaver, Irish soldiers, glad to get revenge for what Scottish soldiers had done to the Irish people in the past.'

'Did Parliament ken?' asked Mary Holmscroft.

'Parliament knew. Parliament had made the laws which said a landowner could do what he liked with his land.'

'Why didn't they fight?' asked Frankie McLellan.

'Peasants can't fight police and soldiers.'

'He's coming in,' shouted Sammy Jackson.

He was too late. The door opened and in bounced Mr Maybole, crouching.

'Really, Mr Calderwood,' he cried, 'I must warn you. You are filling these children's minds with poison. You are undermining their confidence in legally constituted authority. It is a mistake to study the history of one's own country. It divides instead of uniting us, and we must stand united today if we are to curb the dangerous ambitions of the Prussians. Why bother with stuff so out-of-date?'

'It isn't out-of-date, Mr Maybole,' said Mary. 'People are still put out of their houses.'

I remembered the Frames, and my grandfather's judgment on them.

'So they should be, if they do not pay their rents,' cried the headmaster.

The bell rang. He hesitated and then fled. When classes were changing he liked to roam the corridors to make sure no one talked or ran or chewed sweets or held hands.

'Please, sir,' cried Meg, 'did Donald ever find his people again?'

'He did not. They had gone to Canada.'

'And what did he do?'

'He joined the army again.'

As they streamed out, my classmates—they are in front of me as I write, in this old brown spotted photograph—were on the whole relieved, especially the girls. Back in the army, Donald would have no more worries, he would be too busy killing foreigners. Only one boy besides myself saw the irony of Donald's serving again those who had persecuted his people; but he saw it as comic, whereas I saw it as tragic. Here he is, Dugald Galbraith, hair cropped like a Devil Islander's, and grinning cheerfully.

I paused by Limpy's desk. Mary was waiting, too. She often did. She was accused of being his pet, or worse. 'I bet she lets him feel her bum,' I had once heard Archie Paterson say to Frankie McLellan. Frankie had replied, 'I'd raither feel Meg Jeffries.'

'You said it happened all over the Highlands, Mr Calderwood,' I said. 'Did it happen in Oronsay, in the Hebrides, where my mother's people came from?'

'It did.' He turned the pages of a book on his desk. 'Read that.'

I read it, with sorrow and anger; and I resolved that one day I would go to that distant island and see for myself the pleasant fertile sea-meadows where my ancestors had lived happily for hundreds of years, and the harsh, stony, watery places to which they had been callously driven.

ELEVEN

Most Friday afternoons after school Mary Holmscroft and I went to the Tally's in Morton Street, for penny pea-brees and arguments just as hot. We sat in one of the alcoves, scalded our lips and warmed our stomachs, and argued.

One Friday she was subdued. I noticed she shivered now and then. Yet she was wearing a warm enough coat, bought for twopence at a church jumble sale.

'I'm going to Ravenscraig the morrow,' she said.

Ravenscraig was Limpy's big house in the West End. I knew she went there and met famous socialists from Glasgow.

'Teacher's pet,' I sneered.

She wasn't provoked. 'Will you come wi' me?' she asked.

'I don't go where I'm not invited.'

'You are invited. Cathie told me to ask you.'

I felt pleased. I had heard that Limpy's sister was lovely and amusing.

For the bearer of such an interesting invitation, Mary was still too down in the mouth.

'Whit's up?' I asked. 'I thought your sister Isa was better.'

'They want to adopt me. Weel, go and live with them onyway.'

'Who.'

'John and Cathie. They think if I don't get oot o' the Vennel I'll be wasted. They think I should leave Kidd Street school and go to the Academy and then maybe to the University.'

Jealousy was my immediate response.

'Your faither would never allow it.'

'He'd be paid.'

'Paid? How would he be paid?'

'He looks at it this way: if I left school at fourteen I'd maybe get a job at five shillings a week. So if he gets eight shillings a week, as extra compensation for losing my company he says he'll agree.'

I had spoken to Mr Holmscroft once. He had struck me as sly. He called himself a socialist. He liked talking better than working. He'd screw out of the Calderwoods as much as he could.

It occurred to me that Mary herself would be betraying her socialist principles. Living at Ravenscraig she would become one of the favoured people of the West End, whom she'd often accused of cheating the East End poor out of their share. The Calderwoods had a servant, who'd polish her shoes for her. She would be deserting her sisters and brothers, who depended on her.

'You'd have to wear the Academy blazer,' I said.

'That's nothing.'

'You'd have to talk properly. You'd have to say "anyway" instead of "onyway" and "out" instead of "oot".'

'There's nothing wrong with talking properly. It's not Scots we speak, you know, it's a mongrel mixture of Scots and English.'

It annoyed me having Limpy's dictum quoted at me so glibly.

'Whit aboot your sisters? They'd miss you.'

'I'd keep in touch.'

'Maybe you'd try, at first; but you'd gie up trying.'

'Speak for yourself. One day I'm going to be a member of Parliament.'

'So you've said.'

'I need the best education I can get.'

'What's to stop you living in the Vennel and going to the Academy?'

'Lots of things.'

I could think of some of them.

It would be easier for me to go to the Academy. After all, my grandfather was a councillor and knew many important men in the town. I could give my address as Siloam Cottage. The red blazer would go well with my kilt. With luck I could scrape through the entrance exam.

Tears were trickling down her cheeks. It was the first time I had seen her cry. I realised she meant a great deal to me. I would never want to kiss her, as I did Meg Jeffries, but I would always want to know what she was thinking.

'Everybody's got a right to do the best for themselves,' I said.

'I wouldn't be doing it for myself, you fool.'

I didn't argue. I didn't have to. If she were to tell herself a hundred times a day that she was living in the spacious house, sleeping in her own room in a bed with white sheets, and eating food four times a day, all for the sake of the poor whom she had vowed to help, she would not be able to believe it, she was too intelligent, and too honest. After all, if her dream came true, and she did become a member of Parliament, wouldn't she then be even further away from her family and the poor?

We took the tram to Firth Street, and from there walked along the esplanade beside the water which was rough with the wind. Seagulls glared at us with yellow eyes. Mary was wearing the same red coat. I was dressed in dark green jacket, kilt, and tweed overcoat, with a balmoral on my head. I attracted admiring glances. She said it was because I looked like Harry Lauder; even the gulls expected me to do a jig and sing. I never found her jokes funny; nor did she mine.

I had been told Cathie Calderwood was twenty-eight, and wore bright clothes. In my expectations therefore I kept confusing her with my mother, who had been twenty-six and whose costume had been lilac-coloured.

We went through iron gates wide enough for a carriage,

and up a driveway lined with hundreds of daffodils. The grounds were as spacious as six backcourts at least. There were fully grown trees: ash, fir, and sycamore, according to Mary. She expected me to look overawed, so I didn't.

The house was large and square, built of dark grey stone with red ivy growing over the front. I calculated that if it had been divided into single-ends and room-and-kitchens it could have housed, by Lomond Street standards, fifty people, and by Vennel standards, a hundred. Two questions in a hurry collided in my mind: how could Mr Calderwood—it was absurd to call the owner of so imposing a house Limpy—call himself a socialist, a champion of the poor? And why did he teach at a scruffy school like Kidd Street? If I owned a house like this I wouldn't work at all. Nobody would call me idle or unemployed or workshy. Only if you were poor, like Smout's father, and needed help from the parish, did people that mattered call you lazy or good-for-nothing.

On the doorstep was a mat with a foreign word worked into it. Mary said it meant welcome, in French.

Why did I feel so confident? Was it because of my kilt and bonnet? Or because I knew this was the kind of house my mother had wanted me to live in? Or was it because of the stirring in me of ancestral memories? Anyone seeing Mary and me at the door of that fine big house would have assumed I was a friend of the son of the owner, and she a girl from the East End looking for a job as a kitchenmaid.

The door was opened by a small, fair-haired, eager-eyed, fat-lipped, panting young woman, in a dress that even I thought more suitable for a girl of ten: it was light-blue, with an enormous red bow at the waist. Squealing with delight, she put her soft, inkstained hands on my shoulders—I was taller than she—and kissed me on the cheek. She smelled of violets and also, unaccountably for a few moments, of beef. Then I noticed on her high dainty bosom a stain of fairly fresh gravy, about the size of two violets. I was soon to learn ethereal Cathie was as slapdash an eater as my step-sister Agnes, aged two.

'So you are Mary's friend, Fergus,' she cried, clapping her hands. 'Mary has told us so much about you.'

That interested and surprised me, but at the time I was

more taken up with the house, though I took care to look about me politely. Smout would have gaped in awe at so much red carpet, covering all the floor and flowing up the stairs. Used to his single-end, he would have cringed, threatened by so much living space. The hall itself, with its high ceiling, was twice as roomy as his whole house.

I helped Mary off with her coat. I would have done this even if Cathie hadn't been there to be enchanted by my good manners, but perhaps I wouldn't have done it quite so courteously.

John Calderwood came limping into the hall. He wore a dark red velvet jacket, pink silk cravat, and black corduroy trousers. In my innocence I was pleased to see him dressed like a gentleman. I did not know then it was the garb of wealthy socialists.

He had a magazine in his hand and was eager to show it to Mary. It was a socialist weekly well-known then but long since defunct. Evidently he often wrote articles for it. His contribution that week had been written in collaboration with Mary. It was on conditions in the Vennel. Heads together, they read it like conspirators.

'Oh, never mind them and their silly politics,' cried Cathie, taking my hand. 'Come and see my fish.'

She pulled me into a large room so full of plants and flowers it looked, and smelled, like a garden. The fish were in three tanks. Some were tropical, with bright colours and strange shapes. Others were ordinary goldfish, like those you could win at the shows. They did not look ordinary though as they pressed their noses against the inside of the glass, while Cathie flattened hers against the outside.

Nothing was ordinary that Cathie came near. There were birds in the room too, two canaries, in a gilt cage. When she rattled the bars with her fingernails, and sang a cheerful French song, cage and birds, like the goldfish, became exciting and strange. Her neck looked so soft and warm I longed to touch it. One of her canary-yellow slippers fell off, being burst at the back. Putting it on to her red-stockinged foot, as she sat in a big flowery sofa, was for me a keener joy than carrying Meg Jeffries' schoolbag ever had been.

'Sit down beside me, Fergus,' she murmured, 'and tell me all about yourself.'

We were so close a sixpence couldn't have slipped down

between us. I clasped my hands defensively on my sporran. She placed her hand on top of mine, and pressed down, affectionately.

I wondered, at frantic speed, if she knew the physiological effect that delightful pressure could have, indeed was having. I was to learn later that this was a doubt shared by almost every boy and male teacher in the Academy. Some accused her of being a deliberate tease, but the majority thought that the fairest verdict was 'not proven'.

She put her lips to my ear and whispered: 'Mary has told us you have a fascinating history.'

I wasn't sure what she meant.

'Your poor, poor mother.'

It could have been because her hair was the same yellow colour as Jessie McFadyen's, though softer and cleaner, that I suddenly noticed, or imagined I did, another resemblance to that beautiful but glaikit girl. Into Cathie's big blue eyes would come a blankness, the same kind I had often seen in Jessie's, only in Jessie's it lasted nearly all the time, whereas in Cathie's it was gone in a second or two.

Even to her, I did not want to talk about my mother.

'Is it true she drowned herself?'

'No. She got drowned.'

'How sad. Mary says your real father is the son of an earl.'

Smout had said the same thing, but I was five and a half years older now. Thanks to some roughly accurate but somewhat coarse playground and backcourt tuition, I knew what my mother and father must have done to create me. Though I was very fond of John Lamont, I had shrunk from the thought that he, with his hairy chest and hard quoiter's hands, had done that necessary thing with or rather to my fastidious mother; but I had never tried to imagine any other man in his place. Once while he was at work I had searched the house for the photograph my mother had left under my pillow. I had found it in a drawer inside a Bible. It had told me nothing. All it showed was a young man, not much older than Jock Dempster, wearing a cap and white trousers, and holding a cricket bat.

'You certainly look far too distinguished to be an ordinary East End boy,' whispered Cathie.

Then we heard Mary and John Calderwood outside the room. Cathie at once took her hand away and drew apart.

'Don't let on to Mary I told you,' she said. 'You see, I promised her I wouldn't.'

Yesterday I had a visitor. At first I took him to be a Mormon evangelist. A band of these had been in the district a few weeks back. He had the same ecstatic eagerness to talk, and the same exalted determination not to listen. He wore a thick black coat, tightly belted, and a fur hat like a Cossack's. Under his oxter he carried a saddlebag, or so he made it seem.

'Am I addressing Mr Fergus Lamont?' he cried, in an American voice.

I was taken aback and confused. In this place I am known as William McTavish. The only person who knows I am still alive and living here in Blackfriars Street, Glasgow, is Samuel Lamont, QC, and he has sworn never to tell anyone without my permission, not even Betty my former wife, nor Torquil my son, nor my daughter Dorcas, Lady Arnisdale.

'Let me introduce myself, sir. Professor John G. Wienbanger, of the University of South Carolina. Do you recognise this, sir?'

He plucked from his bag a thin volume. The original mauve of the cover was faded to light blue, but the drawing of the Auld Kirk of Gantock was still recognisable. It was my 'First Poems'. Copies are as rare as ospreys.

So many times have I declared that I have no wish for fame and would not shed a tear if every poem of mine was lost forever. Therefore I ought, in honesty, to have handled those first-born with indifference. I could not. Great joy and pride possessed me as I looked at the list of titles: 'Gathering Dung', 'The Puddock Loch', 'Running with a Girr', 'Limpy', 'The Peaver Players', and the eighteen others.

'You will wonder, Mr Lamont,' said my visitor, 'why I have taken so much trouble to find you. I am here in pursuance of an idea, an inspiration, that came to me one day while I was studying the works of Enrico Bardes, a Patagonian poet. You probably have never heard of him. He is not well known even in Patagonia. This idea occurred to me while I was reading a poem called, roughly translated, "The Chewing of Testicles". The reference is to a practice Patagonian shepherds have of castrating lambs with their teeth, and then eating their testicles,

which are considered a delicacy. It seemed to me that that poem, by a series of curious inadvertences, got very close indeed to the innermost essence of Patagonian life.

'*After much pondering, I came to the conclusion that this peculiar insight was not likely to be found in any universally great poet, such as Shakespeare or Dante or Whitman. He would have to be a poet indubitably minor, with no beauty of language or depth of thought, with some humour mostly of the unconscious kind, and native of a small, unimportant country. On further investigation, I discovered, sure enough, such poets in Albania, Iceland, Turkey, Peru, and of course Scotland, in the person of your good self. Your poem "Gathering Dung" is a prime example of what I am getting at. Indeed, it will have a central place in my thesis.*'

There was a time when I would have kicked him down the stairs. But I decided long ago that of all the virtues humility is the greatest, superior even to courage. Nothing would have been easier than to find the courage to chastise this insolent fool, but to smile meekly at him, to shake my head at him sorrowfully and forgivingly, and to beseech him, in a quiet dignified voice to leave at once, this was far from easy, and brought me out in a shivering sweat.

A humble man, in the full glory of his humbleness, is more formidable than a violent man. With cries of fright, Wienbanger shoved the books into his bag and fled.

It is not likely so asinine a verdict of my poetry will be ratified by posterity; but even if it were, to be remembered because of an idiosyncratic mediocrity would be better than to be completely forgotten. I do not fear utter oblivion for my own sake, but for the sake of all the people who helped to make me the poet I was, both those already mentioned, like Cathie Calderwood, and those still to appear, above all Kirstie McDonald, most genuine of women. If it is decided I was a poet of no significance whatever, they will all have lost their immortality.

TWELVE

Aunt Bella seemed the one most likely to be tricked or coaxed into telling me more. Since my mother's death she had had another still-born baby. Grief had made her drink more recklessly. A strange consequence of this deterioration was that she no longer spoke unkindly to Uncle

Tam. Instead of being relieved he had become more anxious.

'It's his own fault,' Bessie had said. 'I hear he even buys her drink for her.'

'He cannae bear to see her unhappy,' my father had replied.

There had been a change for the worse in Bessie too. Where before she had put fairmindedness first, now it was respectability. She often spoke about going to church. When she met Aunt Bella in a shop wearing 'the cardigan she cleans the grate in' she refused to talk to her.

One evening, about five o'clock, wearing my oldest kilt, I paid a visit to Aunt Bella. She took so long to open the door I began to think she must be out. When she came she reeked of whisky and looked half-dressed. She was so pleased to see me she flung her arms round my neck. The buttons of her blouse were undone. Her breasts could be seen.

'It's nice of you to pay me a visit, Fergie,' she said, with some sad sniffs. 'Wad you like a treacle piece?'

'No thanks, Aunt Bella.'

She tried, feebly, to do up the buttons of her blouse.

On the table, beside the bottle of Johnny Walker, lay a doll, as big as a real baby; it had on a pink dress. Aunt Bella must have been pretending to feed it at her breast.

'Weans get aulder,' she whispered.

'I'm nearly thirteen.'

'Past treacle pieces, eh?'

This time she persevered and buttoned up her blouse. Then she picked up the doll and placed it carefully in a basket under the bed.

'Aunt Bella,' I said, 'you once promised that when I was aulder you'd tell me aboot my mither.'

'I was sorry for you when you were a wee wean, Fergie, left withoot a mither. I wad hae adopted you, if your faither had let me.'

'Tell me aboot her.'

She helped herself to some more whisky. 'I tak this for my nerves, Fergie. Maybe I was too hard on your mither. Maybe she missed you mair than I gave her credit for. It was being so bonny was her ruination. She thocht she deserved better than living up a close in a room-and-kitchen, and sharing a lavatory wi' the likes o' auld Strathglass.'

'Was that why she went away?'

'She went awa' because she was selfish and bad. Better women than her hae lived a' their lives in room-and-kitchens. She ran awa' wi' a man three times her age. It was his money she was efter.'

'Was he rich?'

'He used to hae one o' the biggest hooses in the West End. Malcolm he was ca'd, Henry Malcolm.'

'Where did they go?'

'Edinburgh, and ither places. Living in the best hotels. She'd enjoy that.'

'But why did she come back?'

'She said because o' you, but I think mysel' it was because auld Malcolm had dee'd and left her naething.'

Part of the mystery was cleared up.

'Somebody telt me, Aunt Bella, that my faither isnae my real faither.'

'That was a terrible thing to tell ony wean.'

'Is it true, though?'

'My brither's the only faither you've ever had, or ever will hae.'

'Smout McTavish's mither said my faither's faither was a lord.'

'Effie McTavish should hae kept her silly mooth shut. Her ain faither was as drunk as a lord, every Friday night in life.'

'But whit did she mean?'

'I'll tell you whit she meant. When your mither was a young lassie she was sent into service.'

'Became a servant, you mean?'

'Aye, that's whit I mean.'

'Who sent her?'

'Wha d'you think? Her ain faither sent her. He wanted to humble her. She had too high an opinion of hersel' to please him. But don't think it was ony ordinary hoose he sent her to. It was a castle. Corse Castle.'

'Where's that?'

'In Ayrshire. Hundreds o' rooms. It's where the Earl o' Darndaff lives. Your mither went there when she was fourteen. She had to be ta'en awa' when she was eighteen.'

'Whit for?'

'Because she was going to hae a wean.'

'Me?'

'Aye, you. They telt your grandfather that the man responsible was yin o' the ither servants, a footman or something. But she claimed it was the earl's ain son, a lad just turned eighteen. I believed her. Nancy McGilvray put faur too high a price on hersel' to let ony penniless servant touch her. Like as no' she egged the young gentleman on. But there's nae proof in cases like that. Your grandfather's no' the man to gie trouble to a lord. So he made her mairry my brither John, wha'd always had a notion o' her. She had to consent, for she was in terrible disgrace, and she didnae want to be saddled wi' a bastard. But she must hae felt bitter in her hert, for when you were juist three she upped and awa' wi' Malcolm. She met him through the Auld Kirk. He attended it regularly. They tell me there's a painted windae there paid for wi' his money: an angel representin' Hope. Your grandfather used to think highly o' him.'

'But the earl's son,' I asked, 'where's he?'

'Deid. They packed him aff to Australia or New Zealand, I forget which, whaur he had an uncle in a high position. He took badly oot there. He was delicate.'

So at last the mystery was cleared up, but another mystery had been left in its place: me.

THIRTEEN

I was the son of an earl's son, but a shipyard joiner was my father. I should have been living in a castle with large policies; instead I was living in a two-room-and-kitchen with a shared backcourt. I should have been attending a school more exclusive than Gantock Academy, yet I was still a pupil at Kidd Street. My friends' fathers should have been noblemen and landowners, whereas they were welders and caulkers and unemployed. My female friends ought to have been the daughters of gentlemen, not a madcap like Meg Jeffries, whose father was an official in the Orange Lodge, nor a juvenile socialist like Mary Holmscroft, born in a slum. I should have had servants to look after me, whereas I had to clean my own shoes, fetch up coal from the cellar, and even take wee Sammy for walks.

I was a conundrum all right, and I couldn't see how I could possibly be unravelled.

Even before Aunt Bella's, or Mrs Pringle's, revelations, I had been experiencing vague intimations of superiority. Now that these were confirmed they naturally became clearer and more compulsive. I began to find it difficult to speak to people without making it too plain that I thought they were beneath me. Friends like Smout didn't mind, because they were used to me, but foes like Mrs Grier did mind and accused me, both behind my back and to my face, of becoming more stuck-up and conceited every day.

I was at a loss how to deal with John Lamont, who still thought I thought that he was my father. So I began to avoid him as much as I could, considering how close together we had to live. Bessie noticed and scolded me. Often I was on the point of confiding in her, but I was afraid. Archie Paterson had put his eye to a keyhole once, not knowing there was a lighted squib at the other end. It had gone off. His right eye had been permanently damaged. The keyhole I wanted to peep through was the future. I hoped to see a castle, wide green lawns, immense gardens, and aristocratic people who were my relatives; but I might see nothing at all, for there could be an explosion in which all my affections and loyalties would be broken.

I consulted Mary. Our conversation took place in the playground, over the spiked railings. All round us our schoolmates played noisily in the sunshine. She was very happy, though she tried hard not to show it.

Everything had been settled about her going to live at Ravenscraig. Also, through John Calderwood, who knew the factor, her family were to be given a two-room-and-kitchen in Mavis Street, well outside the Vennel. There was the prospect of a job for her father. Her sisters and brothers were to visit her as often as they wished. Her mother was delighted.

Though I had a more extraordinary tale to tell about myself, I listened with pleasure and only a little scepticism. Her rising in the world made my own more spectacular ascent rather less unbelievable. Besides, she was my friend.

'I've been finding things out,' I said, when it was my turn.

'What things?'

'My mother ran away with a man called Malcolm.'

'I knew that.'

I shouldn't have been surprised. No doubt it was common knowledge in the district.

'My name shouldn't be Lamont.'

'Oh.'

'It should be Corse.'

'Why?'

'Because that's the family name of the Earl of Darndaff.' I had been to the library to find that out.

'What's that got to do with you?'

'I think you know what it's got to do with me. My real father was the son of the Earl of Darndaff. I've seen a picture of him.'

'I heard he was an under-butler.'

'An under-butler?'

'Some kind of flunkey, anyway.'

'You heard wrong, then.'

'Maybe. But what difference does it make?'

Before I could tell her how enormous was the difference it would make, and was already making, out came Kruger Jamieson ringing the bell. She walked away at once.

Meg Jeffries came running over. She had bright red ribbons in her long black hair.

'Hello, Fergus,' she cried, and threw me a kiss.

Many boys saw and were envious. Given the choice between being the son of an earl's son or having Meg Jeffries soft on them every one of them would have chosen the latter. They had no pride or imagination. They were content to become shipyard workers. Theirs was by birth the Scotland of tenements and low-paid jobs. Mine was the Scotland of castles, famous families, and heroic deeds.

It seemed to me I must apply to my grandfather for the solution. The trouble was, I did not trust him, and he was not well. He never told me lies, but he always managed to stifle my generous instincts with sermons about Christian duty. As for his pallor and thinness, John Lamont—I must be allowed to call him that from now on—said it was remorse eating him away; but Bessie thought it was more likely to be some disease.

One Saturday afternoon, in May, when the rhododendrons were in bloom, I went up the brae to Siloam.

He was seated in the garden. His eyes were shut, and his lips were moving. Likely he was reciting in his mind some passage from the Bible. Three white butterflies twinkled past his head.

He looked very ill. He had lost weight, and his lips were blue.

I stood watching him for over a minute. I remembered my mother sitting on that seat.

'Hello,' I said.

He opened his eyes. They were blue, like mine, and like my mother's. 'It's yourself, Fergus. I didn't hear you.'

'You don't look weel.'

'A bit tired, Fergus.'

He wanted to shut his eyes and forget me, but he was too courteous. He was always courteous. He would be courteous to sinners roasting in hell.

'Mary Holmscroft's going to the Academy,' I said.

'Is she now? Do I know her, Fergus?'

'I've telt you aboot her. She's the girl from the Vennel. Mr Calderwood, the teacher, is taking her to stay with him and his sister in their big hoose in the West End.'

He did not approve. In spite of his pain and weariness he roused himself to defend his religious principles.

'It is wrong to separate her from her family. No good can come of that.'

Deliberately I fed his prejudice.

'They're a' socialists, Mr Calderwood, Mr Holmscroft, and Mary herself.'

'Not to be content with your station in life is to oppose the Lord, Fergus. That is why socialism is wicked and impious.'

What I had come for was to find out what he thought *my* station in life should be.

'Aunt Bella's told me everything, grandfather. About my mother. About Mr Malcolm. About Corse Castle. About Henry Corse.'

Like a blind man, he rose and went past me towards the house.

I shouted after him: 'Well, what am I supposed to do?'

If he heard me he gave no sign. Going into the house, he locked the door against me, for the second and last time.

FOURTEEN

He died that night. Judging from the fear and anguish on his face, the doctor said there must have been great pain; but I wondered if it had been caused by doubt during those last lonely moments as to whether, after all, he had really pleased the Lord.

The best people in Gantock attended his funeral. Present were: the Lord Lieutenant of the County, Lord Baidland; the Provost of Gantock, two bailies, and sundry councillors; a director of Stewart's, the shipbuilders; three ministers of the Church of Scotland, one of them a leading official in the Orange Lodge; the Sheriff and Chief Constable of Gantock; Mr Kelso, publisher and owner of the *Gantock Herald*, in which appeared a full list of names; and various other citizens, all churchgoers and substantial ratepayers.

Among all these I was chief mourner. The only other living relative, a cousin in the Hebrides, had been written to but had not replied. Therefore I was the one at whom those notables had to direct their stares of sympathy. I took care that they saw, not the grandson of a chief pay clerk, however respected, but the grandson of an earl. Tall for my age, red-haired, kilted, straightbacked, and handsome in a haughty way, I was the most distinguished-looking person there, outshining even Lord Baidland, except when he spoke. From his lips I heard, for the first time, the authentic confident bray of the upper-class, and noted the instant obsequious effect it had on those bourgeois Scots. I knew then that I must acquire it too.

During that half hour at my grandfather's grave I grew up fast. When I stepped away from it I was no longer a simple child.

In addition to Siloam and its contents, my grandfather left me nearly eight hundred pounds, a substantial sum in those days. How he could have accumulated so much mystified us all. Bessie, good at arithmetic, calculated that on his salary of £2 14s he could hardly have saved more than 10/- per week, or £25 per year. At that rate it would have taken him 30 years to save up £800. Where then had all the money come from? She suggested it must have been given him by the Earl of Darndaff as compensation, or as a bribe to keep quiet. John Lamont reluctantly disclosed that when he had married my mother he had been offered money by my grandfather. He was not told how much because he had angrily rejected it. 'More fool you,' Bessie said, sharply. But then, during those weeks after my grandfather's death, when I was turning myself from a Lamont into a Corse, we were all irritable with one another.

Luckily, the Scots are not a demonstrative or ostentatiously philoprogenitive race. In a situation where Italians, say, or Russians, would have wept, wailed, shouted, wrung hands, and appealed to God, John Lamont and I behaved with dignity and good sense.

He admitted he had known all along that I was not his son, but this had not prevented him from becoming fond of me. He had always intended to tell me who my true father was, but had kept putting it off. For a long time he had felt dependent on me, just as he hoped I had felt dependent on him. Now Bessie, Sammy, and Agnes had come into his life; he hoped they had come into mine too. He was sorry he did not think the Corses would ever acknowledge me, but whether they did or not he supposed I would not be content to remain in Gantock all my life, as he and his father before him had done. But then neither he nor his father had ever worn a kilt. I was different. He wouldn't say I was better or worse, but I was different. Whether this had anything to do with my having an earl for one grandfather, and a man of serious religious principles—he really meant a hypocrite— for the other, he wasn't clever enough to say. He had no bitter feelings whatever, and, given the chance, he would do as much for me as for Sammy and Agnes. He was very sorry my father was dead and I would never know him.

He did not tell me all that in one conversation. It took several, most of them in the garden at Siloam; and he did not tell me so much as communicate it to me with stray words, clenchings of his fists as if they were holding quoits, and some rather agitated tugs at his moustache.

I was grateful to him for his example of restraint. I was still too confused to have devised a new mode of behaviour that would impress but not infuriate; but I did my best to let him know that I was fond of him too, and bore him no ill-will for his part in the conspiracy of silence that had kept from me knowledge of my aristocratic birth.

Like him, I was inhibited by the impossibility of physical contact, such as kissing on the cheek, or clasping the hand, or putting an arm round shoulders. When we came in from the garden one evening Bessie said that a stranger watching us would have thought we were both dumb or paralysed.

Bessie was reluctant to leave her two-room-and-kitchen to go up the hill and live in Siloam. She wanted me to sell it. In the end she agreed, but only on condition they paid me a rent, not into my hand or sporran, but into my bank account. I did not protest much. My campaign, already begun, to have myself accepted as a Corse of Darndaff by the world, if not by the Corses themselves, would probably be expensive.

She raised difficulties too over my proposed change of name from Lamont to Corse. She told me not to be insolent. When I was 21 and outside their control I could call myself anything I liked, but until then would I please get it into my head that joiners and ex-shop assistants had as much pride as illegitimate sons of consumptive aristocrats.

Her anger puzzled me. I had expected her to help me in my campaign, and not oppose. She was ambitious for Sammy, whom she wanted to be a doctor, for Agnes, whom she wanted to be a teacher, and for her husband, whom she wanted to be a foreman. It seemed foolish, unfair, and shortsighted therefore not to be ambitious for me.

We reached a compromise. For any purpose where my birth certificate was not required to be shown, I could call myself Fergus Corse Lamont, without a hyphen.

In writing it was easy enough to observe the condition regarding the hyphen, but not in speech. Therefore at Gantock Academy, which I entered at the same time as Mary, as a fee-payer, I was soon known, in playground and classroom, as Corse-Lamont.

FIFTEEN

Though I did not know it at the time, my childhood in Lomond Street had made me poet. Living at Siloam, and attending Gantock Academy, my main concern was to turn myself into a gentleman, as the first stage of my campaign to be accepted, one day, in Corse Castle as one of the family. The poet in me, though subdued, nevertheless persisted.

Head of the English Department was Mr Andrew Birkmyre, a gaunt Presbyterian with a mottled face and a peevish voice. He hated Burns for making fun of the devil, Shakespeare for not giving Lear the consolation of knowing that Cordelia had gone to heaven, and Keats for preferring the ancient Greeks to the ancient Hebrews. Having to teach 'Tam o' Shanter', 'King Lear', and the 'Ode to the Grecian Urn', because questions on them might appear in the examinations set by the Education Authority in Edinburgh, he did it by dictating notes compiled from books written by dry-as-dust academics fifty years out of date. The reading of the poems themselves he did his best to discourage.

If an essay had full stops in the right places, contained no misspellings or abbreviations like 'don't', and was legibly written Mr Birkmyre gave it good marks, however tepid the language or trite the theme. At first I followed this recipe and was commended. But something in me grew scunnered, and I wrote, for the school magazine, an article on 'Quoiting', in my own style, which was more Homeric than Presbyterian. In describing how some older men, in the act of throwing the heavy iron quoit, made noises of stress and expectation, I used the word 'fart'. I was aware Mr Birkmyre might not be pleased, but then every other word I tried displeased me, as being ineffective and dishonest. 'Broke wind' was too polite, more suitable for ladies in church than for tough shipyard workers.

Holding my article between finger and thumb, Mr Birkmyre shouted at me to stand. For the first time in weeks the class was interested. It was also puzzled. Some boys copied from other boys' work, in the school lavatories, where there was scope for exercise-books to be contaminated, but I was known to be too independent and lordly for such a furtive practice.

'Corse-Lamont,' said Mr Birkmyre, hoarsely, his face red as a tomato, 'am I right in saying that you would resent being called a guttersnipe?'

'You are, sir.'

'Then would you please explain why, in this essay, you have used the language of guttersnipes.'

Never before had he interested a class so much. They even asked questions.

'What's the article about, sir?'

'What sort of language has he used, sir?'

'Please read it out to us, sir.'

'Hold your tongues,' he roared. 'It is my opinion, Corse-Lamont, that you deliberately set out to show your contempt for me, for your schoolmates, and for your school.'

'Read it out sir,' they appealed. 'Let us judge.'

His use of the word guttersnipe was making me wonder. 'Fart' was a truthful word, but was it gentlemanly? Was there a contradiction between truth and gentlemanliness?

Would I say 'fart' when talking to Cathie Calderwood? Yes, in certain circumstances, I might. Cathie wasn't my goddess so much as my naiad. She was a naiad too that dreamt of satyrs.

But I wouldn't dare say it to Meg Jeffries, now working in a shop that sold ladies' clothes. She would say it showed I didn't respect her. She would ask me if I would say 'fart' in Corse Castle.

What about Mary, though, lover of truth? I turned and looked at her. Living in Ravenscraig had made her plumper and healthier. But she still had nightmares about rats in the Vennel.

'Come out,' yelled Mr Birkmyre.

I marched out.

'Hold out your hand.' He swung his heavy leather belt over his shoulder.

In my school career I had been belted many times: often enough indeed to learn how, by drawing away my hand at the right moment, the whack would be delivered to the teacher's leg or, in the case of a male teacher who stood with legs apart, to his backside or balls. But in all previous instances it could have been made out that I had done something wrong, even if it was just opening my eyes during a communal recital of the Lord's Prayer. In this present situation it was credit I deserved, not punishment.

'You refuse?' he bellowed.

'I have done nothing wrong.'

'I shall have you expelled. Do you think, because you wear a kilt, you are immune? On the contrary, you are more vulnerable.'

It was the first joke he had ever made, though he hadn't intended to make it. The class laughed at the idea of my getting the belt on my bare backside.

'You and I will pay a visit to the Rector,' he cried. Turning to the class, he gave instructions: 'Grammar-book, page 170, Exercise 91, Analysis and Parsing, do numbers 8 to 15 inclusive.'

In the corridor he hesitated, not sure whether to take me to Mr Fyfe, the Deputy-Rector, or to Mr Beaton, the Rector. He approved of neither, and considered it a disgrace that he, a man of strict morals and a Christian, should be subordinate to, in the one case, a baldheaded philanderer, and in the other case, a classical scholar more likely to quote from Virgil than from Leviticus.

Mr Fyfe might laugh coarsely at my use of the word 'fart' and be content to give me, with a wink, two soft whacks as punishment. He knew I often visited Cathie Calderwood's house. Like most of the male teachers he delighted in Cathie. He had been seen once patting her bottom.

As for Mr Beaton, he lacked what was necessary in a good headmaster, that was, a Jehovah-like perseverance in the punishment of malefactors. Once, when some senior boys had tied a pair of girl's knickers to the school flagpole, Mr Beaton had refused to allow an investigation to take place to root out the culprits. He had contented himself with quoting, at a school assembly, some sonorous Latin.

Mr Birkmyre felt that his honour and reputation would suffer if I did not return to his classroom with bowed head and swollen hands.

The Rector was seated at his desk with a book open. It was in Latin. Though I did not know it then, he was engaged on a translation into broad Scots of the De Natura Rerum of Lucretius. A neat-headed, sallow-faced man, he looked up with a civilised smile.

'Read this, Mr Beaton,' cried Mr Birkmyre, throwing my article on to the desk.

'Whit is it?'

Another of the Rector's failings was that he often lapsed into Scots. He had been brought up on a farm in Ayrshire.

'It is a piece of abominable impertinence.'

'It appears to be an essay on quoiting. I used to watch

quoiting when I was a lad. You catch the atmosphere very well, Fergus.'

'I hope you are noticing that the language used is vulgar and indecent.'

'Vigorous and accurate were the epithets I was thinking of, Mr Birkmyre.'

'What about this word in particular?' He pointed to it, under the Rector's nose.

I was watching, I realised vaguely, a clash between two traditions in Scotland, that of love of learning and truth, and that of Calvinist narrow-minded vindictiveness.

'You believe he deserves punishment for using this word?'

'I certainly do.'

'But in that case must not the nature of his offence be made known?'

'I see no need for that.'

'You have no scruples about being accuser, judge, and inflictor of punishment, all in secret?'

'If I may be allowed to say so, Mr Beaton, you are speaking nonsense. We are dealing with a school-child, please remember.'

'But not with a helot, Mr Birkmyre.'

At that Mr Birkmyre rushed out of the room, with a groan of rage.

The Rector gazed ruefully at me.

'All the same, Fergus, it is only poets who can afford to speak the truth and defy convention. Are you a poet?'

'I don't know, sir.'

'You are a member of the Cadets?'

'Yes, sir.'

'You play rugby?'

'Yes, sir.'

'You always wear a kilt?'

'Yes, sir.'

'You are related, I understand, to the Earl of Darndaff.'

That had been said by others, both pupils and teachers, with sneers of incredulity, or scowls of envy, or coughs of embarrassment, or sniggers of ridicule. Never before had anyone said it with a congratulatory chuckle.

'I was born on a farm not ten miles from Corse Castle,' he said.

One summer's afternoon I had cycled to Darndaff, with Major Holmes, history teacher and Cadet commander. From a distance, and above the tops of mighty beeches, I had seen my ancestral towers.

'I would never have expected you to use the word fart in an essay, Fergus. Perhaps you are a poet, after all.'

SIXTEEN

Major Holmes, who commanded the school cadets, was a thin hollow-chested man of fifty or so, with anxious eyes and a rasping cough. He had been an officer in the Buteshire Highlanders but had been invalided out with bad lungs. Mary Holmscroft and John Calderwood despised him for, as they saw it, encouraging boys to look on killing as a lark. They called him a provider of cannon fodder for the defence of capitalism.

He was really a gentle rather timid man, the least assiduous wielder of the tawse in the school. Other teachers, who disapproved of the cadets as militaristic, belted more boys in a day than he did in a month.

I often visited him in his big, gloomy, chilly flat, where he lived alone except for mice. He loved to smoke big cigars though they provoked fits of coughing that lasted for minutes. I almost asphyxiated myself holding my breath in sympathy. Sometimes, when he was feeling well, he would wear a steel cuirass that he had bought in an antique shop in Edinburgh. It had belonged to a John Prentice, a trooper in the Scots Army in the time of Cromwell. His name and a date, 1651, were incised on the back.

On being told that I was related to the Corse of Darndaff, he remarked that it was a pity I couldn't have got myself derived from a more militarily competent family.

He did some research on my behalf. One of the reasons for the defeat of the Scots army at Dunbar by Cromwell had been the incompetence of Major-General Corse, eldest son of the then earl. He had helped the Presbyterian ministers to badger General Leslie into leaving his advantageous position on a hill. When Cromwell had seen the Scots come rushing down he was supposed to have cried that the Lord God had delivered them into his hands. According to Major Holmes, he had really said Lord Corse.

The Corses had been founded as a noble family in 1593

by Robert Corse, a merchant in the town of Ayr, trading in coal and herring. He had lent James VI large sums of money. In return for the cancellation of these debts the king had created him Earl of Darndaff. Judging by his portrait by the contemporary painter, John Scougall, Corse had been a big, heavy, red-faced man with baggy, suspicious eyes. He had built Corse Castle like a fortress, with walls ten feet thick, and furnished it so austerely that the king, after spending a night in it, had complained his 'banes were sair'.

In the eighteenth century the 15th Earl had commissioned the famous architect Robert Adam to make the inside of the house beautiful, to compensate for the grimness of the exterior. The finest craftsmen in Scotland had been employed; others had been imported from France and Italy. The Earl's heir, fonder of horses and whores than of magnificent galleries and painted ceilings, had looked on in stupefaction as his home within grew more and more splendid, and the family's finances more and more depleted.

The present Earl, however, was rich enough. He had married the only child of Lord Broadfoot, a Glasgow industrialist, whose grandfather had been a crofter in Skye. She had brought wealth into the family, but also plebeian blood.

I felt hopeful. My grandmother at least did not seem too high above me.

'High enough,' said the Major, amidst clouds of tobacco smoke, and between fits of coughing. 'You see, Fergus, your accent's what's wrong. It's too recognisably Scottish.'

I had made such great efforts to learn to speak properly that it was very disappointing to hear him imply that I still spoke, say, like Smout McTavish, now a grocer's message-boy.

'Like my own,' he added. 'Like William Wallace's. Liké Robert Burns's. Like the great Marquis's. Like, in short, that of almost every Scotsman of consequence.'

'Then what's wrong with it?'

'You must bear in mind, Fergus, that the Scots landed gentry are a tribe apart. They do not speak like us. They go to considerable trouble and expense to avoid speaking like us. They are sent to exclusive English schools,

to acquire their characteristic accent and peculiar habits.'

I remembered how oddly but how potently Lord Baidland
had spoken. Even the provost with his gilt chain had
cringed.

'Couldn't I learn to imitate it?' I asked.

'Perhaps you could learn to imitate the sounds they make,
Fergus, but I doubt if you could ever acquire their superb
assurance. You see, they are not aware the rest of the world
exists. They live in the grandest houses, eat the choicest
food, and wear the most expensive clothes, but they know
nothing of stonemasons, or ploughmen, or weavers. They
believe everything comes to them by magic.'

It was hard to tell whether he was condemning them, as
Mary would have done, or admiring them, as I was inclined
to do.

'Aren't you exaggerating, sir?'

'Only a little. It is important that you appreciate fully
what you will be up against. It is not more difficult for
an outsider to sail up the Amazon and be initiated into a
cannibal tribe than it is for him to be accepted by the Scots
landed gentry as one of them. Such things can be done,
of course. Resolute explorers have done the one, wealthy
brewers have done the other. But they are the rarest of
achievements.'

'But I am not an outsider, sir.'

'Even so, Fergus, it will be an ascent as arduous as that
of Kangchenjunga.'

'I shall need help.'

'I shall be very glad to give it. There is one thing likely
to be in your favour. It is pretty certain there will be a
war fairly soon, between Germany and Turkey on the one
side, and Britain and France on the other. You would have
no difficulty in obtaining a commission. You are the kind
of chap, cautious with bursts of recklessness, that wins
medals. As Major or even Captain Fergus Corse-Lamont,
DSO, MC, you would find the great door of Corse
Castle being opened to you. War has been an opportunity
for advancement for young Scotsmen of ability but without
fortune, throughout the centuries. On the other hand, you
might be killed.'

He said those last words not with a sigh of sorrow but

with a smile of congratulation. In his opinion to die bravely
fighting for your country against enemies bravely fighting
for theirs was the finest death: certainly to be preferred to
sitting at home, waiting for the last bloody haemorrhage.

SEVENTEEN

Scotsmen do not find it easy to speak frankly of love,
especially the physical aspects, without some protective
coarseness. We call the act houghmagandy, and, alas, in
the performance we are too apt to make it measure up or
rather down to that crude term. A natural earthiness of
mind added to a Calvinist conscience make a combination
prejudicial to any lover. In my own case as a young man
there was the extra complication that I could never quite
make up my mind whether my approach should be that of
apprentice lordling or neophytic poet.

Whatever their cause, my deficiencies as a lover were
partly to blame for Cathie Calderwood's going mad, and
Meg Jeffries's making an ill-fated marriage.

Out of many scenes of dalliance between Cathie and me
I shall choose two.

One warm afternoon in summer she and I were playing
badminton in the garden at Ravenscraig. I was fifteen at the
time, she twenty-nine. She wore a long loose white dress,
greenish with grass marks, for she kept tumbling down,
and darkened under the oxters with sweat. Her yellow
hair floated about her face, her bare pink feet skimmed
the grass, she smote sunshine more often than she did the
shuttlecock.

Her brother and Mary Holmscroft were in the house, in
his study, discussing the works of Marx or Mill or Proudhon
or some such boring would-be benefactor of mankind. Since
Mary's coming to live at Ravenscraig, John Calderwood had
grown more hopeful and less embittered, with less need of
whisky to sustain his faith in socialism. He reminded me
of a child given an ingenious and complex toy. Fuelled
with economic and political knowledge, it could be made
to perform remarkable tricks, such as coming out first in
all the Academy examinations, and impressing his ILP
friends from Glasgow.

Suddenly Cathie tossed away her racquet, crying she was
too hot and sweaty, she must go and take a bath. Singing

in French, she danced away, with flutters of her arms. I was reminded of butterflies, which I had vowed never to harm.

Temptation stung me like nettles. I wanted to see Cathie naked in her bath. Previously, by rubbing the smarting places with the moral equivalent of a docken leaf, I had managed to soothe them in time. That afternoon no such palliative was effective.

Creeping into the house, I stood at the foot of the stairs. I heard Cathie singing. I also heard water running. The bathroom door must be open. Perhaps she would leave it open while she was taking her bath. It would be the forgetfulness of a dryad in a pool in a lonely wood.

In the stained glass window on the landing above, Ceres, red-cheeked amid the yellow corn, seemed to wink.

Up I crept, sliding my hand along the polished banister, and thinking of silky thighs. Under my feet the carpet was red, with black designs. The sound of a door shutting made me pause. The keyholes had covers like eyelids, one on each side. Earlier that afternoon I had slid the interior one aside, giving myself no reason, but really as a preparation for this present enterprise. Unfortunately, experiment had proved that through the keyhole the bath itself could not be seen or any occupant of it; the lavatory pedestal could, though, and that was a throne I had no wish to see my princess perched on.

I could not have said exactly what it was I wanted to see of Cathie. Not her bosom, really: Aunt Bella's, or rather Mrs Pringle's, bigger breasts, seen when she had been feeding the doll, had made that part of a woman's anatomy more terrible than beautiful. And certainly not her pudenda.

I had seen female private parts before. When Agnes Lamont was a baby I had often seen her being bathed, for Bessie insisted on doing it by the hearth. Also, when I was five or six, in the McFadyens' coal cellar, I had inspected Jessie's. The experience had been peculiarly disappointing, not only because I had kept stumbling over the coal, but also because I must have been expecting appendages of a more marvellous kind than my own, and the reality was an unsatisfactory plainness, as if the whole thing wasn't properly finished.

If then it wasn't Cathie's breasts or pudenda or buttocks

or navel I wanted to see, what could it have been? Something indescribable, something unimaginable; yet something that I knew Cathie had.

Filthy young brute, prudes will say, and if it had been anyone but myself doing it I might have said so myself. Yet why should not a young man, particularly if he is a poet in bud, with his mind in flames, be allowed a cooling peep at a naked woman, if his feelings towards her are tender and affectionate?

On my knees, I put my eye to the keyhole, having first pushed the cover aside. I saw nothing; and while, in some agitation, I was undecided as to whether the nothingness was caused by the inside keyhole cover or by that still more opaque obstruction, black shame itself, a voice addressed me from behind.

'Lost something?' it asked.

It was Mary. She had come up the stairs with her usual nun-like stealth.

I couldn't answer, for I didn't want Cathie to know I was outside the door. In any case, as I got to my feet, I could think of nothing whatever to say.

Mary said no more, but walked past into her own room.

I swithered about going after her and begging her not to say anything either to Cathie or to John. Her attitude towards love, romance, and sex was as much a mystery to me as it was to the boys at school. They whispered among themselves that she had no paps and her legs were bandy. They had to find some fault in her, because she beat them in examinations, and also because she was so nun-like in the plainness of her dress and the austerity of her smiles. I knew, too, what they didn't: that if she had said a grace before meals it would have been 'Lord, forgive me': she felt guilty at having too much to eat while there were millions of people in the world, some of them in Gantock itself, with too little.

She came out, carrying a book.

'Still not found it?' she asked, and then walked, bandily, past me and down the stairs.

Later that evening, as I was about to leave for home, I asked her if she was going to say anything to John.

'What about?' she asked, with only a little contempt.

I was relieved, and yet, as I cycled up the steep streets

to Siloam, I felt indignant too. She had implied that I had done a filthy little furtive thing that was best forgotten, whereas what I had been trying to do was pay homage to something mysterious, beautiful, and precious.

Other men were haunted by that magical quality in Cathie. Mr Fyfe, for example, bald-headed Deputy-Rector. Boys shouted after him in the street 'Old Itchy-Balls', because of the way he ogled good-looking senior girls and young women teachers. After he was retired, when he was living alone because his wife had died, and he was a shrunken old man long since impotent or in no need of potency, he would go for a walk every day rain or shine, just to pass the house where Cathie had lived. He would pick up a stone and throw it over the wall. 'Any kind of stone at all, Fergus. Even a bit of orange peel.'

One Sunday afternoon, when I was eighteen, knowing that John Calderwood and Mary Holmscroft had gone to an ILP meeting in Glasgow, I cycled to Ravenscraig, in the hope that I would find Cathie alone. Sometimes other women teachers visited her, or girls in her classes, or even Mr Fyfe with his moustache dripping scented oil. If an opportunity occurred, I intended to seduce her; or, as I preferred to think of it, to let her seduce me. She had given so many thrilling signs of wanting to do it. So anyway I told myself.

The only defence of my conduct that I could have offered was that Meg Jeffries, after years of being more or less my sweetheart, still allowed me no closer embrace than a brief kiss, so strong was her working-class virtue, and therefore, like most young men of my age, I was in a fairly frequent state of unappeased lust, a condition in no way mitigated by the wearing of a kilt.

Cathie was alone all right, and welcomed me in the little girl's voice she put on sometimes. This time, too, the little girl's dress she was wearing, blue with lots of little white bows, was short. Her stockings were white.

She took me by the hand, crying that if I was a good boy she would let me play with her. The game, though, turned out to be dressing and undressing a doll with real hair and one leg. Tiny dresses were scattered over the carpet in the sitting-room.

I had seen Cathie being childish before, and it had

charmed me; but this was different, there were moments that afternoon, indeed there were minutes, when she didn't seem to be aware that she was pretending.

Her attitude to the doll was so unlike what Aunt Bella's had been. Aunt Bella had wanted her doll to be a real baby, but Cathie, like all the little girls I had ever seen playing with dolls, made it clear that she knew, in the midst of the caresses and endearments, that it wasn't made of flesh and blood, and could be laid aside, thankfully, when play was over. Her imitation couldn't have been more exact.

She got up from her seat on the carpet and carried the doll—she called it Lucy—round the room, letting it peep at the little fish and sing to the canaries. She prattled in the way mothers did to their babies, but I had heard many such mothers and knew that though they spoke nonsense their purpose was serious, they were showing their babies they loved them, and at the same time were encouraging their babies' intelligence to grow. Therefore their prattling made sense, and was delightful to hear. Cathie's was weird. The canaries did not like it: they sulked and would not whistle. I remembered how Rob Roy had died so soon after my mother.

Dropping the doll, she ran over to me where I sat on the sofa and jumped up on to my lap, with her arms round my neck and her head on my shoulder, as if I was a harmless uncle of seventy or so.

Things then happened fast. The sofa was covered with a slippery pink satin stuff. We began to slide off. My hand discovered naked skin at the top of her stocking. I kissed her warm neck. In my nostrils there was an assault of fragrance.

We were on the floor. She lay under me. Her eyes were bright blue; they were blanker than death. She had often teased me about my puritanic restraint; now she said not a word about it. She said nothing at all about anything. My hand, with no experience, knew where to go, what to do. She let her legs fall apart.

Close to us was a table on which was a bowl of goldfish. Perhaps my foot struck one of its legs, making the water in the bowl vibrate; perhaps it was past the fishes' feeding-time; perhaps, conceivably, they were fond of Cathie and wanted, like bull-dogs, to go to her rescue. Whatever the reason, the small fish began to leap out of the water making splashes that, though less noisy and menacing than the hissing of swans or the panting of peeping-toms, were just as arresting to illicit lovers. As I paused, two of the fish jumped clean out of the bowl and bounced, one off Cathie's face and the other off the back of my neck, on to the floor, where they wriggled in what looked like an admonitory parody of myself.

We disentangled ourselves in a hurry, for it had become a matter of life and death. Not waiting to pull up her knickers, Cathie, on her knees, gathered up the fish and cried to me to hand her down the bowl. Though her bottom was bare she was her own self again. I handed down the bowl. She dropped the fish in. One immediately darted about in joy at being alive or at having saved her, but the other floated upside-down for a minute, as if the effort had been too much for it. However, as we watched, it righted itself, and swam about happily.

While I looked away Cathie put her dress to rights and ran to the door, crying in her own voice that she would make the tea: there were cream cookies for it.

She looked round, with her finger to her lips. 'Fish keep secrets,' she whispered, and then laughed gaily.

I wasn't surprised at the quickness of her recovery. Like our western skies, her moods were always brief and swift to change. Indeed, I felt a little vexed at being left to carry the whole burden of remorse myself. Something deep in me warned that even if I lived till I was a hundred I would never be able to forgive myself for having so nearly violated that charming and, though I didn't really know it at the time, afflicted woman.

EIGHTEEN

Meg Jeffries was the most beautiful girl I have ever known. She was also virtuous; and she had a way of laughing that was merry without being vulgar or spiteful. She could have had her choice of fifty sweethearts. Because she chose me I was considered in the East End more fortunate than Mark Antony or Priam of Troy. It should really have been the other way round, she being thought fortunate because I showed her favour, but it was not, I was the one congratulated, envied, and above all warned.

Mrs Grier's warning was jocular. I was still at the Academy at the time.

'They tell me,' she cried, from her closemouth, 'that Rab Jeffries, Meg's brither, wha's a plumber, can lift a lavatory pan wi' yin hand.'

Still small and solemn, Smout McTavish stopped his bicycle laden with groceries beside me.

'I was asked to pass a message on to you, Fergus. Frae Archie Jeffries. Big Archie. Meg's cousin. Tak care. That was the message.'

Bessie Lamont warned me a few days before she and her family left Siloam to live in a five-apartment flat in a red sandstone tenement with tiled closes, in Arran Street, at the edge of the West End.

John Lamont was now a foreman. Bessie herself had been left a little money by an old uncle. She felt able at last to stop being beholden to me. She had never really felt settled in Siloam, though John Lamont, with the help of some workmates, had added to it a proper bathroom and two bedrooms. Arran Street was much nearer the Academy, where the precocious Sammy was now a pupil. Agnes would be able to go to Arran Street Primary, where the children were well-dressed and mannerly.

Bessie wanted very much her family to rise in the world. That was why she did not approve of my ambitions. They made her own more ordinary and more sensible ones seem foolish.

'What about Meg Jeffries?' she asked. 'When you have this big house to yourself her family will expect you to make her an offer.'

I didn't need anyone to remind me that the Jeffries were the most formidable clan in Gantock. They would not hesitate to break the bones of any man who let their Meg down. They were fanatical Orangemen, taking part in every walk, wearing sashes, carrying banners, and playing flutes. They had statuettes of King Billy on his white horse on their window-sills. Their skins turned itchy whenever a priest passed. They were convinced that any Protestant girl who married a Catholic and 'turned' acquired thereby a loathsome cancer of the soul: if she had any children they too would be blighted.

As the grandson of the late Donald McGilvray, well-known anti-Papist, I always felt safe from the Jeffries, provided I didn't get Meg pregnant or give her any promises I had no intention of keeping.

In any case, Bessie's warning was unnecessary. It came a few weeks after Meg had told me she had met someone else, a schoolteacher from Paisley. I had been more relieved than hurt. The woman I married would be aristocratic, gracious, refined, and probably wealthy, Meg had none of these qualities. Besides, she laughed too heartily when I tried out on her my landed-gentry accent.

One wet night at the end of July 1914, when I had been living in Siloam by myself for a month or so, Meg arrived at the door, soaked and shivering.

'Can I come in, Fergus?' she asked, humbly.

Though suspicious as to her purpose in visiting me so late in such weather, I took her in, helped her off with her hat and shoes, and gave her a pair of my slippers to put on.

As she sat close to the fire, still shivering, I could not help imagining her there as my wife. Never had she looked more desirable. Under her red woollen dress her breasts inspired the same old terror, but also a new tenderness.

For a minute I wondered whether, in return for the joy of having her as my wife, I ought to give up my aristocratic pretensions and be content to stay in Gantock, and be a poet.

Suddenly she murmured: 'I'm going to have a wean, Fergus.'

I was shocked: remember at that time I was a prude. I was indignant: remember she had repulsed my advances. I was apprehensive: had she come to beg me to take the blame? I was interested: who was this intrepid fellow that had defied the wild Jeffries? Her tears seemed to indicate that he wasn't willing to marry her.

'Who is he?' I asked.

'I told you.'

'The schoolteacher from Paisley?'

'Yes.'

Better not let the school board know, I thought, or he'd be out of a job.

There were times, too many of them, when I found myself thinking like my grandfather.

'Is he refusing to marry you?'

'No, he is not. He wants to marry me mair than anything in the world.'

'What's the problem then? Don't tell me he's married already.'

'No, he isn't.'

'You don't want to marry him, is that it?'

'Don't be a fool, Fergus. Of course I want to marry him. I love him.'

'Then I don't understand, Meg.'

Understanding came quick as lightning.

'He's a Catholic. His name's John McHaffie, and he's a teacher of geography at St Philomena's School.'

My first thought, so engrained a Scot was I, was that if she married a schoolteacher she would be doing pretty well for herself. My second thought, still more characteristically Scotch, was: Christ help them. However well-hidden and distant their dovecote, hawks would seek it out and harry it.

'I don't suppose your family knows,' I said, feebly.

'I'm feart to tell them.'

So craven is selfishness, it occurred to me that, though telling them would bring disaster on her head, she ought to do it quickly, lest they put the blame on me and come to Siloam with lifted fists.

'I'm no' feart for myself. I'm feart for John.'

Civilisation did advance, even in Scotland. In the old days the Jeffries would have burnt the presumptuous heretic to cinders, with the blessing of the Kirk. Nowadays, if they beat him up, they would be charged with assault and fined. But for destroying his happiness they would receive no punishment.

'I'd dee rather than bring harm to him.'

Walking in the street, McHaffie would never be taken for a miracle-worker. Yet this girl's love for him was miraculous.

'If he gave up his religion, Meg, would your family accept him?'

'I would never ask him to do that.'

'But you'd have to give up yours. You'd have to be married in a chapel, by a priest.'

She was silent. I saw her shudder.

'Why should it be you to make the sacrifice?'

'It's well seen you've never been in love, Fergus, really in love.'

When she left Siloam that night, alas, not much cheered up, she banged the gate, but without spite or anger. She was deeply anxious, but she did not blame me any more than she did the gate for being stiff. She was too brave and honest ever to think that fate was against her. Dogs' dirt on her new shoes, a speck of dust in her eye, her hat blown off by a gust, her finger stung by a bee, at such misfortunes she had laughed. She was never sorry for herself. She was young, beautiful, and merry-hearted, and she deserved to be happy.

I wish I was able to report that Meg married her McHaffie and after two or three years of anguished separation was united with her family again. Nothing so Christian happened. She was married, in a Catholic chapel, by a priest. None of her family was present. The marks of blows discoloured her face. So brave an optimist, she must have hoped to the last minute that her mother at least, or one of her sisters, would come to the wedding. Not even when McHaffie was killed at Paschendaele in 1917, leaving her with three children, did any of her family come to comfort and help her.

NINETEEN

During those years at Gantock Academy, when my acquaintances were mostly the sons and daughters of middle-class professional men, I did my best to keep in touch with Lomond Street and friends like Smout and Jim Blanie. Cycling home from school, I would sometimes go along my native street, though it was well out of my way. To the women at the closemouths I would give cheerful waves. They would wave back and shriek, 'How's your faither?' They did not mean John Lamont. Without intending to, they were publicly acknowledging my aristocratic parentage. In return, I loved them with a poet's compassion, and understood them with a poet's insight.

If a drunkard known to beat and terrorise his wife had staggered past them, they would have eyed him sternly and their 'guid evenings' would have had more admonition in them than cordiality, but they would also have admitted among themselves that he deserved some sympathy, because his wife was fushionless, his home ill-organised, and his children fractious, so that the pub was a haven.

If a rent collector had passed they would have disapproved of him heartily, but they would also have noticed how his hat was stained at the crown or the elbow of his coat darned, indications that his pay was little more than their husbands', and just as precarious.

They were displeased with me because they thought that, like my mother, I was a traitor. She had chosen Henry Corse as her lover, and I had chosen him as my father, instead of John Lamont, a joiner, whose parents they had known, who spoke with the same accent as themselves, who played quoits with their men, and who worked in the shipyard. Henry Corse to them was a creature as remote as an orang-utang, and as ridiculous.

I felt in my bones that these women had had, and were still having, an influence on me that would last all my life.

On the evening of the day that war was declared a feeling of homefelt patriotism caused me to walk home from work by way of Lomond Street.

When I turned the corner, there in Boag's shop window the notice 'No Credit' still appeared, yellow with age but still valid. I was immensely pleased to see, in the sunshine, my native street bedecked with Union Jacks, Lion Rampants, tartan tablecloths, Orange banners, and various improvised flags of honour and defiance. Other streets I had passed through had shown only a flag or two. Here there was dancing. Jock Dempster's brother Sid was playing a concertina. Other youths I knew were scratching their groins and leering at girls. Three small boys were strutting about with sticks for swords and dented chamber-pots for helmets; another sat on the cross-bar of a lamppost.

In its own vigorous, endearingly crude way, Lomond Street was celebrating the challenge flung by the nation to the Huns.

There had always been in my native street this exceptional spirit of camaraderie. The relief of Mafeking had been celebrated here by a party that had gone on well after midnight. Two men had ended up in jail, and a

policeman had lost his cap. (It stood on the mantelpiece
in the Dempsters' kitchen for years, first as a trophy and
then as Mrs Dempster's sewing-box.) Eight at the time, I
had shouted as loudly as anybody, and was hoarse for days,
to Aunt Bella's indignation. Then, when Morag McFadyen,
Jessie's sister, had died suddenly, from meningitis, the
whole street had gone into mourning, with strips of black
cloth hanging from every window-sill. The white coffin
had been smothered in flowers, most of them bought from
florists, but some purloined from public or private gardens.
Jim Blanie and I had picked from the railway embankment
a big bunch of gowans. Their yellow heads had swarmed
with hundreds of minute black insects, but they had not
been rejected.

I was seen. A woman shrieked; 'Christ, there's big
Fergie.'

All the women stopped dancing, wiped sweat off their
brows, pushed back their hair, hitched up their skirts, and
rushed at me, with howls of welcome.

In the van were: Mrs Grier, now white-haired; Mrs
Lorimer, still fat; Mrs Blanie, with the huge red boozy
face Jim was so ashamed of; Mrs Dempster, the strongest
woman in Gantock, able to carry a hundredweight of coal
up her three flights of stairs faster than the coalman could;
and Mrs McTavish, who had given me many 'jelly pieces'
smelling of turpentine.

These, and others, overwhelmed me. For a second or so I
was tempted to flee, through a close; but I reminded myself
that these women were the mothers of my boyhood friends
and therefore in a sense my mothers too. If they inflicted
indignities on me, it would be in good humour, and for my
own good. They knew that I was in need of re-initiation.

In Lomond Street forgiveness and conciliation were
always as turbulent and robust as feud and squabble. In
less dynamic streets my back would have been pounded,
my hand squeezed black and blue, my stomach playfully
punched, and the badger's head on my sporran given a
tweak or two. Such half-hearted gestures could never have
satisfied Lomond Street. I was not surprised therefore when
those female hands, hacked, calloused, and chilblained,
pulled down my stockings, snatched off my balmoral with
its silver badge, tore the birchwood buttons off my tweed

jacket, and, inevitably, lifted my kilt. However, what I could not help thinking excessive even for Lomond Street was when, in the mêlée, a fist (I suspected Mrs Grier, though my only evidence was the peculiar salute she gave me afterwards) grabbed my testicles and gave them a squeeze which, no matter how conciliatory, was still very painful.

The ordeal lasted no more than a minute. During it Mrs McTavish complained that they were going too far. She was a kindly little woman with ill-fitting false teeth.

'Will you jine up, Fergus? Oor Wullie says he's going to. But they'll never tak him, will they? He's too wee, thank God.'

'They'll never tak my Jim,' yelled Mrs Blanie.

She was applauded. To celebrate a declaration of war was one thing, to send out your sons and husbands to be killed was another.

It was then that Mrs Grier stood in front of me and gave that peculiar salute.

She was pushed aside by a small grey-haired dark-faced woman, called Yuill. She lived at the poorer end of the street, outside my territory. I had not known her well.

The fist she shook at me was hostile yet in some way kin.

Once she had summoned the police to deal with her man who had beaten her worse than usual. Blood was pouring from her nose. When they were dragging him off to jail she had attacked them with her shoe. I had laughed, but not any more cruelly than the other boys watching.

'Your auntie's deeing,' she cried. 'When did you last pay her a visit?'

The reproof was justified. I had not been to see Aunt Bella and Uncle Tam for years.

The other women comforted and scolded her all at once, in their characteristic way.

'This is no' the time to bring that up, Aggie,' they cried. 'It's true Bella Pringle's deeing, and he's never been to see her; but if he deserves punishment for that, he'll be punished, don't you worry. Wars were made for the likes o' him. Either he'll come back wi' medals, or wi' an airm or leg missing, or maybe he'll no' come back at a', for snobs get killed as weel as decent men. So let's wish him weel, Aggie.'

All the time, as they were patting and hushing her, they were giving me winks, as an indication that I wasn't to take seriously what they were saying, though they meant every word of it.

TWENTY

I was never a glib passer of examinations or smug collector of prizes and certificates. For generations in Scotland bursary-winners and gold medallists have passed out of the schools and universities, fixed in the belief that nothing has a value that cannot be marked out of a hundred. This is the reason why the Scots have failed as artists and patriots, but succeeded as engineers and theologians. Before a man can enjoy fully the singing of blackbirds, or understand his country's history, it is necessary for him to have felt, when a child at school, the mortification of scoring less than fifty per cent.

In my final year the dux prize for English was withheld from me by Mr Birkmyre and awarded to a nonentity called Wotherspoon, who became a teacher and, later, a headmaster.

There was never any question of my proceeding to university, like Mary. Apart from my not having high enough passes in sufficient subjects to be entitled to a certificate of fitness, as it was called, I had no wish to go where originality and enthusiasm would be quenched. Besides, as Major Holmes pointed out, for the purpose of establishing myself as a gentleman and aristocrat, no Scottish university would have done: it had to be Oxford or Cambridge, or nothing. It was true, he admitted, that when war broke out and I tried for a commission, having been a member of a University OTC might be helpful; but there again, since I would naturally wish to be accepted by some pukka regiment and not by makeshift territorials, it would probably be better not to have been in the OTC at all than in one attached to a provincial university, with the possible exception of St Andrew's, which was half-English, and of which the Major himself was a Master of Arts.

Therefore I took the job of reporter on the *Gantock Herald*, in spite of a letter sent secretly to Mr Kelso, its owner and editor, by Mr Birkmyre, warning him that I could not spell or punctuate correctly, and used vulgar language. Thus, while waiting for war to liberate me, I wrote descriptions, in suitably emasculated and edentate prose, of small local events. At the same time, in Major Holmes's flat, I kept practising my landed gentry accent, and in other ways prepared myself for the election board, which, no matter where it sat, would consist of officers not likely to know anything about Gantock.

It was decided that I would give my address as Siloam House, hinting that its policies extended for many acres. I would also let it be supposed that I had a small estate in the Hebrides. This, like the rest of my story, was not entirely false. There *was* a croft belonging to the McGilvrays in Oronsay that might one day come to me.

It would never do to confess that my mother had drowned herself: gentlemanliness and tragedy were irreconcilables. I would simply say, if asked, that she had died when I was a child. It would not do either to have it known that my foster father was a joiner. Therefore we promoted John Lamont to doctor, basing him on John and Cathie Calderwood's father, of whom I acquired a photograph, just in case. At some opportune moment I would let drop the information that my real father was the son of the Earl of Darndaff. I would let it be assumed that I often visited Corse Castle. Using my imagination, and with the help of some pictures in a magazine, I should be able to display some knowledge of the place.

Everything would depend on whether or not their first glance at me convinced the selection board officers that I was a gentleman and therefore one of them. If it did, they would not pry; if it did not, they would be after me with the zeal and, fortunately, the brainlessness of huntsmen after a fox.

Not only would they not be clever themselves, they would be very distrustful of cleverness in others. Eccentric opinions, however, would not be frowned on; indeed, they would be approved, provided they were not too articulately and coherently expressed.

Since the British Army was made up almost entirely of working class men, my knowledge of these would be regarded as an asset. I would not be so foolish, though, as to let it be known I had acquired that knowledge by living among them. It would be easy enough to give the impression that I knew them in the way every gentleman knew his servants, or a conscientious and kindly keeper his monkeys.

The Major was confident that that quality in me, which caused urchins to yell 'Lord Muck', would, properly controlled, have me recognised and welcomed as a 'demn good chep' in any officers' mess.

Since it was part of every gentleman's education to be able to ride, I spent hours learning in a field near McSherry's Wood, on a fat horse called Jock, that usually pulled a farmer's trap.

When war was declared in August, 1914, and appeals were made for young men to join the army, few were readier than I. But I could not afford to be in a hurry to enlist. I had to wait while Major Holmes made soundings and wrote letters. To that extent, therefore, it could have been said I was not so precipitately patriotic as Smout McTavish.

I was among those at the station seeing Smout off. His mother was weeping. A believer in spiritualism, she was being consoled by others of that faith: if her Willie was killed, she would still be able to keep in touch with him in the hall in Thurso Street.

I remembered how, once, when a boy, seeing flies stuck to flypaper hanging from the pulley in her kitchen, I had remarked that Hindus believed flies had souls. Mrs McTavish had stared at them in horror, wondering whether she should pick off those still moving. Perhaps there in the station she had a vision of the war as a gigantic flypaper suspended from the sky, to which millions of men, among them her Willie, were stuck, bodies and souls together.

Mrs Grier was there, and other women who had known him all his life. They were fond of him, they had brought him presents, but they could not help letting it be known that in their view there were hundreds of men in Gantock with far more urgent reason than he to be grateful to king and country. They had big villas to defend, he a single-end. (This was pardonable exaggeration: the McTavishes had long ago moved into a room-and-kitchen.) Thus they reasoned, aloud, but it was obvious they were proud of him for going before his turn. There being no word in their vocabulary, or in anyone else's, for a hero who was also a mug, they were obliged to season their admiration with disapproval.

I shook hands with him. He hardly came up to my shoulders. He would be given jobs like peeling potatoes or cleaning latrines.

'Good luck, Smout.'

He was embarrassed. 'Thanks, Fergus. Good luck to you.'

Then I was pushed aside by women wanting to pat his shoulder or shake his hand or tweak his cheek or, in one case, kiss him. I was astonished. I had not known that he and Jessie McFadyen were sweethearts. I had not known either that Jessie, bonny as ever, had apparently at long last caught up with her runaway wits, like a boy his girr. Kissing Smout she looked, in the Scots phrase, as 'wice-like' as any lass whose lad is off to war.

Not everyone agreed with me. After the train had gone and we were leaving the station I overheard a woman say to another—I knew neither, they weren't from Lomond Street—that the war would be a blessing for Willie McTavish if it saved him from marrying poor Jessie McFadyen, who as a wean couldn't keep her nose clean and as a young woman couldn't keep her legs shut. The other woman agreed, and added that the war was going to be a blessing to a lot more, particularly shopkeepers: wasn't it scandalous how the price of eggs had shot up already?

TWENTY-ONE

On Sunday morning I was at the station again, this time waiting for Mary Holmscroft. Now a teacher in Glasgow, she came to Gantock almost every weekend to visit her family and the Calderwoods. That day's journey would be a bitter one for her, not only because the German workers had let her down, but also because the train she sat in belonged to the nation, the railways having been nationalised that very week: not, alas, for the benefit of the people, but for the convenience of the army. She would not enjoy that irony. Her bag would be heavy with books and pamphlets showing how war could be abolished and a socialist utopia achieved. She would not enjoy that irony either.

As she walked slowly along the platform her face was

tragic, and she seemed to be in pain. She could have been taken for a young Belgian woman raped by Germans.

She let me take her bag. 'I thought you'd be at church, praying for victory.'

A patriotic service was being held that morning in the Auld Kirk. The pulpit would be draped with a Union Jack. The Lord-Lieutenant, Lord Baidland, was to be present. So was every influential Christian in the town, unless he happened to be a Catholic. I intended to be there myself.

'Haven't you joined up yet?' she asked.

'No. But Smout has.'

'You mean Willie McTavish?'

'Yes.'

'What does he think he has that the Kaiser wants?'

I could have replied: 'His honour as a free man. His right to stand up against tyranny.' But I was merciful. I refrained too from reminding her that it wasn't the Kaiser in person who was robbing and killing Belgians, it was German workers carrying out his orders.

We were approaching Auchmountain Square. It was crowded with spectators watching the dignitaries arrive at the church. From his high pedestal Burns looked down, with the usual seagull on his head. Pigeons strutted and curtseyed about. They reminded me of Uncle Tam and Aunt Bella. I had not been to see her yet. I probably never would.

The Auld Kirk was the heart of Gantock. There had been a church on its site from the days of William Wallace. It was recorded in the town's history that the people had gathered there in 1314 to demand help from God in driving out the insolent English. Perhaps, though, being medieval Catholics and not twentieth century Protestants, they had not demanded but had humbly asked, on their knees on the earth floor.

Arriving in his carriage with his wife was Kirkhope, the grocer: he owned half a dozen shops in the town. A woman in the crowd accused him angrily of having put up the prices of food. A small pompous man in a tile hat (years later he became Lord Kirkhope) he seemed about to deliver a lecture on the necessity of profiteering in wartime. His wife, stalwart in an expensive dark red costume, pushed him on up the steps into the church.

Two other carriages appeared. From one descended Cargill the lawyer and his wife and three daughters, from the other Ettrick, managing director of a firm that made hawsers.

'"The murderers of your mother. The betrayers of Scotland,"' said Mary. 'Do you still call them that, now you're on their side?'

I had meant to leave her there and go into the church, but I felt I had to give her an answer first.

I still believed, or rather felt as a poet, that Kirkhope, Cargill, and Ettrick, and their kind had throughout the centuries set up in Scotland a morality that put the ability to pay far in front of the necessity to forgive and love. I also thought that just as the bourgeoisie in 1707 had sold Scotland to the English for the sake of bigger profits, so their counterparts today still kept up that profitable betrayal. Mary was wrong to say I was on their side: they opposed the Germans on behalf of the British Empire, I on behalf of Scotland.

I was on the side of aristocracy: it was not corrupted by the urge to make more and more money; and of the working-class, who had been poor for so long that they had learned how to make life rich with little money.

I was aware of course that these attitudes of mine might appear contradictory, especially to a doctrinaire socialist.

I found myself walking beside her up Moray Street, away from the square and the kirk.

'Don't look so pleased,' she said. 'If you could stop the war by snapping your fingers you wouldn't, would you? It's the chance you've been waiting for, isn't it? Once you leave Gantock you'll never come back, will you? It'll cause you not one qualm if you never see John Lamont again, or Bessie, or Mr and Mrs Pringle, or even Cathie, your wonderful Cathie. Will it?'

That wasn't the first time she had accused me of hardness of heart, but never before had she done it so bitterly.

It used to be Aunt Bella's opinion that I lacked affection. It was still Bessie's.

Aunt Bella was dying, and I had not been to see her. Yet she had been kind to me when I was a child. So had Uncle Tam. It wasn't just snobbishness that had kept me away. I still visited Lomond Street, and talked to women at the closemouths. Why then did I have this mean determination not to go to 91 Kirn Street, first landing, door on the left?

Mary herself gave me the answer.

We stopped at the close in Mavis Street, where her family lived.

'I'm sorry, Fergus,' she said.

I was taken aback. I had expected another attack, not an apology.

'I shouldn't have said that. About your leaving Gantock and not coming back. You've got a right to hate the place. War's a lot simpler. You just name the enemy and then try to kill as many as you can. When it's your own people that harm you, you've just got to suffer it, there can be no victories then. Ask Meg Jeffries.'

She really meant: Ask Mary Holmscroft.

I was confused. I wanted to protest that I didn't hate Gantock, that on the contrary I loved the town, particularly the East End, about which I intended one day to write great poetry; but I was held back by something, difficult to name.

On the wall beside me I noticed chalk scribbles: 'PL loves NT'; and 'Deos he fuk.' Such accusations of love, and such coarse denials, could be seen on all the walls round about.

'Will I see you at Ravenscraig this afternoon?' asked Mary.

I nodded.

'Good. See you then.'

She went into the close.

After the briefest hesitation, I turned and walked quickly towards the church, and away from Kirn Street.

Yesterday I wept for Kirstie.

In the morning it was cloudy but dry. Thank Christ the schools are not on holiday. An old man can walk through the streets without being insulted or harried. Because I wear a kilt and have a beard and look distinguished, I attract the worst insolence.

Several times I felt tempted to creep back to my den. I had not slept well. But I needed air, even the sour sooty kind that hangs about these city streets; and in the park were trees,

some space, and young mothers with babies in prams. So I persevered.

It is less than half a mile to the park, but I was tired before
I got there, and looking forward to a seat. The first bench I
came to was turned over, with its legs in the air. I remembered
Kirstie's demonstrating to me how, if a sheep fell on its back, it
had to have help to get up on its feet again. With her memory in
my mind, I wanted to think ill of no one, not even of the young
brutes who had couped over this bench for sheer wantonness.
And the next one too. And the next. All twelve of them.

There must have been a rampage the night before. Some
young trees were snapped in two. Plants were scattered on the
path. Two young women pushing prams were agreeing with
each other that the district would soon not be worth living in.
In my rage and grief I wanted to shout that their own children,
in a few years' time, when society had become greedier and more
selfish, would do their share of mindless destruction. It would
have been unfair. Worse, it would have been a betrayal of my
poet's love of humanity; this, like a bird in a cage, no longer
sings but still survives.

Determined not to be defeated, I tried to put one of the benches
on its legs again. It was too heavy. I could not, however I
heaved and pulled, with risk of heart failure or rupture. No
one came to help. I thought of two women I had loved: my
mother, who had said, so bravely, that the young were the best,
because of them there was still hope for Scotland and Kirstie,
who would have lifted this heavy bench with no trouble, just
as once she had set the world itself to rights for me. Tears ran
down my cheeks. I would never see her again, or our croft at
East Gerinish with the yellow irises at the door, and her grave
speckled with tormentil.

Part Two

ONE

I gaze at this old newspaper picture of a wartime wedding outside St Giles' Cathedral. Only the bride's arm can be seen: the rest of her has been cut out. The groom wears the full-dress uniform of a Highland officer, with medals for valour on his chest. Between him and the small anxious boy who once pushed a barrowful of dung up the brae to his grandfather's cottage, what is the connection? And what have I, an old man with shaky hands, to do with either of them?

I do not admire this handsome, successful, arrogant fellow. Nor do I pity him, though I know what he does not, that he is about to enter upon a marriage with as many humiliations as Rannoch Moor has bogs. I whisper the old Scots curse: 'Hell mend ye.'

I am hurrying on too fast. Here is another photograph taken three years earlier. It shows five young men in kilts, against the background of a battlemented castle. An expert would recognise them as junior officers of the Perthshire Highlanders. I am the middle one in the front. Any impartial stranger, asked to pick the one who looks most likely to be of aristocratic origin, would point to me. I can look at this picture of myself and feel proud. I have a right to think highly of myself. The later arrogance was then pardonable self-esteem.

To have passed through an Officers' Training Centre, and then to have been gazetted as a second-lieutenant of the Perthshires did not mean that I had reached, to use Major Holmes's phrase, the summit of Kangchenjunga; but it did represent, for one born in Lomond Street, a precipitous and risky ascent, with stretches of crumbly and slippery rock. Testimonials from Major Holmes, Mr Beaton, and Mr Ainslie, minister of the Auld Kirk, had provided reasonably

good footholds, and hints of my relationship with the Corses
of Darndaff, given out cunningly, gave support like a rope.
Mainly however I had to rely on my appearance, my way
with a kilt, my acquired upper-class accent (only the slightest adjustments proved necessary), my agility with words,
and my confidence in myself. I was helped by the amiable gullibility of most of the senior officers. Fighting the
Afghans and the Boers had not, it seemed, honed their
wits or extended their knowledge of human trickery, in
the way that skirmishing with the closemouth fusiliers had
done mine.

When I became friendly with Archie Dungavel, youngest
son of Lord Gilbertfield, I was almost, as it were, in sight
of the cairn. I looked more of an aristocrat than he, and yet
everybody knew he was one. We joined the Perthshires on
the same day.

In the photograph he has his arm round my neck. He is
the only one not smiling. If the Church of Scotland, like the
Church of England, had been a fit place for a gentleman, he
would have become a minister. He was morbidly religious,
and had very thin legs: two severe handicaps for a Highland
officer. He was eager that I should meet his sister, Lady
Grizel.

Let me introduce the others. They were all sons of landed
gentlemen. They were not as close to me as Archie, but like
him they admired me and were proud of my friendship.
Beside Archie and me in the front row is Charlie Brack.
His father was a baronet, with an estate near Dunkeld.
High-spirited, he took nothing seriously, not even the war.
He was good at comic imitations.

The taller and stiffer of the two at the back is Hamish
Dunloskin. His father's estate was in Argyll. Although
only nineteen, he was haughty even when pissing. The
men in his platoon had several nicknames for him; one was
'Stiff-Erse'. There were times when he seemed to suspect
I was some kind of impostor. Luckily, it was beneath his
dignity to be inquisitive.

Beside him stands Andrew Dalgleish. His father was a
wealthy commoner, with a mansion in Edinburgh and an
estate in West Lothian. Pink-faced and shy as a girl, he
often blushed. He once showed me a photograph of his
sister: she was sweeter-looking than Lady Grizel, but not

more so than himself. After making a mess of drilling his platoon, he would have tears in his eyes.

The boys of Gantock Academy, even those who lived in the largest villas, could not help coming into contact with various members of the working-class, such as char-women and maids, coalmen and dustmen, ice-cream sellers, delivery boys, and shop assistants. They were, indeed, in spite of their pretensions, merely better-off members of the same tribe. My new friends, as Major Holmes had warned me, belonged to a different tribe altogether, one with potent gods. They needed their sergeants not only as assistants, but also as interpreters.

Without having to try, they had all the graces, physical as well as social: so much so it was almost a surprise, in the showers, to see that their navels and penises were not any more refined than a boilermaker's. No boilermaker I had ever met would have been so immodest as to talk about his sister while soaping his genitals, as Archie sometimes did. It wasn't that they lacked modesty or good taste or respect for women; it was simply that, products of a process of evolution more wondrous than that which produced elephants, they did not need mod-esty to appear modest, or good taste to appear deli-cately minded or respect for women to appear respectful towards women. No matter how hard they tried they could not be vulgar.

Discreetly, I patterned my behaviour on theirs. Since the seeds of aristocratic assurance were already in me because of my parentage, I learned with speed and accuracy. What I had to watch out for above everything else was not to seem conceited or stuck up. Aristocrats, I had noticed, were not snobs. Knowing that there was no one in society above them—royalty not counting—they didn't bother about who was beneath them. To appear sublimely indifferent to rank and at the same time to expect deference was not an easy attitude to assume, unless practised from birth. There were times when I found myself stumbling into foolish humility or unnecessary arrogance.

It was of course imperative that I cut myself off from Gantock completely. By not answering letters I made sure no more came. While I was still at the Officers' Training Centre John Lamont wrote telling me his sister, my Aunt

Bella, had died, and inviting me to her funeral. I did not reply.

I knew I would be condemned as a heartless snob. Bessie would tell the very sparrows in the street that she had been right about me. At every closemouth in the East End I would be castigated. They would look up at pigeons passing and say that the Germans were welcome to me. No one, with the possible exception of Sammy Lamont, would understand that this present denying of my native town was strategically necessary, in order that one day, years later perhaps, I would be able to return to it, bringing my honour and fame as tributes.

Among those I had to snub by silence were Smout McTavish, who sent a post card from his Glasgow barracks, Meg Jeffries, now Meg McHaffie, who wrote from Paisley, congratulating me on being made an officer, and joking about her own problems; and Uncle Tam, whose letter I could hardly bear to read: not because it was misspelled and unpunctuated, but because it was full of goodwill and empty of reproach.

I got one letter from John Calderwood. It was a continuation of the peevish attack on 'war-mongers and would-be heroes' that he had launched at me in Ravenscraig, the night before I set off to join the army. Cathie had whispered that I wasn't to mind him. He was really jealous of me: all his life he had seen himself as a resister of evil, and now that the most gigantic evil in history was threatening mankind he was prevented from resisting it by a crippled leg and absurd principles.

In my reply I merely said, with soldierly dignity, that I was sorry he and I disagreed: time would prove me right.

Cathie wrote several times. Her letters were disconcerting. One would be full of cheerful, lighthearted gossip about the teachers at the Academy, scribbled in her untidy, womanly handwriting; the very next would be written in big round painstaking childish characters, and contain prattle about her dolls, canaries, and goldfish. The most remarkable thing of all was that it was the infantile ones that were accompanied by cheques, not for trifling sums either, but for as much as fifty pounds. I was in some doubt as to whether or not these gifts were part of her childish game, not to be regarded as real. However, I eventually cashed them.

Major Holmes wrote once, from hospital, where he was dying. It was a curious letter, written in stately seventeenth-century prose. He seemed to imagine that he was John Prentice, dying of wounds in a tent after the battle of Dunbar. He spoke tenderly of his son and his wife, and commended them to God. The Major himself was never married, and never devout.

I let Archie read it. I explained about the cuirass with the hole in it. He wanted us both to rush off to Gantock and see the Major before he died. It seemed to him so noble and Christian a mission that he was perplexed when I refused. I said I could not bear to watch a brave man dying in pain and distress. If that was so, asked Archie, why was I in the army, eager to be sent to France where I was bound to see many brave men in that condition? In any case, surely I expected to see the Major again in heaven, made whole and happy again?

Every normal child by the age of ten knows that miracles are not possible, heaven is an idea, immortality merely a hope, and love a sad imperfection. At nineteen Archie still had not accepted these bleak but bracing truths.

What of Mary Holmscroft? She and I had agreed to keep in touch. The letters we exchanged were wary and brief. Along with other members of the ILP, she was in danger of arrest, for contravening the Defence of the Realm Act, with speeches against the war that were almost seditious. As an officer of the king, I ought to have disapproved of her as a traitress giving assistance to his enemies; and I did disapprove of her for that. Also, as an aristocrat, I deprecated her excessive passion, and her vulgar assumption that she was right and virtuous, and those who disagreed with her wrong and wicked. At the same time, as a poet and seer, I felt in my heart that it was necessary, for the salvation of humanity, that there should be some voices—not too many—raised in condemnation not only of the present war but of all wars.

Naturally, I did not mention my friendship with her, not even to Archie. When put to the test, I took sides against her.

Sometimes, in the mess, after the senior officers had left, we went wild. In our green and black jackets and yellow and red kilts we must have looked, and sounded, like predatory animals—after all, the regiment's nickname was The Wild Cats. Usually our pranks were of a physical nature, like the 'dockies' of my childhood. I was as reckless and agile as any. Occasionally, though, there was a discussion, or rather a shouting of opinions. One evening somebody brought up the subject of anti-war agitators. Somebody else mentioned 'that beastly little bitch, Holmscroft'; he said she should have been burnt at the stake years ago.

Other extravagant methods of exterminating her were suggested. Their grossness astonished me. When I had first gone to Gantock Academy, I had discovered that the fee-paying red-blazered pupils there were much cleverer at inventing coarse and obscene impertinences, and more effective in delivering them, than my jerseyed friends of Kidd Street board school. Now I made another discovery. My present colleagues, sons of landed gentry, surpassed the most foul-mouthed of the Academy boys. From their flushed, excited, refined young faces there issued, in patrician accents, every known demotic monosyllable of sexual significance, embodied in lewd suggestions as to appropriate punishments for a female denouncer of war.

It was noticed that I was silent. A dozen voices challenged me to say what I thought ought to be done to Mary.

'I assure you,' I said, in my most expert drawl, 'no torture you could possibly devise would be more horrible than what did actually happen to her once.'

They cheered. 'Good old Fergus. Tell us about it.'

Archie looked quite tearful. He shook his head in an appeal to me.

'When she was a child of seven—' there were cheers at this masterstroke of a beginning—'it was discovered one day that the cupboards of her home in the slums were as bare as Mother Hubbard's.' (Sarcastic groans of pity.) 'So was her mother's purse, and her dad's wallet, and her little sisters' piggy-banks.' (More groans.) 'In short, there wasn't a penny in the house. In every grocer's window in the district was a card, prominently displayed, saying "No Credit".' (Cries of 'Quite right, too.') 'Nevertheless, our Mary, aged seven as I have said, volunteered to take a basket and go round all those shops, begging for food. Her father hastily put in a suggestion that she should

ask for a packet of Woodbines for him as well. There are
no greater optimists, you see, than the very poor.' (Loud
cheers.) 'But our little heroine refused: she would subdue
her pride to beg for food, but not for cigarettes. So off she
went, with her basket. History does not record what form
of words she used to soften the hearts of those capitalistic
provision merchants; whatever it was, it did not succeed.
Picture her humiliation. Picture her weariness. Picture her
disappointment. Picture her reluctance to go home, with
her basket empty.'

Never was a more despicable act applauded so heartily.
My reputation for not caring a damn about anybody or
anything was established.

Only one of my audience looked puzzled, as if he couldn't
make up his mind whether or not my heartlessness was contrived, to conceal my true pity for Mary, and my contempt
for those laughing at her, including myself.

His name was Baxter. He came from Perth, where his
father was a lawyer. He was killed at Loos.

Charlie Brack went down on his hunkers, until he was
about the height of a seven-year-old. Holding out his
sporran, he shuffled from one officer to another. They
entered into the game and spurned him like hard-hearted
grocers.

It was regarded as the most entertaining night ever in the
mess. After it, my lack of sentimentality towards the poor,
or rather my courage in expressing it so publicly, was held
in awe. That I had once been one of the poor myself, that
I considered them to be richer in humanity than lords or
lawyers, and that I intended one day to write apocalyptic
poetry about them, was not likely now to be suspected.

On our way to our quarters, over the cobbles and under
the moon, Archie upbraided me.

'Let me tell you, Fergus, I rather admire this woman
Holmscroft.'

'If she had her way, Archie, Gilbertfield Castle would be
turned into a home for worn-out scrubber-women.'

'Well, wouldn't that be a more Christian use for it?
I know what you're thinking. You're thinking I know
nothing about the poor.'

'Well, do you?'

'Once, on holiday from Eton, I made a jolly big effort to get to know what it feels like to be poor.'

'In a castle? With fifty servants?'

'Let me tell you, Fergus, the part of the house where we live is horribly draughty in winter; and this *was* winter. I wore a sack next to my skin to get the feel of rags. I ate so little I felt hungry. I didn't have much money, only a few shillings, but I threw it all into the lily-pond.'

'But, surely, Archie, the agony of poverty isn't suffering it yourself, it's watching people you love suffering it.'

'By Jove, Fergus, that's well said. That's very wise. That's the sort of thing you should have been telling them tonight.'

'They'd have laughed still louder.'

'Anyway, do you know the conclusion I came to, after my experiment? I decided that morality can only exist in a society where wealth is fairly divided. I mean, what temptation is there for a rich man to steal?'

'The temptation of wanting to be even richer.'

'Don't make cynical jokes, Fergus. Basically, you're as serious as I am. When you make jokes they're always heartless. There are some things shouldn't ever be joked about. One's war. Another's poverty. The trouble with you, Fergus, and all the others, like Charlie, is that none of you knows anything about the poor.'

I winked up at the moon.

'I admit I don't know very much myself, but at least I've tried. I've talked to lots of farm workers, and chaps that work on the estate. You can't say they're not poor.'

'Why, don't they get paid decent wages?'

'No, they don't. I've complained about it, you know. That's the only reason why I wish I had been born the eldest, so that I could pay decent wages, and be an example to all other landowners.'

He assumed that there would always be owners of vast estates. His concern for the poor was genuine, but he would have been similarly concerned if, at the zoo, he had seen lions in cages as small as single-ends, and monkeys dim-eyed from semi-starvation. The poor to him were not just a huge alien tribe, they were a lower species. They had weird habits, such as sharing lavatories and eating bread-and-margarine. It was the duty of Christian gentlemen to be kind to them.

My profounder loyalties, I was glad to see, though of necessity kept secret, were alive and developing.

TWO

In the wilds of Afghanistan there is a game called buzkashi. It is a kind of rugby on horseback, with a dead kid or calf for a ball. The contestants are bearded men with fierce eyes and high-heeled boots. They respect no rules. Lady Grizel Dungavel, Archie's twenty-one-year-old sister, would have excelled at buzkashi.

This was the gentlewoman Archie was so eager that I should meet.

She was waiting for us with a trap drawn by a handsome high-stepping pony. The train from Glasgow to London passed through Dungavel land, and stopped whenever a member of the family wished to get on or off. There was no proper station, only a small platform in the midst of a great moor. The guard hurried along to help us alight. Other passengers looked out with interest. I wore over my kilt a tweed cape, for though sunny it was also cool. On some of the highest hills shone patches of snow.

I had hesitated before accepting Archie's invitation to spend a few days with him at Gilbertfield Castle, before we set off for France to join the regiment. Up to now, it had been easy enough to have my credentials as a member of the landed gentry accepted, because none of my fellow officers had been interested enough to ask difficult questions. Women, though, might be different. Lady Gilbertfield and Lady Grizel had never stood at a closemouth in their lives, and they would not have raucous voices, but they might well be as determinedly inquisitorial as Mrs Grier and her cronies.

As soon as I saw Lady Grizel, or rather as soon as I heard her, I knew she would not be dangerous, as an inquisitress. Only if I had had four legs, hooves, and a tail, would she have queried my pedigree. She was a hippomaniac.

'How do?' she said, gruffly. 'Been sitting here thinking tomorrow would be a good day to ride to the top of Spango yonder.'

She pointed with her whip to a distant hill dappled

with sun, shadow, and snow. There appeared to be no rocky precipices; nevertheless, to climb it, especially on horseback, struck me as the most useless achievement I could think of.

She drove us at a reckless speed along the rough track.

'There's been no rain to speak of for three weeks,' she growled. 'So the going should be good. I don't know why you didn't join a cavalry regiment. Wearing a kilt must soften the backside.'

She said it without a hint of jocularity.

Her own backside, I thought, would be as hard as leather. Fatness of buttocks had never greatly attracted me in a woman, but neither had conquistadorial leanness.

Now she was telling, with grim seriousness, how a few days ago one of her favourite hunters had come a cropper jumping a drystone dyke. Luckily he had broken no leg, but he had badly bruised his genitals. They had had to be rubbed with a mixture of castor oil and egg yoke. The treatment seemed to have been efficacious, for he was beginning to take an interest in fillies again.

From the way Archie nodded and smiled, she might have been talking about the arranging of flowers.

I realised how foolish and rash I had been in thinking that I had the hang of landed gentry ways and could possibly imitate them. I had never suspected that their women worshipped horses and had hard behinds. Other surprises, even more disconcerting, might be in store for me.

In nearby fields white-faced ewes bleated.

Since that stuffy afternoon in Limpy's classroom ten years ago, the ghost of Donald of Sutherland had troubled my imagination. Now, through the sheep, it spoke, to rebuke me for associating with the kind of people who had betrayed him so cynically, and to warn me that such association would blur my poet's vision and numb my poet's conscience.

For a minute or two I was minded to order Lady Grizel to stop the trap. I would throw down my bag, and leap down after it. I would bid them goodbye, without bitterness. Then I would walk until I found some shepherd's cottage. There I would be given a cup of tea and a bannock. If he and his wife showed me too much respect I would gently reprove them. I was on their side, I would tell them, on

the side of the poor and humble, and against the rich and
powerful. He would take me in his cart to the nearest
station. I would catch the first train to Glasgow, and then
one to Gantock, where I would spend my leave among my
own folk.

Of course I had no intention of making any disastrously
premature return to Gantock. So I listened to Lady Grizel,
with a few haw-haws of appreciation.

About half an hour later, we passed through large ornate
iron gates, sped up an avenue lined by magnificent trees,
and came in sight of the house itself, larger and more
gracious than a church, with a vast lawn in front.

At long last I had, symbolically speaking, come home.

I held my own during that short stay at Gilbertfield
Castle, even with Lady Grizel.

Her parents' curiosity was after all easily assuaged. They
had, excessively, that sure sign of high breeding, an aversion to showing anyone a second's more attention than they
thought he deserved.

Lord Gilbertfield often disappeared like a mole to pursue
some arcane activity. Archie said it was to read, but I never
saw him (or anyone else for that matter, except a maid
dusting) in the library, where the walls, from floor to lofty
ceiling, were lined with thousands of books, all bound in
leather.

Lady Gilbertfield spent most of the time pretending
she wasn't worried about Archie, her youngest and her
darling; but there were moments when there appeared on
her powdered face an aristocratic version of the sorrowful
apprehension that Smout's mother had shown in Gantock
station.

Archie took me on a tour of the house. Amidst its
magnificence and splendour I was encouraged to see, in
a portrait of an eighteenth-century Dungavel lady, painted
by Raeburn, a strong resemblance to Mrs Blanie, Jim's
mother. She wore a dress of shimmering white satin and
showed more of her bosom than Mrs Blanie would have
thought decent, but she had the same flushed, heavy face.

Because it was known I liked poetry, I had been given
a bedroom once slept in by Sir Walter Scott. A portrait
of him hung in it. I studied this for some time, for he
was a Scotsman who had done with success what it was

my ambition to do: that was, write about common people and assort with nobility. There were times when I saw on his face the sly smirk of the lawyer who had toadied to the Prince Regent and the then Earl of Gilbertfield; at other times I saw the wise, courageous smile of the creator of Dugald Dalgetty, and the author of 'Proud Maisie'. I had the advantage over him of having aristocratic blood in my veins; he, perhaps, had the advantage over me of superior talent.

I did not look forward to the ride up Spango. But it was no use praying for rain: Archie had said Grizel would go even in a tempest. The cook had been told to have sandwiches ready, the butler to put out bottles of wine, and the stablemen to have the horses at the door at nine o'clock.

Grizel was alone in the breakfast room when I went there about half-past eight. She was eating a smoked haddock and studying a map.

'Morning,' she said, with her mouth full. She did not bother to look up.

Bessie Lamont would have called her rude. But then Bessie did not know that for aristocrats the worst vulgarity was to invade people's privacy by being needlessly polite to them.

I helped myself to scrambled eggs.

'Windy,' I remarked.

When I had stuck my head out of the front door a gale was blowing from the east, with ice in it. But one trick of landed gentry I had learned and could do as well as they was to understate excessively.

'Archie's cried off,' she said. 'Got a cold.'

Again Bessie would have been shocked. She would have found it necessary, in the interests of truth and self-respect, to point out that last night, before going to bed, Archie had shown no sign of a cold. Thus she would have demonstrated her honesty, but also, in Grizel's eyes, her commonness.

'Sorry about that,' I murmured.

'No need. He wasn't keen.'

'Doesn't care much for horses, does he?'

'Never has liked them.'

I remembered the Co-operative galas in Gantock, when children were carried to some picnic spot in lorries drawn by big handsome Clydesdales with tails and manes pleated with coloured ribbons. I had liked horses then.

'Going to change?' she asked.

'Well, no.' I had decided not to wear the breeches provided for me. It was not likely I would impress her as a horseman; therefore I would have to compensate with some dashing dottiness.

Her brows went up, but she said nothing.

I had already been introduced to the horse I was to ride. Grizel had pointed out that it was a gelding. I didn't think of course that she had herself wielded the knife or scissors or whatever the castratory instrument was, but I wouldn't have been surprised to hear she'd watched it being done. From a remark she had dropped, I had gathered that she'd supervised at least one equine copulation.

The stableboy holding my horse found it easy to keep his face straight. Serving aristocrats, he had seen too much odd behaviour to find it funny.

At first we cantered across green fields among lambs and ewes. Almost immediately, I became aware that the warning Grizel had given me, with that lifting of her brows, was justified. I ought at least to have worn thick underpants. Even for a more practised horseman than I, it would have been difficult to appear at ease, while all the time trying to prevent skin being rubbed off my backside or, worse, my scrotum. Watching Grizel bouncing up and down freely, I reflected that women, by their shape, were more fitted for riding.

She leapt a low dyke. Low though it was, I cast my eye desperately along its length to see if there was a lower part still or even a gap. There was none. My horse seemed to have no apprehensions—was this because it had nothing left to lose?—and jumped over with ease. I was the one to suffer. The skinning had begun.

Soon we took to the hills. Out of remote shepherds' cottages children appeared. I waved to them, like Cortes to skulking Aztecs. They rushed back into their stone huts.

After an hour, still some way from the top, we stopped, to rest the horses, as Grizel said. As soon as she dismounted she climbed over a wall into a wood. I wondered if 'resting the horses' was an aristocratic euphemism, equivalent to the plebeian 'pouring the tatties'. She soon came back with twigs clinging to her, and sat beside me. From there we had a fine view of the castle amongst its trees far below.

'Can't see Archie as a soldier,' she said.

'Why d'you say that?'

'He says he's not going to kill anyone.'

'Not all soldiers kill, you know. Wouldn't be anybody left on either side if they did.'

'He used to lock himself in his room if there was a deer shoot on.'

'Takes his Christianity seriously.'

'Rot. Christians don't mind killing. We had a bishop once staying with us who'd shoot anything.'

'I expect you're right.'

'The Germans are Christians, aren't they?'

'I suppose so.'

'They've got lots of churches and cathedrals. I've seen them.'

'Perhaps it doesn't follow.'

'Archie says his duty is to be killed, not to kill. That's rot.'

'Yes, that's rot.'

Probably it was Christian rot, but I didn't care to say so.

'Shouldn't we be pushing on?'

'If you wish.'

All the rest of the way up to the summit cairn, we did not speak. The horses often snorted, no doubt in complaint.

The wind whistled round the cairn. The tips of Grizel's ears were blue. I felt as if I had been making love to a demented woman with long sharp nails.

I remembered another cairn, on top of Stony Hill, overlooking Gantock. I had climbed there once, with Meg. She had scraped both our initials on one of the stones. I had kissed her, not because I wanted to but because it was what a poet ought to do. 'What a dutiful kiss, Fergus,' she had said, laughing.

If I kissed Grizel, how would she describe it? Probably as stupid.

'We'll eat somewhere below,' she said. 'Too cold up here.'

We found a sheltered spot beside a stream. There was

grass for the horses. I busied myself getting out the food
and pulling the cork. Because of the pain of my skinned
scrotum I could not help walking with my legs more apart
than usual.

'I warned you,' she said.

'What about?'

'I always carry a first-aid box.'

'I'm all right, thank you.'

'I saw you grimace.'

'The cork was jolly hard to pull.'

'Before that. You've taken skin off. See, you moved and
you winced.'

'Sat on a thorn.'

'Silly suffering all the way down again. Not fair to your
horse, whatever else. I warned you, what a kilt does.'

'Good wine, this.'

'Are you prudish?'

'Modest, shall we say?'

'I shall insist, you know.'

She was after me all right, but in what conceivable role?
Hardly as a first-aid enthusiast looking for practice. Nor
as a girl claiming a sweetheart. Perhaps as a gentlewoman
scenting an impostor? How, in that case, to react, so as
to have her decide I was genuine? Would Charlie Brack,
baronet's son, simply turn his back, lift his kilt, and let
her minister? Possibly. But what if the nature of his hurt
was such that he would have to face her while she was
tending it? In short, how did an aristocratic young man
comport himself when an aristocratic young woman was
applying salve to his skinned scrotum? I just did not know.
This was a contingency that had never occurred to Major
Holmes.

It was of course possible that she was teasing me, not as
an aristocrat at all, but as a mischievous young woman confronted by a young man whose prudishness amused her.

I was on the point of saying, as nonchalantly as I could,
'Go ahead', when she got to her feet and said it was time
to start for home.

That evening Archie came into my room before dinner.

'Grizel says you let her down, Fergus. What happened?'

'We rode up to the cairn and down again; that's all.'

'She's a rum one.'

'You wouldn't say then that she's typical?'

'Typical of what?'

'Of a gentlewoman of 21.'

'Good Lord, no. She's too fond of horses, for one thing.'

'Are not all gentlewomen fond of horses?'

'She overdoes it. She's had a passion for them since she was five.'

'For one thing, you said. Is there another?'

'Dash it, Fergus, you shouldn't be quizzing a fellow about his own sister.'

'I'd like to know in what way I disappointed her. I jumped every fence she did.'

'She said she'd seen more stylish horsemen, but you did all right, so far as that went.'

'Did she say in what respect I did not do all right?'

'You see, she puts people to tests, without letting them know.'

'What sort of tests?'

'It depends on what she thinks their weaknesses are. She used to drop beetles on me, to see if I was too squeamish to kill them. What did she drop on you, Fergus?'

Young women, it seemed, whether aristocratic or bourgeois or plebeian, were illogical, perverse, mischievous, and unfair. Meg Jeffries had often been offended when I had expected her to be pleased, and she had found funny ideas I had put forward in all seriousness. Fiona Cargill, the lawyer's daughter, and Margaret Kirkhope, the grocer's, and other middle-class girls in the Auld Kirk bible-class had giggled in delight that I was the grandson of an earl; yet when I had assumed an air of superiority appropriate to such lineage, they had been huffed.

It seemed to me that by refusing to let her tend my skinned scrotum I had passed Lady Grizel's test. If I had assented she would have been shamed. Why then had she said I had let her down?

It was another reason for being glad of the war. In France I might be killed or maimed or blinded or castrated, but at any rate I would be safe from female perversity.

THREE

During the Great War I was an ambitious and enthusiastic officer. That I won the MC did not necessarily mean that

I was outstandingly brave or exceptionally competent. In situations that were nearly always muddled and confused, competence in the usual sense of the term could hardly exist. More often than not, it took the inspired form, in a junior officer, of leading his men to where they were not meant to go but where they were comparatively safe, and not to the right place where they would all have been killed, himself included.

As for bravery, this too could hardly exist, as a conspicuous feature, in situations where ordinary men, clerks, teachers, barmen, roadsweepers, etc, went rushing heroically across acres of mud with shells exploding about them, to reach, first of all, thickets of barbed wire, and then, if that was passed without crippling hurt, trenches, where the enemy, similarly clerks, teachers, barmen, roadsweepers, etc, were waiting to massacre them with machine guns, grenades, rifles, and bayonets. Heroes were ten a penny then. No wonder it was said, with cheerful cynicism, that those who were given medals were like raffle-winners: lucky indeed, since in the hat or helmet were so many names.

Though I admired this wholesale courage, I found it personally a disadvantage, in that it made opportunities to excel not easy to come by. The war would be pointless if I could not make use of it to distinguish myself, so that the Corses, when I finally made my approaches to them, would be pleased and proud to welcome me. Where heroism was commonplace, distinction was difficult.

Another complication was that, as an officer and a gentleman, I had to be careful not to do anything ostentatious, no matter how valorous it might be. In that case it would not only win no medal, it would be condemned as vulgar and vain-glorious. Moreover, the opportunity had to arise of itself: to do anything purposeful to bring it about would be to run the risk of appearing ill-bred. Gentlemanly heroes had not only to be modest, they had to be seen to be modest. Sometimes privates and NCOs slaughtered Boches with revengeful gusto, if their own mates had just been killed, but officers, gentlemen at all times, had to show the required refinement, even when thrusting a bayonet into an enemy's belly.

I had one important advantage.

In peace-time, where death comes from cancer or thrombosis or cirrhosis, no young man ever thinks he is going to die; but in war, where death's agents are swifter and more impatient, this confidence, in the majority of cases, is greatly weakened. Not, however, in mine.

I never thought I would be killed. This conviction did not spring from faith in the God of the Auld Kirk of Gantock: I saw too many men killed with bibles in their pockets and crucifixes round their necks. Nor did it come from the equally superstitious belief in the protective qualities of a photograph of someone I loved. Many men before a battle looked at such photographs. Afterwards they were counted among the dead.

The reason for my confidence was that I felt I had a greatness in me, too valuable to be lost. I had no idea what supernatural power was interested in preserving me, but all the time, whether in safe billet behind the lines or on a night raid or going over the top, I was sustained by that strong assurance of deserved immunity.

Therefore for me to be buoyant, in the midst of shells, whiz-bangs, mines, bullets, grenades, poison gas, mud, barbed wire, gangrene, trench-foot, lice, rat-bite, blistered feet, and pneumonia, was easy enough. When the danger was greatest the voice within reassuring me was at its most convincing. Men with contrary intimations, who felt that their luck had run out and the next attack would be their last, came to look on me with envy. It was whispered I was worth keeping close to; but men were shot dead with their arms round my neck.

The men in my company called me anointed. They intended sarcasm and achieved truth.

The opportunity I had been waiting for for months came at last.

I was in the front trench with my platoon. At any moment a whistle would blow, the signal for us to clamber up over the sandbags and charge the enemy trenches.

The colonel came along, patting backs and muttering hoarse, whiskied encouragement. He had cotton-wool in his ears, for the racket of our artillery barrage was tremendous.

He had just reached me and had his hand on my arm when we heard a peculiar whoosing sound, not so loud as the roaring of the big guns, but for us a more intimate and terrifying noise, since it was made by a large round black bomb with fizzing fuse, lobbed, God knew how, into our midst by the ingenious enemy, smashing the helmets and the heads of the two unfortunate soldiers on whom it landed.

'Christ Almighty,' cried the colonel. His subordinates, from major down to newest private, echoed the cry, as if he was a bishop and they his acolytes. They would have fallen on their faces in the mud, in the devoutest of obeisances, if there had been room.

While my comrades pressed back and blasphemed fervently, I made for the bomb. If it had gone off it would have blown me, and fifty others, to bloody bits, for, though ludicrous and unusual, it was no doubt powerful: ludicrous indeed, for it reminded me of the anarchists in the comics of my childhood, with hats over their eyes and bombs like this, only smaller, in their pockets, with the fuses hanging out.

I had no idea if it would instantly go off, or be made harmless, when the fuse, or what I took to be the fuse, was pulled out. Others, peeping in horror, were equally doubtful, for when I seized the part and began to tug at it, with the delicate force of a dentist pulling a tooth, there were groans of horrified anticipation, and warning cries. Out it came. For a few moments I waited, and everybody waited with me. All about us was the hellish din of war: we had a perfect silence.

Then the whistle was heard. At once, uttering my battlecry, I climbed quickly out of the trench. Still distrustful of the bomb, my men followed, not gladly, but with some relief. Thanks to me, they were still alive, they still had that blessed chance to come through. They thought of me then with a greater gratitude than they had ever felt for their mothers or fathers or wives. So, fortunately, did the colonel, back in the trench, though in a different part.

In his report he recommended me for the MC, and promotion to captain.

FOUR

It might have been expected that I, born in a room-and-kitchen in a tenement, would have been more popular with the men, most of them also born in similar proletarian places, than Archie Dungavel, born in a castle. I had played the same street games as they. Until I was thirteen I had gone to the same kind of board school. Like them, I had spent my Saturday pennies on comics and sherbet dabs, and had paid for admission to the cinema with jelly-jars. My childhood, the most formative part of our lives and the one where the strongest loyalties are forged, sometimes against our wills, must have been very like theirs. No doubt they had relatives living up closes, and uncles that kept pigeons or played quoits. It was true that after I had learned who my true father was, and had gone from Kidd Street school to the Academy, I had drawn apart from working-class ways, except for my ceremonial visits to Lomond Street, and my 'winching'—a word quite unknown to Archie—of lovely Meg Jeffries. But, though I had then consorted with the sons and daughters of bourgeois bankers and lawyers, I had never forgotten the ways of that other, more primitive, more exuberant, and earthier tribe.

Archie, on the other hand, had spent his childhood at Gilbertfield Castle, in the nursery with his sister Grizel, being educated by governesses and tutors. He had come into contact with members of the working-class only in the shape of servants, invisible except when needed. Then he had gone to Eton, where among the subjects he had studied had certainly not been the habits of close-dwellers. It would have been fair to say of him that he knew as much about the Fiji Islanders as he did about the Scottish working-class: probably more, for in some book or other he might have come across something about the former.

Yet his men liked and cherished him more than mine did me. They were proud that he was the son of an earl, and cut out of a magazine a picture of his elder sister, Hetty, a society beauty, married to Lord Knapdale.

To please him, they moderated their profanity and restricted their grumbles. Blasphemously contemptuous of chaplains, they even tolerated his saying a silent prayer before they went into action. They did, though, draw the line at letting him tend their blistered feet. They did everything they could to protect him, but were gloomily convinced he would be killed: only swaggering bastards like me were allowed to live.

It was true I swaggered. It was partly deliberate. Unlike Archie's, my social superiority was still to be confirmed. Therefore I had to assert it brashly. My fellow officers attributed my aggressive pride to my Highland blood, and were amused. I let it be known I had spent much of my childhood among Hebridean bogs. The private soldiers, however, and the NCOs, according to Hector McNaught, my batman, suspected there was something, not spurious exactly, but 'a wee shade odd' about my patrician airs.

Since Gantock was a fairly large town with its share of young men of military age, and the Perthshires were a fighting regiment that often needed replacements, it was always on the cards that there would be sent to my company some native of the East End acquainted with my history. I did not bite my nails in anxiety, waiting for that to happen. I was no snivelling impostor. I had killed Germans who had done me no harm, except of course that they were trying to kill me: I was certainly not going to cringe before malicious Scots seeking to lower my pride.

In the meantime my well-directed barrage of arrogance kept would-be exposers and detractors under cover.

In a lull during what the soldiers called the battle of Paschendaele, in autumn, our battalion rested and, among other things, incorporated drafts of new recruits. These were conscripts who had never been in the line before. They arrived with their caps stiff and their buttons shining. Among the batch assigned to my company I noticed the name Samuel Jackson; his address was given as Cowglen Street, Gantock. I remembered it as the street where the woman with the rotted nose lived. He must be the Sammy Jackson who, thirteen years ago, in Limpy's classroom, had kept watch at the door, to make sure old Oh-ho Maybole didn't come crouching in and catch us unawares.

Sammy's father was a railway porter. He himself, after leaving school, had worked at the pier. I had heard that his mates there gave him all the heavy ends to hold. His muscles had developed more than his brain. I remembered him as the kind of boy always given the role of goalkeeper, especially if the goal area was muddy, and at 'hunch-cuddy-hunch' that of pillow or cushion, where no honour or glory could be won, but much pummelling of one's stomach had to be endured.

I saw him first along with the others in the batch, when as company commander I welcomed them with my customary brusqueness. It was my belief that men did not think much of an officer who despatched them to the trenches or chose them for suicidal missions, with compassion in his voice. Hell was bearable only if everything in it was hellish.

I gave Sammy the same attention that I did the others. Though he hadn't yet been in action, he had been a soldier long enough to know that when a private was addressing an officer he had to offer no sign at all of human complicity. Therefore he neither grinned nor winked. He did give me one or two peculiar glances, but then all his mates did too. This was usual. In welcoming new recruits I always made it clear what was expected of them: that was, to obey orders and uphold the honour of the regiment. Other company commanders made the mistake of indulging in friendly chats, as if instructing beaters in a deer drive. The business of war was to kill the enemy. The more Germans that were killed the sooner the war would be over. That was my message, brusquely stated.

Archie, one of my platoon commanders, was, as usual, saddened by my harshness.

'I don't understand you, Fergus. Surely you could have shown them a little kindness?'

'What has kindness to do with war?'

'Oh, a great deal. Everything. How could we stand it, if we didn't show kindness to one another?'

It seemed to me kindness was far too poor a word to describe what soldiers in battle felt for their comrades. In any case, I now found it difficult to have sympathy with Archie. About six months previously he had been wounded in the arm. It was the kind of wound many soldiers longed for, unlikely to cause permanent damage, justifying a return to UK, and entitling the sufferer to wear a stripe of gold braid. Archie, with his influential connections, could easily have used the spell at home to get transferred, honourably enough, to some non-combatant post. I had advised him to do that. No doubt his mother had pleaded with him. Perhaps Grizel, with a sneer, had joined in. He had defied us all and returned to active service as soon as his arm was

better. In a man who recognised that Germans had to be
killed if the war was to be won, his attitude would have
been praiseworthy; but not in a man who thought it nobler
to die for one's country than to kill for it.

I did not assign Sammy Jackson to his platoon. Under
Lieutenant McSween Sammy would be made to work
harder to keep himself and his rifle clean, but he would
also have a better chance of surviving.

I soon found an opportunity of having a private chat with
Sammy.

'Well, how's it going?' I asked.

Still careful to be properly respectful, he couldn't help
a congratulatory grin. Evidently it delighted him that an
old schoolmate was getting away with a clever and daring
masquerade.

'We heard you'd won a medal, sir. In Gantock, I mean,
sir.'

He would break heads to prevent my fraud, as he clearly
thought it, being discovered; but the head I had most to
fear from was his own. Nearest to the door, I reflected,
had been bottom of the class.

'I see Mary Holmscroft's goin' her duster tae, sir.'

He meant that she had been in jail for making seditious
speeches to munition workers on strike. She had been
abused in every newspaper. Lloyd George himself had
called her an irresponsible and foolish young woman. I
would have expected Sammy to share in the general disgust,
but no, here he was grinning, and trying hard, without
winking, to let me know that in his opinion her defiance of
the government and the army was, like my impersonation
of an officer and gentleman, a ploy worthy of admiration,
and a credit to Kidd Street school.

'Her comin' frae the Vennel, sir. Some cheek, eh?'

'What are they saying about her in Gantock?'

'Och, sir, maist say she ought to hae sterved to daith in
jile. Things like that, sir. I heard her making a speech in
Auchmountain Square, frae the steps o' the Auld Kirk.'

'And what had she to say?'

'Weel, sir, yin thing she said was that efter the war
there'll be thoosands like Donald o' Sutherland. Mind
Donald o' Sutherland, sir? In Limpy Calderwood's class?
He came back frae the wars and found his hame burnt to

the ground and his folk evicted to Canada. He was a good teacher, Mr Calderwood. But he got the sack. Did you ken that, sir?'

I knew it. Mary had mentioned it in one of her brief notes.

'Seems he was telling the weans the war's juist a waste o' lives and money.'

Sammy grinned, listening to the thump of shells in the distance. Even a dunce like me, his grin as good as said, knows old Limpy was right.

'His life's safe enough,' I said, sharply.

'That's so, sir. My mither said she wished I was a cripple. They say his sister's no' weel: Miss Cathie. Aff her heid, they say.'

It was time to shut him up and send him back to his duties.

He was killed ten days later.

Archie Dungavel died too, in that same attack. It was the kind of death he wanted.

In a dreary landscape of mud, craters, broken walls, splintered trees, and stinking bodies of mules and men, he found himself confronted by a German sprawled on the ground, weeping with pain. Seeing the danger as I rushed up, I shouted to Archie for Christ's sake to shoot the bastard. He held out his revolver but did not pull the trigger. He looked as if he wanted to plead with the German, as one Christian to another. I fired several times, but too late: the Boche had his rifle under his body; he fired two bullets into Archie's face, shattering his skull and splattering his blood and brains. They must have died almost at the same moment.

In the German's pocket was found a bible, inside which was a letter from his wife, full of pious phrases. While burying Archie, I wondered if, in his instantaneous heaven, he and his Christian killer had entered hand-in-hand. What compromise uniform had they worn? When confronted by their new Commanding Officer had they saluted in the British or German fashion? Or, as in terrestrial armies, had they, as newcomers of lowly rank, been received by intermediaries?

No one expected me to shed tears because my friend had been killed, and half my company with him. Some, though, may have looked for a small sign of special grief in me, and because they could not see it were confirmed in their belief that I was ruthless.

I let Lieutenant McSween write to Sammy's parents. I myself wrote to Archie's.

About a week after Archie's death came the note from Mary with the news that Cathie Calderwood had been moved to an asylum. I read it by candlelight in a dug-out that shook with the explosion of shells. Captain Sinclair was cutting his toe-nails. Lieutenant McSween was trying to shave. Lieutenant Johnstone was simpering over a novel. In the men's quarters they were singing 'Loch Lomond' lugubriously. There was a stink of mud, shit, candle grease, and cold sweat.

Hardly a hundred yards away the Germans were similarly occupied. In a few hours they would be trying again to slaughter us, and we them.

Yet poor Cathie had been certified mad for playing with dolls.

'Bad news, Fergus?' asked Sinclair. 'Has she chucked you for another chap?'

They all waited with grins for my answer. They knew I seldom got letters or sent any. (My correspondents were Mary, once a month, Cathie, once every three months, and Sammy Lamont, still a pupil at the Academy, who sent me occasionally what he said was a report, requiring no reply.)

It was also known I had no sweetheart, and disliked strange women making up to me, especially whores.

I went out and stood in the rain, smoking and thinking.

If, among the thoughts that came into my mind, was surmise about Cathie's money, who will blame me? After the war I had a campaign of my own to wage, for which money would be needed. It would be futile to approach the Corses as a journalist or clerk: to have any hope at all I would have to do it as a leisured gentleman. The money I was saving up, from my pay and Cathie's cheques, would keep me in that style for no more than a year.

There was another possibility: I could marry a wealthy woman.

I often assessed myself as an inspirer of love in a woman with money. The result was always disquieting. I had no

difficulty in finding in me a number of attractive qualities:
I was tall and handsome; my eyes were bold and blue,
my moustache red and soldierly; I had the reputation of
being a hardened, experienced, and able officer; I had
aristocratic blood in me; I had won the Military Cross.
This was a good deal, but it did not seem enough. Nowhere
in me could I find a magical core, an irreducible lump of
lovableness. In some dismay, I wondered if every man, if he
was equally truthful about himself, would have to make the
same alarming admission. On the other hand, perhaps I was
being naive in looking for some rare angelic quality. Could
not lovableness be merely a combination of excellent but
mundane attributes? It would certainly seem so, judging
by the happily married men among my fellow officers. If
it were so, it would be a relief, and yet a disappointment
too. Even if I did not have it myself, I wanted there to be
that magical magnetic core.

(Among my assets I did not include my potential greatness.
This, if it was ever realised, would be the business of all
humanity, not of any one woman, even if she was my wife.)

Having, more or less, satisfied myself that I was as
eligible for love as any man, I then had to consider whether
or not I wanted to be loved. My brief experience with Lady
Grizel had shown me how little I understood, and indeed
was captivated by, aristocratic young women. I remembered how working-class Meg Jeffries had once interrupted
my far-reaching and satirical disquisition on the hypocrisies
of bourgeois Scotland, by asking me to admire her new
hat, and once my passionate annunciation that I might
be the champion Scotland so badly needed, by plucking
a buttercup and holding it under my chin. Fiona Cargill,
Marion Kirkhope, and other girls who lived in West End
villas had been trivially minded too, but in a more petu-
lant way. As for Mary Holmscroft, she had professed to
understand and profit intellectually from long sociological
tomes that I found incomprehensible and repellent. My
fervent discourses and aspirations, which had bored but
impressed Meg, Fiona, and Marion, Mary had, with a few
sharp words, revealed as puerile.

In any case, I was not recklessly keen to bind myself, body
and soul, for life, to a female creature that left hair in combs,
face-powder in wash-hand basins, and stockings everywhere.

While I was lusty enough to enjoy the prospect of being in bed every night with a body as soft as marshmallow, I was apprehensive about the mind as hard as steel that might well inhabit that body, if I was not careful in my choice. Moreover, I did not want to have taken from me certain small freedoms, not of great importance perhaps but nevertheless necessary if a man was to live at ease: freedom to belch, fart, scratch, drop ash, and eat with a view to enjoyment and not to elegance. Above all, I could not look forward without horror to having sticky-fingered, damp-bottomed brats climbing on to my lap and calling me da.

Perhaps, I kept warning myself, my aversion was simply that of a soldier at war, whose life for the past three years had been a mess of mud, blood, guts, and shit.

It had not escaped me how men with wives and sweethearts returned from home strangely relieved. Their women, they said or rather hinted, had become curious creatures, hard to recognise, far less love. They were too obsessed with cleanliness, too preoccupied with ordinary things, too politely unwilling to listen to tales of carnage, and above all too readily reconciled to their hero's having to return to the slaughter, once his leave was over.

'I tell you, Fergus,' said one officer, 'if I'd wanted to take to the hills or hide in a cellar, they wouldn't have let me, my wife, my mother, my sisters, my mother-in-law, my aunts. There they were at the station, the whole coven of them, seeing me off. They were sad I admit, but if I shouted, "Bugger it, I'm not going, I'm staying at home. I've had enough, I've done my bit," they'd have looked a whole lot sadder, they'd have outdone one another in reminding me of my duty, to my king, to my country, to my regiment, to my class, and to them. You're a wise fellow, Fergus, keeping well clear of women.'

I was often teased about my attitude of high-minded caution as regards women, but if McCrae had winked his eyelid black and blue I still would have known that though he wasn't entirely serious he wasn't entirely humorous either. He showed me later a photograph of his wife. She looked pleasant and amiable enough, but then there would have been no need for her to assert dominance over the photographer. That was what I really feared most, being married to a woman who dominated me.

FIVE

I first heard of Betty T. Shields when I was at Stank Castle. Lying open on the adjutant's desk was a book in which he was so engrossed that he kept on reading it while speaking to me. Being interested in literature, though I did not read many books, having neither the time nor the inclination, I asked him what it was called. Its title, he replied warmly, was *The Heirs of Crailzie*, and its authoress was Betty T. Shields. It was one of the noblest and most inspiring books he had ever read. If the Army Council took his advice they would disseminate thousands of copies among the troops. Indeed, it ought to be translated into German and dropped on the German lines, where it would weaken their resolution to resist more than bombs or shells, for it would let them know what kind of people they were up against.

When I came to read *The Heirs of Crailzie* some weeks later I saw what Captain McHolm had meant, but I also felt a little uneasy and suspicious. Somehow it all seemed too good to be true.

Set in Midlothian, during the Boer War, the story portrays people, including the villain, as fundamentally good, unselfish, and well-intentioned. The Ures of Crailzie, noble-hearted but impecunious landowners, go without wine for a year so that their tenants can have water in their cottages. Jack Ure, a Guards officer on active service in South Africa, writes home saying that the Boers were really splendid chaps at heart: once they were defeated they would see that to be part of the great British family was the best thing on earth. Jack is later blinded, and returns home to Crailzie House to break everybody's heart with his gay, dauntless laughter. Madeleine, the heroine, after the villain, a neighbouring baronet, has taken liberties—this part isn't clear, but he appears to have placed his hand on her foot as she climbs over a stile—rebukes him so sweetly that, exalted, he goes off to India and spends his great wealth on chapattis for the poor.

(Years afterwards Campbell Aird, most sardonic of critics, summed up Betty as a novelist.

'She's no simpleton, your Betty. She looks at humanity as boldly as Balzac. When she has carefully noted its selfishness and greed, its prurience and lust, its vindictiveness and spite, she turns all this inside out, so skilfully as to make us think, consciously in the case of the subtle among us, unconsciously in the case of the simple-minded, that it is the vice and not the virtue which is being celebrated. When she depicts a scene of innocent dalliance, look how she always brings in goats; consider *The Heirs of Crailzie*; or sparrows; consider *Airlie Place*. Lust is always lurking. This is the reason why her books are so widely read in manses, ladies' colleges, and nunneries. Have you noticed how fond she is of scenes of forgiveness? Yet if you listen hard you will hear black-winged nemesis hovering overhead, like a vulture.')

Since *The Heirs of Crailzie* Miss Shields had published three more novels, and become famous. It was said the King and Queen, and members of the Cabinet, were among her admirers. It was, indeed, her latest, *Airlie Place*, that Lieutenant Johnstone was reading in the dug-out the evening I received Mary's news about Cathie.

Like most of her readers, I imagined that the successful authoress was a white-haired old lady, perhaps the wife or widow of a clergyman. In the magazine she edited, *The People's Companion*, there appeared every week on the page where advice and comfort were dispensed the picture of such a sweet old lady, called Aunt Martha. It was never stated that this was Miss Shields herself, but most people assumed it. I certainly did. Many soldiers had *The People's Companion* sent them regularly by their mothers or wives. My batman was one. Sometimes he passed his copy on to me.

It was the page of poems that interested me. Some were by soldiers at the front. Miss Shields, in very small print, claimed the right to 'edit' contributions. It was obvious she did not mean by this simply correcting grammar and spelling. She meant the substituting of gay laughter for howls of protest, flowers for lumps of flesh, and nightingales for rats. I did not know of course at that time of the principle of opposites in her books. I regarded her prettifying of poems of carnage as an insult to all soldiers, dead or alive. So I sent her a poem I had written, 'The Burning of the Boots', and challenged her to print it without altering a word.

This poem, it may be remembered, tells how a night patrol stumbles into a field littered with scraps of decomposed bodies and dollops of human excrement. Evidently a mass grave and a huge latrine had been blown up together.

Such freaks happened. Afterwards they could not get the stench of mortality off their boots, which had to be burnt. But, to their horror their new boots, no matter how frenziedly dubbined, gave off the same sad stink.

Sooner than I expected a reply came from Miss Shields. She thanked me for my 'powerful and tragic poem', which was, she was afraid, unsuitable for the *Companion*. She had passed it on to a friend of hers, Mr Campbell Aird, who edited a literary magazine. He liked it so much that he intended to publish it in the next issue of the *Caledonian*, even if it meant running the risk of a prosecution for obscenity. She ended by saying that if I should happen to be in Edinburgh on my next leave she hoped I would call in at the office of the *Companion*, where she would be delighted to see me.

I could not help wondering at the casual way she mentioned obscenity.

I wrote, rather stiffly, thanking her and giving permission to Mr Aird to publish my poem, provided he made no changes.

Thus began my correspondence with Betty. With her third letter she enclosed a photograph of herself. I looked in astonishment upon a tall, strapping woman of no more than thirty: like a farmer's daughter accustomed to mucking out byres; or, more imaginatively, like a Viking princess capable of strangling, with one of her thick plaits of hair, any lover who failed her. Her smile was so keen it made me feel I was running over stubble with bare feet.

I thought at first it was a mistake, or a trick: she had sent a photograph of her daughter instead.

The autograph at the foot, Betty T. Shields, looked as if it had been dashed off with the point of a dirk.

She had asked me to send her a photograph of myself. Looking through my small store, I came upon the one taken with my four friends at Stank Castle. They were all dead. Hamish Dunloskin would never again shoot pheasants in Argyll, Archie Dungavel would never again pity the poor; Charlie Brack would never again imitate a hard-hearted grocer; and Andrew Dalgleish would never again blush like a girl. I thought of sending this photograph to Miss Shields, with a ring drawn round my head, and on the back a debonair scribble to the effect that I was the only

one of the quintet left alive. I drew the ring, I scribbled the
remark, but I did not send the photograph. Miss Shields, I
suspected, was a lot less sentimental than her books made
her out to be.

I sent the photograph of myself, in full-dress uniform,
taken after I had been presented with my Military Cross.

Not long afterwards the colonel sent for me and told me
I was wanted at divisional headquarters. He wouldn't say
why, but he looked impressed.

The brigadier's headquarters were in a fine chateau about
twenty miles from the front. I made sure, as I entered the
big handsome house, that no staff officer got a chance to
regard me with disdain. I was as good at putting hauteur
into a salute as any man in the army.

Brigadier Sir Ronald Lockerbie-Smith was a man of
about sixty, with a white moustache stained with tobacco.
He was said to do crochet work to pacify his nerves.

'Relax, man,' he said. 'Sit down. This is a friendly
chat.'

I sat down, still at attention. If he liked discipline
slackened, I did not.

'I'm sending you home,' he said. 'Our masters there
think they have a job for you more important than the
one you're doing here, and doing very well too.'

I was astonished. I even wondered if the Earl of Darndaff
had been pulling strings on my behalf.

'What kind of job, sir?'

'Is this news to you? Hasn't Miss Betty T. Shields mentioned it to you?'

'I do not understand, sir. Mentioned what?'

'You're acquainted with the lady, aren't you?'

'I correspond with Miss Shields, sir.'

'She hasn't said anything in her letters about your accom-
panying her on a morale-boosting tour of industrial areas in
Scotland?'

'Not a word, sir.'

'Odd. Well, she's asked especially for you, and it seems
she's got her way. I expect you know there's a lot of unrest
at home. They're a bit tired of the War. Then this bloody
business in Russia has given agitators a chance to stir up
trouble. Miss Shields apparently believes that if she were

to go round factories and shipyards and that sort of place she'd inspire the workers to produce more and grumble less. I can't stand her books myself—sugary saps—but I'm told working people, particularly women, put more faith in them than they do in the Bible. She wants some handsome young fellow to accompany her, and she's asked for you. To be frank, Colonel Knox and I would have suspected you'd put her up to it if you hadn't shown any number of times you're too damned stiff-necked to be devious. In any case you deserve a jaunt home as much as any man. So you go with our blessings and congratulations.'

Was it premonition that made me hesitate?

'Must I go, sir? Is it an order?'

'More like a benefaction, if you ask me. I understand Miss Shields is a very handsome woman.'

'I'm afraid, sir, I don't relish having to flatter or humour scrimshankers.'

'I'm sure you don't. But I wouldn't think you'd have much talking to do. From what I gather Miss Shields intends to do most of it herself. All you'll have to do, I suppose, is look brave and handsome. Don't look so glum, man. It could be jolly interesting, and—you never know, it could be useful too.'

There is a public library about half a mile from where I live. The reading-room is warm and airy. Thanks to the kindness of the librarian I am allowed, or have been allowed, the use of a small table and a chair in a corner, away from the draughts caused by the opening of the door. This is done mainly by decrepit pensioners, some of whom peer in at what must seem to them as uninviting as a church, and then creep away to a street corner where talking or coughing up phlegm is not forbidden. Others, interested in the world's depravities or the day's racing, come stealthily in and creep over to the up-right boards on to which the newspapers are firmly clamped. There they take their places, as in a urinal, among others as palsy-fingered and weak-eyed as themselves.

Through snotty handkerchiefs they squint at my pencil as it fills line after line, and page after page. They shake their heads at what appears to them an unprofitable obsession: a man clever enough to write all that ought to be studying form and backing winners. Perhaps it is as well talking is illegal, otherwise they would pester me with questions. They discuss me in slavery, illicit whispers. There is a belief among them that I am a renegade lord.

Recently there has been a change of management. The new librarian is a woman. It is obvious that she objects to smelly, arthritic, half-blind old men who slaver all over her newspapers. She has been awaiting an opportunity to apply a senility or dotage test; it came three days ago. A regular attender, no more than sixty-five, was gloating over a picture of a half-naked young woman with big breasts, when he collapsed. He was dead before the ambulance arrived. I heard one of his mates mutter: 'Juist like Tam, tae gang afore his turn.'

After that those likely to die on the premises were politely discouraged.

Yesterday, as I was warming my hands on the radiator before beginning my morning's stint, the librarian appeared.

'Good morning,' she said, sternly. 'I'm Miss Braidlaw, the librarian in charge.'

'How do you do, Miss Braidlaw?' I replied. 'Chilly again this morning.'

I used an educated Scots accent, with only a trace left of my old landed-gentry haughtiness.

'I understand you have been using this table and chair for months.'

'That is so. I come here as often as I can. Coal is so expensive nowadays. I am writing my memoirs.'

She glanced with impatience at the twopenny jotter on the table. Certainly it was crumpled, certainly it was stained with tea and jam and other spillable comestibles, and certainly it did not look part of a masterpiece; but, as an expert on books, she ought to have known it was not the outside that mattered.

'I'm sorry,' she said, 'but it is my duty to inform you that the facilities of a public library are for the use of the whole community, and not of a few who monopolise them. The reading-room must not be used as an office or a writing-room or a refectory. There are regulations in print.'

The dig about the refectory was because of my habit of bringing sandwiches.

'You must give up this practice,' she said, and marched off, thank God, before I could start whining about my MC, *my kinship with the Earl of Darndaff, my wife, the once famous*

Betty T. Shields, my nephew Samuel Lamont QC, *my friend Mary Holmscroft* MP, *recently deceased, and my two volumes of poetry.*

I felt a tap on my shoulder. It was an old fellow with bleary eyes and nervous snorts.

'She telt me aff tae, mister,' he wheezed. 'Me, that's been a Glesca ratepayer a' my maiirit days. I'm gaun tae complain tae Wullie Erskine, the cooncillor for this ward.'

There was a smell off him. Was there one off me too? Sometimes food got lost in my beard. There is no bath in my room-and-kitchen. In winter I follow the Eskimo practice of not removing my clothes, especially those next to my skin. Do I therefore smell? The old chap did not seem to mind, but then no Eskimo finds other Eskimos rancid.

'I stay wi' my dochter, you see,' he muttered. 'She likes me to get oot o' the hoose for a while every day. My wife's deid, you see. You're a stranger, but I'm telling you I still miss her.'

'My wife,' I said, 'is at this moment sitting on the terrace of her villa, in the province of Alicante, overlooking the Mediterranean.'

He shrank back. He thought I was mad.

'But the woman I miss, my friend, is dead, like your wife. She lies buried in the Hebrides, in a place where seals can be heard barking.'

'Jessie's in Janefield. It's only dugs that bark there.'

He crept away then, out of the reading-room. I do not think he will complain to his councillor. If your pride as a man has been hurt, what compensation is it to assert your puny rights as a voter?

As for me, I have no intention of being driven away. If the police are summoned I shall knock off a helmet or two.

Part Three

ONE

I arrived by train in Edinburgh, in late afternoon, in mid January, with snow falling. I did not know the city, having visited it only a few times before, with Archie Dungavel and Charlie Brack; and it did not know me. Gantock, no more than seventy snowy miles away, felt further than the Arctic.

There would be no one on the platform to welcome me home. That was the risk I had deliberately run. Freed from all impeding associations, I could become the kind of man I wanted to be.

I was wrong, though, in thinking there would be no one to meet me. Conspicuous on the platform, in a long white fur coat with hat and gloves to match, was a tall woman. Even from fifty yards away I recognised her as Miss Shields. As she hurried towards me, waving her hand and calling my name, I felt more apprehensive than flattered. Under her hat her hair was Viking yellow, and her eyes were as blue as the seas the longboats had foraged. Other men, officers and porters alike, watched us, admiring her and envying me. They thought she and I were old friends or even sweethearts, reunited after long separation by the brutal war.

'You look tired, Captain,' she murmured. 'Please come. I have a car outside.'

'Where are we going?' I asked, as she drove us through the dim white streets.

'To my house. I hope you don't mind. It seemed to me the most convenient arrangement. In any case, Edinburgh is full-up.'

'But, Miss Shields, I have to report to my superiors.'

'You can do that tomorrow, or the next day. Besides, Colonel McKenzie has said you are in my hands.'

One of those hands kept dropping on to my knee, with curious inadvertence.

127

I kept reminding myself that my companion was revered throughout Scotland, from single-end to castle, for her virtuous and wholesome books. In her house I should be as safe as in a convent. Yet, as she turned to smile at me, I felt, as I had done the first time I had looked at her photograph, as if I was running over stubble with bare feet.

Her house was in a handsome Georgian terrace. I learned later that on one side her neighbour was a High Court judge, and on the other an expensive physician.

An old manservant tottered out into the snow. As an officer I could not carry my bags myself, as a considerate young man I could hardly let someone almost three times my age carry them for me. Miss Shields resolved the dilemma by telling him to carry them one at a time.

In the hall we were met by two grey-haired white-capped women servants, eager to help us off with our outdoor garments. I caught them exchanging glances of prim lubricity. Evidently I was not the first young officer their mistress had brought home.

With her coat removed, Miss Shields was seen to be wearing a tweed skirt and a cashmere cardigan. She was boldly bosomed. My childhood fear of mammality stirred in my subconscious.

In the hall there now appeared a tall, middle-aged woman with girny face. Miss Shields introduced her as her mother.

Mrs Shields sniffed at me, as if, like a dog, she judged by her nose. Slowly her spaewife ill-will turned to what was ever more disturbing, spaewife pity.

'So you're the yin,' she said. 'God help ye.'

'My mother has a sense of humour that strangers find rather alarming,' said Miss Shields, grimly.

'You'll find keeping her in order a lot harder than killing Germans,' said her mother.

'Mother, Captain Corse-Lamont's tired, after his long journey. He would like to rest.'

As she spoke Miss Shields laid her hand fondly on her mother's head; yet it was easy to imagine, in her other hand, behind her back, a muzzle or even a hatchet.

In my room, with the initial panic subsided a little, I considered my position more rationally. If Miss Shields wanted me, whatever such wanting might involve, if with

her romantic novelist's imagination she saw in me something to love or at any rate to desire, would I not do
well to submit? Judging from her house, with its elegant
furniture and its many pictures with gilt frames, she was
comfortably off. It was true she was a few years older than
I, but the strain of the trenches had put bags under my eyes
and pallor in my cheeks, whereas she was pink and fresh
and youthful. What her mother had meant by her being
difficult to keep in order was easily conjecturable, but I
had just come from commanding a company of some of
the most pugnacious soldiers in the world, in the bloodiest
war in history. Surely the management of one woman, no
matter how many sharks were in her blue eyes, was not
beyond me.

I did not venture out that cold, snowy night. My hostess
suggested I might like to write letters, and showed me into
a study where there was a big stag's head. To put her off
the scent, and also in an effort to re-orientate myself, for
I still felt astray, I sat down and for three hours wrote
letters, to John and Bessie Lamont, Thomas Pringle (Uncle
Tam), John Calderwood, Mr Kelso, my former employer,
the Rev Mr Ainslie, minister of the Auld Kirk of Gantock,
and Mary Holmscroft. That I had no intention of posting
any of them did not prevent my taking care with them all,
but especially with the one to John and Bessie Lamont.

That night Miss Shields and I dined alone, by candlelight.
The old fellow who had carried in my bags attended us. His
hands were so shaky that in handing us our cockaleekie soup
he spilled some on the tablecloth. Perhaps, I thought, it
wasn't senility that was making his hands shake, or at least
not senility in itself; perhaps it was senility tormented by the
sight of his mistress's breasts, rising like two full moons out
of her dark-blue velvet dress.

Though strong drink was deprecated in all her books, in
her house it flowed. Before dinner we had drunk whisky;
during it much wine.

'Fergus is such a virile name,' she murmured.

'My mother happened to like it, that's all.'

'She is dead, is she not?'

'How did you know?'

'There was such a sad, beautiful little break in your
voice.'

I had hiccuped, and she knew it.

'Tell me about your mother, Fergus. Has she been long dead?'

'As long as I have been alive.'

'She died giving birth to you, is that what you mean?'

Launched upon lies, I would have to be as crafty as a chess-player. Already I knew her well enough not to be deceived by the triteness of her mind into thinking she was not dangerous: she stalked by instinct, like a lioness.

'You do not remember her then?'

'No.'

'Poor Fergus. Is that why you're so distant with women?'

She was right. I had never been able to get close enough to any woman, not even to Meg Jeffries or Cathie Calderwood or Aunt Bella or Bessie Lamont.

'Never mind, Fergus. I think I can cure that. Were you and your father a comfort to each other?'

It occurred to me her own father was kept well in the background.

'He died when I was ten. In Australia.'

'So far away? Among the platypuses? Was he there on business?'

'He was paying a visit to his uncle, Lord Drumelzier, then Governor of New South Wales.'

Conceit made me say it, though within caution whimpered and self-respect groaned.

She sipped wine.

'So your father was well-born?'

'Youngest son of the Earl of Darndaff.'

I saw what I was doing: providing her with an opportunity to turn me into one of her heroes. She would insist that I live by the absurd standards of Roger Wintercleuch and Ronald Glenartney. I would be expected to find my greatest happiness in kissing the hem of her skirt.

It was not too late to escape. None of her heroes was a bastard, or had a boilermaker's daughter as an ex-sweetheart or a socialist agitator as a friend. A little truth might still save me, even if served up with a dish of lies.

'I'm afraid I am illegitimate. You see, my mother was only 18 when she met young Henry Corse. He was 18 too; he had just left Eton. They fell in love. She became pregnant. The Earl was willing that they should get married,

but her father, my grandfather, was not. He was a stern
Calvinist. He refused to let her marry the man who had
seduced her: that was how he saw it. So my father, young
Henry, was packed off to Australia, where he took fever and
died. My mother was married off to a man almost twice her
age, a doctor, who in due course became my foster father.
He was called Lamont. I must admit he was kind to me.
He died five years ago.'

I had rehearsed it so often I believed it myself. Tears
were in my eyes. If I was making myself more appetising
to the lioness, I could not help it.

'Poor Fergus. Still, you must have had many sweethearts
to comfort you.'

'Only three.'

'Tell me about them.'

'One married a Catholic, another went mad, and the third
became a socialist agitator.'

My intention was to scunner her off me, but what I really
did was to make her more voraciously interested.

I was to learn later that she distrusted Catholics as much
as my grandfather or John Knox did. There is not one in
all her thirty-three novels.

Also she was afraid of going mad. Campbell Aird was
to tell me, in his exaggerated way, that she kept bringing
off a transformation, more difficult and a greater strain on
her sanity, than that attempted by medieval alchemists:
they tried to turn lead into gold, Betty turned shit into
sugar.

In addition, as a feudalist, she looked on socialists and
communists and levellers of all kinds as anti-Christs. In
her books at least three clergymen, with their creator's
approval, refer to Christ's remark that the poor will be
with us always.

'However did you come to be acquainted with a female
socialist agitator?'

'Among other things, she's devoted to seeing that the
poor all have inside lavatories.'

'How old is she?'

'Twenty-five. She has already been in jail for her principles. You may have heard of her. Her name is Mary
Holmscroft.'

'I have *not* heard of her.'

'You cannot read the newspapers then. Lloyd George himself has done her the honour of denouncing her.'

'I do not read about political termagants.'

'She was born in a hideous slum.'

'Is she one of those dreadful Clydeside traitors?'

'Her people are the poor. Only if she were to betray them would she be a traitor. She would suffer her breasts to be cut off first.'

'Has she any to speak of? You have not answered my question: how did you come to know such a creature?'

'Some day, Betty, I may tell you. Some day I may even have the pleasure of introducing you to each other.'

'I think you're drunk, Captain.'

'My head may be floating, my speech may be slow, but I am not drunk.'

'Time for bed.'

When I rose I found my legs shaky. She had to help me up the stairs. I wondered how it was that she, who had drunk as much as I, was so steady in her speech and on her feet.

The servants, and her mother, slept downstairs, at the back of the house.

She pushed me, with some impatience, past my room and into hers.

I was in no state, nor did I have the time, to assess the morality or tactics of my being in my hostess's bedroom at half-past eleven on my first night in her house, or of my acceding to her suggestion—it sounded very reasonable—that we should get undressed, or of my stroking my hostess's breasts (more like one laying a ghost than enjoying a treat), or of my permitting her to make serviceable what, alas, no longer deserved the innocent appellation of pintle.

Afterwards, when it was over, when the bizarre deed was done, on my part not too satisfactorily, she kept me awake in order to assure me, grimly, that when we were married she would see to it, for our children's sakes, that I obtained my rights from the Corses of Darndaff.

TWO

Among the places on Betty's list were the shipyards of Gantock. I told her I would go anywhere she liked, except there.

'But, Fergus, Gantock makes ships, ships are very necessary if we are to win the war. I cannot see why, having agreed to visit Kirkcaldy, you should jib at Gantock.'

'You forget I was born there.'

'All the more reason, I should have thought, for including it.'

'That may be so, Betty, but all the same I will not go.'

'You sound like a man with something to hide.'

'Let it be enough for me to say, the place has memories too painful.'

'But, Fergus, I would like to see your native town. I would like to see Ravenscraig, the house on the sea-front where you were born. I would like to see the Auld Kirk where your grandfather was an elder. I would like to see your mother's grave. I would even like to see the slum in which your friend Mary Holmscroft was born.'

'Later, Betty. Not now.'

'I should think Gantock would be eager now to welcome back its hero.'

For a minute or two I was tempted. All the influential citizens would certainly want to honour me because of my medal. There would be no need for me to be bothered by people like John and Bessie Lamont, or Mrs Grier and the other inhabitants of Lomond Street: these would be kept well back in the rear, as they always were. Even if one or two did push to the front, with characteristic thrust and impudence, they would want to applaud me: like Sammy Jackson they would look upon my distinction as in some way theirs too.

But it would not do, it was not enough, I was not ready for that momentous return. I had promised myself to go back when I had become famous. Military decorations did not represent the kind of fame I had meant. These would put me at a distance from the folk of the East End, whereas I wanted to be brought as close to them again as I had been long ago as a child of eight.

Also, for my mother's sake, I must not go back among her destroyers until I had been acknowledged by the whole world as the grandson of an earl. Only then would I be able to clear my soul of the terror and ignominy of her death. It was not revenge I sought, but purgation; with this would come release of the stores of charity, faith, and hope locked up in me.

When I went back to my native town therefore it must be, not just as hero, aristocrat, and poet, but as absolver and redeemer.

'Don't,' said Betty, with a sudden stridency in her voice that I had already come to expect, 'don't when I am trying to reason with you, don't ever hide behind a fatuous, secretive smile.'

As a description of my smile, how meanly unfair that was; and she knew it.

'Very well, Fergus, I shall agree to leave out Gantock, in the meantime, provided you give me an assurance that your reason for refusing to go there is not connected with the woman you knew who went mad.'

'She is not in Gantock, Betty. She is in an asylum outside Glasgow.'

'I see. Well, when we are in Glasgow we may pay her a visit. Please do not say no. You have denied me once already. Once is quite enough.'

'Yes, Betty.'

Thanks perhaps to my grandfather's Calvinist influence, I have always been slow on the sexual uptake. Filthy innuendoes that others have instantly sniggered at, I have often never even noticed. Invitations by women to make love to them, conveyed by lewd smiles and blue-lidded winks, I only became aware of afterwards, when they were pointed out by more observant friends. In the same way, I was never proficient at the preliminaries to love-making, the nibbling of lobes or the pinching of nipples or the griping of buttocks, etc. More often than not I found these more inhibiting than stimulating. It was furthermore always an amazement to me how intelligent men and women could regard as wonderfully special an act of such frequency. Once I lay in bed, after another addition to the score, trying to calculate how many times the deed of venery had been done by human beings, leaving out the animal and insect kingdoms. It came to a figure exceeding the number of stars in the universe.

Nonetheless, in spite of my sexual greenness or inno-cence, it was obvious to me that the reason why Betty was given such quiet hearings and afterwards such hootings of applause, by grimy-faced workmen with horny palms, was that every one of them in his imagination was stripping her naked, implanting on her breasts oily kisses, and vigorously bestriding her. I noticed too how aware she was of those imagined ravishments, and encouraged them, so that it was no scowling face her ravishers saw beneath them, but one radiant with satisfaction.

When they went back to their machines and benches it was probably true that those men worked a bit more enthusiastically for an hour or two. To that extent the newspapers were right in saying she was successful in her efforts to increase production. But it was not her patriotic speeches or her readings from her novels which caused her to succeed. It was the voluptuousness of her appearance and her voice. She would have done even better if she had just recited the alphabet, naked as a snail.

Long before Campbell Aird warned me, I knew Betty was a monster.

I felt sure that women who worked long hours at dreary jobs in bleak chilly factories would see through her as a fraud or at any rate a hypocrite. She came to them so fresh, so blooming, so fragrant, so expensively and warmly dressed. She spoke to them as if they were semi-imbecilic. She read out passages from her novels that might as well have been about cannibals with bones through their noses for all the relevance they had to working-class women worried about their men at war and their children sleeping three in a bed in room-and-kitchens. Yet, to my astonishment, they listened to her with rapture on their haggard faces, showed their bad teeth in smiles of delight, and clapped their work-worn and lumpy hands in delicate applause.

That was something I never understood: how Betty could transform tough-minded, rough-speaking, physically uncouth women into radiant, happy, and sensitive ladies. It was a trick of the monster's that remained incomprehensible, though I saw her bring it off many times. It worked too on women I would have thought particularly insusceptible, such as Mary Holmscroft.

One cold wet evening, in a Templars' hall in the East End of Glasgow, our little troupe was performing. It consisted of Betty (wearing her white fur coat), me (in uniform, with medals on my chest), a fat contralto who was to sing

patriotic songs, and some jingoistic middle-class ladies, who
included the chairwoman, wife of a local Tory MP. The
audience consisted mostly of middle-aged, working-class
women, devout readers of *The People's Companion*. It was
easy for me to pick out among them counterparts of Mrs
Grier, Mrs Lorimer, Mrs McTavish, Mrs Blanie, and Mrs
Dempster, those Gantock women who had influenced my
childhood. I ought therefore to have looked on them with
friendly gratitude and twinkles of humour. Instead, I stared
at them through, as it were, a monocle of disdain; and
when it was my turn to address them, on the fellowship in
the trenches, I used my landed-gentry accent. The result
was, paradoxically, that I was as great a success as Betty.
They saw me as a hero of one of her books still to be
written. If those women ever had libidinous fancies, the
men they imagined as fondling their breasts were no doubt
like Roger Wintercleuch, Ronald Glenartney, Sir Ralph
Balmanno, and Captain Fergus Corse-Lamont, who would
make love, not in animal fashion, like their own husbands,
but chivalrously and high-mindedly.

Sometimes they asked Betty questions. These had nothing to do with the war: they were all about her stories. A
typical one might be: 'What kind of dress did Madeleine
Ure wear at her wedding in St Giles' Cathedral?' (Evidently
in *The Heirs of Crailzie* Betty had forgotten to describe it.)

That evening, though, she was asked a question that
involved the war. A woman at the back—I could not see
her because of a pillar between us—cried in a hoarse voice:
'Miss Shields, in your books there is no violence, and death
is beautiful. I'm thinking of the death of Lady Crailzie, for
example. Why then are you going about urging people to
produce more shells to blow men to pieces?'

Leaning to the side, I saw the woman, and recognised
Mary. I had not heard from her for months. It was no
surprise to see her there: I had been half-expecting her
to turn up to scarify us. What was a surprise was the mild
irony of her question, which seemed to take Betty and her
books seriously.

'Who is she? Does anyone know her?' whispered Betty.

'Looks like Holmscroft,' whispered the chairwoman. 'But
she wouldn't ask anything so reasonable.'

'It *is* Holmscroft,' muttered another lady on the platform.

Betty gave me a smile. Then she faced the audience.

'I understand I have been addressed by the notorious Mary Holmscroft. You know, my friends, what she cannot know, for she is blinded by treacherous hates, that my books, with their lack of violence and their message that death is not to be feared, portray life as it will surely be after the threat of the barbarous Hun has been lifted forever from the fair face of humanity.'

As a girl of 13 in the Tally's in Morton Street Mary would easily have demolished that preposterous statement. Yet now, a seasoned campaigner with many speeches and a spell in jail behind her, she just shrugged, gave me a wave (I was sure it was for me, and so was Betty), and left the hall, to the accompaniment of hostile cries from members of the audience whose dreams of paradise she had bespattered with blood and guts.

'Well done, Miss Shields,' cried the chairwoman, standing up and clapping vigorously.

Everybody in the hall got up and clapped too.

I remembered how, in the Rector's room at Gantock Academy years ago, I had witnessed, in the persons of Mr Beaton and Mr Birkmyre, a conflict between the humane scholar and the vindictive Calvinist. The scholar, wonderfully, had prevailed. Here was another similar conflict between two aspects of the Scottish soul: in the one corner, represented by Betty, mendacious sentimentality, and in the other, represented by Mary, ironic truthfulness. Victory had gone, in the very first round, to the former.

THREE

To our Glasgow hotel came my former employer, Mr Kelso of the *Gantock Herald*, eager to write an article about me in his newspaper, and also to invite Betty and me to Gantock.

Luckily Betty had gone out to buy a new hat for our visit to the asylum that afternoon.

In the huge black and gilt hotel lounge I received him as the Emperor Napoleon might have some princeling who in his early days had slighted him.

Four years and millions of deaths ago, when I had told this fat white-haired bourgeois gentleman that I had been accepted for the Officers' Training Centre he had congratulated me and then had deducted from my pay for the days I had had to take off for the interviews. Surely, he had urged, no man of honour would want to be paid for work he had not done. It was most commendable that I was going off to fight for king and country, but so were thousands, many thousands he hoped, of other men. If all of them demanded to be paid for days of absence before setting forth to join up many employers would be ruined and the country brought to its knees economically. Patriotism consisted in other things besides jaunting off to kill enemies.

Since then I had advanced a lot further in my tenets than either the Allies or the Germans had on the battlefields. One of the positions I had reached was this: any man, no matter his age, rank, wealth, or reputation, who had made a profit out of the War, whether financial, political, or social, I considered myself bound to treat with less respect than any soldier, colonel or private, who had served in the trenches. That the keeping of this resolution might oblige me to offend various influential people I realised very well. Another of my forward positions was: since I knew myself to be a Corse of Darndaff, it would be craven not to comport myself as one, in all circumstances.

Therefore I quickly made it clear to fat and prosperous Mr Kelso that in the meantime I had nothing to say to him or his readers, and also that Gantock was not yet ready for (it was obvious I meant worthy of) my return.

He departed in a rage, mumbling that I was a disgrace to my medals and too big for my breeches. No satirical wit was intended by the latter remark: he was a man who always used clichés for their own sakes.

Before setting out for the asylum, Betty spent some minutes in reading a page or two of one of her own books, as devoutly as a nun. This was her way of sustaining faith in her own God-given abilities. I was to learn later that most authors did the same, including some whose writing, God help them, was feebler and falser than hers.

She spent rather longer in front of a mirror, trying on her new hat. This, it seemed to me, was unsuitable for our purpose: of yellow velvet, adorned with artificial hyacinths and primroses, it represented the freshness and gaiety of Spring. When I suggested that black or dark purple would be more appropriate she replied that if I wore a black or dark purple kilt she would wear a black or dark purple hat. It was then that I became aware, though not yet fully, that this visit to the asylum, which she insisted on making, was frightening her, in a private part of her mind. She was putting herself to some painful, abstruse test.

I should have sympathised, because I too was eager to go and see Cathie, and at the same time I shrank from the ordeal. Many times as an adolescent I had thought that the secret of happiness for the human race was not to be found in the dull worthy books John Calderwood and Mary Holmscroft read and discussed, but in Cathie's laughter. Listening to it, I had always felt happier and more hopeful. Like every soldier come from years in the trenches, I needed reassurance as to what was really mad and what really sane. The Cathie of old would have given it in a minute; the Cathie I was going to see might leave me benighted and insecure for years.

Situated about twelve miles out of Glasgow, the asylum called itself Hazelside Private Nursing Home for Ladies, in gold letters on a board at the gate. The relatives of its unfortunate inmates were evidently willing to pay a substantial amount for the avoidance of any mention of mental derangement, and also for, as we soon discovered, luxurious comfort. A large, handsome red-stone building with extensive well-kept grounds, it had once been the home of a Lord Provost of Glasgow.

We were received by the doctor in charge and the matron. They addressed themselves to Betty, as if it was she who was Miss Calderwood's friend; and when they were searching their minds for discreet words to describe Cathie's condition, it was Betty who stopped them, with a regal lifting of her yellow-gloved hand. We would prefer, she murmured, to judge for ourselves: sometimes surprise sharpened insight. She hoped Miss Calderwood had not been too carefully prepared for our visit.

Impressed and charmed, they assured us that even if Miss Calderwood had been, she would have forgotten: her memory, alas, was not good.

With a heavy sigh that reminded me of many I had heard from men waiting at dawn for the signal to attack, Betty said meekly that, if there was no objection, she would like first to meet a few of the other patients. Some of these, perhaps, had heard of her; if she could bring a little joy into their lives she would be grateful.

Her face was pale and anxious. Again I was reminded of the trenches, where, as the whistle sounded, many men suddenly felt a need to empty their bowels.

The matron, a big muscular woman, inured surely to every known eccentricity of the female mind, nevertheless had tears in her eyes as she listened to Betty. She had a copy, under her oxter, of *The Heirs of Crailzie*, which she had asked Betty to sign.

As squeamish as a general venturing among the dead, Betty went into the sitting-room. Like an attentive aide-de-camp, the matron kept close, whispering that there was no need to be alarmed, none of the ladies was violent, or incontinent, or unpleasant to look at. The delusions they suffered from were harmless. One, for instance, imagined that she was Mary, Queen of Scots. If we found her kneeling on a cushion, waiting for her head to be chopped off, we were to pay no heed. She would kneel like that for hours: she had been given pads for her knees.

The drawing-room, large and comfortably furnished, reminded me of the one in the living quarters of Gilbertfield Castle. I remembered Lady Gilbertfield's habit of staring at people as if their heads had changed places with their feet, and Grizel's obsession with horses.

I remembered too Betty in the throes of love. It was difficult to reconcile that nocturnal creature of talons and manic grunts with this pale, anxious, woman holding a flaccid hand here, patting a bowed head there, murmuring consolingly, and listening compassionately.

Knowing that she was, as it were, under shell-fire, I had to admire her calmness. I thought that marriage to her might after all be a challenge, and not a tribulation.

One of the women, with chalky-white face and long grey hair, crept over to me, reached up, and took hold of my moustache. Another came and stroked my kilt. Both had sad lost eyes. They were no older than my mother would have been. Yet it was not the sorrowing son, or the pitiful poet, who tholed their attentions; it was the courteous officer. I stood to attention as the matron removed their hands from me.

Sudden as a pain, a feeling of inadequacy overcame me such as I had never experienced in the trenches. War, as Mary had said, was simpler. There, if a man had courage, he would do. Here, in this quiet room, not only courage was needed, but all the power and versatility of love. That was why I fell far short. Upstairs, too, there waited an even severer test.

The staircase was of marble, softened by red carpet. We passed eyeless busts. On the walls were paintings of scenery. I could not help wondering what it cost to keep a patient here. Cathie's fortune must be dwindling at the rate of hundreds of pounds a year. She was not yet forty either. Some of the ladies, the matron had told us, lived to a ripe old age. Within these walls they were safe from the pressures of the world. Most of them didn't know there was a war on. In a way, were they not lucky?

'How long has Miss Calderwood been here?' I asked.

'About six months.'

'Has there been any improvement? What is being done to help her?'

'A great deal, sir, I assure you. Dr McCallum, you know, has a world-wide reputation as a mind specialist.'

'Do many of the ladies go home cured?'

'Quite a few.'

She said it too snappishly for it to be true. No doubt quite a few of the ladies were sent home, not because they were cured, but because their relatives could no longer afford to keep them here.

An attendant passed us. Like all the others I had seen she was as burly as a jailor. Did any of those sad-eyed ladies ever try to escape from this depressing luxury?

The matron stopped at Cathie's door, her knuckles raised to chap. 'When did you last see Miss Calderwood?' she asked.

'I have never met the lady,' said Betty. 'She is Captain Corse-Lamont's friend.'

'Four years ago,' I said.

'You will find her much changed. Still, she enjoys her food.'

With that cryptic remark she knocked and entered. An

attendant who had been sitting knitting got up and went out.

'Does she always have to have someone with her?' murmured Betty.

'No, no. She gets herself into a mess, you see. Ordinarily it doesn't matter. But visitors prefer to see her—well, tidy.'

I had not yet dared to look at Cathie. 'Does she get visitors often?' I asked.

'No, I wouldn't say often. A Miss Holmscroft comes regularly once a week. They tell me she's a notorious socialist, but I must give her this credit, she's the kind of visitor we like, no tears, no hysterical scenes, no upsetting the patients.'

'What about Miss Calderwood's brother?' I asked. 'Does he come?'

'The gentleman with the bad leg? Yes, about once a month. It used to be about once a week. It is difficult for him.'

'Anyone else?'

'Sometimes ladies from Gantock call in when they're in Glasgow shopping.'

During this conversation Betty and I whispered as if in the presence of someone dying, but the matron spoke normally and cheerfully.

Then at last I looked at Cathie.

She was seated on the carpet playing with painted wooden blocks. But it wasn't the infantilism of what she was doing that appalled me, it was her appearance. She was enormously fat, and she was busily chewing, with brown slavers running down her chins.

'She lives in a world of her own,' said the matron. She bent over Cathie and clapped her hands. 'Miss Calderwood, people to see you.'

Cathie looked up, with the bland, friendly, brief interest that children under five are so good at.

Was it put on, I wondered, was she teasing us all, behind that pasty pudgy face was the old slim, playful, womanly Cathie watching us in amusement?

'I had no idea that she was so old,' whispered Betty.

Only cruel malice or profound sympathy or a mixture of both could have produced so startling a remark.

I remembered peeping through the slit in the bathroom door, in happy Ravenscraig, and Mary asking me if I had lost anything.

'Courage is largely callousness.' Archie had said that once to rebuke me, because it had seemed to him that I had got too easily used to the bloody deaths of men I had known and admired. I had merely answered that we were trying to win a war.

That necessary callousness of the soldier was not possible here. Without it I was not brave. I could not bear to look and had to hurry out of the room.

Betty did not come with me. She stayed a few minutes more. When she did make up on me, on the stairs, beside a bust of Plato, she was not smirking in any kind of triumph; on the contrary, she looked stricken and was in tears.

She had caught a glimpse of hell. The matron, beaming, thought that this was Miss Shields of the noble heart moved to pity.

As we drove back into Glasgow, after a long silence Betty said: 'Let's not talk about her. Not now anyway.'

I could not have talked to Christ Himself about Cathie then.

FOUR

Even before we were married, Betty began what she called our Eve and Adam sessions. These were conversations or consultations about personal matters, conducted in her bedroom, before a fire if the night was chilly, she seated on the floor on a soft plush cushion, I on a straight-backed chair with a cane seat, and both of us stark naked. It meant, she explained, that we had to be absolutely truthful with each other, for in her view other parts of the body were more tell-tale than the face or hands.

It took me some time to feel at ease with her breasts, which always seemed more naked than the rest of her. Often I wondered why they intimidated me while other parts with more obvious menace did not. The reason, I thought, must lie in my childhood. Then I had been scolded for tearing pieces out of soft, white new loaves, or picking the cherries off cakes. Once I had come upon a huge toadstool and had lain down to sniff it, to find out if it was a mushroom. These, though, and others similar, did not seem adequate explanations.

Then, one morning, as I was striding up the Royal Mile on my way to the Castle, with my kilt swinging, I saw a young woman in a shawl suckling her baby. At that moment it came back to me. When Smout McTavish and I were five, we were invited by Jim Blanie into his house to see his new little sister. Mrs Blanie was sitting on a stool feeding the baby. As we came close to peep at the baby she took the teat out of its mouth and, squeezing her breast, squirted milk all over our faces. If it had been vitriol we could not have been more shocked.

Among the matters discussed in these circumstances, so inhibiting to me, so stimulating to Betty, was the form of our engagement announcement. We decided, or rather Betty did, with my hesitant concurrence, that I should be styled thus: 'Captain Fergus Corse-Lamont, MC, only son of the late Hon. Henry Corse, of Corse Castle, and of the late Agnes McGilvray.' If the Corses objected whether privately or publicly, it would be seen as an acknowledgment of my claim to kinship; if they did not, it would amount to an acceptance. (I myself thought that in the latter case it would simply mean that the Corses read newspapers with aristocratic inattention.)

Later we discussed the arrangements for our wedding in St Giles. The Army had agreed to supply a piper, a guard of honour, and some senior officers as guests. The occasion was to be used as a means of uplifting home morale, at that time depressed by German advances on the war front. There would be pictures in newspapers. With luck none would appear in the *Gantock Herald*. My snubbing of Mr Kelso had probably ensured me a dearth of publicity in my home town. Snubs of equal efficacity were ready for other editors and reporters.

Providing a bridesmaid was easy for Betty, who had many women friends available, but all the men I would have preferred as my best man were either dead or in the limbo of Gantock. Among the writers I had so far met was none whose appearance would suit an august ceremony. I decided that if I could not have a man devoted to me at least I could have one grateful: so I nominated Captain Hugh Sinclair, of my own battalion of the Perthshires,

then in France. Uxorious to a distressing degree, he would
be overjoyed at the chance of an unexpected leave.

Betty showed no surprise, and scratched no part of her
anatomy irritably when I insisted that there was no one
from my home town I wished to invite. 'Not even Miss
Holmscroft? Or Mr Calderwood, with the bad leg? Or the
provost, with his chain? Or one of your old school friends?'
'None, Betty.' 'As you please, my dear.'

Her mother did not take it so calmly. She was shocked.
'Guid God. Even a murderer has freen's and kin. Are you
worse than a murderer?'

At that period in my life I was stiff, cold, and aloof. (To
use a Lomond Street word I was a puke; a puke with style
certainly, but a puke nonetheless.) Yet my situation was
the most enviable in all human experience: a soldier back
from the war garlanded with praise, and honourably free
from any obligation to return. In addition I was young,
unscathed, handsome in a kilt, and engaged to a beautiful,
talented woman with money.

In the course of my duties as an inspirational adviser
on trench warfare, I had to address companies of soldiers
about to set off for France. Among them were many men
who would have been more useful in building tanks and
ships but who had been snatched from their factories and
yards. Some no doubt were from Gantock, but none of
these dared to present himself to me. My instructions were
to minimise the miseries and dangers of the trenches, and
emphasise the fellowship and fun. Naturally I obeyed: not,
however, without some inward amazement at how different
were my encouraging addresses to my poem 'The Burning
of the Boots', fortunately not yet published. Only private
individuals, I realised, could afford to tell the truth; and
of all individuals poets had to be the most private.

I sometimes wondered, if Mary too, in her public
speeches, knowingly dishonoured truth.

What I really needed most from Betty, and what she never
gave me, was tenderness. She gave me concupiscent love,
more than enough, respect (she would kiss my medal as if
it was a crucifix), encouragement, support, and sympathy,
but not tenderness. She did not withhold it, she simply

did not have any to give. Later, when we moved into the country and kept dogs, these used to brace themselves, with whimpers like prayers, for her pats and strokings, which were more like buffets. Even with our children, whom she ruined with indulgence, she found it difficult to be soft-handed in her caresses.

I was disappointed but not surprised. Experience had not shown me that women as a sex were particularly tender. As a foster-mother, Bessie Lamont had been fair-minded and dutiful; as a sweetheart Meg Jeffries had been cheerfully affectionate; as a friend Mary Holmscroft had been staunchly truthful: none had been tender. Even in the way Cathie Calderwood had rubbed noses with me had been a certain roughness. No woman teacher had ever treated me tenderly, and no woman neighbour: not even Mrs Grier, when she had seized my testicles, an act crying out for tenderness.

The only exception had been soft-witted Jessie McFadyen. As a child she had been kind even to snarling dogs; as a girl in her teens, if rumour spoke truth, she had let all manner of males, some old enough to be her grandfather and some scarcely pubescent, abuse her. Those cynical rapes, which was what they amounted to, carried out amidst dustbins or in coal cellars, would have been unspeakably sordid but for the gentle, unselfish loving-kindness Jessie was sure to have shown those abusing her. That was true tenderness. No wonder I had found it rarer than four-leaved clovers.

(How heroic and good a man had my friend Smout been! By taking Jessie as his sweetheart he had strengthened her wits. All that marvellous tenderness would have been his. Even in a single-end, he would have been the happiest of men. If only he had not been killed!)

It is not the goodness of saints that makes us feel there is hope for humanity: it is the goodness of obscure men, like Smout McTavish, and Hugh Sinclair, best man at my wedding.

When I look again at this picture of my bride (though she has been cut out I can imagine her well enough) and me outside St Giles, under the swords of the guard of honour, I am able to forgive myself for my contumelious smile when I see, past my right shoulder, Hugh's jolly grin. I am able indeed to forgive all blundering humanity. Though it would have been possible for him, who loved his wife to dangerous excess, to find some sufficiently honourable reason for staying safe at home, he returned to France and was killed at Cambrai, two months before the armistice.

The ceremony was conducted by an ex-Moderator of the Church of Scotland, and attended by three other ex-Moderators, one of whom gave Betty away. I wondered what they would have said if I had told them that the bride, shimmering in virginal white, had not waited for their Lord's permission to drag the bridegroom into bed with her, but had done it months ago.

Our honeymoon was spent in Argyll, beside a sea-loch, in a shooting-lodge lent by a friend of Betty's. (Gradually I was finding out that she had numerous such friends, well-placed wealthy men eager to do her favours.) Since the purpose of a honeymoon is to make love I ought not perhaps to have felt peeved at having to make it so frequently, in and out of doors. Readiness was all, according to Betty. Discomfort did not deter her. Once, in a cave, we were both dyed bright green with slippery slime: it took hours of scrubbing to get it off. Nor did she mind being seen, by rabbits, seagulls, stonechats, or lurking peasants. We were, she said, god and goddess celebrating love in a time of war, and demonstrating how the world could be replenished.

In contact so often with such beautiful and combustible flesh, my own sometimes caught fire. Betty would whisper into my ear afterwards: 'Seventy-five per cent, my love;' or, on one occasion, in a glade of tall foxgloves, 'Ninety.'

Though I discovered a great deal about her not to her credit during those ten days of rut, at the end of them I was fonder of her, more grateful, more dependent, and more understanding. If all that did not quite amount to love, it came close. Certainly it enabled me to catch glimpses of the terrors in her mind.

Once, as we were climbing the hills hand-in-hand, on a sunny day with blue sky above and blue loch below, she suddenly let out a groan, and her nails dug painfully into my palm. I thought she had been stung by a cleg or even bitten by an adder. But she gazed at me with horror in her blue eyes as she whispered: 'Don't ask me why, Fergus, but I just thought of your friend, Miss Calderwood.'

It was not the fear of growing fat that was terrifying her. Fatness could be avoided by eating less. It was the fear of going mad.

Campbell Aird was to tell me later that Betty, like Shakespeare, had moments of melancholy insight when she saw all human existence as a pervasive madness. Therefore her determined portrayal of it as an oversweet sanity must be an enormous burden. If she let go God knew what chaos would descend.

I was, he pointed out delicately, in the best position to know. Did she not hope to find in love, or at any rate in its physical expression, a great deal more than pleasure for the body and illumination for the mind? Did she not also hope to find obliteration of those glimpses of hell?

Though I did not much approve of my bedmate's being analysed by a shilpit grey-haired man of fifty-five whose own venereal partner at the time was a plump young barman, I had to admit that his analysis was acute.

FIVE

For many years now Campbell Aird has been soliciting among the cherubim: with more success, it is to be hoped, than he enjoyed in his later years among the catamitic youths of Edinburgh, who found his lank grey hair, vast brow, soiled velvet collars, and slouching walk too offputting. But if there are no books in heaven the sweetest of cherubic bottoms will not compensate. No man loved books so much, or could tell, so quickly, almost from sniffing, whether one was true or false.

In the Sunday newspapers and literary weeklies books were often acclaimed in terms that would have been hyperbolical applied to *King Lear* or *War and Peace*. 'Kach,' Campbell Aird would say, with a snort, and sure enough, a year or two later, those masterpieces were everywhere recognised to be kach and flushed away for ever. On the other hand, if a book was good, if it really was the life-blood of a master spirit, he would cry 'Manna!' In any one generation there are no more than a dozen such books. Among these Campbell Aird included my two volumes of poems, the one dealing with my childhood in Gantock, and the other with my experiences during the War.

As well as editing the literary magazine *The Caledonian*,

and writing articles for various journals, including Betty's *People's Companion*, he was employed by Betty's publisher, Pettigrew and Strang, as a reader. Despising public taste, he could tell at a glance what would gratify it. Two other readers, and Pettigrew himself, had wanted to reject Betty's first novel *The Heirs of Crailzie* as too foolishly romantic, but Campbell had called it the first shovelful of nuggets out of a goldmine. Very soon he was proved right.

During that last year of the War, and the years following it, our house in Traquair Row was a meeting-place for Scottish authors. Prominent among them was Hamish Sievewright. Today, nearly sixty years after its publication, it is incredible that his two hundred and fifty page-long philosophical poem, 'A Prey to Dede', a dialogue, in archaic Scots, between Mary, Queen of Scots, in her prison in England, and her husband the Earl of Bothwell, in his dungeon in Denmark, or rather between their disembodied spirits that meet like sea-mews over the North Sea—or so it seems, for much is unintelligible—was ever taken seriously, and indeed proclaimed as the profoundest exploration of the Scottish soul ever undertaken in literature. The first time I read it, or to be honest tried to read it, for as with so many so-called masterpieces, contemporary and classical alike, I found the going unendurably dreary. Trying again later, I thought it turgid, stilted, and inert. This last was really some sort of achievement, considering the exciting lives and tragic deaths of the two protagonists. 'Kach or manna?' I challenged Campbell Aird. He was reluctant to answer, for he liked old Sievewright, who certainly looked like a poet, with his silvery hair and beard. Pressed, Campbell answered, with a scowl: 'First-class kach, of course. But don't tell him I said so. He's a nice old man.' I remonstrated, insisting that for the sake of maintaining standards the perpetrators of bad writing ought to be told it was bad, plainly and conclusively. He agreed, with a groan.

Years later, in an article on Scottish poetry, he wrote: 'It is a melancholy fact of literary life that the nicest of men do not write the best poetry. In order to be able to write good poetry it is necessary to have what the poet himself will call god-like confidence, but what seems to the rest of us to be infernal conceit. The great poet offers us his work as if it had been handed to him by the Lord on top of a mountain. Mr Sievewright's, we feel, was composed in a pleasant library, with the sun shining through tall windows on to books of reference piled up on the leather-topped desk, and a decanter of choice companionable Glenfiddich. We have the impression that his poems were not hindered but rather were helped along by interruptions from congenial friends, whose talk flowed as golden as the whisky. We think of Mr Sievewright as a gracious host, not as a poet with a daemon in him. We love to be in his company, but we would rather not read his poetry. With Mr Fergus Lamont it is precisely the opposite: we feel we must heed his poetry because it has on it all the authentic signs of the divine scorching; but we have no urgent desire to seek his company. In mundane circumstances that god-like confidence without which admittedly great or even good poetry cannot be written becomes insufferable. Robert Burns, in Poosey Nancy's tavern, and on the stony fields of Mossgiel, could set it down for the time being and become a convivial imbiber in the one case and a farmer with a sore back in the other. Mr Lamont, it seems, cannot set it down . . .'

Astute though he was, he was unable, like everybody else, to see that my perennial stiffness and aloofness which he castigated so humorously were simply the hard, necessary husk, inside which a true humility was slowly growing to ripeness.

I am obliged to say something about Alisdair Donaldson, though he is a novelist, and I have never had any interest in novels. Though in uniform, he never served abroad because of knock-knees, and for the same reason seldom wore a kilt. When I first met him he was a corporal clerk in the Castle, and smelled of carbolic soap, because of the primitive ablutionary arrangements in his quarters. At that time he had published only one novel, a gloomy tale of the killing of gannets in his native Lewis, in the 18th century, written in a sing-song prose supposed to represent the surge of the sea and certainly inducing some sort of squeamishness. Most of his subsequent thirty or so novels, however, were set furth of Scotland, with Englishmen for heroes. He believed that as a people the Scots had long ago lost their individual flavour, and were now as wersh as stale baps: consequently it was unprofitable, artistically and financially, to write about them. I agreed, but only as far as the money-loving, hypocritical bourgeois Scots were concerned. There was, I assured him, plenty of pungent flavour left in the proletarian Scot and the aristocratic Scot. In illustration of the latter claim I mentioned Lady Grizel Dungavel's poulticing of her horse's genitals. He listened with a pout of incredulity, but in a later novel purloined the incident.

Today, living in the South of France on the proceeds from his best-sellers (now dismissed as mostly kach) he probably maintains that Fergus Lamont was a minor poet, with some robustness of language; but it is jealousy speaking. Even when he was having ecstatic reviews and I either none or frivolous ones, when his books were making pounds and mine maiks, when his marriage, to the younger daughter of an English baronet, was solid and mine disintegrated, when his children were proud of him and mine ashamed of me, even then he was jealous. Many years afterwards, when he sought me out in the Hebrides where I had exiled myself, he came, so he said, to pity my hardships and obscurity, but it was really to rejoice over them.

In front of the shops in Buccleuch Street, round the corner from Lomond Street, were iron gratings in which the spaces were small enough to keep heels from getting stuck in them, but big enough to let coins fall through. The gratings were intended to give light to basements under the shops, but most of those basements were shut up and disused. Women out shopping with cold fingers, children running too fast with precious but slippery pennies clutched in their fists, and drunk men reeling home with their change rattling in their pockets, passed over the gratings every day. Therefore coins, keys, rings, brooches, etc, were always being dropped among the litter of fag-ends, sweetie papers, tram tickets, and withered leaves, where they glinted tantalisingly.

We had a method of recovering them. A piece of clay, about the size of a man's nose, would be kneaded so that it could be pushed through one of the spaces. Its flattened end would be wetted with spittle, to make it more adhesive. It would be lowered, with much care, on a length of string until it was suspended directly over the lost treasure. Then it would be let drop with a hopeful thud. After a few seconds of prayer it would be brought up, inch by inch, usually with the coin or whatever it was adhering. Sometimes this would fall off and the whole thing would have to be done again, with still greater caution. Sometimes the clay would disintegrate and have to be renewed. Sometimes some too eager coadjutor would step on the manipulator of the string, who lay flat on his stomach; or the shopkeeper would dash out and chase everybody away. Sometimes the object being salvaged, when falling back, would be lost to sight amongst the rubbish: but only after many attempts, spread out over months, would it be abandoned.

Our trade was recognisable from the clay on our hands and the tips of our noses, the rust on our knees, and the temporary crossness of our eyes.

My imagination was those dauds of clay, bringing up, out of my Gantock childhood, poems like 'Gathering Dung' and 'Stairhead Lavatories'.

It is amazing that I wrote those poems, so rich in sympathy for the poor, during the three years after the War when I still looked on myself as an aristocrat. One incident will be enough to indicate the kind of person I was at that time.

One evening Betty and I were guests at a dinner party in Heddleston House, home of Sir James Mutt-Simpson, one of her admirers, and later her lover. When the ladies had withdrawn, we drank port, smoked cigars, and discussed, with indignation, the miners then on strike, who spent their days playing cards and their nights poaching. Our host owned three coal mines. We were all agreed that whatever the War had been fought for it hadn't been to make life easy for fellows unwilling, in the country's interests, to work a bit harder for a bit less pay.

As gentry, we took for granted that we were owed the best of everything, not just because we were personally worthy of it, but also because that was how the Almighty had arranged things. It seemed to us a sacred and sensible arrangement, and any attempt to alter it would be impious and foolish.

Dressed like a Highland chief in a Raeburn painting, I was the most scathing in my criticism of the Scottish working man. My companions were impressed. They supposed that I had acquired my knowledge and insight during the War. One of them suggested that I should stand as a Tory MP: men like me were needed to counteract the dangerous nonsense spouted by the Clydeside revolutionaries, including 'that abominable woman Holmscroft'. What, asked another, did I think ought to be done about the thousands of demobilised soldiers going about the country grumbling that promises given them of well-paid jobs and good houses weren't being kept: not having the honesty to admit that such promises would never have been necessary if they had been prepared to do their duty for duty's sake alone.

'They're all right at heart,' I replied. 'They need discipline, and a purpose, that's all. Winston Churchill's right. They should be put back in uniform and sent against the Bolsheviks.'

While they were chorusing 'Heah, heah', the butler came in with a message from McCulloch, Sir James's head gamekeeper. A poacher had been caught. McCulloch wanted to know if he should be handed straight over to the police, or did Sir James want to see him first.

Instead of pleased, Sir James looked sheepish. I was not surprised. A tall round-shouldered baronet with gold-rimmed spectacles and a melancholy neighing voice, he liked to think of himself as a humanitarian. He had not fought in the War because of bad eyesight. When out shooting he was more of a danger to the beaters than to grouse or roe-deer. Left to himself, he would have given his colliers what they were asking. In some ways he reminded me of Archie Dungavel.

Ashamed, perhaps, of appearing disloyal to his class, he ordered the fellow to be brought in.

We approved heartily.

'Quite right, old man.'

'Should be fun.'

'Good to hear what these fellows have to say for themselves.'

'Let Corse-Lamont have a word with him.'

'Pity is he'll get off with a paltry fine,' said Sir Hubert Cuthbertson, a magistrate. 'It's all wrong. In my view, the severer a punishment is the kinder. What I mean is, in

Muslim countries, you know, the penalty for stealing is to have the right hand chopped off. Pretty drastic but damned effective, I should think.'

We agreed. We looked round to make sure that everyone of us showed that agreement. Gentlemen had to stick together, particularly when they were obliged to adopt attitudes or support views not quite gentlemanly.

Two gamekeepers came in, holding their prisoner. All three had their caps in their hands. Their clothes were wet and their boots muddy. Sir James looked anxious about his carpets.

The poacher had a red coarse face, sly downcast eyes, and a pimply nose. He had allowed bad housing, cheap food, and worry about money, to degrade him. Mary Holmscroft would not have been pleased. She was always exhorting the poor to hold up their heads and look their exploiters in the eye. This one looked us in the foot.

'Would you like to speak to him, Corse-Lamont?' muttered Sir James. 'You know how.'

'Certainly.' I addressed the poacher. 'Stand to attention in the presence of gentlemen.'

He stood to attention.

'What's your name?'

'Muir, sir. Donald Muir.'

For a second I was taken aback, but there could be no connection between this whimperer and Donald of Sutherland, that brave and unselfish patriot.

Meanwhile Muir had taken out of his pocket a bronze medal. It wasn't the kind given for valour, but it did show he had served in the War: that was to say, if it had really been awarded to him. I had heard of similar medals being swopped in pubs for glasses of beer.

'What was your regiment, Muir?'

'The King's Own Scottish Borderers, sir.'

'Did you see any action?'

If his whining but boastful tale could be believed he had, a good deal.

'But no' as much as you, sir. That's the MC ribbon, isn't it, sir?'

If I had been loyal to my principle of honouring men who had fought in the trenches above baronets, magistrates, and coalowners who had not, I would of course have taken Muir's part and denounced my companions. But, like everyone else, I had learned when to uphold an awkward principle, when to modify it, and when to ignore it altogether.

'Aren't you ashamed to let your regiment down?' I said. 'Especially those of your comrades who never came back. They gave their lives to keep the Boche from coming here and helping themselves. Yet isn't that just what you've been doing?'

'Juist twa or three rabbits, sir. Fermers say rabbits are vermin, sir, like rats. If it was rats we took and ate naebody wad complain. When we were in camp once Captain McNiven use to tell us to go and snare rabbits. He was killed later, at Vimy Ridge.'

'That was war-time, Muir. War-time's different.'

He began to whine that it wasn't his fault he couldn't get work, he'd dig ditches for the sake of a job, he had four children, one was sick, rain came through the roof of his house.

'Being up against it is no excuse for stealing,' I said.

'It's a' right for you to talk, sir.'

He was being humble, but in his humbleness there was, to the trained ear, an unmistakable note of insolence.

Once, against the advice of my sergeant-major, I had passed on a deserter to be tried by higher authority. He had been sentenced to be shot, but it had been commuted to ten years' hard labour. He was still serving it. As he was being marched away he had shouted: 'It's a' right for you, you big stuck-up red-haired bastard.'

'If I was you, Sir James,' I said, 'I'd let the police have him.'

I felt sorry for him of course, and would have liked to send him away with a five-pound note in his pocket, to feed his family and buy medicines for his sick child; but if I had done anything so self-indulgent I would have let my side down, especially my little red-haired daughter, Dorcas, whose good opinion was very important to me. Socially precocious, at two and a half, she already had people divided into classes, those above her (very few), those on the same level as herself (a not very numerous élite), and those beneath her (countless millions).

Sir James, however, did not have the courage to take my advice.

'Not this time,' he mumbled. 'Let him go, McCulloch. He's had his warning. Next time, though, it'll have to be the police.'

The gamekeepers were not pleased. They had evidently spent long wet cold hours lying in wait for the fellow. No doubt they had already given him a good kicking, and as soon as they got him outside they would give him a still better one, but they wouldn't feel appeased. The working-class are their own most implacable enemies.

'Thank you,' whined Muir. 'Can I keep juist the yin for the pot?'

'All right, all right. Let him have one, McCulloch.'

Going out, McCulloch gave me a grin that showed he thought me a proper gentleman. Muir, even more complimentarily, looked at me as if, given the chance, he would shoot me in the back. A few men in my company had had that wish too. They had resented my brusqueness: being too unimaginative to understand that if I had used kindness instead it might have unmanned them. Just as Muir could never be able to see that by suggesting he ought to be prosecuted I had been showing no ill-will towards him personally, but simply had been protecting the foundations of society.

'Sorry about that, gentlemen,' muttered Mutt-Simpson. 'It was his mention of the officer that asked him to catch rabbits.'

'Probably a lie,' remarked one of us.

But we rallied round our comrade who had faltered, for such honourable motives.

Only arid perfectionists would have expected me to be as understanding of and compassionate towards the poor in my capacity as an ambitious social being, as I was in my capacity as inspired poet. In his poetry does not Burns pour scorn on seducers of innocent young girls, and did he not, in his active life, seduce any such girl he could lay his hands on, whether on the flowery banks of Doon or on mucky straw in a byre? In his novels Scott rejoices in mad-women and fishwives, but it was duchesses he entertained at Abbotsford. Shakespeare calls money trash, but amassed as much of it as he could.

Poets have a hard enough task showing mankind what truth and love are, without their having to be truthful and loving themselves, at any rate all the time.

SIX

First Poems was published by Bob Gilzean, because no other publisher in Scotland would do it. He had inherited from his father a prosperous printer's business in the Haymarket. This he had brought to the edge of ruin by preferring to print, instead of lucrative tickets, books of so-called Scottish literature, most of them, alas, painfully uninspired and all of them disastrously unprofitable.

As a book to hold in the hand, *First Poems* was shoddy, with coarse yellowish paper full of skelves, and innumerable foolish misprints. Betty had provided a subsidy of fifty pounds, and this ought to have ensured better paper at least, but into Bob's office one day rushed a berserk novelist called McWheep, who seized him by the throat and demanded payment of an advance five years overdue. Some money had to be given him. He left behind a hole in the glass door that any enraged poet could have clambered through. Some did, and snatched their share of what was left of Betty's fifty pounds.

I did not like the title: it sounded too jejune. I suggested *Gathering Dung, and other poems*. Bob would have agreed, but Campbell Aird counselled against. ' "Dung" was a name that could stick,' he said.

Naturally I wanted to be called Corse-Lamont. Bob, though, the mildest nationalist I ever met, turned dour and sulky over that hyphen: it was English, he said, and went with monocles and shooting-sticks, not girrs and quoits. To my surprise Betty supported him. She pointed out that it was really Fergus Lamont who had written the poems. When I came to publish my poems about the War it would be in order then to call myself Corse-Lamont. Besides, it would be prudent not to let our society friends like Sir James Mutt-Simpson and Sir Hubert Cuthbertson know I had written poems that revealed an inside knowledge of working-class ways: mere eccentricity would not explain that. Whatever doubts they had about my origins would be stirred up. Above all, she said, I should bear in mind that, given the choice of having for her father either a famous poet or an accredited gentleman, Dorcas would without hesitation choose the latter.

So Fergus Lamont it was that appeared on the title page.

150 copies were printed. Of these 40 were sent out for review. Of the remainder, how many were sold, how many given away, and how many destroyed in the furnace as valueless lumber by Bob's liquidators, I never knew. Today they are, as I have said before, rare as ospreys. What I did know was that I received not one bawbee. This was expected. What was not expected, what came as a shock, in spite of Campbell Aird's warnings, was the abuse heaped on me, instead of the admiration and praise I had been looking forward to.

Consider the solan goose, or gannet. Gloriously down the sky he plunges, folding back his beautiful black-tipped wings, and cleaves the sea, vanishing for a minute while the whole world waits, and then rising again with a fish in his beak. Stupid, callous men nail a fish to a floating board. The brave bird dives, strikes impenetrable wood, and breaks his neck. In a moment he is turned from a splendid creature of sea and sky to a bunch of sodden feathers, which will be washed up on some forgotten shore.

I was the solan goose, my poems the daring and thrilling dive, the stupidity and callousness of critics the treacherous floating board.

In a corner of a pub in Rose Street Campbell Aird tried to explain.

'You must understand, Fergus, these critics, particularly the Sassenach ones, come from a class of society where humanity, if this be defined as warm, rumbustious relationships, is chronically deficient, in comparison certainly with the red-blooded vigour of your East End streets. Therefore, though they giggle so wittily at your poems, they are in their hearts bleating with envy. Most are would-be poets themselves, with subjects restricted to their souls' torment or meditations, say, on earwigs. They would much rather write about running with a girr or gathering dung or throwing quoits, if they knew anything about these.

'Their language is as anaemic as their humanity. They snigger at what they call your vulgarity, but what they know to be your robustness. They have all the allusions, all the appropriate quotations, all the scraps of foreign languages, all the smart references to foreign poets, all the wit, all the polished phrases, and all the elegant metaphors. What they do not have is life. Take your poem "Reinitiation", for instance, where the young man is caught by the balls by the harridan. Suppose such a thing had happened to them. They would have made of it merely a contrived Rabelaisian flourish, complete in itself, a dead end. They would be quite incapable of making it, as you have done, an act from which there flows an intricacy, a whole delta, of rich, comic human relationships.

'If you had written about Greek peasants, or Australian aborigines, these critics would have shown some interest and sympathy; but no section of the whole human race is less congenial to them than the Scottish working-class.'

A copy of the poems was sent to the socialist weekly, *Advance*, of which Mary was then assistant editor. I felt sure it must appreciate how I had shown the lives of working-class people to be in many respects richer than those of mercenary bourgeoisie or effete aristocrats. Instead, there appeared a peevish diatribe. Sneered at as 'member of the officer class', and accused of portraying the poor as 'exhibits in a menagerie', I was advised to write about the kind of people I let myself be photographed with in the *Scottish Tatler*. The initials at the foot were CKK, those, as I ascertained, of the Honourable Charles Kinnoull, Mary's friend and probable lover, and the renegade son of the Earl of Strone. He had spent years abroad and knew many European socialists. His sympathy for the poor was, I felt sure, merely tactical.

I wrote to Mary. She replied that she had read my poems and agreed with Charlie Kinnoull's opinion of them. In her opinion, the first and foremost function of literature was to show up the immorality of a society in which some people had far more than they needed while others had a great deal less. If that criterion was applied to my poems, they failed utterly; indeed did they not make jokes out of abominations like stairhead lavatories?

Such misinterpretation staggered me. It was true that I had treated stairhead lavatories humorously, but surely it was plain that I had done so in order to make the humiliations they caused bearable?

In common with most provincial Scottish newspapers, the *Gantock Herald* seldom paid attention to books. It needed all its space for advertisements, pictures of weddings, and accounts of sheriff court proceedings. Thinking however that an exception might be made for my poems I had a copy sent. The outcome was a short paragraph, at the bottom of an inside page under a huge advertisement for Kirkhope's groceries: it stated that a book of poems had been published recently purporting to be about life in Gantock; but, though the drawing on the cover could well be that of the Auld Kirk in Auchmountain Square, the poems themselves revealed no knowledge of Gantock ways and were amateurish. Mr Kelso, it seemed, had not forgiven me.

Sammy Lamont, then studying law at Glasgow University, still reported to me. He wrote that his father and mother had been offended by my poems. He had tried to read 'Gathering Dung' to them, but his mother had made him stop. Uncle Tam, though, had enjoyed it, and sent his regards.

As always, Sammy himself passed no judgment. As always too he dropped a hint that he was still waiting for an invitation.

What disappointed me most was that my fellow poets did not shout hosannas. Sievewright, Tushielaw, and the rest knew in their hearts that my poems were as good as any in Scotland since Burns. They ought therefore to have hailed my achievement, not for my sake, but for their own: they could have found some sort of fulfilment in the thought that their own work, with all its limitations, had prepared the way for mine.

Writers find it too painful to admit a contemporary's superiority. They are much happier overpraising the dead. Campbell Aird pointed out that my shortcomings as a man, or what my detractors regarded as my shortcomings, were too conspicuous, too constantly up everyone's nose. To begin with, I always wore a kilt, the garb of stage comics or caber-tossers or anglified lairds, but not of poets. I did not respond to whisky as I ought. After no more than two halfs I did not turn belligerent or lachrymose, either of which would have been normal, but Rechabitic, which certainly wasn't. I had no gift of intimacy. Not even with a fellow poet, drunk and in tears, with his arm about me, praising me and belittling himself, could I be close. I claimed friendship with the redoubtable Holmscroft, but I so manifestly did not give a damn who went cold and hungry.

That was how they saw me, said Campbell, and to be truthful, he jestingly added, that was how I was. I should not wonder therefore that my fellow writers, who considered themselves large-hearted, idealistic, and knowledgable, should find it quite intolerable that their own poetry was so much inferior to that of a selfish, ignorant, conceited, unconvivial, aloof, and unsympathetic bastard like me.

I had reason to be grateful to Betty. Unable to give me as a man tenderness, she more than made up for it by giving me as a poet unflinching support. In her position, that was to say, as maker of the money and keeper of the purse, most women would have badgered me with taunts of idleness. Writing poetry, they would have girned daily, was just a hobby, like fretwork or golf: no self-respecting able-bodied man would ever think of making it his full-time occupation.

Though in her novel *Mark Eglintoun's Vow* she portrays the poet Marmion Stream as a consumptive sipper of absinthe, with fragrant locks and a penchant for far-fetched witticisms in archaic language, Betty knew well that in real life the composing of good poetry was both physically and spiritually exhausting.

Alas, while she was encouraging the poet she was at the same time betraying the husband.

SEVEN

After the War there came on to the market a number of country estates at bargain prices. One of these was Pennvalla, about twenty miles out of Edinburgh. It consisted of a fine substantial house of some twenty rooms and policies of over one hundred acres, which contained within them the ruins of a fourteenth-century abbey. The village nearby was called Abbey. With the help of a loan from Mutt-Simpson Betty bought Pennvalla. The title deeds were in her name, but in the eyes of the world I passed as owner. At last I had a home worthy of my lineage.

The stone with which the house was built was a beautiful

reddish colour, like that of azalea leaves in autumn. Once I was so overcome by gratitude that I kissed it when I thought no one was looking. Dorcas, however, was. Only four, she was always spying on me and thereafter clyping, with her tiny forefinger pointed in accusation.

Betty and Mutt-Simpson bought Pennvalla for Dorcas so that she could grow up a lady, and for Torquil not yet born so that he could grow up a gentleman. They also bought it for me, in the hope that I would be so engrossed in my new role as a laird that I would not notice their philandering.

But, as they say in Gantock, I did not come up the Clyde in a wheelbarrow. I saw what was going on all right. Since the situation was more advantageous than grievous for me I did nothing to end or even to moderate it.

One afternoon a day or two before Christmas when Betty was seven months pregnant I was pacing about the lawn in front of the house composing my poem 'A Taste of Brains', which describes the death of Archie Dungavel. Dorcas's Pekinese Roger kept snapping at my brogues, which he pretended were rabbits. I had now and then to tread on his paws.

Suddenly two faces one close behind the other appeared at the window of Betty's bedroom upstairs. Hers was the one in front, Mutt-Simpson's the other. They were not snatched away. On the contrary, they were kept in view the whole five minutes. I recognised the beatific smirks on Betty's.

There was no doubt in my mind that they were engaged in sexual congress. This approach from the rear was made necessary by the bigness of Betty's belly. It was practicable enough with perseverance, as I knew from experience.

I am well aware of the enormity of what I am saying. My wife was renowned throughout the country, indeed throughout the world, as the authoress of books in which chastity, decency, purity, innocence, and Christian faith, always prevailed. Edwin Hinshelwood's painting of her with Dorcas aged ten months in her arms was thought by many people to illustrate the beauty and dignity of motherhood better than any outlandish Renaissance Madonna and child.

As for Mutt-Simpson, he was a baronet, a product of Eton and Oxford, a wealthy landowner, a philanthropist and humanitarian, and a potential High Commissioner to the General Assembly of the Church of Scotland.

It will be objected by the incredulous that two faces
in suspicious juxtaposition at an upstairs window fifty
yards away was hardly enough evidence on which to
base a charge of adultery, and not very straightforward
adultery at that. It will be suggested by the naive that
they were merely gazing down at me and Roger, with
seasonable smiles.

The incredulity and naivete of the masses as regards
the erotic activities of the rich and powerful have always
amazed me. Whatever the evidence to the contrary, and the
sensational press contains plenty, they keep on believing
that these pre-eminent ones live private lives of marmor-
eal virtuousness. Stories of royal, prime-ministerial, and
archiepiscopal profligacies they read with relish and then
mysteriously disregard, as children do with fairy-tales full
of violent deaths.

If a deputation of clergymen's wives, say, visiting
Pennvalla, that shrine of chastity and married purity
as they thought it, had looked in and seen Betty and
Mutt-Simpson naked from the waist except possibly for
their shoes, coupling so nefariously, they would have
smiled, apologised for intruding, and tiptoed away. Because
what they had just seen was so different from what they had
come to see, and from what they had wanted to see, and
from what they ought to have seen, they would have had no
difficulty in convincing themselves that they had not seen
it at all.

I offer this excuse for Betty. That feat of transubstanti-
ation which she performed in her books, of turning evil into
mush, must have imposed so great a strain that to relieve it
she was driven in her own person to commit every so often
deeds of deliberate vileness.

I felt no hatred for Mutt-Simpson. He would be sufficiently punished by finding himself in the role of contrite
cad.

EIGHT

Torquil was born in mid-February when the ground was
iron-hard with frost.

During her lying-in Betty liked me to sit at one side of
her bed and Mutt-Simpson at the other. She held my left
hand, his right.

I overheard one of the nurses whispering to the other:
'You'd think Sir James was the father, to see him!' Her
older colleague replied: 'You're no' feart the Lord will
strike you down, Whitehouse, for hinting such a thing
about Betty T. Shields.'

In the drawing-room, when the birth was imminent,
Mutt-Simpson was maudlin. 'The most precious, the most
sincere, the most beautiful lady in the land, Fergus. God
give her safe and easy delivery.'

In came Dorcas wearing a new dress. I held out my arms
but she made for Mutt-Simpson. She did not ask how her
mother was, she asked if he liked her new dress.

Though only four she was already so conceited that she
would stare at herself in a mirror for an hour at a time,
practising curtseys; so snobbish that she would sulk if
some farm labourer's child of her own age offered to play
with her; and so imperious that she had to have her way
in everything: up to the age of three she had insisted on
sitting on her chamber-pot in the drawing-room, like a
seventeenth-century princess.

It breaks my heart to have to write so censoriously
of my little red-haired daughter, who was so like my
mother.

Mrs Shields came in and made for the drinks tray.

'You can relax,' she said. 'A boy. Baith weel.'

It was to Mutt-Simpson that she raised her glass.

He put his hand on Dorcas's head. 'You have a little
brother, my dear.'

'I don't want a little brother.'

She did not say it wistfully, as if afraid she would no
longer be loved so much. She said it spitefully, and scowled
at me as if I was to blame.

'She wants to see you,' said Mrs Shields.

Naturally I assumed she meant me. Impudently he
assumed she meant him. We both made for the door.

Dorcas refused to come with us. We left her kicking
the leg of the table on which the drinks tray stood. Her
grandmother would soon stop that.

Betty looked tired but not confused. She gave me her
hand to kiss, Mutt-Simpson her cheek.

A nurse was holding the baby in a shawl. She let us
peep at it. We babbled greetings. As usual, they sounded

ridiculous. Mutt-Simpson's, it seemed to me, sounded triumphant too.

All new-born babies look alike, being as yet only the raw material of humanity and not individual humanity itself. Friends who cry how like the father or mother or this uncle or that aunt the child is are simply welcoming the new creature into the human race.

What of course ought never to be said is that the newcomer resembles some man not a blood relation and known to have been on close terms with the mother. Therefore no one in the room, not Betty nor the doctor nor the nurses nor I nor Mutt-Simpson himself cried how very like Sir James my son looked. All of us, however, showed it on our faces.

True, Mutt-Simpson with his scanty hair and his habit of grimacing in aimless goodwill resembled every new-born child; but in this case there was something extra.

Among civilised people what can a husband do on discovering that the child just born to his wife is probably not his, but a wealthy rival's? There must be primitive tribes somewhere in the world where in such circumstances the wronged husband would dash the babe's brains out against the nearest banyan tree; then, while his sanctified rage was still hot, he would chop off his wife's head and his betrayer's genitals. All this to the applause of onlookers, pleased at seeing justice done according to ancient tribal custom.

As a civilised man I had no such relief for my feelings. I had to suffer the child being put in my arms while I simpered paternally. I had also to suffer Mutt-Simpson's congratulations. Worst of all, I had to tell Betty our son was beautiful, that I was proud of him and her, that I was the happiest man in Scotland, and that we would all toast her health and the child's with the champagne that kind Sir James had brought.

I must add in fairness that the older Torquil grew the less he looked like Mutt-Simpson and the more like my grandfather, Donald McGilvray. He had the same grave pious air. Only it wasn't a retributive God that Torquil worshipped: it was the beauty of artistic creation. At five his favourite painter was Botticelli. All my attempts to interest him in girrs and quoits failed. In his favour, however, it has to be said that he never looked down on me in the way his sister did.

NINE

A bizarre situation developed in Pennvalla. Mutt-Simpson was often a guest, if the term could be applied to one who at bed-time always went upstairs with his hostess after bidding his host a cordial goodnight. As for Betty, she gave me either a waggle of her fingers or a feather-light kiss on the brow. Any stranger present would have been a little surprised, but it would probably never have occurred to him that once upstairs and out of sight they would slip into the same bedroom. It did not occur to me until it had been going on for months.

On the night of discovery I felt a desire as I passed Betty's door to go in and talk to her. She and I had been sleeping in different rooms for some time, but now and then before I was safely asleep she would appear in mine and, as she put it with a chuckle, claim her connubial rights. Rather less frequently I would go into hers, not for amorous reasons, but out of a fear that if I did not show willing once in a while I might lose suzerainty.

That night my wish was just to talk. I felt lonely. So, after the least lustful of taps on the door, I opened it and whispered into the darkness: 'Betty, my dear, are you asleep? I would like to talk for a few minutes.'

After a pause her voice came from the bed, drowsily indignant. 'Go away, Fergus. Observe the rules, please.'

'What rules?' I asked, puzzled.

'The rules of civilised behaviour. Once a gentleman has accepted an arrangement he does not interfere with it.'

'I don't understand, my dear. What arrangement?'

Another pause. Then a snort; definitely hers. Then a sigh; not hers at all, being too gentle.

The bedside lamp was switched on.

Before I saw Mutt-Simpson in the bed beside her I noticed his trousers on the carpet.

He was using her left breast as a pillow. Never had his hair looked so infantile. His uppermost eye was open. It reminded me of a listening horse's.

I could not help admiring the calm way in which he was gathering his resources. Breeding told.

'Surely you knew, my dear?' said Betty, still on her back.

'Knew what?'

'That James and I are lovers.'

Of course I must have known. Had I not suspected him of being Torquil's father? But there was a big jump from furtive adulteries behind my back to this sleeping with her in relaxed husbandly fashion.

She whispered in his ear. Then they both sat up. They were naked.

Her hair partly covered her breasts. Her fingers gripped her right nipple, as if it was the pin of a grenade. Her smile, though, did not seem hostile.

I had seen Mutt-Simpson show breeding even in stirring a teacup. Now, caught in the act of illicit love, he tried to look like a gentleman. The intrinsic indignities of the situation defeated him, but not nearly as much as they would have commoner men.

I did not know what to say.

'What was it you wanted to talk about?' asked Betty.

'It doesn't matter.'

'Surely tomorrow would do?'

'Yes, of course.'

'I would like to have a talk with you myself, Fergus,' said Mutt-Simpson.

His grandfather had kept as his mistress one of the most celebrated actresses of the day. Mine had been a rigid Puritan who wouldn't keep even a canary lest it should sing on Sundays. Small wonder it was I who looked the more guilty.

'Well, goodnight, my dear,' murmured Betty, sliding down under the bedclothes.

'Goodnight, old man,' said her paramour, doing likewise.

She switched off the lamp.

There was nothing for it but to say goodnight too and take my leave. Grabbing him by the throat, dragging him out of bed, and kicking him in the balls would have been in order if he had been, say, a plumber's mate and I a caulker. But since we were both blue-blooded gentlemen any such expression of natural passion was out of the question.

Outside in the passage I wondered if what I had just

seen had been hallucination or reality. Coming to Mutt-Simpson's room I went in, half-expecting to find him innocently asleep and half-determined to wake him up and apologise; but the bedclothes weren't even turned down. It seemed no one in the house except me had expected him to sleep in his own bed.

Next morning Betty and Mutt-Simpson went off to Edinburgh in her car. An onlooker would have taken them for man and wife, and me, tamely waving from the doorstep, for some privileged kind of servant.

TEN

Mrs Shields had a small sitting-room of her own. I found her there drinking gin, though it was not yet eleven o'clock in the morning.

I sympathised with my mother-in-law. She reminded me of limpets which could be knocked off their rocks only by a certain sudden artful skiffing kind of kick that not everyone knew how to apply. Betty had tried all kinds of tricks to dislodge her mother from Pennvalla; none so far had succeeded.

She refused to be packed off to a cousin in New Zealand; she refused to be set up in a flat of her own in Edinburgh; she refused to modify her Scots accent; she refused to keep out of the way when we had titled guests; and worst of all in Betty's eyes, she refused to give up her grandmotherly duty of giving Dorcas a disciplinary skelp now and again.

'I'd like a few words with you, Nellie,' I said, 'if it's convenient.'

'If it's to complain about catching her in bed wi' Jimmy don't bother.'

I was taken aback.

'For guidsakes, the haill hoose has kent for lang enough. It's kept her happy and quiet.'

Being confronted by aristocratic blackguardism with its roots in ancient royal example was one thing, being confronted by the insouciant acceptance of her daughter's outrageous immorality by a woman who'd once mucked out byres was quite another.

'Don't you regard marriage as a sacred trust?' I asked sternly.

'I'd be a fool if I did, seeing I was never mairit myself.'

Seldom was a bombshell of information tossed so casually.

'But you call yourself Mrs Shields.'

'If it suited my purpose I'd ca' myself the Duchess of Buccleuch.'

'But if this is true it means that—'

'Betty's a bastard? That's richt. So she is. You've never had a guid look at your mairrage lines, have you? Her faither was a young fellow wi' hair like corn. I let him put poppies in mine aince too aften. I was juist sixteen.'

'I see.'

What I saw was what gave Mrs Shields her sticking-power. It was blackmail.

'You keep my secret,' she said, with a wink, 'and I'll keep yours.'

I crept away, not daring to ask what she thought my secret was.

That evening I tackled Betty in her bedroom while she was dressing for dinner. In white corsets and pink crepe-de-chine knickers she sat massaging wrinkles out of her puffy face.

She frowned at me in the looking-glass.

'I hope you're not going to be tiresome and common,' she said.

'Is it common to feel hurt when one finds one's wife in bed with another man?'

'It is always common to make a fuss. I shall be frank, Fergus. When being made love to a woman wants to be made to feel precious, exalted, and favoured above all other women. You, I'm sorry to say, make me feel like a prostitute with a client who is so busy grudging the money and the effort that he forgets he is supposed to be enjoying himself. You lack tenderness. Why look shocked? You handle my most sensitive and fastidious parts as if they were nuts and bolts.'

What shocked me was not so much her accusation that I lacked tenderness as her assumption that she possessed it. After all, her simile of nuts and bolts applied far more accurately to my sensitive and fastidious parts.

'I do not think,' I said judicially, 'that the Very Reverend Mr McBeagle who married us in St Giles would consider an alleged inability to make an act of holy and mystic adoration out of an activity that we have in common with camels, an excuse for your dishonouring the Christian institution of marriage. Be honest, Betty. Would he?'

'I've wondered,' she said, as she powdered her oxters, 'what was in your mind at the time. So it was camels. But to answer your artless question. Publicly, from his pulpit, wearing his Geneva bands and addressing the common herd, no, he would not; but in private, speaking to intelligent people who know the difference between claptrap and truth, yes he certainly would. He would, you see, grasp what you do not seem able to: that my sleeping with James has saved our marriage. In realistic theology, Fergus, infidelities that save a marriage are not the same as infidelities that wreck it.'

I was well aware, from observing my own at work, that the human mind is the trickiest thing in nature, easily able, if it so wishes, to justify the slaughter of millions, far less a few adulteries.

'Just tell me this, Betty,' I said. 'Suppose Roger Wintercleuch had found Madeleine Ure in bed with Justin Sundhope, would he have forgiven her?'

'If he had been as financially dependent on her as you are on me, my dear, he would not have had the impertinence to condemn her, let alone forgive her.'

She stood up then, snapping the elastic in her knickers. This was her peremptory way of letting me know that the interview was over.

ELEVEN

A few days later I cantered over the fields to Heddleston House to have it out with Sir James. Under my kilt I wore specially padded underpants. My pony was small and unambitious. The day was sunny, the fields unhilly and all the gates openable. So I was able to do some thinking as I jogged along.

Usually I made do with a hazel switch, but that afternoon I took with me a proper riding-crop, the kind with which cads who lead innocent young girls astray are traditionally thrashed. Betty was no innocent young girl and I had no intention of thrashing Mutt-Simpson, but I needed a symbol the sight of which would make him cringe with guilt. For I was faced with a difficulty: my wife's seducer

was in many respects a better man than I. His reputation
as a Christian gentleman was deserved. While it was true
that his store of goodwill towards humanity was not locked
up in him by harsh circumstance as mine was, and that
he had plenty of money of his own to be generous with,
the fact remained that in his place I would have been
less charitable. He was the only landowner in the county
who allowed tinkers to camp on his land. The rest of us
grumbled at having such thieves and pests in our vicinity,
but he refused to have them driven away. He even gave
them permission to use his wind-blown timber.

He was far more likely to help a friend than harm him.
He had done me many good turns.

I took the whip into the house with me, stuck down my
stocking, as if it was part of the accoutrements of a kilted
horseman. The butler looked bemused.

Sir James was in the library listening to music louder
than massed pipe bands. Leaping up to shake my hand, he
informed me, in a reverential whisper that had to be roared,
that it was Wagner. He bent down to take a closer look at
the riding-crop as if to compare it with the conductor's
baton he held, not as weapons in a possible duel but as
indicators of idiosyncratic zest. Both of us then settled
down to listen, myself with fortitude, he with winces of
pleasure.

'You don't realise, Fergus,' he said, when there was
silence again, 'you who fought so bravely in the War,
how a timid non-combatant like me needs music to give
courage.'

Courage no doubt to face a friend whose wife he slept
with.

'Tea will be brought in in a few minutes,' he said.

Had he guessed that the drinking of tea was for me what
smoking the pipe of peace was for Red Indians? So many
times as a child had I watched adults overcoming their
distrust of one another by drinking tea together.

'Did you motor over?' he asked.

'I rode.'

'I'm glad you came. I need your help, old man.'

Since we were both Christians, myself nominally and he
seriously, it was in order I supposed for him who had
wronged me to ask my help in finding forgiveness.

'I thought I was the one who needed help,' I said.

He nodded sympathetically.

The butler came in with the tea.

'What's your trouble, Fergus?' asked my host as soon as we were alone again. 'Try a buttered pancake. They're delicious.'

I tried one. It was tasty enough, but not to be compared with those that Jim Blanie's mother had made long ago.

'What's *your* trouble, James?' I asked.

'Well, you see, Fergus, I'm getting married.'

I saw at once why he needed courage. He was afraid to tell Betty.

'That's no trouble, old man,' I cried. 'That's splendid news. Congratulations. Do I know the lady?'

'As a matter of fact, Fergus, you do. She met you once. You knew her brother. Lady Grizel Dungavel.'

I could not help grinning at the idea of this timid music-lover being yoked to that handmaiden of stallions.

'I didn't know you knew the Dungavels, James.'

'They've been friends of my family for many years.'

'Is she still as fanatical about horses?'

'She still hunts, if that's what you mean.'

'I expect you and she have ridden to the top of Spango many times?'

'Only once.'

'She used to be fond of putting people through tests.'

'I don't understand.' But he closed his eyes for a moment, in instant prayer. 'You knew her brother, I believe. Archie, who was killed.'

'Yes.' But I did not want to talk about Archie. He, like Gantock, must be put off until I was more worthy of him. 'Well, James, in what way does a man so fortunate need help?'

'Betty doesn't know. I haven't quite got round to telling her.'

'Keeping it secret from her must have been difficult considering how close you and she have been recently.'

'I'd rather you didn't adopt that tone, old man.'

'What tone would you say is appropriate for a husband to use speaking to a friend and neighbour who has debauched his wife?'

'Really, Fergus, it's true that you have an awfully vulgar streak in you.'

'It is petty to resort to abuse. Surely you do not deny sleeping with my wife, in my own house?'

'No, I do not deny it. I'm sorry, Fergus. I would have explained long ago but I didn't want to hurt your feelings. You see, old man, Betty came to me in some distress. It seemed that you were suffering from some delayed effect of your experiences during the war: some kind of shell-shock. It took the form of making you averse to the making of love. Your marriage was suffering. Betty's very sanity was in danger. What I was asked to do was an act of therapy and compassion. Perhaps other elements did enter into it later. I may have been mistaken, but if so it was in good faith.'

He had spoken, and was now staring at me, with pity or irony or barefaced cheek: all three are well-nigh indistinguishable on artistocratic faces.

Making a fuss, Betty had said, was common. Mutt-Simpson would agree. A gentleman in my predicament ought to sympathise with a gentleman in his.

I had to take care lest I throw away with a few plebeian barbarisms what since leaving Gantock I had schemed, lied, deceived, betrayed, and even killed, to achieve: that was, my status as an officer and gentleman.

As always, Sir James was eager to help.

'In any case, old man,' he said, 'my part is over. Not only because I'm getting married but because Betty's got her eye on someone else, someone I may say more suitable.'

'Who?'

'Sir Jock Dunsyre.'

'Isn't he a Member of Parliament?'

'Yes. For one of the Glasgow constituencies. Oxford rugger blue. Huge chap. His place is in Lanarkshire. His wife died about three years ago. She was a daughter of Lord Gleneagles.'

I felt furious with Betty, yet I felt proud of her too. Good for the byre-woman's bastard, I could not help thinking.

'They'll be awfully discreet, Fergus. She has her readers to think of, and he his constituents.'

By this time we were both on our feet. He held out his hand. For a moment I was tempted to pull the whip up out of my stocking and give him at least one symbolical slash across the face. But it would have been like striking the Good Samaritan. So I took his hand.

'Be a brick, Fergus, and break the news to Betty.'

'I'll do that, James.'

'Knowing Grizel should make it easier for you.'

'So it should.'

'Please do it as gently as you can.'

'Surely.'

'Much obliged, Fergus.'

'Much obliged, James.'

TWELVE

Though she seldom showed me any sign of affection I continued for a long time to have a father's anxiety about Dorcas and her social ambitions. It worried me that she was doing all her practising and posturing in the middle of a mine-field.

Her grandmother, Mrs Shields, had never been married. Her other grandmother had committed suicide. Her mother was an adulteress. Her father had been born in a room-and-kitchen. These were mines, any one of which could blow to pieces her confidence that one day she would be a great lady. Therefore Betty and I joined forces in trying to keep her clear of them.

I had put so wide a desert between me and Gantock that there was no danger of anyone from there arriving with a packful of disillusion. Betty's own past was well hidden away; but there was one person who could with a few words drag it out into the open. This was Mrs Shields. That was why Betty and I kept urging Dorcas to be nice to her grandmother. That was why after every display of pertness we held our breath and waited for the bang.

One day I had a talk with Mrs Shields as she lay sick in bed. She stank of gin and camphor. Her voice was a painful croak. But she looked capable of living for another twenty years at least. The older she got too the more touchy she would become. Like a mine, indeed.

'How are you feeling, Nellie?' I asked.

'I'd be deid long ago if I was depending on visits frae my grandweans to keep me alive.'

'I thought Torquil came to see you.'

'He came to paint my face. He said it's mair interesting when it's yellow and thin.'

'Yes, he takes his painting seriously. But didn't he blether away to you while he was doing it?'

'When did you ever hear Torquil blether? He talks like an auld priest that used to come to oor hoose when I was a wean. I thocht he was the Pope himself.'

I showed my surprise.

'You didnae ken that I was born a Catholic?'

'I certainly did not.'

'Weel, I was.'

So the bomb she represented was even more powerful than I had thought.

'When did you turn?' I asked.

'Wha said I turned?'

'Do you mean, you're still a Catholic?'

'My religion is my ain business.'

'But you never go to chapel.'

'I said my religion was my ain business.'

'Betty's never said anything to me about this.'

'She's nae babbler aboot her background. But neither are you.'

'There are good reasons for our reticence, Mrs Shields.'

Her mind was sharp. 'You mean Dorcas?'

'Yes.'

'Don't worry aboot that one. Naething can hurt her. She's got a hert o' ice. I hear she's been saying she hopes I dee.'

'If she said it it must have been a joke.'

'Some joke.'

'She's only nine.'

'That's whit frichtens me. She's like a tree covered wi' snaw.'

I knew what she meant. 'Snow melts when the sun shines, Mrs Shields.'

'Some snaw doesnae. The snaw at the tap o' mountains. That's the kind on her.'

'What rubbish,' said Betty, when I reported to her. 'Not snow. Cool white blossoms. Once she's sure her roots are firm she'll show masses of affection.'

But she too, I saw, had her apprehensions.

She would have died rather than say that Dorcas must take after my mother, but I was sure she often thought it.

THIRTEEN

Sir Jock Dunsyre, Betty's new lover, was the stupidest man I ever met. In the House of Commons, if one of the Clydeside members was telling of some family living on bread and margarine in a single-end over-run by rats, or a humane Liberal was describing the miseries inflicted on Germans by reparations, Sir Jock, his big red face beaming, would bellow 'Sob-stuff!' and then roar with laughter. Or if some Socialist was being too clever on the subject of economics, the bellow would be 'Jew!' and the laughter just as stentorian. Afterwards, in the smoking-room, he would approach the man he had insulted, thump him matily on the chest, and offer to buy him a drink. If this was refused, as it nearly always was, he would shake his bullish head and snort what a pity it was those Socialist chaps were such poor sports: it was the result of their not playing rugby when they were young.

Six-foot-one in height, and sixteen stones in weight, he could still at forty-five charge through a thick hedge and throw a ball a hundred yards: feats which he performed at Pennvalla for Torquil's benefit and to Torquil's disgust.

It amazed me that other aristocrats, like the Mutt-Simpsons, did not abhor one of their number who let them all down by his boorishness. On the contrary they were very tolerant of him. I came to the conclusion that he reminded them of days when noblemen wielded battle-axes more mightily than their henchmen and so proved their right to the great mansion and the many acres: superior brawn and more enemies mangled being more creditable reasons than theft or chicanery.

Once, when befuddled, he boasted to me that at a hunting party at Gilbertfield Castle he had kissed Lady Grizel's bare behind. She had challenged him to do it and he had done it.

On the whole, I preferred him to Mutt-Simpson as my wife's lover. He was often in London attending Parliament, for he believed that his presence there was important to the nation. Also it was a point of honour with him never to sleep with a man's wife in that man's own house.

He had first been elected to Parliament at a time when even in Glasgow the working-class voted Tory. The War, however, had damaged the reputation of the upper-class for political as well as military competence. In constituencies that contained a large number of working-class voters Tory MPs began to be asked questions that only those with agile minds could evade convincingly. A mastodon like Sir Jock was in danger of extinction at every election.

Even at the General Election of 1931 when he stood as a National Government candidate, his position was insecure. This was because he was again opposed by Mary Holmscroft, who at the previous election had reduced his majority to less than 200 votes. This time too also standing were Alisdair Donaldson, as a Scottish Nationalist, and Andrew Keith, a well-liked local independent Liberal. If these two took some middle-class votes from him he could well be squeezed out. In desperation he asked Betty for her support. She not only gave it, she promised him mine too.

Usually she claimed to be above politics; but since it was a time of national crisis she felt that her participation would be seen by her admirers as having patriotic motives.

'You could be useful, Fergus. You knew this Holmscroft creature. You must know things to her discredit.'

I pointed out that if I had any political sympathies at all they were for the Scottish National Party.

'That may be so, but this particular candidate of theirs you do not care for.'

'I have nothing against Alisdair except that he has written a number of mediocre novels and been highly praised for them.'

'Would he make a good Member of Parliament?'

'He would have to be stupefyingly bad not to be better than Dunsyre.' That was mumbled under my breath.

'The country is facing ruin. It is no time for an irrelevancy like Scottish Nationalism.'

'Will it not be difficult for Dunsyre to convince people that the country is facing ruin when it will be only too obvious that he himself is not suffering the slightest drop in his very high standard of living? Should he not be emaciated and in rags to make his lamentations credible?'

'Your political opinions are childish.'

'How then can I be of any use?'

'Because you will say what you are instructed to say.'

I had to submit. Like Scotland I was not yet ready for independence.

Soon after her arrival in the Central Station Hotel in Glasgow reporters came to interview Betty in the same lounge where twelve years ago I had rebuffed Mr Kelso, envoy from Gantock. Unable to bear the adulatory questions and the so sweetly reasonable replies I went out for a walk in the streets. There it suddenly occurred to me that it would be a good idea to pay a visit to Mary's campaign headquarters.

A taxi took me there. Like all members of the working-class the driver could not make up his mind what to think of me. I had the voice and bearing of a colonel of Guards, I was dressed like a Highland laird, I lounged like one used to spacious rooms, and yet I gave the impression that I was willing to be, not friendly (I was too aloof for that), not comradely (I too manifestly insisted on my superior status), and not neighbourly (my kilt was too splendid for his drab breeks) but nevertheless kin of some kind. I could see various doubts flitting across his tough face, like wind ripples on a pond littered with bricks and old bicycle tyres. He knew Mary was a Socialist, but if I was one he himself was a Turk: thus might he have expressed it to his wife that night. Yet here he was driving me to her committee rooms, which turned out to be a derelict shop in a grimy tenement in a stony leafless street that could have been Lomond Street itself, if among the many smells had been that of the sea.

'Are you famous or something?' he snarled, as I was paying him.

He did not say 'Sir', but then very few Glasgow or for that matter Gantock men ever did. The English were always saying it. If I had been asked to sum up in a sentence the difference between the Scottish and the English peoples I would have said: 'The English say "Sir" all the way up the hierarchies; the Scots, who recognise no hierarchies, do not say it at all.'

I preferred the English style: if more servile it was also more gracious.

He drove off without waiting for an answer.

Inside the shop some men and women were busy folding election addresses and putting them in envelopes. They wore hats, coats, scarves, and gloves, for the place was unheated. They sported red rosettes. Their dedication, however, to the abolition of poverty, privilege, injustice, and war was not so easily displayed. I did not hold it against them, for my own mirror had made me aware that the human face, if it tried too consciously to light up with idealistic zeal, succeeded only in looking demented.

As I entered they all looked surprised and one woman in a green hat said 'My, my!' quite loudly.

A grey-haired man with spectacles asked me what I wanted. I said I had come to see Miss Holmscroft.

'She's out chapping on doors. I'm her agent. Can I help?'

'No thank you. It's a personal matter.'

'Suit yourself. Take a seat. Name's McGregor. What's yours?'

I thought him rude. He thought himself sturdily independent. What a disservice Burns did his countrymen when he wrote his democratic rant 'A man's a man for a' that'.

'Captain Fergus Corse-Lamont,' I replied, courteously.

At the same time I sat down grandly on the cheap chair.

After a minute during which they kept stealing dumbfounded glances at me the woman with the green hat asked if I was any good at folding paper. It was her sly way of trying to find out if I was one of the elect.

I shook my head.

A pink-faced middle-aged woman coughed genteelly. 'Excuse me,' she murmured. 'Aren't you Betty T. Shields' husband?'

'Miss Shields is my wife.'

'Is it true,' barked a much grimmer woman, 'that she's going to speak for big Dunsyre? If she is then she's got no right to.'

Her comrades chided her. In a free society everyone must be allowed to speak for whoever he or she wished. It was a small demonstration of the purity of their principles, which caused them to be so ineffectual.

A car plastered with posters stopped outside. Out of it stepped Mary.

She wore a black coat and hat that looked as if they had

been bought from Lumhat Broon or his Glasgow equivalent. People gathered round her on the pavement. They laughed at her quick replies. I remembered that quickness. Often my own mind had had to scamper to keep up. What I did not remember, though, was her making people laugh. She must have mellowed.

Her devotees were working-class women. Their faces were bright with fondness and trust.

I thought how marvellous if when I went back one day to Gantock, to the East End, the women there looked at me like that.

With a last wave she came into the shop. As she was pretending to dab sweat off her brow she caught sight of me.

Surprise, anger, puzzlement contended on her thin earnest face, but in the end they were all replaced by rueful affection.

I felt greatly relieved. If she had disowned me I would have been desolate.

'Hello, Mary,' I said.

'Where have you sprung from?'

'I'd like a chat with you.'

'I'm pretty busy. I'm fighting an election.'

'Couldn't we go somewhere for a cup of tea? You look as if you could do with a break.'

She hesitated.

The woman with the green hat came over and pinned a big red rosette to my breast.

'No, Eleanor,' said Mary. 'Not for him. He's not one of us.'

'Och, it'll do him good then to wear it for a wee while.'

'Leave it,' I said.

But Mary took it off me. It was a medal I did not deserve. It was a badge of comradeship and I was not her comrade.

'All right,' she said. 'There's a café along the street. We'll get a cup of tea there.'

'Lots to do, Mary,' warned her agent.

'I know, Jim. Just ten minutes.'

The café was only fifty yards away. Yet during the minute it took us to walk there Mary was hailed by at least a dozen women wishing her luck. For all my grandness I was hardly noticed. One old woman who did notice me gave me a friendly smile for my companion's sake.

I was beginning to understand why Sir Jock was so afraid of losing his seat.

We sat and waited for our tea and chocolate biscuits just as in a similar place long ago we had waited for our penny pea-brees.

'Well, Mary, it's been a long time,' I said.

'I hear your wife's going to speak for Dunsyre.'

'Betty knows nothing about politics.'

'Maybe not, but I wouldn't mind if it was me she was speaking for. Those women you heard wishing me luck think very highly of Betty T. Shields or anyway of her books.'

'But, Mary, those books are all romantic humbug, and nobody knows it better than Betty herself.'

'They've given pleasure to a lot of hard-working women.'

And therein lay the mystery.

'Do you keep in touch with Gantock?' I asked.

'Of course. My people are still there.'

'Do you see John Calderwood very often?'

'Fairly often. He thinks your poetry's wonderful.'

'You're joking.'

'No, I mean it. He can recite most of it by heart.'

The woman bringing us our tea and biscuits, a stout Glaswegian with fat forearms, was transfigured. In their gold and red wrappings the biscuits were gifts from the gods. Such was the effect on me of hearing that someone besides myself thought my poems were wonderful.

'Why don't you go and see him?' said Mary. 'It's not far.'

'Far enough.'

'I see.'

I wondered what it was she saw. Very fond of her own mother, did she think that it was my mother's unbearable death which made Gantock further than the moon for me?

'They'd get the pipe-band out for you,' she said.

'Do you think so, Mary?'

'Especially if your wife was with you. They'd hang out of their windows in Lomond Street and cheer you as you drove past.'

'Do you ever hear anything of the Lamonts?'

'My mother keeps me well informed. She knows everything that's going on. She's a real Gantockian. John Lamont's doing well, in Stewart's: one of the lucky ones. Sammy's a lawyer here in Glasgow. And Agnes teaches in the primary department of the Academy.'

'And Bessie?'

'Leading light in the kirk guild.'

'The Auld Kirk?'

'Where else? Terrible Tories all of them.'

She glanced at her watch again.

'I visited Cathie once,' I said. 'In the asylum.'

'So I heard.'

'I never went again. I couldn't bear it. Do you still go regularly?'

'She's dead.'

'Dead?'

'About two years ago.'

'Dear Christ.'

'Just as well really.'

'I was very fond of Cathie.'

'We all were. She'd have been proud of you, Fergus, looking and talking so grand. The old Cathie, I mean.'

'With the meat stains on her dress?'

'And on her chin.'

We smiled at each other. For a few moments we came very close, remembering Cathie.

'Tell me about your children, Fergus.'

'Torquil's seven: he wants to be a painter. Dorcas is eleven: she's got red hair like mine.'

'I was told she's the image of your mother at the same age.'

'Who told you that?'

'An old enemy of yours. Mrs Grier. She saw a picture in a magazine and cut it out.'

'Is she still to the fore?'

'Very much so. Well, Fergus, I'm sorry but I'll have to go. It's been nice talking to you.'

Out on the street she was again surrounded by well-wishers.

'I'd like to see you again,' I said.

She frowned and shook her head. 'What's the good? We

might not be so friendly next time. You've gone your way and I've gone mine. We're really a million miles apart. Goodbye.'

She left me then and went into the shop to join her friends and comrades.

I felt abandoned. I thought I would never get safely back to Gantock without her help; and though I could see her through the shop window she was already a million miles away.

FOURTEEN

Next morning Sir Jock joined Betty and me at breakfast. In a smart light-grey suit with a sky-blue cravat he looked dressed for a race meeting. He gazed wistfully at Betty as if she might have a good tip that would help him recoup his losses. Things weren't going well. According to the latest from the course it was going to be a damn close thing.

'She *must* be a fraud,' he muttered, as he chewed his kipper, 'because, in the last analysis, we all are. Question is, how do we nobble her? She dresses like a charwoman off-duty. She lives in a ghastly working-class tenement. She's paid less for working on that damned socialist rag than I spend in a week on cigars. She's too bloody good to be true. Now it's possible that she's the one incorruptible socialist. I've watched them all succumb, you know. I've laid bets on them and won. Good luck to them. Not, mind you, that her showing herself to be incorruptible would do her much good. Nobody likes anybody to have higher moral standards. Still, that's all very well. If she wins I'll be out in the cold.'

'Couldn't you find a safer seat somewhere else?' I asked.

'The fact is, Fergus, it might not be so easy. There's a whisper going round that I'm the wrong sort of Tory for a Scottish constituency. Christ, my people have been Scotch for hundreds of years. We helped to knacker Bonnie Prince Charlie. The sort that's going to be wanted in the future, they're saying, is some fucking bank manager or grocer with Tory views but a Scotch accent: educated too at some dreary Scotch school absurdly called an Academy.'

'Mind your language, my dear,' whispered Betty.

Heads were turning and eyes blinking.

'Sorry. But it's a bloody awful prospect. Sorry, again.'

'All is not yet lost,' she said. 'I have still my contribution to make, and Fergus has his.'

He looked at me and shook his head. I was a faithful hack, without any turn of speed. Then hope lit up his face, like the sun shining on a plate of mince.

'You're from Gantock, Fergus, and so is she. I forgot that. Are you telling me you once . . . ?' He winked lewdly. But the sun then went behind a cloud and the mince looked dull and fatty. 'It wouldn't help much if you had. That's not the kind of thing we want. After all, there's me and you, Bess.' He laughed like a horse with a cold. 'If we raked up that kind of mud about Holmscroft what's to stop her raking it up about us? No, it's got to be about money.'

'I can tell you something about her and money,' I said.

He didn't look hopeful. In his view I was too tame, my wind and spirit both broken.

'She was born and brought up in a hideous slum.'

'Christ, that's no secret. She mentions it in every speech.'

'One day there was no food in the house.'

'Not even a mouldy crust? For Christ's sake, no mealy-mouthed exaggerations.'

'Their usual grocer refused to give them a penny more credit.'

'You know, I believe I've heard this story before.'

'So young Mary, aged seven or thereabouts, volunteered to go round all the other grocers with a basket.'

'This sounds familiar.'

'Her father wanted her to ask for cigarettes for him but she refused. Only for food would she degrade herself.'

'Bloody little prig. And she came back with her basket empty? Yes, I've heard it before. It's a good laugh, nothing more. It wasn't exactly to her discredit, was it? Showed guts. And after all she was just a kid. It won't do. Christ, it might even get her a few votes from some sentimental old hags. What do you think, Bess?'

'I think Fergus can do better than that.'

I nodded. 'When she was thirteen she went to live in the West End of the town with a well-to-do schoolteacher and his sister.'

'She'd have been a damned fool not to jump at the

chance,' said Sir Jock. 'I take it there was nothing indecent about this schoolteacher's motives? Anyway, we've decided that that kind of muck won't do.'

'It meant her enjoying bourgeois comforts while her family continued to rot in their slum.'

'Yes, that's nearer the bone. That might do. I mean if she let her side down once she could do it again. What do you say, Bess?'

Betty smiled at me with fond contempt. She could not help liking me for being so abjectly in her power.

'Dorcas once had a little dog that attacked people with brown shoes,' she said. 'Fergus is a bit like that with people professing principles. Yes, I think we can turn him loose on Holmscroft.'

'Can't say I blame you, old man,' said Sir Jock. 'Show me a man or a woman—especially a woman—that makes a fuss over principles and I'll show you a damned nuisance.'

So it was agreed that at a big rally in his constituency that night I would speak a few words. Betty would help me prepare my speech.

FIFTEEN

There was an audience of over four hundred, most of them lower middle-class women. In their homes loving mothers and submissive wives they were in that hall draped with Union Jacks rabid imperialists. They clapped ecstatically when I was introduced as Captain Fergus Corse-Lamont, MC, husband of Betty T. Shields the famous authoress.

In the front row reporters sneered. They expected from me a braying of the usual Tory twaddle.

'As an aristocrat,' I began, in my most aristocratic manner, 'I share with Plato the philosopher a contempt for democracy.'

I paused, while the audience applauded, a little hesitantly; the reporters gaped at one another in astonishment; Betty behind me hissed 'Stick to the speech'; and I myself remembered the bust on the staircase in Cathie's madhouse.

'Plato believed in excellence, as I do. He advocated that the State should be governed by a body of men recruited from the aristocracy and selected for their wisdom, ability, impartiality, and discretion. He called them Guardians. We call them Members of Parliament.'

Again I paused, not to let the clapping die down for there was not much clapping, but to let suspense build up and bewilderment increase.

'Let us consider each of the candidates in respect of his or her suitability to be a Guardian of the State. Take Mr Keith, Liberal. I do not know Mr Keith personally, but I understand he is the owner of an engineering firm specialising in making valves. Judging from reports of his speeches, and from his photograph in his electoral address, he appears to be well-intentioned but naive. He thinks that the ills of society would be cured if its members were all less selfish. In my opinion any maker of valves with such simplistic views is not fit to be a Guardian.'

Another pause. The frowns of the audience showed that they would have preferred Keith to be dismissed with less fancy palaver, but their hands approved of his dismissal nevertheless.

'I come to Mr Alisdair Donaldson, Scottish Nationalist and novelist. Leaving aside the mediocrity of those novels, let us consider Mr Donaldson's belief that the Scottish nation is no longer supine but is on its feet ready to throw off the English connection and take control of its own affairs. Would it were so. But it is not so, and anyone capable of so egregious a misjudgment must be ruled out.'

They were beginning to catch on. Idiosyncratically perhaps but decisively enough for all that, I had rejected two of Sir Jock's opponents as not worth voting for. Since they had already come to that decision themselves they approved of it. They applauded therefore, but not wholeheartedly: my approach was just a shade too eccentric, possibly as a consequence of my being an aristocrat.

A glance round showed me that Betty, though displeased, was far from suspecting that her kilted worm was about to turn. Sir Jock's huge grin suggested that he thought me a pompous bugger but I was doing all right so far.

'As for Sir Jock Dunsyre—' I had to wait then, but I did not mind: the pause would make all the more dramatic what I was about to say— 'I do not have to waste any words on him. He is more fit to be an ostler than a Guardian.'

There was some applause because not all of the audience were sure what an ostler was. Those that knew the usual meaning of the word smiled uncertainly, wondering if I had used it in some peculiarly aristocratic, obscurely complimentary way.

I went on. 'There remains Miss Holmscroft. She was born in a slum but you will recall that Plato made provision for gifted individuals, however lowly born, to be promoted into the aristocracy and chosen as Guardians, provided they had the requisite moral and intellectual superiority. Miss Holmscroft is such an individual. I recommend therefore that you all vote for her.'

I bowed to show that I had finished and then sat down beside Sir Jock.

Probably I had not lost him a single vote. Betty had jumped to her feet to mend any damage that I might have done. She explained that her husband had a whimsical sense of humour. Those women understood at once and smiled at me in fond forgiveness. Their own husbands often said whimsical things too.

Sir Jock was more puzzled than angry.

'What the hell d'you mean, an ostler?'

More mutters followed at intervals.

'An election's a serious matter, you know.'

'First time in my life I ever heard anybody mention Plato at an election meeting.'

'Can't make you out, Corse-Lamont, simply can't.'

'Holmscroft's been in jail for making seditious speeches, for Christ's sake.'

At last, smiling and waving like a queen, Betty was done. She sat down to tremendous cheering. She was even more queen like, with a threat of execution or banishment in her voice, when she hissed: 'No one shows off at my expense. No one makes me look a fool. Especially not you, Fergus.'

Sir Jock lost his seat. The majority was tiny, but the shock considerable. Mary was immediately famous and he demoralised. He sobbed in Betty's arms: he had nothing left to live for except his estate, his racehorses, his income of ten thousand a year, his other mistresses, and her.

It was possible that I contributed a little to his defeat. One newspaper had carried the headline: NOT FIT TO BE AN OSTLER. Glasgow, city of few ostlers, had enjoyed the joke. Some transient interest was shown in me. It was remembered that I had published a few years ago some unconventional poems about the War.

The day after our return to Pennvalla Betty summoned me to her study. On the desk in front of her lay an open cheque-book. She looked baleful.

'No woman has ever been more tolerant and patient than I,' she said. 'But there is a limit. That limit has been reached. You have acted in collusion with a dreadful woman to make me look a fool in public. That I cannot tolerate.'

I remained cool. I was ready for her.

'May I sit down?' I asked.

She would have preferred to keep me standing or to order me to kneel.

I sat down and arranged my kilt modestly over my knees.

'May I smoke?' I asked.

'You certainly may not.'

I took out a cigar but did not light it. I just let her see it. It was one of a boxful that Sir Jock had given me.

'You have often expressed a wish to travel,' she said.

'I do not recollect ever expressing such a wish. I am a happy stay-at-home, my dear.'

'I have decided that you are to go to Australia, or some place as far away. For not less than three years. Here is a cheque for three hundred pounds. Requests for additional funds will be ignored. If you need more money work for it. This decision is final. Dorcas fully supports it.'

'Does Torquil also support it?'

'He is too young to be consulted.'

'Has Sir Jock been consulted?'

'I shall expect you to leave Pennvalla within three days.'

As an ex-soldier I felt sorry for her, making so puny an attack on a position so strongly held.

'I'm afraid you have it wrong, my dear.' I said.

Her neck swelled with rage. I noticed how fat she was all over. She must have loosened her corsets and girdle for the fray.

'If anyone is leaving Pennvalla I'm afraid it will have to be you, Betty.'

'There are times when I am convinced you are not right in the head. Why on earth should I leave my own home?'

'Because you would be afraid of my making certain matters public.'

'What matters?'

'Your various adulteries.'

'No one would believe you.'

'That would make no difference. The accusation itself coming from your gallant husband would be enough. The champion of purity and chastity must be far removed from the merest whiff of scandal.'

'Would you stoop so low?'

'Lower, if it was necessary.'

'So your low-bred nature and origins have come uppermost?'

'On the contrary. My low-bred connections would be shocked by my setting up as a blackmailer.'

'So you admit it is blackmail?'

'What else? Great estates have been acquired, and illustrious families founded, by even less savoury means. It is the aristocrat in me that you are dealing with.'

'What if I were to make public the fact that your mother ran off with a man three times her age?'

'I should simply sneer like Lord Wolfelee.'

He, it may be remembered, is a depraved nobleman in *The Heirs of Crailzie.*

'If I was to let it be known that she took her own life?'

Even against that despicable threat I was proof.

'Aren't you forgetting what such a disclosure would do to our sensitive daughter?'

'You are a villain, Fergus.'

'I am a gentleman determined to hold on to his privileges.'

'You have not heard the last of this.'

'Perhaps you'd like us to continue the discussion in bed tonight?'

'You would not dare!'

But dare I did. So did she, by leaving her door unlocked. We were more tender to each other than we had ever been before. There were no nuts and bolts, no awarding of percentage marks. We were as loving and loyal as we could: all the more so because we knew that next day she would despise me as an unscrupulous blackmailer and I her as a would-be evictor. Suspended animosity, we proved, could make for more tenderness in the act of love than love itself.

SIXTEEN

Three days later a letter found its way to me from a Mr Malcolm McPherson, a lawyer in Lochmaddy. In it he informed me that my great-uncle, Mr Angus McGilvray, had recently died at East Gerinish, on the island of Oronsay in the Outer Hebrides. By law his croft should descend to me as his nearest male relative. It consisted of a dwelling-house with a tin roof, its furnishings, two and a half acres of semi-cultivatable land, and grazing rights over some hundred acres of hill. There was also a small sum of money.

I felt tempted to go to Betty, take the cheque, and hurry off, not to Australia but to my ancestral home in the Hebrides. What deterred me was not only the difference between twenty-roomed Pennvalla set in pleasant parkland and the hovel with the tin roof up to its window-sills in drenched bog, it was also the fear that if Betty and Dorcas ever got me out they would never let me in again.

The very next day after getting that letter about my inheritance I was walking in the cool sunshine among the mossy stones of the old ruined abbey, smoking the last of Dunsyre's cigars, when Buchanan, the chauffeur who was also the gardener, came running frosty-breathed to tell me that I was wanted on the telephone.

I did not hurry, few urgent calls ever came for me.

'Very good. Thank you, Buchanan.'

As I strolled slowly back to the house I felt reasonably content. It did not matter that my wife and daughter were scheming to get rid of me, that the small stir created by my two books of poems had long ago passed and I had been able to write no worthwhile poetry since, and that I seemed to have no close friends. The small boy creeping past all the lavatory doors had come almost as far as his mother would have wished. I now had the choice of three lavatories, all private and all inside. Servants obeyed me: not perhaps with happy zeal but smartly enough. This fine large red-stoned house was as good as mine: not by virtue of my name on the title deeds but for other reasons quite as cogent.

Betty was in her study, writing. Dorcas and Torquil were at school in Edinburgh. Mrs Shields was lurking in her own quarters. I had the morning-room to myself as I picked up the telephone.

'Hello. Captain Corse-Lamont speaking.'

'Hello, Fergus. This is Sammy Lamont.'

I frowned. It had been agreed that he would never make a direct approach to Pennvalla.

'I'm sorry to bother you, Fergus. I'm telephoning on my own responsibility. Mum and Agnes don't know.'

'Well, what is it?'

'Dad's ill. In fact, he's dying. He might be dead now. A stroke. He's in the infirmary. Gantock Infirmary. He can't speak but he can write or scrawl anyway. He scrawled F-E-R-G on the bedsheet. I saw him. He meant you, I'm sure. He wants to see you. If you came Mum and Agnes might try to stop you seeing him. I'm warning you. Anyway, I thought I ought to let you know. It's up to you now. The number's Gantock 3497.'

Then he hung up.

Long ago in the peerie season John Lamont had made me one, bigger and better than any sold in the shops, and a whip to keep it spinning. Acquiring skill, I had been able to keep it going for half an hour at a time until my arm tired. When I had stopped plying the whip the peerie had spun slower and slower until it had begun to stagger, as if dying. I had felt weak and dizzy in sympathy.

After that telephone call from Sammy my thoughts were like that peerie reeling to a stop.

As a child I had loved John Lamont, and he had loved me. I should be weeping and getting ready to rush to him to beg his forgiveness before he died. But going to him meant going to Gantock and I was not yet ready for that. What distinctions I had, my medal, my poems, my famous wife, and my ascension into the ranks of landed gentlemen, were not enough, though Mary Holmscroft had seemed to think so. I needed to take back with me much more. I would not feel at peace by my mother's grave. I would not feel at home in Lomond Street, nor in the Auld Kirk. At the War Memorial Smout McTavish and Jim Blanie would not remember me as their friend. I would need all my arrogance to protect me from my own unworthiness.

With these anxieties whirling in my mind I went to Betty's study though the rule was she must not be disturbed before twelve.

She went on writing.

'I've just had a telephone call,' I said. 'I'm afraid it means I have to go to Gantock. John Lamont's dying. He's in the infirmary.'

Still she did not look up, but her pen travelled more slowly across the page.

'I'd like Buchanan to run me into Edinburgh, to the station.'

I asked meekly enough. Blackmail could only be honourably used to safeguard my right to remain at Pennvalla. All lesser rights had to be requested.

She dropped her pen. She looked sympathetic.

'I'm sorry to hear this, Fergus. Who telephoned?'

'Samuel Lamont.'

'But I thought you had vowed never to go to Gantock again.'

'I never made any such vow. I just wanted to wait until I was ready.'

'Are you ready now?'

'I want to see him before he dies. I owed him a great deal once.'

'Far be it from me, Fergus, to discourage filial gratitude in you. How long do you expect to be away?'

'I don't know. Two or three days.'

'So short a time! Won't you have to wait to see if he gets well, or to attend his funeral if he doesn't? And aren't there many old friends to look up, many old haunts to revisit?'

I did not answer.

'Where will you stay?'

'There's a hotel.'

'I see. What about money?'

'Perhaps I could do with a little.'

'Of course.' She got out her cheque-book and wrote me a cheque for twenty pounds. I was surprised. I had expected five at most. I thanked her.

'Do you want me to go with you?'

I could not help looking aghast.

'Why not? It's not an unusual thing for a man to have his wife with him when he goes to see his dying father.'

'He is my *foster* father.'

'So he is. Are you leaving immediately?'

'Yes.'

'You may tell Buchanan I said he has to take you. No. Wait. I'll tell him myself. He can do some shopping for me and then pick up Dorcas and Torquil. You go and pack. And good luck.'

She gave me her cheek to kiss. I felt grateful, but I did not trust her. Gantock would be a hard enough battle to win without treachery in my rear.

According to our arrangement of meeting twice a year Samuel Lamont and I met yesterday 15th June at eleven o'clock in the usual place, the Glasgow Art Galleries, in front of Rembrandt's 'Man in Armour'.

As a well-known QC Samuel is the kind of man for whom policemen, hotel commissionaires, and Art Gallery attendants make concessions. We were not likely to raise our voices but if we did there would be no requests to be quiet.

His hat and coat were dry, though outside the rain was heavy. He had been brought to the door all the way from Edinburgh in his big black car.

He has a way of pressing his lips tightly together that reminds me of his mother long since dead.

'You look tired, Fergus,' he said.

I am seventy-one, he ten years younger. Long ago I pushed him in a pram along Lomond Street. He still hopes to be made a judge.

'Some months ago,' I said, 'a fellow, an American, a professor of literature he called himself, came to see me. How did he find out where I live?'

'Yes. I'm sorry, Fergus. It was a mistake. No harm done, though. If he writes anything about you it will be for some esoteric magazine that no one ever reads. Your secret's safe. I hope he wasn't too much of a nuisance.'

'I threw him out. Please make sure it does not happen again.'

'I already have. But—let me say it once again—are you being fair? To yourself most of all, but to your son Torquil too. He admires your poetry. He keeps telling me how much he wishes he had known you.'

'He knew me once.'

'He was just a child then.'

'Does he still live in Paris?'

'Yes. You know, Fergus, you could live somewhere in the sun just as cheaply as here. You'd soon get rid of that cough.'

He gives me this advice every time we meet. He seems to have some vague idea of my becoming reconciled with Betty, now an old half-crazy woman of seventy-five.

I stood up. In Rembrandt's painting the man in the helmet gravely smiled. I liked that smile. It gave me courage. It reminded me of Kirstie.

He followed me out. We passed through the hall of statues. Laocoon wrestled with serpents.

'Can't we go somewhere for lunch, Fergus? I've an hour or so to spare.'

'No, thank you.'

It was still raining. His car was waiting. The chauffeur was reading a newspaper.

'Can I give you a lift home then?'

'The bus is convenient.'

'At least let me drop you at a bus-stop.'

'There's one not a minute's walk away.'

'So it's goodbye again?'

'Goodbye, Sammy.'

At the bus-stop in the pouring rain with the roar of traffic about me I thought of Kirstie and East Gerinish and waves breaking on a rocky shore.

Part Four

ONE

I had spent so much time in acquiring authentic aristocratic attitudes that I had necessarily been dilatory in the
cultivation of cordial feelings, particularly towards those
beneath me socially. In Gantock the people who mattered
most to me, the Lamonts and the denizens of Lomond
Street, would, I felt sure, be flattered if I condescended
to them, provided I could make it clear how fond I was
of them. Suppose I met Mrs Grier, say, and treated her as
any officer and gentleman must any seventy-seven-year-old
crone of the lower orders, she would not feel insulted, for
she had lived long enough near the bottom of the social scale
to be realistic about such things; but if I could also convey,
by unspoken subtleties, a reminder or rather a suggestion
that once as six-year-old children her weak-witted grand-
daughter and I had inspected each other's private parts in
a coal cellar by the light of a defective torch, she would be
secretly but sufficiently gratified.

I felt I could manage the condescension confidently
enough, but not the implicit kinship. There would be
scope unfortunately for all sorts of contretemps.

In Glasgow Central Station since there was some time
to wait before the next train to Gantock I telephoned the
number Samuel Lamont had given me. He had been uncharacteristically vague, but I had supposed it was the number of
the infirmary. Therefore I was disconcerted when, instead
of a stranger's voice, I heard Bessie Lamont's, not quite
the old Bessie who had lived in the room-and-kitchen in
Lomond Street, she was too primly bourgeois for that, but
still immediately recognisable as the woman who had tried,
so conscientiously, to take the place of my mother.

'Mr John Lamont's residence,' she said, with an attempt
at haughtiness that I, expert and connoisseur, knew instantly to be the consequence not of snobbishness but

of fear and anxiety. She was not trying now to hide the fact that she had never got beyond elementary school. What she was trying to make clear was that her husband's dangerous illness was her and her children's business, though any outsider who showed the right kind of sympathy would be properly thanked.

'Who is this calling, please?' she asked.

I hesitated. Important things were involved. I was about to speak to a woman who at a time when I needed love and encouragement more than I ever would in my life again had given them generously. I had repaid her by ignoring her existence for many years. If I said the wrong things now, or even if I said the right things in the wrong way, I would stop the stars in their courses: just as my grandfather had done, all those years ago, when he had refused to go into the garden to speak to my mother.

'It's me, Bessie,' I said.

God knew I tried as hard as I could to sound affectionate, letting hauteur speak for itself.

It spoke too strangely. She did not at once recognise me.

'You? Who are you, please?'

'Fergus, Bessie. Fergus Corse-Lamont.'

'Oh!'

It was more like a cry of pain than a sign of recognition.

'I hear John Lamont's seriously ill,' I said, as gently as I could.

'If you're the person you say you are, you're talking about your own father.'

'Yes, Bessie. I'm speaking from Glasgow. On my way to Gantock. How is he?'

'It's late in the day to be concerned, is it no'?'

'Yes, Bessie. But not too late, I hope.'

'I think it is. Yes, I think it is.' She was weeping. 'Not because he's dead and past all caring, but because shame between the living grows too great, if you see what I mean.'

I thought she meant that he was dead. A man passing glanced into the kiosk. He looked unhappy. I was to remember his face for the rest of my life.

I listened to her weeping. I remembered her rushing out

into the garden at Siloam to take in her washing, before the sudden rain soaked it.

'When did he die?' I asked, humbly.

'Don't be in such a hurry to hae him dead. As far as you're concerned we've a' been dead for years.'

'I'm sorry, Bessie. I misunderstood.'

'He's still critical, they say, but he's no' dead. I don't ken how he is. They don't seem to ken themselves. They tell me nothing.'

All I could say was, 'I'm sorry.'

It was inadequate, yet it seemed to mollify her. Whereas if I had been eloquent and passionate she would have been further offended.

'How did you know?' she asked. 'Was it Sammy?'

'Yes. He telephoned.'

'He wasn't supposed to. But he's always taken your part. Is your wife with you?'

'No.'

'I see.'

I thought I knew what she was thinking. If I had intended this to be a permanent reconciliation I would have brought my family.

'I would have liked to meet your wife,' she said. 'She writes beautiful books. You've been very lucky. I hope you appreciate that.'

I let it pass.

'I'll have to go, Bessie. My train leaves in three minutes. Could I have a quick word with Sammy?'

'He's not here at the moment. I'll let him ken you telephoned. If he kens you're coming I expect he'll be at the station to meet you. Goodbye.'

She hung up before I could say goodbye to her. I was left not sure whether or not she would be willing to meet me when I got to Gantock.

TWO

In the train, smoking a cigar, and looking out at scenes that grew more and more familiar, I reviewed that preliminary skirmish with Bessie and decided on future tactics. No matter whose feelings were hurt, including my own, and no matter what last ties of loyalty were strained or broken, I must use my landed-gentry manners and accent, even in Lomond Street itself. Surely the last thing anyone in Gantock wanted was for me to return humdrum and humble. Any distinction I brought would be shared by all. It was therefore for everybody's sake that I should speak as lord to serfs, hero to cravens, and poet to groundlings, though always with undercurrents of affection.

Consequently, when the train arrived in Gantock station, though many memories immediately assailed me, I was not overwhelmed. There was the stone pillar where Smout McTavish, Sammy Jackson, and I had scratched our names with a rusty nail. There was a barrow very like the one I had helped to push. There was the advertisement for Haig's whisky under which I had said goodbye to Smout and he had kissed Jessie McFadyen, that tender silly girl. I saw those things and was moved by them, but outwardly I appeared to be gazing disdainfully at nothing in particular: in contrast to the Gantockians in the station who gaped at me in aboriginal disbelief.

Sammy Lamont, or a solemn-faced young man in a dark suit that I took to be he, came gliding—he had a peculiarly smooth walk, as if on wheels—up to where I stood with my suitcase at my feet.

I had already demeaned myself, and in the circumstances taken a risk, by lifting it down from the rack on to the platform. The one porter in the distance, chatting to a friend, had heard my shout and turned round incredulously, as if expecting to see a hippopotamus dancing, and not simply a gentleman asking for his suitcase to be carried.

'Sammy Lamont,' said Sammy. 'Hello, Fergus.'

We shook hands.

He picked up my suitcase. 'Porters don't carry them here,' he said.

'So Gantock is still as uncouth as ever?'

'You could call it that.'

As we walked through the chilly station people did not come rushing up to me to wish me well, as they had done to Mary in Glasgow. I regretted this, but perhaps it was just as well, for I would have had to snub them, as grandly as I could.

'Do they know who I am?' I asked.

'They're working it out.'

He had explained that his father appeared to be a little better. There was still hope.

He had a small motor car outside. We set off for the infirmary through streets that, if I had not like the Lord hardened my heart, might have had me shedding premature tears.

'If you'd brought your wife,' he said, 'they'd have been cheering.'

That was a loaded remark best ignored.

'Mum and Agnes think she's wonderful.'

I remembered his sister Agnes as a greeting-faced little girl who was always catching colds: just the kind who'd grow up to admire Betty's preposterous romances.

'She's a schoolteacher,' he added.

We passed through Auchmountain Square. Pigeons strutted up and down the steps of the Auld Kirk, as if mocking the pompous burghers seen there every Sunday.

I asked if Thomas Pringle still kept pigeons.

'Uncle Tam? No, he gave them up after he became blind.'

'Blind? Did you say "blind"?'

Those were yelps of astonishment and horror. My Scotch accent showed through.

'I'm afraid so.'

'What happened?'

'A brick fell on his head.'

A situation that I had often chuckled at in the comics of childhood. Lumps like eggs had appeared on skulls. But no one had been hurt, no one had been made blind. Some of those comics Uncle Tam had bought me.

'I didn't know a blow on the head could make you blind.'

'I'm afraid it can.'

'When did this happen?'

'About five years ago.'

'Is he ever likely to get his sight back again?'

'Who knows?'

'Where is he?'

'Still in Kirn Street.'

'Living by himself?'

'Yes.'

'But how can he, if he's blind?'

'Neighbours help.'

I understood that. No man was ever better liked.

'How old is he?'

'In his middle sixties, I should think.'

'Does he keep well, apart from his eyes?'

'He gets headaches.'

I felt my hand shrinking to childhood size, and being enclosed by one as hard and rough and reliable as a brick.

I dreamed of taking him back to Pennvalla with me.

'Dad wanted him to come and live with us, but he wouldn't.'

'Why not?'

'Well, you know how proud and independent he's always been.'

Did I know that? All I knew of him was that he had been kind to me. That was all I had wanted to know.

'Do you still visit him?' I asked.

'Whenever I can. My office is in Glasgow, you know. He often mentions you.'

I felt very small. 'He wrote to me once, when his wife died. I never answered.'

'He didn't expect you to. Well, here we are. We'll probably meet my mother.'

He put it like a warning.

I had been in Gantock Infirmary once before, when I was about seven. A boy in our street was ill with diphtheria. His face had looked as green as the tiles on the walls. Two days later he had died.

It was very quiet in the room where John Lamont lay: so much so that Bessie's intake of breath as I entered sounded like a sob of pain.

It had been seventeen years since we had last met. She had been close on fifty then. Yet I always kept remembering her as the young woman with dark-brown hair, honest eyes, and firm mouth who had become my stepmother. It was disturbing to see her with white hair and eyes not quite so frank.

What was giving her courage not only to face me boldly but also, as it turned out, to forgive me, was the improvement in her husband's condition. I, who had looked on many dead and dying faces, knew at a glance that John

Lamont's was that of a man sleeping, and not of a man dying.

I did not want to look at him too closely with those others watching. I might have given myself away, not only to them, but to myself too.

The Sister conducted us out.

'Sorry,' murmured Sammy, 'if you think I've brought you back to Gantock unnecessarily.'

'It was high time he came,' said his mother. 'You'll come back to the house with us, Fergus?'

Before I could think up a dignified and tactful refusal, she added, as we passed the open door of a ward where old women lay ill, 'There's an old friend of yours in there, dying. Of cancer.'

I stopped. 'Who?'

'Mrs Grier. Surely you remember Mrs Grier, Maggie they called her, that used to live in Lomond Street? Terribly vulgar woman, but good-hearted enough. If she was on one pavement you'd cross to the other so as not to have to pass her.'

I wanted to hurry away from the stricken ogress, but found myself saying, 'Do you think they'll let me see her?'

Bessie looked shocked. Evidently she thought there could be only two reasons why I should want to see a woman who had once terrified me: either I wanted to jeer at her now that she was very old and dying; or else the humanity in me wanted to pity and honour the humanity in her, all grudges forgotten. Since the second reason was most unlikely, considering the heartless snob I was, it must be the first.

'I wouldn't think so,' she said. 'Without her family's consent, I mean.'

'I'd like to.'

Suddenly I needed to. If I did not make my peace with this old enemy before she died, my Gantockian triumph, if it ever came, would not be complete.

I stopped a young nurse coming out of the ward.

'Excuse me,' I said. 'Is it possible for me to see Mrs Grier, just for a minute?'

'Mrs Grier?' She sounded incredulous, and looked it too, as she stared open-mouthed at my kilt, my cape, and my jewelled skean-dhu.

'I know she's very ill, but I would very much like to see her.'

'Sister said nothing about anybody coming. You're not a relative, are you?'

Oh yes, I was. All of us in our section of Lomond Street had been in a sense one family; that was why our quarrels had been so bitter, our reconciliations so boisterous.

'She's got the screens round her. They think she'll die today.'

'Come on, Fergus,' whispered Bessie.

I saw, though, that she was proud of me: only a genuine upper-class person would insist on so impertinent and inconvenient a request.

Sammy said nothing but his discreet smile seemed to be warning me that sentimentality was a dangerous game to play. If I wanted to convince Gantock that I was a genuinely upper-class person I ought not to be seen wasting time or pity on the likes of old Maggie Grier.

But no genuine upper-class person would be intimidated by a lawyer's warning. Nor would he wait for official permission. Neither screens nor the imminency of death would deter him. He would not mind being stared at by toothless ill old women. He would simply stride over the polished floor, smile at the two ancient hags inviting him into bed with them, make for the bed in the far corner with the white screens round it, and look in, paying no heed to the clatter of indignant heels in pursuit.

I recognised her immediately. Age, illness, and pain had shrunk her once massive head and throat, bleached and thinned her hair, and robbed her hands of their devilment, though not of their courage. Her devil's spot on her chin had dwindled with the rest of her face. The stiff hairs that once had sprouted from it were now subdued.

She was not likely to waken. If she had, I felt sure she would have known me as quickly as I had her.

She had laughed evilly when Mrs Lorimer had spat in my mother's face. But had she not afterwards apologised? When she had gripped and squeezed my balls during the celebrations in the street on the day war was declared, she had been letting me know that she was sorry and wished me well, stuck-up young bastard though I was. It had been her way of giving me her blessing.

'Excuse me,' said a stern voice behind me. 'You've got no business here.'

It was the ward sister. Her cheerful face belied the sternness of her voice. She was impressed too by my appearance and manners, but most of all by my tears.

Those were momentary, but genuine just the same. They must have seemed to her as miraculous as if they had been in the eyes of the badger on my sporran.

'You've split a few stitches,' she said, as we crossed the ward, to the accompaniment of some screeched ribaldry.

'They don't seem to be showing much grief for their companion who is dying.'

'Gracious me, two days ago Mrs Grier herself was the worst of the lot. Goodness, the things she'd have said about that beautiful kilt!'

THREE

Still hardening my heart, I turned down Bessie's invitation to come in and have lunch. I said I had not yet made up my mind how long I intended to stay in Gantock. If John Lamont's improvement continued I might return to Pennvalla tomorrow. There was no possibility of my wife and children joining me.

Aristocrats never explained, no matter how outrageous their conduct.

She was hurt, but I could not help it.

Sammy said little, but as he drove me to the hotel he became quite loquacious.

'Pretty convincing,' he murmured.

'What do you mean?'

'You hurt my mother's feelings, you've hurt them for years, and yet I'm ready to wager that at this moment she's thinking of you with more pride than anger. I would say that was as good a test as any.'

'Of what?'

'Of hubris. To make people whom you've insulted feel they have been honoured.'

'I did not insult Bessie.'

'Ah, so part of the secret lies in not being aware that you've been obnoxious.'

In extenuation of his impudence, I had to remember that in the days when I was being coached by Major

Holmes, Sammy, then aged about ten, had been my eager accomplice. I had tried out my landed-gentry accent on him. He had offered sensible suggestions.

Perhaps therefore he had earned a right to criticise. 'Your wife wrote a story, didn't she,' he said, 'in which a duke's heir was brought up in a tinker's tent? I should think the people of Gantock are more likely to think of you as some creation of your wife than to remember you as the boy born up a close in Lomond Street.

'Some people think,' he went on, as we stopped outside the hotel, 'that you threw away the chance of a greater distinction.'

'What do you mean?'

'As a poet. You'd be surprised at the number of people who have told me what a pity it was you gave up writing poetry. But perhaps you didn't choose to stop. The life of a country gentleman with a wealthy wife must be very comfortable and self-satisfying, but I shouldn't think it as inspiring, say, as Lomond Street thirty years ago, or the Great War.

'Well, if you want to get in touch,' he said, 'you know where we are'; and he drove away, leaving me to carry my suitcase up the brass-bound steps of the Gantock Hotel.

I had been told that irreverent Gantockians referred to the angel on their War Memorial as Glaikit Mary, because of the attitude and expression of silly supplication that the sculptor had inadvertently given her. Intending her to be beseeching heaven to deal kindly with the souls of the dead soldiers, he had succeeded in making her look as if she was pleading with the gulls not to shit on her.

The Memorial was situated in a public park near the iron drinking fountain put up to commemorate victory over the Boers. The water came gushing out of four lions' mouths, and had to be drunk from thick iron cups attached to chains. As boys, we had warned one another that we would catch diseases which would cause our lips, tongues, and pintles to rot and fall off. We used to tell the most delicate-minded among us that the cup they had just drunk from was the one used by the noseless woman from Cowglen Street.

I paused at this fountain, not to drink, but to take out of

my pocket my MC medal and pin it to my breast. This was not done out of conceit. It was to honour all the Gantock men who had been killed.

Close by some little girls were playing with skipping-ropes. I was pleased. Their presence would give a resonance and poignancy to my homage to the dead. In the gaslight their young faces and shrill voices chanting the numbers were ancestral. They could have been the daughters of men killed at Flodden.

Despite her appeal, the gulls had much defiled the angel's face. Luckily, this had the effect of giving her a rather desperate, harassed look, and therefore a resemblance to many a Gantock housewife. It was easy, by ignoring her wings, to imagine her standing at a closemouth, offering doleful contributions to the conversation.

'That big man in the kilt's awfully interested in Glaikit Mary,' cried one of the girls.

'Maybe he wants her for a click,' said another.

They all shrieked with laughter.

These were friendly observations: the dead men would certainly have appreciated them. All the same, I hoped there would be no more, and moved round the Memorial to where I would be out of their sight.

There were over a thousand names on the four sides of the plinth. The town's grief must have been very great. Yet I had not been here to help it grieve.

Lomond Street had suffered as much as any other. Of my close friends there were Private William McTavish, Private James Blanie, Private Samuel Jackson, Private Robert McIntyre, and Corporal John Dempster; and also, though not from our own particular sector, eight others I remembered.

With tears in my eyes, I hoped that during the exchanges of hope and sorrow at all the closemouths in those terrible years, some kindly mention had been made of me.

I was standing at the salute when I heard spurts of giggles behind me.

'Wheehst, Jeanie.'

'Don't punch me, Isa.'

'He's talking to himself.'

'I think he's greeting.'

'Dae you ken whit I think? I think he's a ghost.'

'Jees, Mary, you're richt. He's the ghost of a sodger that was killed.'

Their squeals of terror then were only half-feigned. They dashed past me, making for the gate. The boldest came close enough to put out her hand and touch me. I got a look at her face. It was merry and impudent. It reminded me of Meg Jeffries.

They were nearly half a mile from their homes in the East End. They would enjoy the journey home along the gaslit streets, stopping to look in shop windows and in prams, returning with interest abuse yelled by boys, yodelling snatches of songs, pulling up stockings, and at the end from their respective closemouths shouting arrangements for tomorrow's play and goodnights. As they ate their teas they would tell their families of the ghost of the soldier they had seen talking to himself at the War Memorial.

They had interrupted a conversation between me and Smout.

I had tried to conjure him up as the shy twenty-one-year-old volunteer with the very short haircut who had so defiantly kissed Jessie McFadyen in the station, but I had not known that Smout very well. It was the skinny-shanked, solemn, patient, little Snout with the holes in his breeks who came and stood beside the angel.

I asked his advice.

It was the same as it had always been. Be grateful for what you've got; or, in the words of a hymn that the Salvation Army used to sing at our street corner, and in which he had joined enthusiastically, to the consternation of all his friends: 'Count your blessings'. With his ragged clothes, and his mother preferring to talk to the dead and play whist rather than sew or cook, he had struck us as having very few blessings of his own to count. Yet no one had ever heard him whine with envy or self-pity.

'You live in a twenty-room-and-kitchen, Fergus. When you're in the lavatory with a sore belly nobody's going to come and bang on the door. If you're fed up with corned beef and butter beans you can eat something else. If it's raining you don't have to stay in because your boots are leaking. You've got a bed to sleep in.'

'It's true, Smout, that I don't have to suffer the hardships and humiliations of poverty.'

'You never did.'

'What other advantages would you say I have?'

'Well, you've got a big fat bonny wife.'

Like Rubens, he had had no time for skinny women. At the station Jessie had looked quite voluptuous.

I could have pointed out that my big fat bonny wife had been unfaithful to me, but it would have been useless saying that to him, who, if he hadn't been killed, would have married daft, tender, promiscuous Jessie.

'You won a medal. You became a toff. You got what you wanted.'

'Not quite, Smout. My real family, the Corses of Darndaff, have never acknowledged me.'

'Who cares aboot them?'

'And my daughter hates me.'

'Have you taken her to Lomond Street, to see where you were born?'

'I could never do that, Smout. She would hate me all the more. I might, one day, take Torquil my son. He might find the sordidness interesting. He wants to be an artist.'

'I used to like drawing trains.'

'I'm in a bit of a fankle, Smout. What should I do?'

'Yin thing you could do, for me: look efter Jessie.'

'I'll do what I can, Smout.'

'That's a promise.'

It was then that I heard the girls giggling.

FOUR

Back at the hotel, after a bath, and a change into an evening kilt, and a couple of whiskies, I telephoned first the hospital where they told me John Lamont was maintaining his recovery, and then Sammy Lamont whom I astonished by asking if he knew what had happened to Jessie McFadyen.

I had to make some effort to keep my promise.

'Jessie who?' he asked.

'McFadyen. She lived in Lomond Street, up the next close to ours. Mrs Grier's her grandmother. Pretty girl, fair-haired, lovely skin, but a bit weak in the head. I believe she was often taken advantage of, for she was too kind-hearted to say no. Before he joined up Smout McTavish considered himself engaged to her.'

'Well, my goodness,' murmured Sammy.

'What's the matter? Is she dead?'

'No, no. Well, she may be, for all I know. It's just that your local knowledge, and your extraordinary interest in such odd people, never cease to surprise me. I keep forgetting you wrote those poems. I'm afraid I can't help. I left Lomond Street before I was four, and I've never been back. I never knew the people there the way you seem to have done. To be truthful, I never wanted to. Mum might know. She never goes there but by some mysterious means she seems to keep in touch. Jessie McFadyen, did you say? What do you want to know about her?'

'Just what's happened to her.'

'All right. I'll consult Mum and then ring back.'

But it was Bessie herself who telephoned.

'Is that you, Fergus?'

'Yes, Bessie. I hear John is still gaining strength.'

'Yes, thank God. We're visiting him in the morning, before we go to church. Would you like to come?'

'To the hospital yes, to the church I think not.'

'You'd cause quite a stir. Of course, you'd cause a great deal more if you had your wife with you. You were asking about Jessie McFadyen?'

'Yes.'

'Why that trollop, for heaven's sake? Of all the people from Lomond Street to pick on the McFadyens, and especially Jessie. There were a lot of respectable folk living there at that time, Fergus. The Colquhouns, for instance; and the Ritchies.'

She had mentioned none of my closest friends' families.

'If you remember, Mr Colquhoun worked for Williamson, the plumber. Well, he went into business for himself and has done very well. They have a nice flat in Menteith Terrace where that teacher you were fond of, Major Holmes, lived. And the Ritchies, they went off to America, to Milwaukee, soon after the War. I believe they were getting on very well there before this depression. The McFadyens, I'm sorry to say, were scruff then and are scruff still; and the McTavishes too, though I admit that wee Willie was the best of the bunch.'

'What happened to Jessie?'

'She's the worst disgrace of all. Maybe it wasn't altogether her fault, her being so soft in the head, and I expect
if she had come from a more respectable and responsible
family she'd have got the help and protection she needed.
If you remember, Mrs Grier was her grandmother. By the
way, *she's* gone; died an hour or so after we left. Anyway,
Jessie, after she left school, was nothing but a trollop; *before*
she left, some said. My goodness, the things they said that
silly little thing was up to in coal cellars with boys still in
short trousers; and with men too. Some said she didn't
know that what she was doing was wrong, that she was
just being kind, but in my opinion she knew very well;
every woman knows that. Of course, that doesn't excuse
the boys and the men. If anything, they were worse than
her. Do you know that when she was 15 she had a wean by
a man of 55? It was put out to adopt. There were rumours
that old Dr McBride—he's dead now, so it can safely be
said—had her sterilised; otherwise she'd have flooded the
parish with illegitimate weans.'

'Where is she now?'

'Well, I'll tell you, for it's not likely you'll be rushing off
to pay her a visit. You'll not remember old Mr and Mrs
Strathglass who lived next door to us in Lomond Street.'

'I remember them well.'

He had smoked in the lavatory for hours. She had sent
me to the shops for such small quantities of things that I
had been ashamed. 'An ounce o' tea, son. Tuppence worth
o' butter. Twa tatties, medium-size.'

'Well, Jessie McFadyen, now Jessie McCreadie if you
please, lives there now, in the Strathglasses' house. They're
both dead. Of course the whole place, Lomond Street I
mean, is a slum. All that part of Gantock has gone down
the brae. It's mostly scruff that live there now. All the
decent folk have moved out.'

'Who was this McCreadie that Jessie married?'

Was he a man of wisdom and compassion who valued
tenderness above all else?

'I don't really like to talk about this, Fergus. It's sordid,
that's what it is. Well, McCreadie was a widower who used
to live in Kirn Street, next close to the Pringles, as a matter
of fact. A caulker in Stewart's. After the War, when wee

Willie McTavish was killed, McCreadie bought Jessie from
the McFadyens. I know what I'm saying: bought her. They
say the sum that changed hands was a hundred pounds.
During the War he made good money. He was a lot older
than her.'

'Was it out of kindness, to give her the help and protection you said she needed and never got?'

'Are you joking? It was for a very different reason altogether. Her brain might never have developed but her
body certainly did. That's what McCreadie was buying:
her body. He'd hardly let her out of the house in case
other men as much as looked at her. He'd have put a
padlock on her if he could. That was years ago, of course.
He's well over seventy now and still as jealous as ever, but
she can manage him now. She pleases herself now.'

'Poor Jessie.'

'Well, maybe.'

'She used to take my hand in playground games of
ring-o-roses.'

'I'm surprised a man in your position would want to
remember a thing like that. But that's enough of Jessie
McFadyen.

'Listen, Fergus, why don't you ask your wife and children to join you now that you're here in Gantock? My
goodness, if she were to come tonight or early tomorrow,
in time to go to church with us, why, you know, it'd make
up for all the years you've kept away, it really would. Betty
T. Shields in our pew in the Auld Kirk! I'd be the proudest
woman in Scotland. Telephone her, and ask her. Will you
do that, Fergus? For me? And for John?'

She was suddenly weeping. To calm her I promised I
would try and coax Betty to come to Gantock, with the
children. It was a lie. If Betty came it would not be to bring
reconcilement; it would be to investigate and expose all my
lies, evasions, and deceptions, and so leave me helpless in
her power.

Sammy spoke. 'Mum's been under a strain this past
week.'

'I understand.'

'If you explained I'm sure your wife would come. I mean,
she's used to doing good deeds, isn't she?'

That sounded ironical, but it was hardly likely that a

provincial lawyer had heard of Betty's infidelities with noblemen.

As I put the telephone down I realised the danger I was in, especially now that I had been shut out of Ravenscraig. All my married life I had been careful never to let Betty inveigle or bully me into taking her to my native town. If she were to descend upon it now I would be caught like a rat in a corner. All my pretensions would have their backs broken, their heads snapped off.

Thank Christ there was no likelihood of her coming. Dorcas would not allow it. Dorcas had an instinctive fear of Gantock. Though she had never heard of people like Jessie McFadyen and Smout McTavish she had smelled them off me. I had seen and heard that horrified sniffing. To Dorcas Gantock was not merely a sleeping dog to be let lie, it was a dead dog with many maggots: it was the maggots that had to be let lie.

Just in case, however, I decided to leave Gantock next morning by the first train, even if it meant not seeing John Lamont or keeping my promise to Smout's ghost.

I was at dinner in the sepulchral dining-room when there appeared in the doorway, wearing a long fur coat and looking red-cheeked and vigorous as if she had just come across snowy wastes on a sledge pulled by horses, my redoubtable wife. In my imagination I heard wolves baying.

I was not surprised to learn that she had wielded the whip herself, in other words that she had left Buchanan at Pennvalla and driven herself.

She had also left Dorcas and Torquil at home.

'They didn't want to come.'

What she meant was they had preferred not to be in at the kill.

FIVE

We did not share the same room that night. We met at breakfast, at half-past eight. This was her arrangement. I came prepared to discuss terms of surrender, she to receive my unconditional capitulation. Therefore over the porridge and kippers it was I who did most of the talking. I noticed she ate well. It was a bad sign.

Piteously, I told her I was going to visit poor John

Lamont in hospital that morning, and begged her to come with me. Not only he, but all the other patients, would be comforted and cheered up by a visit from the well-loved Betty T. Shields.

Her response was to order more toast.

I mentioned how eager Bessie was for her to go to the Auld Kirk. All the people in Gantock who mattered would be there. She would have the profoundest satisfaction of demonstrating that her prestige and popularity far outshone mine even among my own people.

Inwardly I was convulsed with rage, fear, and frustration. If only my poetry had received the praise it deserved; if only the Earl of Darndaff had publicly recognised me as a member of his family. As a famous poet or an acknowledged aristocrat, or better still as both, I could have challenged her to go anywhere in Gantock with me, yes even to Puddock Loch or Lomond Street itself.

I was not nearly famous enough. Therefore I was not panoplied against insult and shame.

We had just finished eating when I was summoned to the telephone.

'It'll be Bessie Lamont,' I said.

'So?'

'She'll want to know if you're coming to church with us.'

'I am not.'

'She's sure to invite us to lunch.'

'I intend to lunch at Pennvalla.'

'That's not fair, Betty.'

'Fair?'

What an enormous amount of sarcasm and disgust she put into that whispered little word.

'I shall be ready in ten minutes,' she said. 'I want you to be ready too.'

'Where are we going?'

'You will find out.'

Now was my last chance to resist.

Instead I bowed my head and crawled away.

It was Bessie on the telephone.

'Hello, Fergus. So she did come!'

'How did you know?'

'I asked Mr Kirkwood, the manager. How wonderful! Did you invite her to come to church with us?'

'I'm afraid, Bessie, she isn't staying. She has to hurry back to Pennvalla.'

'Oh.'

'Dorcas, our daughter, isn't very well.'

'I'm sorry to hear that. Nothing serious, I hope?'

I nearly whispered: 'She hates me: that's all that's the matter with her.' What I did say was: 'A touch of flu, Betty thinks.'

'What a shame! But couldn't you and she call in at Cowal View for a few minutes? It would be an awful pity, Fergus, if we didn't meet your wife, after all these years.'

'I'll mention it.'

'If she had been anybody but a wonderful woman like Betty T. Shields I'd have been inclined to think it was just a way of putting us off.'

She laughed, nervously. 'You must have some influence, Fergus. After all, she *is* your wife.'

Again I was silent.

'Did she come in her own car?'

'Yes.'

'I expect you'll be going back with her?'

'Yes.'

'Well, we'll be waiting in hope,' she said.

Betty too was waiting, in the entrance-hall, with so relentless a face that I decided not to mention Bessie's invitation to call in at Cowal View.

I picked up my balmoral from the hallstand and followed her down the steps into her car.

She did not immediately drive off.

'You know, Betty,' I said, 'you have a reputation to keep up. Like thousands of other women Bessie Lamont believes you are the soul of goodness, kindness, and wisdom. To disillusion just one admirer could be dangerous. It might spread.'

She started the engine and drove off.

'Where are we going?' I asked.

'You'll find out.'

SIX

Luckily it was a cold, bright, sunny morning. Washed by recent rains, Gantock was looking at its best. There was still the feeblest chance I might yet survive.

Driving through these wide avenues with the limes and
sycamores, past the well-kept villas, she was bound to be
impressed by the town's substantiality and dignity. The
shipyards themselves, from a distance, would be impressive
too, with their gantries, cranes, and half-built ships. In this
charitable sunshine the tenements of the East End would
seem much less dreary and degraded than in dull weather
or pouring rain, especially as this Sabbath morning few
people would be about and all the closemouths would be
deserted.

She drove as if she knew where she was going.

Soon, out of the West End, we were bumping along
the cobbled Main Street, past closed shops and empty
pavements. The one tramcar we passed had few people in
it; probably they were Catholics on their way to early Mass.
Since they had only one church they had to worship in
shifts. That thought made me realise how many Protestant
churches Gantock had, twenty at least. In an hour or two
all their bells would be ringing. As children once, gathering
mushrooms in the fields above the town, we had listened
to those bells, and looking at one another had wondered
if, when we went back down, we would find Jesus and
His disciples in the streets, performing miracles. Now,
as we arrived in Auchmountain Square, the heart of the
town, I found myself, childish again, being amazed that
the piety issuing from all those churches, over many years,
had not so impregnated the air that malevolence, such as
Betty's towards me, was not immediately converted into
goodwill.

In the Square late roses bloomed. Outcasts sat on
benches, looking as if they had been there all night.
Not welcome at home, they probably crept out early
every morning, sunshine or rain, to where the pigeons,
gulls, sparrows, and stray cats did not make them feel
that they were holding on to life too long.

The grey stone of the Auld Kirk had recently been
cleaned. With its six thick pillars, its spacious steps, and its
square tower with the four golden-handed clocks, all telling
the same time, it seemed to be putting forth a massive
effort, on behalf of the whole town, to make substantiality,
dignity, and permanence, amount to holiness.

I could not hide my pride.

'The Auld Kirk of Gantock,' I said. 'There was a church on this site before the battle of Bannockburn.'

She stopped the car at the kirk steps.

'Is it your intention to return to Pennvalla?' she asked.

'Where else? It's my home. It's where my children live.'

'Your children do not want you.'

'That's a very cruel thing to say.'

'What is more, you do not really want your children.'

'That's crueller still.'

Two old men had got up from their bench to come over and inspect the big purple car. They paid no heed to its occupants.

'Look, Wullie,' said one, 'it's the colour o' the feathers on that pouter's neck.'

'I had a muffler once that very colour,' said the other. 'Mollie knitted it.'

'You don't seem to realise, though to everyone else it has been obvious, that for years you have been a parasite.'

'Proving me a true aristocrat, wouldn't you say?'

'Whit wad you say a caur like that cost, Wullie?'

'This nauseating pretence of being an aristocrat! You have the manners of a navvy. Ask Grizel Mutt-Simpson.'

'A thousand quid at least, Erchie.'

'That anointer of stallions' genitals!'

'Exactly what I mean. No person of breeding would utter such obscenities.'

'Mair than that, Wullie. The only time you and me will travel in a caur like that will be on the way to the boneyard.'

'A man of pride would not stay where he wasn't wanted.'

'Why am I not wanted?'

'Because you yourself want no one. I don't think you ever have. Go to Australia, where it will not matter to the kangaroos that you are so flagrant a fraud.'

This was the tar-boiler calling the pot black.

Wullie rapped on the window at Betty's side. She nodded graciously.

'Yes, Fergus, a fraud. What does the old fool want?' Wullie was rapping again. She rolled down the window. 'Is there anything wrong?' she asked, sweetly.

'It's juist that a big dug's juist lifted his leg against your shiny back wheel.'

'Oh, thank you so much for telling me.' She rolled up the window again. 'Filthy old brute. Your sort, Fergus, vulgar to the core.'

She went on: 'Campbell Aird used to say a poet with no interest in literature or in people must be a fraud.'

'He admired my poetry.'

'He thought you must have produced it fraudulently. Otherwise, he used to ask, how could you, without a spark of sympathy for anyone and with no sense of humour to speak of, have written sympathetic and humorous poems? And I've spoken to officers who served beside you in the War. They said your men hated you, you never showed pity, your only concern was to build up a reputation for efficiency. So your poems about the War were fraudulent too.'

Wullie and Erchie, weak with laughter, returned to their bench, hand-in-hand. If I went and sat beside them, and chatted about Gantock, would *they* pronounce me a fraud? It was very likely. But they had a right.

'And of course the Corses have always thought you a fraud.'

I knew well enough why she and Dorcas wished to get rid of me. By themselves they would be invited to houses where I would never be welcome: it could well be Corse Castle itself was one. Dorcas would bloom in society if I with my dubious origins was not there to cast a blight. At first it would be enough for them to let it be known that I had gone to Australia, or to Oronsay, which was just as far away. Soon, since few would enquire, they would not have to mention me at all. Within a year I would be forgotten.

'Let me show you proof,' she said.

SEVEN

Even if I had been blindfolded I would have known that she was making for Lomond Street. Into her voice had come a note of pity, without which cruelty cannot be complete.

She and I both knew, like her old paramour Sir Jock Dunsyre, that every human being practised fraudulence at one time or another, from the baby in its cot pretending pain so that it would be lifted and made a fuss of, to the white-haired statesman knowing in his heart that the fine words applauded by his countrymen were mostly lies. Every

man excused himself with the plea that he would be honest
and truthful always, if only he could depend on all other
men to be honest and truthful too, otherwise he would be
shamefully taken advantage of.

Was I not being persecuted by one who had made a reputation and a fortune by the most fraudulent or hypocritical
of performances?

Why though was she so confident that by driving along
Lomond Street she would bring me to heel, whimpering?
Even if the place had gone down the brae, as Bessie had
said, and all the respectable and semi-respectable families
had left, it would still be short of squalid or bestial. In the
sunshine and Sabbath quiet it might even have a quality
of grimness, of the same kind that Corse Castle had, and
therefore be suitable enough, in an ironical way, as the
birth-place of a poet who was also a mislaid aristocrat.

The trouble was—I was driven back to this time and
again—I was not famous or rich or successful or dead
enough.

If the world decided to shower fame on a man it liked
nothing better than to pretend that his origins were much
lowlier than in fact they were. The higher it raised him the
more generous it appeared itself.

Because I was not sufficiently famous, any scabby-faced
child seen in my native street would be simply a scabby-
faced child, with no mystical significance whatever.

What Betty was seeking to do was, in the Biblical phrase,
uncover my nakedness. Afterwards, she hoped, I would
be so shame-stricken that I would agree to anything she
suggested.

The car was so big, the streets so narrow, and the corners
so tight, that she had frequently to slow down almost to
walking pace. She looked apprehensive lest I should take
advantage of one of these opportunities to leap out, and
surprised that I did not. It never occurred to her that
these streets through which we were now passing might
be remembered by me with love. In all of them, often with
Smout to help, I had pushed my barrow, gathering dung.

Bessie was right, though. In the past twenty years the
district had greatly deteriorated. The defenders of respectability had retreated from it to other areas of the town that

still held out. The Goths and Vandals from the Vennel and other slums had come in and taken over, bringing with them their tribal habits. They would not bother to go down the stairs with their rubbish, they would simply throw it out of the window: the conscientious among them would wait till dark. If the lavatory on the stairs was occupied, as it would be much of the time, or if there was frost in the air, they would not stoically wait or suffer, they would use the jaw-box (as I had done myself more than once, to be fair) or improvised chamber-pots.

Any boy living here now who wore a kilt would need ten times the courage and resolution I had had to show.

By this time the car had been spotted, for there were more people about than I had expected. The puzzled but respectful glances it at first attracted, because in those parts opulence in motor-cars was associated with death, quickly changed to scowls when its occupants were seen to be members of an alien clan.

We passed a gang of boys. As jealous of their territory as baboons, they immediately yelled insults and snatched up off the street whatever messy or injurious missile they could find—the variety was remarkable—and pelted us. Naturally Betty, who saw nothing of anthropological interest in their behaviour, and felt no painful stirrings of kinship, accelerated, as much as she dared. Provoked, the baboons bounded after us, yelling and throwing. More joined them, leaping out of closemouths. When we turned into Lomond Street and stopped outside No 437 there must have been at least a dozen in pursuit.

Standing at the closemouth were two women, one of whom I thought I recognised. Gap-toothed, hair in paper curlers, with a squint in her eye, and hugely pregnant, she had on her thin face an expression of bewilderment so intense and extravagant that it looked more the effect of a physical disease than of intellectual confusion. She must surely be Elsie Tweedie, still seeing the same visions of chaos and damnation. 'Elsie,' her mother used to shout, 'stop looking as if you'd seen the deil wi' his tail in his mooth.' She had been sweet on Archie Paterson, one of my mates in Limpy's famous class. In spite of his bad eye, he had not been quite so enamoured of her. I wondered if they had got married.

The other woman looked like one of the invaders from the Vennel. With black hair, flat nose, big teeth, and long powerful arms, she snarled at us like a she-gorilla guarding her tree.

'Excuse us, please,' said Betty, preparing to enter the close.

The she-gorilla barred the way. 'Hey, juist a meenute,' she growled. 'Wha the hell are you? Whit d'you want?'

'It's a' right, Annie,' whispered Elsie. 'Maybe they're looking for somebody.'

'I ken fucking fine whit they're looking for. Slums. That's whit they're looking for. Slums.'

Meanwhile the boys, joined now by a few girls, fiercer creatures, were gathered round the car, kicking its wheels, jumping up and down, showing their teeth, and uttering baboon-like cries of menace. I thought I recognised in one a resemblance to a family I had known. This tall boy with the florid face and white eyelashes looked like a mad Murchison.

Betty tried sweetness. 'We wish to visit Mr and Mrs Orr,' she said.

So she had done some preliminary investigation. These Orrs, whoever they were, wherever they had come from, must occupy the room-and-kitchen where I had been born.

'They're no' whit you wad ca' early risers,' giggled Elsie, 'especially on Sundays. No' that Eddie has ony work to go to ony day. Are they expectin' you?'

'No. But they will be pleased to see us, I think.'

'Don't be sae fuckin' shair,' muttered Annie.

'Eddie Orr,' explained Elsie, 'is a man no' likely to welcome unexpected visitors, except of course if they were bringing him money. Forby, wee Isa's in the family way, like me, and then she's got wee Gary wha's cross, I believe, wi' sair ears. Whit I'm trying to tell you is, the hoose will no' be whit you'd ca' tidy.'

'I have something here that will sweeten Mr Orr's temper,' said Betty, opening her gloved hand and revealing a five-pound note.

'Jesus Christ,' said Annie, subdued.

Betty smiled at her. 'If you would be so kind, Mrs—?'

'Blackburn, Annie Blackburn.'

'Thank you. If you would be so kind, Mrs Blackburn,

as to do us a small service I would be pleased to reward you for it.'

'Whit sma' service?'

'Help to ensure that our visit to the Orrs is reasonably private. I mean, by preventing these children from following us up the stairs and creating a nuisance.'

'Hoo much is this reward?'

'Two pounds.'

'You're on. For twa quid I'd bre'k their fucking legs.' And she thereupon demonstrated her prowess as a guardian of the closemouth by skelping across the face a boy who'd ventured too near, and by warning the others off with ferocious threats.

'Whit aboot me?' asked Elsie, wistfully. 'My name's Mrs Wishart, by the way.'

So Archie had escaped. I remembered Gavin Wishart, though he had been noted for nothing but nose-picking.

'I'm no' wanting money,' said Elsie. 'Don't think that. I'd juist like to oblige you. I could show you whaur the Orrs live. They've got nae nameplate, you see.'

'I think we know where they live,' said Betty. 'But thank you just the same.'

As nonchalantly as I could, I whispered: 'All right. No need for further bloodshed. I give in. You win. Let's go.'

'No, Fergus. We must go through with this to the end. You must be beaten to your knees. I don't trust you.'

She led the way into the close. I tamely followed. Behind us we heard Mrs Blackburn threatening to break legs. I wished she had broken mine.

'For two pounds,' giggled Elsie, coming with us, 'Annie really would. She's an awfu' woman.'

In my recollections the close had never stank quite so rankly of cats' piss. Nor had the walls been so fearfully defaced, not merely with chalk, but with knives, and, in some places, with hatchets apparently. In my day Mrs McNair who lived in the close, though unable to keep out smelly toms had kept out destructive boys. She had been proud of the cleanness of the close. 'I wouldnae say you could eat meat aff it, but your dug could, if I was to let your dug in, which I wouldnae. Your freen's, whaever they micht be, neednae be affronted passing through.'

We began the ascent to hell. Betty had her handkerchief

soaked in scent at her nose. Elsie kept
fur coat.

'I keep thinking,' she whispered to me, 'th
ken you? Should I ken you?'

We passed the first lavatory. Thank Christ the
was shut.

On the landing above it a door opened and a woman
looked out. Dirty grey hair covered her face. She was
yawning.

'It's you, Mrs Wishart,' she mumbled toothlessly. 'Whit
the hell are the weans making a row aboot?'

Then she saw Betty and me. Astonishment had the effect
of making her itchy. She clawed her head, and then hauled
up her dirty white nightgown to claw her leg. We caught a
glimpse of that pale flabby limb; on it varicose veins were
intertwined with whirls of paler dirt.

'Don't,' whispered Elsie, as we mounted, 'judge the rest
of us by the likes of her. Or by the Orrs, when you see
them. Are you sure it's the Orrs you want to see?'

'Yes, I'm sure,' said Betty.

We came then to the next lavatory, that indeed into
which I had trespassed at my mother's bidding, more than
thirty years ago. The door was open; in fact it was hanging
off, since one of its hinges was broken. Any sensitive
person—God pity any such who had to use it—would
be in danger of rectal rupture trying to hold the door in
place, while at the same time doing, in haste, what brutal
nature made necessary. The chain, I noticed, had been
replaced by a length of slimy-looking string, and the seat
looked permanently sodden.

'Some folk hae nae pride in whaur they live,' sighed
Elsie.

Still, I thought, the beautiful and romantic Mary, Queen
of Scots, at Holyrood Palace must have had a chamber of
easement not much less primitive than this.

'You'd hardly believe,' whispered Elsie, 'that this building used to be one o' the maist respectable in the district. I
live up the close next to this one, but it's juist as bad. A' the
folk wi' pride hae left. Me and my Gavin hae had oor names
doon for a cooncil house for years, but the list's as lang as
your airm. I don't want to bring up a wean in a dump like
this, but if you're poor and oot o' work and fond o' each

ose. Weel, this is whaur

amonts lived. Some of the
been when, on cold wet
to this door, blue-knee'd,
a poke of bonbons in my
en with me, or Jim Blanie.
vas, encouraged me to bring
e there to open the door for
vork: even the tap in the jaw-
er had been any hot water—
big coal fire in the grate. We

stroking Betty's
t I should
door
221

would ⎯⎯⎯⎯⎯⎯⎯ n the hearth rug, reading our
comics, chewing our ⎯⎯⎯ and drinking Irn Bru. It had
been heaven.

In Elsie good manners were now struggling with curiosity.
She had brought us to our destination, her duty was done,
she should now withdraw and leave us to knock on the
door ourselves—Betty had already done so, firmly— and
conduct our business, whatever in God's name it could be.
This was the tale her face pathetically and grotesquely
told.

'They'll no' be up,' she whispered, after Betty had got
no response to her imperious rapping. 'Wee Gary's seldom
weel, as I telt you. If he's sleeping, they'll no' want to
wauken him. And like me, as I telt you, Isa's expecting.
She's no' weel either. Orr, I'm sorry to say, is no' very nice
to her.'

I had already deciphered the name in Gothic letters on
the brass plate on the door adjacent, where in my day the
Strathglasses had lived. It was McCreadie. I could not make
up my mind whether or not I wanted voluptuous Jessie to
come out.

'Chap louder,' advised Elsie, and showed us how.

The door opened an inch, just enough to let out a whiff of
stink. A timid, hoarse, defeated, female voice that sounded
as if it belonged to a woman of seventy asked us what we
wanted.

This was Mrs Orr. She showed her face. She was no
more than twenty, yet the impression of exhausted senility remained. There was a purple bruise under her left
eye.

Amazement overcame fear and listlessness. Making an effort she again asked us what we wanted.

'This is a five-pound note,' said Betty. 'It is yours if you allow us into your house for two minutes. That's all, just two minutes.'

It seemed a flicker of pride was still left in the young housewife.

'But whit for?' she asked. 'Whit d'you want to see my hoose for? There's naething to see.'

'My God, Isa,' whispered Elsie, 'even if it is a bit untidy, and wha's hoose isnae on a Sunday morning? surely it's worth it for five pounds?'

'But whit's it for? Whit's she want? Orr's in bed.'

From within came a surly male voice. 'Will you get that fucking door shut? There's a fucking draught.'

'That's Orr,' said Mrs Orr. 'I'll hae to ask him first. Juist a meenute.' She shut the door.

'Eddie Orr thinks he's a bit of a joker,' said Elsie, in warning. 'But he's terribly short-tempered to be sich a young man. He hasnae worked for years. He'll no' turn doon the chance of five pounds wi' nae work attached. You'll see.'

We saw. In a minute Mrs Orr was back. This time she had her head covered with a shawl, with which she tried to hide the side of her face that was marked.

'He says you've to show him the money first.'

Elsie was dubious. 'He's liable to tak it and then slam the door on you.'

Betty handed over the bank note.

After another brief wait Mrs Orr came back. 'A' right. But juist twa meenutes. He says if you exceed the time it'll cost you anither five pounds. No' you, Mrs Wishart. Juist them.'

Handkerchief at nose, Betty strode in. I followed. Mrs Orr closed the door behind us, leaving poor Elsie stranded on the landing.

In the kitchen, which was also the living-room, on the hearth, in front of the rusty cold range, an infant of about three, sat sound asleep, hands over ears, on a chamber-pot the enamel of which showed several black bruises as if it had once been used as a helmet. There were other stenches, but the worst came from the unfortunate child. The second

worst came from the set-in bed, the very one where I had
pretended to be asleep with Mrs Grier bending whiskily
over me, and where, it suddenly occurred to me, I had
been born. In it now, under a jumble of tattered and
unclean blankets, lay the man of the house, Orr himself,
smoking a cigarette. The five-pound note, folded up, was
tucked behind his ear. Though he certainly looked brutal,
especially when unshaven, unwashed, and unbreakfasted,
he had also about him a touch of coarse humour. When he
saw what a grand-looking woman Betty was, and when he
smelled her expensive French perfume, he did not cringe or
hide his face. What he did was, under the bedclothes, take
hold of his penis. It was his way of showing that, whatever
the situation was, he was in control of it.

With the instinct that all women from queens to bus
conductresses have in such matters Betty and Mrs Orr
were well aware of what he was doing. Betty's disgust was
hidden behind her handkerchief, but Mrs Orr smiled. Isn't
my Eddie an awful devil? her smile seemed to say.

'Whit's this aboot then?' asked Orr. 'Are you writin' a
book or something? Are you on whit's ca'd a sociological
survey?'

If I had needed to be convinced that the maintenance of
civilised standards among the respectable poor depended
on an effort of will more enduring and courageous than
that shown by any army of soldiers, comparison between
that living-room under poor Mrs Orr's jurisdiction and the
same room under, first, my mother's, then John Lamont's
and for a short time, Bessie's, would have been enough.

'Your twa meenutes are up,' said Orr. 'You're on the
dear rate noo.'

Betty decided to be Betty T. Shields, majestic and compassionate.

'We have seen quite enough, thank you,' she said. 'I
must apologise once again, Mrs Orr, for this inconvenient
and indeed unpardonable intrusion. As a housewife myself,
I know how awkward it can be for people to burst in
unexpectedly. If I may be allowed to offer a little advice, my
dear, I would suggest that your little darling requires now
to be lifted and cleaned. As a mother myself I found grey
powders very useful in the treatment of infant diarrhoea:
any chemist will advise you as to the required strength. But,

of course, I do not have to tell you that strict cleanliness is the best preventative.'

Mrs Orr was charmed and saw us to the door with dignity. Such was the miraculous effect of Betty T. Shields on women.

'Come again,' shouted Orr.

Outside on the landing, who should be waiting for us, but Jessie McFadyen, or rather Jessie McCreadie.

If Meg Jeffries, with her raven hair and red cheeks, had been the bonniest woman I had ever seen, fair-haired Jessie, with this magnificently mature bosom and these ample houghs, wrapt in a red dressing-gown, was the most sexually tempting, outdoing even Betty herself before she'd gone to fat.

I had no doubt that next door, Orr, probably now on top of his wife, would have preferred Jessie's riper favours. Bessie had said she pleased herself nowadays. Certainly she gave the impression that she might well still stir up lust, but would not as in her old tender days quite so readily appease it. She would have ambitions above an Eddie Orr.

She recognised me at once.

'If it's no' big Kilty Lamont,' she cried, and held out a hand that was needed to help her other hand to keep her dressing-gown closed. This opened, and gave a glimpse of hair as flaxen as that on her head.

I gave her a bow for Smout's sake, and then raced downstairs.

'Whit a shameless creature,' gasped Elsie, in envy.

I thought of what poor Smout had missed.

Then we were at the closemouth again.

Mrs Blackburn was still keeping them out. She was evidently a woman of her word, who gave service for money. Though the pavement was thronged by some of the most malapert children in Christendom none dared to try and push her aside.

Since her contract had been to keep people from following us up the close, she had made no attempt to protect the motor car. Perched on this were half a dozen boys, while others were engaged in scratching their initials on the paintwork with various sharp objects.

There were some women in the crowd and one or two men. No doubt some of these were parents or aunts or uncles of the young vandals. Perhaps they had voiced a word or two of protest or reproof, not really expecting or indeed wanting to be heeded. Without ever having heard of educational psychology they were inclined to believe that their children ought to be allowed to express themselves in any way they pleased, always providing that any property or persons damaged in the experimentation belonged to someone else.

Betty's calm was admirable when she saw what they were doing to her car. Inwardly no doubt she was calling them a shower of young cunts. Outwardly she smiled and waved her hand in blessing, as if the contentment of boys and girls with baboon habits was more important to her than any thousand-pound car.

The crowd, to begin with, was more interested in me. There were shouts of 'Kilty Lamont!' I was asked if I had come back to see the house I was born in. In the three or four minutes it took to pay Mrs Blackburn, push aside many cadging hands, dislodge the boys, climb in, and drive away, I recognised two of the women. One was Mrs Blanie, Jim's mother, no longer so boozily red in the face or so massive in the arms. She stared at me with a mixture of surprise, resentment, and wonder. She had never expected to see me again, so she was surprised. I was still alive and her Jim was dead, so she was resentful. I had once eaten her pancakes, so she was filled with wonder that I had risen so high in the world as to own, for so she would think, so beautiful a car.

Driving away, we heard a woman yell: 'If that was Lamont then the woman must have been Betty T. Shields, for didn't he mairry her?'

'Betty T. Shields!'

They had all heard of her. She was better known than the Prime Minister.

All the church bells began to ring. Within a minute the town was reverberating with the ding-dong-dell. I remembered how Smout had told me that when the bells were ringing he used to lie on the ground and press his ear against it. God knew what visions he had seen.

People in Sunday dress were walking towards the churches. Others rode in cars. They all looked pleased with themselves. They had God mastered.

If we had been at Pennvalla we would ourselves have strolled to church, across our own grounds, and entered the kirkyard by our own private gate. We would have sat in our own private enclosure.

We stopped outside the hotel. We had said nothing to each other since leaving Lomond Street.

Betty took an envelope out of her handbag. 'Five hundred pounds,' she said.

I took it and made sure it did contain a cheque, properly made out, for that amount. 'Thank you,' I said.

'Where is it to be then? Australia?'

'Oronsay.'

'I would prefer Australia.'

'Oronsay.'

'Very well. I'll send on your things.'

'Don't bother.'

'As you wish. No correspondence, remember. No contact of any kind.'

'That suits me.'

'For at least three years. Goodbye, Fergus.'

'Goodbye, Betty.'

We did not kiss or shake hands. I got out. She drove away.

I was never to see her again.

For weeks now I have not been feeling well. Mrs McRorie, the widow who lives next door, has been more importunate than ever in pressing on me her home-made broth, mealy puddings, and septagenarian favours. She waylays me on the landing and stairs, and drops hints how her husband, Alfred, died years before his time because he had given up much too soon the invigorating exercise of love-making. As considerately as I can, for in spite of her dried up whiskery face she is a ladylike old woman who goes to church and reads the Sunday Post, I point out that it has been the consensus of sages throughout the ages that sexual abstinence is more likely to prolong life than to shorten it. I take care not to let dab that if I did have any carnal desires they would be for the cheerful plump-buttocked young woman upstairs.

Nevertheless it is true that I do feel ill. I have had to give thought to what is to be done after my death.

Let me say as clearly and humbly as I can that, though

I long daily to be reunited with Kirstie, I do not believe in personal immortality and have no hope of ever seeing her again. To resuscitate a body to the last hair and haemorrhoid after it had mouldered into dust is, surely, beyond the powers of God Himself. As for reviving us as souls only, which of us would recognise or like the look of his or her disembodied soul if it came floating past? I consider myself a wonderful and unique piece of creation, but believe nevertheless that for the Creator to perpetuate me, even in an improved form, for all eternity, would be an abuse of His powers. He has, I hope, better things to do.

We linger for a while in the memories of those who knew us: perhaps those who disliked us or were jealous of us remember us longest. If we wish to encourage this remembrance we shall ask to be buried in some convenient graveyard that can be kept tidy and visited after tea on dry Sundays. If we wish to discourage it we will have our ashes scattered any old where, like a tinker's tealeaves.

Whenever I feel hopeful of humanity I want to be buried in the kirkyard at East Gerinish, beside Kirstie, because in that case anyone wishing to visit my grave would have to make the journey across the Minch to a place that I loved. I should be bestowing on him a gift more precious than rubies. But when I am pessimistic and feel sure that the human race will destroy itself if not in the next ten years then certainly in the next hundred, I decide to be cremated here in Glasgow and have my ashes dumped into the nearest dustbin.

Yesterday afternoon I called in to see Mr McSpeug, the undertaker in the district where I live.

My mood was optimistic. At the public library in the morning I had watched two very old frail men, one half-blind and the other half-deaf, minister to each other lovingly. Between them, after five minutes' hard effort, they gleaned from the newspaper what the rest of the world already knew: that the President of the United States had been shot the day before. Though the news had disturbed them they had remained far more anxious about each other than about the famous man lying dead in Washington. They had sat at a table and attended to each other like monkeys. I mean great respect by that comparison, for to pick lice off a comrade and eat them seems to me as useful and intimate a service as one creature can do for another, and I once saw monkeys do it at Edinburgh Zoo, with delicacy and love.

The effect on me of watching David and Jonathan in old age with cloth caps and Glasgow accents was that I felt a surge of confidence in the decency of my fellow men, and wanted as many of them as possible to visit East Gerinish, where their generous feelings would be refreshed.

I chose Mr Hector McSpeug for three reasons: his premises are within easy reach, in his advertisements he states 'Distance no object', and his name interested me.

I had never heard the name McSpeug before. His was the only one in the Glasgow Telephone Directory. Of what clan the McSpeugs were a sept I could not discover. If it hadn't also stated in his advertisements that the firm had been established in 1881, I would have suspected that the family had come from Poland or Lithuania during the War, with some unpronounceable name that they had had to render into a Scottish form.

Speug of course is Scottish slang for a sparrow. I pictured him therefore as a small, alert snapper-up of business, in smart but drab clothes. To my surprise I found him, that dull November afternoon, more like a turkey-cock, with red face, tufts of black hair, a dapper grey suit with a flower in the button-hole, and a fragrance of the wildwood.

A jolly-looking girl in the outer office, in order to prevent my seeing her employer in so unfuneral a condition, was cheerfully telling me that he had gone to supervise the arrangements at a wedding reception, that being a function he combined with undertaking, when he appeared from within, smoking a cigar and beaming like Bacchus.

'No, Maggie, no,' he cried. 'Do not turn the gentleman away. All deference, girl, all deference to a man in the garb of old Caledonia.'

'I just thought, Mr McSpeug—.' She could not help laughing and giving him a look that showed how proud she was of his joie-de-vivre, reckless and inappropriate though she knew it to be for a man in his profession.

On my way into his office I caught a glimpse of stores of coffins in the dim interior of the premises. Shutting my eyes, I could have imagined I was in a forest of pines, after rain. Pinewood, I knew, made the cheapest coffins. Our district was poor and hard-headed: it saw no sense in squandering on expensive wood money that could be more joyfully spent on providing drams for the mourners.

'*Well, Mr McTavish, what can I do for you? You do not mind if I smoke, do you?*'

I was not sure yet whether or not I approved of so happy an undertaker.

'*I wish to arrange a funeral.*'

'*Ah yes. Your dear spouse has departed?*' *He said it with a chuckle.*

Was it the wine, I wondered, or had he, in his experience of bereaved husbands, learned that they preferred their loss to be talked about with a little manly jocularity, not out of callousness—well, not out of callousness in most cases—and not out of any inspirational understanding that death to some extent was comic, few men being capable of such an inspiration, but perhaps out of a cagey admission that since the burial was to be Christian, with everybody believing or pretending to believe that the dead woman had gone to a happier land where there was no cancer of the womb, no deaths of children, no drudgery of housework, and no dominance of males, then unmitigated solemnity might well seem, in the Lord's eyes, ungrateful?

'*The burial I wish to discuss is my own,*' *I said.*

Not a bit nonplussed, he cried: '*Do you know, Mr McTavish, what I said the other day to my dear wife? "Rachel," I said, "show me a man who is not concerned about his remains and I will show you a man who has lost interest in living."*'

'*Your advertisements say: "Distance no object".*'

'*Do you wish to be buried on top of Everest? It would be the most expensive interment since that of the late King Solomon, but, if the funds were available, it would be done.*'

'*The place is called East Gerinish. It is in the Outer Hebrides, on the island of Oronsay.*'

He took a map of Scotland out of a drawer. '*You are a native of East Gerinish? And your dear wife is already buried there?*'

'*My wife need not be mentioned.*'

'*As you please, sir. East Gerinish? I don't see it.*'

'*It is too small to be shown on a map of that scale. It is in any case a derelict township. No one lives there now.*'

'*Ah, it is the ancestral burial-ground of the McTavishes! Is that it? Let's see now. By road or rail to Oban: beautiful journey. Across the sea to Lochmaddy: wonderful voyage. By road to our sad destination.*'

'*Except that at one place there is no road, only a track across*

*the sands, passable only at low tide and then only if there is no
sea-mist or the imminency of such.'*

'Mr McTavish, if I am still to the fore when the time
comes I shall myself ferry you to your beautiful and remote
last resting-place.'

'There is also no road into East Gerinish itself. There used
to be a cart track, but it will be overgrown now.'

'There would have to be portage then. A common enough
practice in the Highlands of not so long ago. Sometimes distances
of ten miles and more were involved. There were, I believe,
recognised stopping-places where the carriers were changed and
drams consumed. How far in this case?'

'About two miles.'

'Since East Gerinish is now derelict, do we recruit porters
from places round about, or do we take our own?'

'I think I would prefer you to take your own.'

'Is there a graveyard, a plot of hallowed ground?'

'Yes.'

'Administered by the local authorities?'

'Administered by the wind, rain, and curlews.'

'In other words, abandoned. Do you own a lair? Or does
one, as it were, help oneself?'

'There is a particular grave where I would want to be
buried.'

'That of your parents no doubt? I do not ask out of impertinence, Mr McTavish. Immense difficulties can arise out of
placing remains in graves to which their right is not secure. By
the way sir, I have a bottle here, of Chivas Regal, and two
glasses. Would you care to join me?'

I said I would.

We sipped the good whisky.

'This, Mr McSpeug, is the grave of a woman I loved
long ago.'

'But not your wife? My dear sir, Everest might not be in it
for difficulty if that dear deceased lady has surviving relatives,
who might object to your being buried beside her.'

'She has no surviving relatives.'

'Still, there might have to be a search, just to make sure. We
would not want to find a sheriff's officer waiting for us with
a writ, would we? Besides, what of your own relatives?'

'They would not be consulted. They would not even be
informed.'

'Hm, hm, hm. There again we could find ourselves in murky legal waters.'

'I would leave you written authority.'

'That would help no doubt, but a determined wife, or a stubborn daughter—I have had troublesome experiences with determined wives and stubborn daughters, I assure you—could make obstacles.'

'It would be all over before any of them knew.'

'All over for you, lucky fellow! You would be well out of it. I, on the other hand, might find myself obliged to dig you up again and rebury you in another place, at my own expense. What of mourners? Friends?'

'There would be none.'

'There again I must warn you, Mr McTavish. As a living man you have a right to demand complete privacy at your burial, but as a dead one you would find that right open to dispute. Determined wives, my dear fellow! Stubborn daughters! You would of course leave instructions as to what form of service was required.'

'There would be no religious service. A poem might be read, a pipe tune played.'

'May I ask which poem and which pipe tune? I am very fond of pipe music myself.'

'A poem written by myself. The tune is one called "Leaving East Gerinish". It is not very well known.'

'Could you hum me a snatch? I may know it.'

I hummed a little of that beautiful, haunting, brave melody. I remembered Kirstie singing Gaelic words to it. I shed tears.

'More whisky, Mr McTavish. To East Gerinish.'

We drank the toast.

'My name is not really McTavish,' I said. 'It would be revealed at the time.'

'At the time would do well enough.'

'It is possible I may change my mind and decide simply to be cremated here in Glasgow.'

'I hope not. Tell me, would it not be a good idea if all the bearers wore kilts?'

I had not thought of that. 'I would prefer it, yes.'

'It would be done. We must discuss this again, Mr McTavish. You are going to be with us for some time yet, I sincerely hope, but, you know, I haven't ever seen that lonely graveyard at East Gerinish, but I can imagine it'— he hummed the tune—

'*I can imagine the whole scene, the kilted carriers, the piper, the curlews, perhaps a little rain and a little mist. After so many humdrum interments in the city yours, Mr McTavish, is something to look forward to.*'

We were on our third glass and humming the tune confidently together when Maggie knocked on the door and came in to say it was five o'clock and she was going home.

Part Five

ONE

When I wrote that I was not worthy to return to Gantock
I had of course meant morally worthy. Too much of the
grease and soot of selfishness obfuscated my soul. I needed
scouring, like a pan that a conscientious housewife is only
satisfied with when she can see her smiling face in it. In
me too few people saw themselves smiling.

Too harsh a scouring though might, with souls as with
pans, not only mar the surface but also damage the sub-
stance. Therefore, I thought, in the beautiful Hebrides the
simplicities of life over a period of, say, a year—I did not
take Betty's sentence of three years seriously, I was too
confident of remission—would gradually, day by splendid
day, cleanse, sweeten, and purify me.

Thus I thought, and seeking no one's advice, set off forth-
with. Pledged now to humility, I travelled to Oban in a
third-class compartment which was not well heated. I
made considerable efforts to speak as an equal to my companions. Unfortunately, I could not quite so soon decide
what aspects of my upper-class Anglicised accent to shed
and with what egalitarian Scotch crudities to replace them.
Small wonder then that I found myself at times mumbling
morosely to those shivering boors.

At Oban, where the wind was howling in from the dark
sea, I was obliged, through the dereliction of porters, to
humph my own case from train to boat through a jumble
of fish-boxes. I learned what I ought to have known already:
that if one's arms feel as if they are being wrenched out
of their sockets, and one's fingers are cramped with pain,
it is not easy to entertain thoughts of goodwill towards
fish-boxes, far less towards one's fellowmen.

As I struggled up the gangway I overheard an anxious
passenger asking if the crossing was going to be rough.
'Rough enough', was the crewman's laconic and, as we

were all soon to learn, criminally understated answer.

Sharing the cabin with me, and occupying the upper bunk, was a commercial traveller in hotel supplies from Glasgow, the sort of fellow who would have been sent round to the tradesmen's entrance at Pennvalla. In the hell of groaning, whining, bumping, and banging noises, and of lurching, sliding, rising and falling movements, I had the best of opportunities to show consideration for a fellowman in distress, especially when he vomited over me. Alas, I did not take it. On the contrary, when he moaned that he was going to die, I shouted, 'The sooner the better, you careless bastard!'

Crossing the Minch in the dark in a storm on a rolling boat with a commercial traveller's vomit all over one's pyjamas is not an experience likely to increase anyone's store of loving-kindness.

Nor is disembarking at Lochmaddy pier at six o'clock on a cold, wet, windy December morning.

Particularly if like me you are on the verge of what is too glibly called a nervous breakdown.

For those first few minutes after arrival I thought that I must have died without noticing it—I had seen many men die like that—and had been ordered to this corner of hell where it was always raining, and the wind was always blowing, and instead of sunshine there were these feeble lamps, and the inhabitants were black and yellow seal-like creatures who spoke in unintelligible grunts and completely ignored me as if, not yet properly enrolled, I was still invisible to them. In the background all the time were plaintive bleatings.

The fresh air, in bucketfuls, soon revived me. Things became themselves. The pier was busy with the arrival of the steamer. People, wrapped in oilskins, had come to welcome friends and relatives and take them home. They were speaking in Gaelic because it was their native tongue. They paid me no heed for the good Hebridean reason that they did not know me; besides, since I was wearing a kilt, they assumed that I was some English toff come to stay with one of the lairds, and therefore all the more none of their business. The bleatings came from sheep waiting to be put on board. As for the rain and wind, these would surely abate, and the sun would come out.

I saw my commercial traveller climbing unsteadily into a car which then drove off into the darkness. I hadn't time to go over and apologise.

At the agent's office I was told a bus would be leaving at nine o'clock. It would drop me off at East Gerinish road-end. That was to say, if Big Ian didn't think it was too stormy to cross the big strand. Was I sure, though, it was East, and not West, Gerinish, I wanted to go to?

'I'm sure,' I said. 'Won't the weather clear up?'

'Not for the next twenty-four hours, they're saying. It can go on like this for days, you know, weeks even. You'll get breakfast at the hotel. The bus leaves from there anyway.'

'How far is it to the hotel?'

'Just a step, up the brae.'

It turned out to be at least two hundred yards, and the brae was steep, made more so by the buffets of wind. These kept hurling seagulls about the still dark sky.

I could not help thinking that it might have been wiser to have gone to sunny Australia.

Other passengers were having breakfast. One was the commercial traveller. He was wolfing into bacon, sausages, and eggs. I felt relieved, not for his sake but for my own. If a peddler of soap and napkins could recover his self-confidence so quickly, there was no reason why I couldn't.

My hands, though, kept shaking.

Only three times in my life had I felt so close to being demoralised. The first time was when I had been told that my mother was dead. I had had John Lamont and Uncle Tam to help me then. Indeed, one of the things I needed to purge my soul of was ingratitude towards those two good men.

The second time had been when Archie was killed, and the third time when I had seen Cathie Calderwood in the asylum.

Six other passengers were hoping to take the same bus as I. It stood outside, with dirty windows and bald tyres: hardly a fit vehicle in which to attempt a journey that, according to jocular remarks exchanged, was little short of heroic. No one, however, seemed to think that Big Ian would call it off.

I expected therefore a stalwart Viking, with fair hair and bronzed cheeks, whose brawny hands would handle

a steering-wheel as his ancestors' had tillers out on the
wild, unknown Atlantic. Instead, there arrived, shortly
before nine, a tall, thin, pale, hollow-cheeked man, whom
I would not have trusted to steer a girr along a sunny level
street far less an aged bus across miles of dangerous sands,
in a gale, through sheets of rain.

I soon learned that I had misjudged him. Not only was
he the only one to show no surprise when I told him I was
bound for East Gerinish, he smiled in a friendly way and
said that when I saw Kirstie I was to be sure and give her
his regards. He did not mention her second name.

I had met men like Big Ian before during the War.
They too had undertaken arduous and dangerous tasks, and
carried them out with unassuming competence. Achilles
and Hector could not have outdone them.

The difference between those small Glasgow toughs and
Big Ian was that they had blasphemed often, whereas he
was as grave as a priest.

Often he would stop his bus, in the midst of that drenched
gusty desolation, where by the side of the road a woman
would be waiting, with a coat over her head and Wellingtons
on her feet. He greeted her in quiet friendly Gaelic, like
a blessing. If her parcel was too heavy for her he would
carry it to her house, though this was no part of his duties
and probably her husband was sitting snug in front of the
peat fire.

Every time he climbed back into the driving-seat he was
like a father returning home, bringing with him confidence
and security, though most of the passengers, including
myself, were older than he.

When we left the hard road and took to the soft sand at
the big strand, the old man by my side, feeling me shudder
and thinking I was afraid, assured me, in a mixture of Gaelic
and English, that I had good reason to be.

Yess, yess, there were posts marking the way, but chust
the same you had to pe knowing where those posts were,
pecause pe damn they would not come and look for you if
you got lost. If you did get lost you would find yourself
heading out for the open sea, as if it was a poat you were
in, not a leaky pus, or you would get stuck in sand that
was too soft. If you got stuck you would pe well and
truly drowned when the tide came in. It did not come

creeping in like a cat either, but came roaring in like a pull.

Put there was no need for me to be frightened. Big Ian could cross blindfolded. It was true, chust the same, that the pus was old and a week or two pack had trouble with its gaskets or some such thing, and might take it into its head to stop, in the prute way that cattle and sheep and puses just stopped. If that happened, well, in his opinion it would be petter chust to sit and wait and be drowned like chentlemen.

The others in the bus listened with secretive smiles.

I did not blame them for not knowing that my shudders had nothing to do with fear of crossing the big strand. How could they have known that more terrifying tides than those of the Minch and the Atlantic were threatening me? Admissions of my own blameworthiness, and realisation of the loneliness I had let myself in for in this howling wilderness, were gathering, and soon would come roaring in upon me from all sides.

We got safely across.

The old man, with a wink at the others, told me that I'd better relax now. I'd need a good rest if it was really East Gerinish I was going to.

At the East Gerinish road-end, which had no distinguishing feature such as a gate, a sign-post, a fence-stob, or even a wheel mark, Big Ian set down my case in the inadequate shelter of a stone that, eczema'd with lichen, looked as if it belonged more under water than on land; as did all other stones in sight. Round it grass and heather raced like demented creatures. Wherever I looked, and it needed strength and determination to stand up and look anywhere, I could see only bleak sodden moorland, but not much of it because of swirling curtains of rain, that wasn't rain either but dispersed sea. My lips tasted salt. Balls of brownish spume kept flying past. The beast from whose back they had been torn was the fierce Atlantic. I heard it roaring. I also heard, in my mind, Betty and Dorcas laughing.

'It's none of my business,' said Big Ian, 'but maybe you'd be better in the Inn at Cullipool, that's three miles along the road, till it clears up anyway.'

I thanked him but said I was determined to go to East Gerinish.

'Well,' he murmured, staring into the rain, 'she should be along soon. She knows you're coming. In any case, she'll be for the bread.'

He meant a cardboard box which he had put off with my case. It had the name of a Glasgow baker on it.

Dry and comfortable, I would have found amusing this Gaelic way of muddling the sexes in English. No doubt the carter from East Gerinish was a hulking fellow with hands like shovels. Crouching behind the stone, I could manage only the feeblest of grins, as I watched the bus disappear along the road in a cloud of spray.

TWO

'Ciamar a tha sibh?'

The words, and particularly the voice in which they were spoken, roused me from my dwam of misery. Gruff, yet with an odd trace of sweetness, it was the voice of either a virile woman or an effeminate man. Looking up, I saw a bulky figure wearing a long black oilskin coat kept closed by a length of tarry rope round the waist, a potato sack over the shoulders, a yellow sou'wester tied round the chin with more tarry rope, and shaggy crotal-coloured trousers tucked into big Wellington boots. A man, I thought. The face, as much of it as could be seen, was a mixture of humour and melancholy, with blue eyes, longish nose, and wide mouth. Yes, a man. The cheeks, though, were smooth and tanned, and the lips red. A woman, then. But he or she was smoking a stubby pipe. So a man, surely.

'I was not thinking,' he said, speaking slowly in what was a language he did not use often, and tapping my suitcase with the toe of his rubber boot, 'that you would be having so big a case.'

I wondered if this was the East Gerinish idiot on the loose. I had read that, because of generations of inbreeding, tuberculosis and imbecility were rife in the townships. In Big Ian I had seen evidence of the one, here surely was evidence of the other.

'I am waiting,' I replied, 'for the carter from East Gerinish. My name is Fergus McGilvray. (This was the name I had decided to give myself.) My great-uncle, Angus McGilvray, had a croft in East Gerinish. I have come to live in it.'

My diagnosis was confirmed by the way his top-heavy head (he seemed to have a cloth-cap under his sou'wester) began to sway from side to side in an idiot's gesture of uncalled for silent mirth.

'I am the only carter there is in East Gerinish,' she said, for the balance had swung in favour of her being female. 'My name is Kirstie McDonald.'

So this was the Kirstie Big Ian had mentioned. It was not, though, a propitious time to pass on his regards.

She held out a hand as hermaphroditish as the rest of her: long and fine-boned like a woman's, with the strength of a man's, and a strong man's at that. If she had wished she could have squeezed tears into my eyes. For a moment or two it looked as if she would wish.

If not quite an idiot, she was certainly enjoying some kind of idiotic joke at my expense.

She took the pipe out of her mouth to spit, delicately. The rain spat much harder against her oilskins. I remembered I was a gentleman. No woman, however peculiar, should have been out in such weather. Her male relatives ought to be ashamed of themselves.

'I think maybe it is better for you to go to the inn at Cullipool,' she said. 'Till the weather clears up.'

'Is there no inn at East Gerinish?'

She laughed as if I had asked a very droll question.

'Well, no matter. I intend to go there anyway.'

She murmured some Gaelic. I learned later that it meant: 'God help the man!' In English she added: 'You carry the bread. I will carry your case.'

'Haven't you got a horse and cart?'

'Glas is too old for such weather. He's twenty-two, and he's got rheumatism. So has Djilas my dog.' She laughed. 'We all have rheumatism. You will have rheumatism yourself soon. I did not think you would bring so big a case.'

'In my letter to McBrayne's agent I made it clear I would have a fair-sized suitcase with me. However, it is out of the question your carrying it. I shall carry it myself. It can't be all that far.'

'It's quite a step.'

I remembered with a shiver how long the step from pier to hotel had been.

'No more than a mile surely?'

'A bit more.'

'Good God. Well, help me get it up on to my back, please.'

It may well be imagined with what gnashes of dismay I got ready to take on my back that big heavy suitcase. Since becoming an officer and gentleman seventeen years ago I had hardly ever carried anything heavier than a cane or a thin brief-case.

Together we heaved the case up on to the stone, on its end. I crouched with my back to it. She lifted it on to my back. My fingers tried to grip. I staggered forward, struck my foot against a small stone, and fell on my face, with the case flattening me into the wet heather.

'Ach, it's too heavy for you,' she said.

'If it's too heavy for me, you glaikit bitch,' I mumbled into the heather, 'then it's too heavy for you.'

I was soon proved wrong.

With quick powerful movements she got it on to her back. Shouting to me to remember the bread, she set out along what passed for the road to East Gerinish but which was just a track overgrown with heather, grass, and reeds, littered with stones, and crossed by roaring burns. There was no shelter from wind and rain. Even stumbling along without a burden would have been an ordeal. Soon my feet were soaked, my back sore, and my legs aching. However much I tried to hurry, reeling and gasping and shouting with rage, I kept falling behind. She marched on ahead with witch-like speed and strength.

I needed a rest long before she allowed me one. Peering into the rain, I at last saw, to my surprise and relief, that she was seated on a stone by the side of the track, talking to someone wearing a red sou'wester. Doubtless he had come to help. I hurried, for there was something I wanted even more than to hand over the box of bread to someone else to carry: this was to talk to someone normal, someone whose sex was beyond doubt, someone who would represent East Gerinish a lot more favourably.

I was within twenty yards of the person in the red sou'wester before I realised, with incredulity, that it wasn't a person at all, but a posting-box for letters, fixed to a wooden post, at a place where another track branched off.

At that junction there should surely have been houses in sight with smoke coming from the chimneys, and people living in those houses who wrote letters and posted them, and who had kettles steaming on hobs. But I saw only desolate moors, interspersed with even more desolate lochans.

I made out the name East Gerinish on the rusted white plate, and the hours of collection. These were Mondays and Thursdays at 3pm.

This reminder of civilisation made all the more unbearable the cold, wet, windy wilderness all round.

'Where in God's name are all the houses?' I asked.

She waved her pipe. I noticed how blue, indeed how beautifully blue (milk-wort blue as I discovered later) were her eyes.

'How big is the township?' I asked.

'There used to be thirty crofts worked once.'

'How many now?'

'Two. Just two.'

I knew about the depopulation of the Highlands and Islands, and had expected her to say that the number had been halved, but two was the answer of imbecility.

I reminded myself that not many miles from this place another gentleman had had once to endure rain and gibberish.

I knew that I ought to offer at least to take a turn of carrying my case. Charles Edward Stuart would not have offered, so I did not.

We moved on. Soon I saw the first building of the township. From a distance I thought it was a bunch of cattle, but surely not even Highland cattle would be so stupid as to huddle up there, exposed to the full violence of wind and rain. Nearer, I saw it was like a jail, with very small windows.

'The church,' shouted my companion.

I saw then the stone cross on the gable-end. I also saw that part of the roof had fallen in. No service had been held there for many years.

No doubt another church had been built, in a more sheltered spot, with more generous windows and more comfortable pews. Even in East Gerinish religion must have moved with the times.

I trudged on. We were now in the midst of the township.

Every croft seemed to have been abandoned long ago. No dogs barked at us, no cocks crowed, no sheep bleated, no cows lowed, no children laughed. There was only the sound of the wind howling round those forsaken walls.

Further along Kirstie had put down her load again and was seated on a big mossy stone, as comfortably as if it was an armchair in front of a warm fire.

She watched me calmly as I struggled angrily past what had been a gate once, formed out of a bed end with one brass knob still attached, and went up a muddy and stony path to the nearest croft house. Everywhere were signs of life past, none of life present. A zinc bucket that once had contained tar. Fragments of wool on rusty barbed wire. The broken-off handle of a spade. An old boot. A chipped tinny. At the door, which was open, was a shrivelled rowan tree, warder-off of bad luck.

The turf on the roof had fallen in and covered the floors. Heather grew inside the house. Among the scorched blackened stones of the fireplace lay a rusty poker. In what must have been the pantry I found a bent spoon.

Outside again, I easily saw why the people of that house had been discouraged and gone away. There were still signs where the unwilling earth had been cultivated. Backs must have ached here often, and bellies too.

I plodded along to where Kirstie sat smoking happily, as if the sun was shining. If the exodus had been gradual, over a period of years, she must in her lifetime have seen many families leave.

'The bread will be getting wet,' she remarked, calmly. 'But sit down. You look distressed.'

I sat down beside her.

We were the only living creatures in sight. Not even a gull or hoody crow could be seen.

She offered me a puff of her pipe.

Thanking her, I took out my cigar case. My hands shook. She watched with child-like interest as I lit a cigar. It needed ten matches.

This, I thought hysterically, was the only way to live with dignity, here or anywhere: be in no hurry, keep calm always, ignore wind and rain, forget soaked feet and aching legs, don't worry about where you were going to sleep or what you were going to eat.

'So East Gerinish is an abandoned township,' I said.

'They've all gone.'

'Except two, you said. Your own family, I suppose. And what other?'

'I have no family. Just myself.'

Knowing no better, I felt sorry for her. After all, I was an intelligent man in possession of my right senses, with a cheque for five hundred pounds in my pocket-book; and she was a hermit with the simplicity of a not very bright child, and very little money. It seemed necessary to be sorry for her.

'Did your husband die?' I asked.

'I never was married.'

'Your parents then?'

'My father died three years ago. These are his clothes.'

'He must have been a big man.'

'He was very strong, even in his old age. This stone we are sitting on, he could have lifted it without breaking wind.'

'I see. You must have inherited your strength from him. When did your mother die?'

'When I was three.'

'So long ago!'

She chuckled. 'What age are you thinking I am? Are you thinking I am more than forty?'

More than fifty was more like it. Still, those absurd clothes would put years on anybody.

'I am thirty-five years of age.'

Four years younger than I therefore. Yet I believed her. She was as simple as milk. She would always tell the truth.

She rose. 'You will be as stiff as a board.'

That she was right I soon proved, being hardly able to stand. I was shivering too.

'It is not so far now to old Angus's place,' she said, heaving my case on to her back again, not, however, without breaking wind.

THREE

Since I had already made up my mind to make for Cullipool Inn as soon as I had had a rest, I suffered only slight disappointment when Angus's place, mine now, turned out to be a small, bleak stone cottage with a tin roof, beside a small reedy lochan with two stoical swans in it.

A path of pebbles led up to the front door; this was thick, with a lock fit for a jail or castle. It needed all the combined strength of Kirstie's two hands to turn the key.

What in God's name was there to steal, I wondered, and where were the thieves.

Kirstie murmured that old Angus had been a bit of a miser.

Rain spouted from a burst rone-pipe. The house would be as damp as a sea-cave.

I almost wept with relief that I had money to go and buy hospitality in a dry, warm inn. Glancing at my wrist-watch, and finding that it was now half-past two, I felt panicky. I must set off within the next half hour. I would take out of my suitcase what I needed for the night. Kirstie could carry the suitcase back to the road-end tomorrow. I would pay her for it.

She refused to enter by the front door. Her boots were too muddy. The custom, she said, was for visitors to be let in by the front door only on Sundays.

She spoke as if the township was still populous.

A passage with a stone floor led through to the back door; this I found secured by three big iron bolts. I skinned a finger pulling these back.

The damp in the house could be smelled. I touched a sofa. It was wringing wet.

Sou'wester in hand, but cloth cap still on head, Kirstie stood sniffing the dampness. Her cap was bulky, as if she had a lot of hair under it. I noticed that she was tall for a woman.

'Welcome home,' she said.

At the same time her stomach rumbled.

Or perhaps it was mine. I felt hungry. She, who had worked so much harder, must be hungrier. I also needed to relieve nature.

'How long do you think it'll take me to reach the inn at Cullipool?' I asked.

'It is too late now. You would not get there before dark. I do not think you would get there at all. You would fall in a burn and be drowned.'

She was right. I had neither the resolution nor the

strength to walk five miles in this weather. I was too
tired, too hungry, too cold, and too depressed. I was in
a trap. If I spent a night in this damp house I'd die of
pneumonia. Yet if not in it, where? I had noticed some
bits of peat outside, but they were all sodden. It would be
impossible to light a fire. Also, what could I eat? Kirstie's
soppy bread? With cold water from the lochan to wash it
down?

I had insanely assumed that there would be a shop in
East Gerinish, the kind where anything from firelighters
to sausages could be bought.

Perhaps, though, this other family she had spoken of
could put me up for the night.

'Their house is smaller than this one,' she said. 'They do
not have upstairs. And they have two little children.'

'Good God. How can children survive here? How am I
going to survive tonight?'

'Come with me. My house is warm. There is food.'

I accepted. It was not her fault she was a freak. If I had
lived here all my life I would be a freak too.

Earthy soul that she was, she divined my other, more
urgent need, and pointed out of the window at the sentry-
box of a lavatory.

No attempt had been made to hide it behind a tree; there
was no tree, in any case. Nor behind a wall, for there was
no wall either. In clear weather it must be seen for miles.

As I hurried over to it, she shouted after me that there
was sphagnum moss beside the burn; it was softer than
paper.

The door had to be held shut by hand: there was no
lock, not even a bit of wire. There was a board to sit on,
with an oval hole in it; it fitted, not too securely, over the
pail, which looked unbalanced. The floor was uneven; in
fact, the whole thing had a tilt. A kilt proved more of a
hindrance than an advantage. In my hand the wet moss
looked, and in practice proved, not efficacious.

All right, I thought, as I stepped out into the rain again,
all right, I came to East Gerinish to learn humility. Here
endeth the first lesson.

There would, however, be no more quite so drastic.
Tomorrow or the day after I would take the boat back
to the mainland. From the most luxurious hotel in Oban I

would telephone Betty and warn her that I was on my way home to Pennvalla. She would scream denunciations of me as a liar, a fraud, a breaker of promises, and a worm with no pride. I would retort that she was a monster of cruelty as well as of hypocrisy. She would say that Dorcas would be furious. I would tell her that Dorcas could go to hell.

FOUR

I was sobbing as I thought of that telephone conversation with my wife. I did not know I was sobbing until Kirstie patted and soothed me, as if I was an unhappy child.

She helped me to take out what I needed for the night. Her delight was touching as she stroked my silken blue-and-white pyjamas (not those spewed on), the pigskin case containing my shaving equipment, the two flasks that contained my eau-de-cologne and Parisian talcum respectively, my white mohair dressing-gown, my slippers and my socks. She laid them, carefully, in an old brown suitcase that she found in a cupboard littered with mice dirt.

I would never have thought that a woman in such uncouth men's clothing would have roused my poet's imagination, so long torpid. But she did. I saw her as an old maid grieving that she had never borne a child; and as the ugly virgin in a fairy-tale administering to the handsome prince.

Quite unaware of these fanciful roles in which I was picturing her, she remained herself, simple as milk, strong as a bear, and as unlascivious as a whelk.

As her guest I might have to undergo some tribulations, including bedbugs or fleas, but not, thank God, amorous embarrassments.

She stuffed the small case 'up her jooks', to keep it dry.

Her croft was about half a mile away, nearer the sea, for this could be heard roaring above the howl of wind and hiss of rain. I had not expected her to be a diligent or capable housewife either indoors or out, but even so I was taken aback by the untidiness all round her house. It appeared to be her habit, as it had once been her parents' and grandparents' before her, when getting rid of any household utensil that was no longer of use, to open the door and toss it out, or up, for there was an old frying-pan amongst the nettles on the thatch of the roof.

No wonder she wore Wellingtons. The mud everywhere was ankle deep: so much so that the old grey collie that came limping to greet us kept lifting its paws to shake them. Its barking, though elegiac, was a welcome sound, as were also the melancholy lowing and neighing that came from a low stone shed (where as well as the cow and the horse the privy was kept, as I was soon to be told), and the crowing of a handsome cockerel that strutted about among the debris, with his harem of hens.

I had heard that it was almost a ritual requirement in those parts to lift a peat from the stack outside the house and take it in, as a gesture of friendship and goodwill. Whimsically therefore I picked one up. Instantly the cock and his hens, in the hope that I was about to scatter food, darted towards me. When he discovered that it was only crumbs of peat I was dropping he showed his disgust by leaping on to one of his hens, with intent to tread her. She, equally disgusted, threw him off with a flutter of angry wings. Crestfallen, he sauntered off, pretending that he had had his pleasure, like half the husbands in Scotland.

Djilas's reaction to my presence was just as dramatic. After a few sniffs at my knees, he lifted his head into the rain and howled, in passionate lamentation. Whatever it was that he thought would bring back to his legs the spring and ease of youth and to his eyes clear vision, or would simply make the sun shine warmly again, I was not it.

For the first minute or two Kirstie's living-room appalled me as much as the Orrs' had done. There was no sick smelly infant asleep on a chamber-pot, but as against that the floor was of earth covered with reeds that squeaked when tramped on, either because they were dried up or because there were nests of mice or voles beneath them. Also, there was no putrid stench, but there was a great deal of peat reek that made me cough and caused my eyes to smart and water. There was no unshaven wife-beater in the set-in bed, but there was a broody hen.

It did not take me long, however, to appreciate the great difference between this living-room and the Orrs'. This was a home, where after a while the very discomforts would be cherished; yon was a hell-hole of degradation. Here were earth and growth, yonder dirt and sterility. Here a man might become kippered, or have sore eyes, or walk stiffly because of rheumatism, or even grow feeble-minded, but he would always feel closer to old traditional ways of living and his soul would be continually refreshed.

Naturally these were thoughts in general terms. My own destiny lay far elsewhere. Still, as I sipped the generous dram of whisky that Kirstie poured for me, into a tumbler out of which a speck of peat or a dead insect had first to be fished by her pinkie, I felt more and more enthusiastic about the dignity of living so close to nature, and more and more scornful of the previous inhabitants of the township who had abandoned it to seek the illusory benefits of so-called civilisation in Glasgow or even, God help them, in Australia.

Kirstie, who had poured a big dram for herself too, asked if I would like a hot bath. I replied fervently that nothing would please me more. Thereupon she pulled out from under the bed a zinc bath, not unlike the one I had been washed in as a child, only larger and shallower.

'The water in the pot's nearly on the boil,' she said.

So it was, for the scum on top of it kept trembling.

As an experienced campaigner, I considered the situation. Though I would have to bath in a foetal position, I would be cleaner and fresher afterwards, more able to enjoy whatever repast she offered. There was another room in the house, but it had no fire lit yet, so the sensible place for the bath was right here in the living-room, over by the dresser, say, out of my hostess's way as she prepared the meal. Modesty would not come into it, certainly not on my part, and surely not on hers either. Though she had taken off her oilskins she still wore the cap, a thick green sweater, the hairy trousers, and the Wellington boots. In any case, the peat smoke would make a screen.

'Where do we get the cold water?' I asked.

'From the spring. I shall bring it.'

'Thank you.'

I did not feel ungentlemanly. It was her house. She knew where the spring was. She had on Wellington boots. It pleased her as a woman to serve me as a man.

When she went out with the two buckets I pulled the bath away from the hearth. Then I seized the handle of the cauldron, intending to lift it and coup the contents into the bath; but I had to let it go in a hurry, not only

because the handle was hot but also because the weight
might have caused heart-failure or rupture. Resourcefully
enough, I was carrying the hot water in panfuls when she
returned. With hardly a grunt she heaved up the huge heavy
pot and emptied it into the bath. Next, pushing aside my
offer to help, she poured in the cold water, testing with
her finger. Soon there was quite enough pleasantly warm
if not scrupulously clean water for an adequate bath. Out
of a kist she got a towel, rough as a sack but clean. I used
my own cake of scented soap.

Feeling more like a soldier in camp than a guest in a
house, I was not a bit squeamish about taking off my
clothes, though I did her the courtesy of turning my back.
That there were no sexual currents flowing about the room
was easily proved, for my indicator of such remained at
minimum. In spite of the draughts, and the peat smoke,
and the dog that crept in and, apparently in contrition,
licked my back, I did not hurry. I took time to do, with
decorum, what I had learned to make a practice of during
the War, and which I had always done since, with Betty's
approval: that was, wash behind my foreskin.

More like a batman than a housewife, Kirstie busied
herself at her proper tasks, peeling potatoes and boiling
them, doing the same with turnips, frying fish, and cutting
bread. Whether she ever keeked at me, I could not have
said, but I certainly did not catch her at it. Now and then I
glanced round at her. That stout sweatered back and those
baggy breeks would have been reassurance enough for the
most prudish of men.

By the time I was dried, shaved, powdered, combed,
and dressed in pyjamas and dressing-gown, the meal was
ready. An oil lamp had been lit, adding more smoke to the
atmosphere. I had wondered if she would ask me to eat
first, by myself, while she attended to my wants. If such
had been her intention I had been going to urge her to join
me; after all, it was her house and her food. True, I was now
fit for a duchess's boudoir, while she, from heaving sooty
pots about, was sooty herself; and she seemed determined
to keep her cap on.

As a hostess, she had done her best. The tablecloth
was clean enough, though badly scorched through careless
ironing. My fork had relics of food embedded between the

prongs. The blue delf was heavy and cracked. The table rocked, because of the unevenness of the floor. All the time I had an apprehension of mice running up my legs: reminiscent of the time when, seated on my grandfather's front steps, I had been afraid of the bumble-bee stinging my pintle.

Nevertheless, I enjoyed the meal. The fish was plentiful and fresh, the potatoes not too hard, the turnip not too watery, and the sour milk not too sour; but it wasn't really the food that made the meal so enjoyable, indeed so memorable, it was the knowledge that in that wilderness of moor and loch, on the edge of the stormy sea, with the wind still roaring and the rain lashing, we were as remote as Eskimos from the petty worlds of social pretension and of literary gossip-mongering.

Why not, I mused, stay here and become a poet again?

(In Glasgow I had bought a book on how to grow good crops and raise fat cattle in the wet and windy West High-lands. All that was needed were years of back-breaking work, prodigious luck, and lots of capital.)

During these somewhat wistful cogitations, I did not pay much attention to my hostess. I now hastened to make amends.

'Well, Kirstie,' I said, belching loudly and picking my teeth with a matchstick, 'that was excellent fish. I notice you get your bread from Glasgow. Where do you get your fish?'

'I caught them, with Dugald.'

'Dugald? Who is Dugald?'

'Dugald McLeod. He has the other croft, him and Màiri and their two little children, Ailie and Hector. We have a boat, you see, but it is an old boat. If we had money we would buy a better one with an engine, and then we would catch more fish and maybe lobsters and sell them to the hotels. That is Dugald's idea. Or maybe it is Mairi's idea. She is the clever one.'

She spoke earnestly, and looked so dignified, in a primi-tive kind of way, that in respect I stopped belching and picking my teeth. She was not a lady; she was scarcely a woman, in those mannish clothes; but she loved her native township and this vision that she and the McLeods had of reviving it, though foolish, was praiseworthy. In a boat she would be very useful. With strength like hers to row what need of an engine?

'Mairi and Dugald said they would want to talk to you if you came.'

'They will have to be quick if they want to do that. I have decided to leave tomorrow at nine o'clock. What do they want to talk to me about?'

'About the boat, and other things. I could tell you better in Gaelic.'

'I'm sorry I do not have the Gaelic, though my grandfather did. Tell me in English.'

'It is a great pity, Mairi and Dugald think, that all the pieces of ground that were once cultivated years ago with much hard work, should be going to waste. They think it could be turned into good pasture again, or crops could be grown. Also they think that if the hill was drained it would grow good grass. In my great-grandfather's time there were over a hundred head of black cattle in the township. They had their own bulls too.'

It seemed a pity to douse her hopes, and my own dreams, with a bucketful of cold realism.

'If there was that much prosperity in your great-grandfather's time, why did the people subsequently go?'

'Mairi says there were too many people, too many mouths to feed. She thinks six crofts would be the best number. In those days there were more than thirty.'

I was beginning to feel impatient with this optimistic and opinionated Mairi. Another bucketful had to be poured.

'But surely the abandoned crofts, or at any rate their land, have reverted to the landowner?'

'Mairi says that the laird has never done anything for East Gerinish. Therefore he has no rights.'

'Perhaps not. But that wouldn't prevent him from ordering you off or demanding rent. He would have the law on his side, too.'

As the Countess of Sutherland had had, when Donald of Farr's people had been burnt out of their homes.

'Dugald says he will shoot anyone who comes to order him off or ask him for rent.'

Suddenly I did not want to hear any more about this braggart Dugald and his visionary wife. Perhaps I felt too ashamed.

I rose, belching again, and went to the back door where I pissed out into the rain. To spare the feelings of a feeble-minded peasant woman I was not going to soil my slippers with mud, sharn, and dung, by using the privy in the byre. After all, she herself probably pissed like this at the back-door on stormy nights, though for physiological reasons her posture would be different and she would have to advance a step or two further into the rain.

Since it was still not seven o'clock I decided to read for a while before going to bed. So, while my hostess was busy lighting a fire in the room I was to sleep in, and warming the sheets with two earthenware pigs, I sat by the fire in an armchair with a sagging seat and grubby arms, and read the Bible.

It was large and heavy. On the frontispiece were written in faded ink the names of Kirstie's family since 1829, over a hundred years ago. Between the pages were the remains of flowers. Perhaps Kirstie as a child had put them there: if, that was, so odd a woman ever had been a normal little girl.

I amused myself by imagining Kirstie as a woman of the Old Testament. Sarah laughing in simpleness at the Lord? Rebecca carrying her pitcher to the well? Leah stealing into Rachel's bed? No, she would never have been one of the principals. Her role would have been that of a bondswoman, belonging to Abraham, say, whose task was to rub the patriarch all over with aromatic oil, to keep his venerable limbs active, and particularly his organ of procreation. The lusty centenarian, testing his faculty or keeping in practice, would have bade her lie with him on the smelly goatskins. He would have mumbled no endearments or compliments, and she would have expected none. No likening of her eyes to 'the fishpools in Heshbon' or her nose to 'the tower of Lebanon'.

I rebuked myself. Making fun of any woman, and especially of my hostess, was not gentlemanly. But I could not help smiling, for as Abraham's bondsmaid she would have had to do her share of looking after his goats and sheep, and here she was stumping out to feed the horse and cow, and here she was lumbering back in again with armfuls of peat for the two fires.

She had refilled the cauldron on the fire. Evidently it

was her intention to take a bath when I was out of the way.

Seeing me occupied, she kept quiet, as Hagar would; but when I yawned and stretched my arms, and said I was ready for sleep, she offered eagerly to make me a cup of tea and bring it to me in bed. Fearing no ulterior motive, I consented.

My bedroom was still chilly, the fire and lamp still smoky, so I was glad when she brought the tea and a home-baked scone, on a tray with a stag and hinds painted on it. No hint was intended: probably it was the only tray she had. She poked the fire. She gave a kick under the bed to let me know there was a chamber-pot within reach. She showed me how to turn out the lamp. She asked if I was warm enough. Like Abraham's bondswoman, when she had finished her ministrations she did not linger. She did not quite go out of my presence backwards, with her brow low to the ground, but she went humbly enough. She was that most reassuring of creatures, a woman who knew her place.

When I left in the morning I would give her a couple of pounds; no, three, for she had still to carry my suitcase back to the road-end.

The tea was too strong, the bap too hard. I drank little and ate less. The bed was lumpy. My bladder, chilled, needed frequent emptying. The chamber-pot, handleless, was not easy to find or use in the dark. I had in front of me a soldier's night. There was even danger, as well as hardship, for she had warned me that her thatch needed renewing and could fall in any day.

Between her room and mine was only a narrow passage, and the inside walls of the house were thin. I heard the splashing as she poured the water into the zinc bath, and also her singing.

Picturing her naked in the bath was something I did not want to do, nor did I at first particularly want to listen to her singing; but the song, a Hebridean lament, was so moving that I had to listen, with my heart chilled with a peculiar anguish, just as my bladder was with sheer cold. The song told, I was sure, of some tragic incident in the history of my mother's people, and therefore of my people too.

In tears I felt that I ought to stay here in East Gerinish,

use Betty's money to buy a boat and anything else that was needed, help Kirstie, Dugald, and Mairi to reclaim the old pastures and drain the hill, become their friend and partner, and encourage them whenever their hopes ebbed.

I knew that as soon as the inspiring song ceased the blaze in my mind would die out, and all the old, dull, cautious, selfishnesses would revive.

Tears flowed down my face.

One thing I could do, what I must do, was to apologise to my hostess for the condescension with which I had repaid her kindness.

I got up, put on my slippers, nearly knocking over the chamber-pot, and crept to her door. From the light under it I saw that her lamp was still lit. But she wasn't singing any more.

I knocked.

She spoke in Gaelic.

'I just had to tell you, Miss McDonald, how sorry I am for treating you so lightly.'

I could not stop sobbing.

There was a pause.

'The door is not locked.'

I hesitated. If she was in her night clothes she might well look so grotesque that my self-reproach and gratitude would dribble away again.

At last I opened the door, and got the biggest surprise of my life. Who was this tall, strongly built, stately woman in the white nightgown, brushing hair, black as outer space, that came well below her waist? She was Kirstie McDonald all right, with the same wide mouth and longish nose; but though she was still as sadly droll as ever—more so, for she was in tears—she was also beautiful, in a strangely noble way. Beside her all the aristocratic women I had met would have looked common.

With the men's clothes she had put off every trace of masculinity. She still looked magnificently strong, but in an exciting, feminine way: thus might the Queen of the Amazons have looked, except that she would have exerted her strength as a menace, whereas beautiful meek Kirstie carried hers like an adornment. Her nightgown was loose and hid her figure. Yet so high and firm were her breasts, wonderfully so in a woman of thirty-five, that they stood out proudly. I remembered Betty's: for all the massaging (in the early days much of it done by me) and the creams and salves, and the ingenious and expensive corsets, they had lost shape and firmness so that, if let loose, they sagged to her navel. Kirstie's were like a girl of eighteen's. Her very feet were strong and lovely.

FIVE

Whether or not I would have gone in to comfort her, and to be comforted, if she had been as uncomely in her night as in her day clothes is a matter that like the songs of the Sirens can never be determined. What I can say in my favour is that if she had not been in tears I would probably have taken my amazement and chilled bladder back to bed, after stammering out the apology I had come to deliver. I can also say that in my going in and walking over the squeaky rushes to where she stood with the brush arrested in her hair, there was too much solicitude for there to be any lust: my indicator at that point being still at minimum.

It would be insulting to her as a woman with breasts and to myself as a man with balls, to pretend that to me then she was only a sad symbol, and that when I was clasping all that muscular loveliness I was thinking exclusively of our ancestors, hers and mine, driven first from their fertile machairs by tyrannical landlords and then from their penitential bogs by the brutality of the earth and weather. I was very well aware (without any need of an indicator) that this was a woman in my arms, and a beautiful, strange, and instinctively artful woman at that, for, with a few gymnastic shrugs that loosened but did not break my embrace, she let her nightgown slip to the floor and, since she wore no chemise or undershirt, stood in front of me as naked as a swan. It took little detection to tell that in the summer time she had not always covered herself in thick men's clothing, for her arms up to her shoulders, and her legs up to the thighs, and her neck down to the tops of her breasts, were still golden. Only her belly was white, but of so splendid and unblemished a whiteness as to remind me of Solomon's phrase 'a heap of wheat set about with lilies'.

Eager to give comfort, I was still more eager to receive it. All the vexations I had suffered, all the wrongs I had endured myself or had inflicted on others (why had I called the children of Lomond Street baboons?), all my crippled and blinded expectations, howled about my soul, as the wind howled about the house.

It was weeks later before she told me how low-spirited she had herself been feeling that day when she had come upon me sheltering behind the stone at the road-end. She was never good at describing her deepest feelings, at any rate not in English, and I was too old, with a mind not agile enough, ever to pick up enough Gaelic. She suffered stoically, like a beast, but more deeply; and she was happy, not like a skylark that soars but like a corncrake that hides.

Kirstie was not what the world calls bright. At school she must have been a dunce. People called her feeble-minded. I called her so myself. All that was true. Yet I found more pleasure in her silences than I ever did in the spoutings of men regarded as brilliant.

It was not the act of a feeble-minded woman to hope that, if she revealed her unexpectedly beautiful body, a man like myself, a gentleman, possessed of the appurtenances of civilised living, like silk pyjamas and mohair dressing-gown, would be so overwhelmed and confused by admiration and desire that he would be impetuous to do to her what the cockerel had tried in vain to do to the hen. It was the act of a religious-minded unhappy woman who had lived too long alone, and who saw in me her salvation.

But something else ought to be said, in justification of her willingness to participate in what was soon to take place. She had fallen in love with me. Not having the eloquence to show it by telling me that my eyes were 'as the eyes of doves by the rivers of waters' or that my legs were 'as pillars of marble set upon sockets of fine gold' she had more effectively demonstrated it by carrying my suitcase more than two miles without complaint, by giving me food and shelter, and by singing her saddest songs in my homage.

Not that night, but one night weeks later, she confessed to me that when she had seen me crouching behind the stone, weeping—had I really been weeping, though, or had she mistaken raindrops for tears and sneezes for sobs?—she had thought me the handsomest man she had ever seen; but she would not have fallen in love with me because of handsomeness alone, she had also thought me the most sorrowful man she had ever seen.

SIX

She was not a virgin. This was more of a relief to me than a regret. With her strength it was not likely that any lecherous Hebrideans had taken advantage of her simpleness, so she must have given herself willingly. One of my predecessors was Big Ian of the bus. She told me that, years later, when we heard that he had died, vomiting blood like Major Holmes. There had been a young fellow of about twenty whom she might have married if he hadn't gone off to the War and been drowned. There had been too the laird, when both he and she were eighteen. (I was always sceptical about her and the laird until he turned up at her funeral.)

That first night, when we were in bed together, I remembered just in time that what we were on the point of doing, however fondly and innocently, could have bitter lifelong consequences. I panted out a warning.

If we had had to desist, or be content with, so to speak, half the cake only, I would have been as chagrined as any man in similar circumstances, but I would have borne it more philosophically than most, for to be truthful the suddenness of the situation, the lumpiness of the bed, and the claustrophobic smallness of space, were intrusive factors that I could not help finding irksome.

However, I had no sooner called halt, than Kirstie stepped out of bed and bounded over the rushes, with firelight on her firm buttocks. From a small drawer in the dresser she took a tiny square packet, the contents of which were easily conjectured. Not giving me time to feel, far less express, astonishment that she should have such a thing so readily available, she returned to bed and gently rolled this rubber protector on to my pintle; which, I humorously reflected, tholed the indignity with the same patience that Floss, a chihuahua once owned by Betty, had shown when being garbed on frosty mornings with a knitted jacket.

What followed was not a fuck or copulation or even a love-making. There is in no language, not even in Gaelic, which was spoken in Eden, a word to describe a union of male and female bodies, not intended to produce offspring or assuage lust or revenge adultery or prove a theory or explore the subconscious or annihilate the universe, but simply a gesture of comradeship, dependence, and loving-kindness, leaving behind it no sense of disappointment or futility or frustration, only a continuing sense of comrade-ship, dependence, and loving-kindness.

That was what happened between Kirstie and me.

Cynical Betty had accused me of seeking what was not possible: the rose of love without the thorns of disillusion-ment. What I really wanted, she used to say, varying the metaphor, was not the tempestuous sea of love but the haven of maternal affection. That was why I was such a timid and conscience-stricken lover. I was Oedipus in a kilt.

I smiled at those taunts as I lay hand-in-hand with Kirstie, listening, without much irritation, to her snores. I had found a new way of life, and a perfect companion to share it with. Deep ancestral longings in me would be satisfied, and I would be a poet again.

SEVEN

When I awoke Kirstie was making porridge and frying eggs, amidst sunbeams. She had on her clothes of yesterday. Affectionately, I lay and wondered if I should exercise the influence I had acquired last night to persuade her or if need be command her to wear skirts and dresses in future. In fairness, I took time to consider what were the advantages, first, of the cloth cap: it kept her hair from getting stoury and being blown about by the wind; second, of the thick sweater and trousers: they kept her warm and protected her splendid body from the many dunts it must sustain in the course of a day's work; and third, of the Wellington boots: after yesterday's deluge there would be floods and glaur everywhere.

Other advantages occurred to me. No other man would see her loveliness, and I myself would have it revealed to me every night in a ceremony of surprise, as if I was not only her lover but her high priest too.

As for her smoking a pipe, how could I object if I smoked cigars?

Better then, on balance, to let her go on as before.

I could not see my kilt. Last night it had been draped

over a chair in front of the fire to dry. I assumed she
had put it out in the sunshine. Then a suspicion struck
me. Perhaps, not being as tolerant as I in the matter
of what she considered suitable dress for her lover, she
had thrown it out or torn it up. She might well share
the local prejudice that a kilt was for a laird with an
English voice, or for a jessiewillocks. That she was probably as stubborn as a stot might have to be taken into
account.

She dispersed this particular doubt and anxiety by going
out and coming in again with my kilt clasped in her arms
like a baby.

Another kind of warning bell began to ring in my mind.
She might, this strange simple woman, take it into her head
that she wanted me to give her a child. With a woman of
normal strength tactics of avoidance could be resorted to,
delicately and tactfully, but not with her. Nor would she
be able to understand if I were to tell her that, already
martyred by fatherhood, I had no wish to be nailed to
that cross again. She would comfort me, but she would
still demand my unstemmed seed.

She poured warm water into a basin for me to wash. She
kissed my back, saying it was soft and smooth.

As we ate the porridge (full of rubbery lumps) and the
fried eggs (black from an unclean pan) she said that we
should flit to my house. It had wooden floors, a tin roof,
and rooms upstairs. It had always been one of the best
houses in the township. We would live together like man
and wife, whatever Mr Caligaskill might say or do.

Naturally I asked who this Caligaskill was. It appeared
he was Free Kirk minister of the parish that included East
Gerinish. He had once knocked off the head of a cock with
his stick because he had caught it treading a hen on the
Sabbath. He had just meant to knock it off the hen, but
though he was small he had terrible passions in the service
of the Lord.

He had nine children; eleven really, for two had died in
infancy. Mrs Caligaskill was always ailing.

Without having seen this Caligaskill I hated him. Let
him come to our cottage and I would break his stick over
his head. I would tell him I encouraged my cock to tread on
Sundays. He represented that mixture of sanctified lust and

hypocrisy which had soiled and stunted the soul of Scotland
for centuries.

Kirstie gave out information like a hen pecking, a word
or two at a time, with many head-tilted thought-suspended
silences in between. It was a slow method, and until my
own mind learned to creep at the same pace it could well
be exasperating.

Compared to Dugald McLeod's her speech was garrulous
and pell-mell.

He turned up, with a dog, as I was basking in the sun,
waiting for Kirstie to come with my suitcase. She had
decided to carry it rather than disturb her old rheumaticky
horse; in any case her cart had spokes missing and one shaft
was badly spliced with wire.

I had intended to make myself busy tidying up the
precincts, but the sun was warm, the sky blue, and the
radiance on the surrounding lochans hypnotic, so that I
soon gave up and rested in an old basket chair outside the
door, smoking a cigar. Above me geese honked in from the
Arctic, and at my feet a robin hopped about. Less than
half a mile away the sea's gentler pounding on the rocks
was soporific. There were many things to do, but there
was plenty of time in which to do them; even if they did
not all get done, or if most of them got only half done or
even quarter done, well, what difference would it make in
a hundred years' time? Thus, so soon, was I succumbing
to the Hebridean spell.

I have mentioned before that Lowlanders in Scotland
have a prejudice against Highlanders going back hundreds
of years. The word 'Hielan' in the Lowland vernacular is
synonymous with wrong-headed or bovinely stupid. The
Lowlander thinks of the typical Highlandman, fresh from
the heather, as beefy-faced, slow-brained, thick-tongued,
and huge-footed. This is probably in revenge for the
Highlanders' view of Lowlanders as gallous, quick-witted,
belligerent midgets. In reality Highland men, particularly
Hebrideans, are usually handsome, in a refined black-haired
Celtic way, or in a square-faced yellow-haired Norse
way.

Yet when I opened my eyes, there, glaring down at
me was a perfect example of the Cowcaddens idea of a

Highlander, except that it was tufts of black hair and not of heather that sprouted from his ears.

It might appear arrogant of me to call stupid a man who could do so many useful things better than I: handle a boat or a plough, for instance, dig drains, build a jetty or a dyke, sow seed and plant potatoes, milk a cow or fleece a sheep, and—his masterpiece—carve up a carcase; but in spite of all these skills stupid Dugald undoubtedly was.

It took the form of refusing to admit, or worse still of being unable to see, that there were other skills and qualities more valuable than his own, and that I possessed them. Because he could work fourteen hours a day while I fell exhausted after eight, he thought that he was, not just the stronger man, but the better. When he came to hear that I had published two volumes of poetry his only question was: how much money did they make? On my proudly answering that they had made no money at all he strode off, eyes asquint with the pressure of two opinions: that writing poetry was a job for unmanly fools, and that, even so, I must have been bad at it.

Though he disliked Caligaskill he really shared his Deuteronomical morality, and believed that a married gentleman who slept with a crofter's unmarried daughter deserved to be pelted with stones.

Born in East Gerinish, he had gone at the age of 14 to work in a butcher's shop in Inverness. After 19 years there he had come back to inherit and work his father's croft, bringing with him his wife Mairi and his baby son Hector. That had been three years ago. Since then his daughter, Ailie had been born. Mairi's own forebears were from Oronsay.

This then was the big, ruddy-faced, ex-butcher glowering at me that sunny morning.

'Eh? Where's Kirstie?' he demanded.

He prefaced almost every utterance with that 'Eh?' In reproducing his speech I omit it to avoid tedium.

I stood up, politely. The ruder he was the more urbane I must be. That was the aristocratic creed.

'Miss McDonald will be here shortly,' I said. 'You are Mr McLeod, I presume? My name is Fergus McGilvray.'

I held out my hand. He looked at it as if assessing its worth as meat. But he shook it, after rubbing his own on the backside of his trousers that were splattered with sharn.

'Fergus? That's Irish.'

Others had said so, beginning with Aunt Bella long ago. My mother had liked the name, that was the reason why I had it. I liked it too. It meant, in the Gaelic, supremely choice.

'Not many Ferguses about,' he added.

Like many of his remarks, that was impossible to reply to. So I patted his dog's head. It looked more intelligent than he. At any rate it was treating me with more respect and friendliness.

'So you're old Angus's nephew?'

'Great-nephew.'

'And you've come here?'

'I've come here.'

'What for? You don't look as if you've done a hard day's work in your life.'

Again I made a fuss of his dog.

'Working a croft's hard work.'

'I'm sure it is.'

'Are you going to stay here and try and work it?'

'I may do so.'

'A man in Lochmaddy has a boat for sale, made in the Orkneys, with a Kelvin engine. It's going cheap.'

'That's interesting.'

'Our boat's done. It's not safe. Are you any good in a boat?'

I had once rowed a boat across Rothesay Bay. That was the extent of my seamanship.

'I suppose I could learn.'

'Did you spend the night with Kirstie?'

'Miss McDonald was kind enough to offer me hospitality.'

'Kirstie's not the cleverest woman in the world.'

'Who would want to meet such a creature?'

'What d'you mean? You've met her. You just spent the night with her.'

'Not with the cleverest woman in the world.'

'No. Don't get smart, Mr McGilvray, just because you've got on a kilt.'

I could see that for some time he had been wanting

to laugh at my kilt, but laughter, that concession to the humorous side of life, was not something he did lightly or readily. I was so soon to learn that by the time he had made up his mind to laugh the risible situation was well past, and he found himself the only one laughing.

We saw Kirstie approaching, bent under the weight of my suitcase.

'Did you sleep with her?' he asked.

'That is my business, and hers.'

'Her father is dead. She has no brothers. She is a woman on her own.'

'I know that, Mr McLeod.'

'She has no men-folk to look after her.'

'Is she not able to look after herself?'

'She is not so like a man as you would think.'

Had he then seen that beautiful hair and those splendid breasts? No. His leer was sly, not lewd. He would rather be sly than lewd any day.

Kirstie arrived. She did not set down the suitcase. He addressed her in Gaelic, no doubt discussing me. She replied in the same language. In an attempt to indicate to them how rude they were being I threw a few remarks in French to the two dogs.

Kirstie gave me a wifely smile and then took the suitcase into the house.

'Sometimes she is more like a child than a woman,' said Dugald.

'It is a wonderful thing to have the innocence of a child.'

He sniffed at that like a dog offered meat by a stranger.

'I don't know about innocence,' he muttered. 'But if any man did her wrong I would choke him with my own hands.'

'I should think she could do her own choking.'

After a long pause—the conversation had been full of long pauses—he grinned. 'That is true, that is very true.'

Then, mercifully, we were interrupted by the arrival of his wife and children.

Apart from Kirstie, Mairi McLeod and her two children, Ailie and Hector, were the reasons why I stayed so long and was so happy in East Gerinish.

I loved Kirstie, and was more contented in her company

than in anyone else's; but there were times when some of
her habits, such as her pipe-smoking and her breaking of
wind (admittedly only when out of doors and engaged in
strenuous work) caused my heart to sink a little. Also she
could be quite aggressively possessive and treated me more
like her child than her lover. In those moods she would
even try to feed me with a spoon.

Mairi McLeod was an unmarred delight. Quick to laugh,
kind and frank, shrewd to advise, brisk and red-cheeked,
she reminded me of Meg Jeffries, except that in Meg there
must have been a tragic or unlucky element—why else
would she have married McHaffie, a man as dangerous for
her as Antony for Cleopatra?—whereas Mairi easily sur-
vived marriage to a man without imagination and humour,
with her own imagination and humour in no way stifled.
Daughter of a farmer, she was the best agriculturist of us
all. As a good wife should, and as a clever wife will, she
let her husband think that her bright ideas were really
his own.

As for fair-haired cheerful little Ailie and black-haired
earnest Hector, they and I were to have many happy times
exploring East Gerinish. Because they were so young, and
I was a newcomer, we were at the same stage of getting to
know and love the place. Dorcas, and to a smaller extent
Torquil, had helped to extinguish the poet in me; those
two did a great deal to revive him.

EIGHT

Handing Ailie to me to hold—Dugald would be sure to let
her drop, she cried cheerfully—and encouraging Hector to
make a fuss of poor old confused Djilas, Mairi gave each of
them a home-baked scone out of a pokeful she had brought,
and then went into the house to say hello to Kirstie and help
her make tea.

She was evidently the kind of woman who could make a
home out of a wet cave and a feast out of whelks; or, more
realistically, out of a single-end and a stale loaf.

I remembered poor silly pregnant Elsie Wishart.

What helped little Ailie to become friends with me so
quickly was hearing from the house her mother's laughter,
though it seemed to me, not knowing Mairi then, that
the laughter was a bit too frequent and merry considering

that she had only serious-minded Kirstie to joke with. I couldn't help suspecting that much of it was provoked by the gentlemanliness of the bedmate that Kirstie had landed this time.

After drawing back her head and studying me, especially my moustache, for a long minute, Ailie suddenly shoved her scone into my mouth, ordering me, in infantile gibberish, to take a bite. My interpreter was her brother Hector, who was sharing his scone with Djilas and the cockerel.

Their father had gone over to have a close look at Kirstie's old grey horse. It stood in a dwam, enjoying the sunshine. I guessed that he was telling it not for the first time, that it wasn't worth its feed any more.

Still, it was, all in, a happy scene. The cockerel showed he agreed by fluttering up on to the peatstack and uttering his most triumphant crow of the morning.

Mairi came to the door and cried that tea was ready. She had taken off her old brown raincoat and was seen to be wearing a pink jumper and yellow skirt. She loved bright clothes. She could be seen coming a mile away. It made the pleasure of her company all the sooner.

We made for the house, even Djilas and the McLeods' dog and the cockerel, the last in the hope of a few more pecks at Hector's scone.

Mairi had, in a few minutes, tidied the living-room, made the bed, laid a fresh cloth on the table, set out the best china, and instead of the sooty tin teapot with string round the handle, produced a handsome china one with a carriage and pair painted on it. Her most magical trick, though, had been to transform Kirstie, whose hair was now held up by two red combs in Spanish fashion, and who wore a white blouse, black skirt, and black shoes with silver buckles.

Even Ailie was impressed. She stretched out her arms towards her Auntie Kirstie who lifted and embraced her with a fondness charming to see but also ominous as a warning, for there were undoubtedly maternal longings in it.

'Well,' said Mairi, 'I was just telling Kirstie that it's silly to have nice clothes locked up in a drawer.'

'Nice enough,' grunted Dugald, 'but they will not do for lifting stones.'

Kirstie had explained to me that the job she and McLeod had in hand was the repair of their jetty.

'We may not have very much in East Gerinish to be proud of,' said his wife, 'but one thing we do have is the finest-looking woman in the whole Long Island, and it's a shame if we never get to see her.'

I waited for her clod of a husband to pay the obvious, and justified, compliment. He did not, so I paid it myself. 'The two finest-looking women in the whole Long Island,' I said.

She laughed. 'Me? Och away. I'm like a wee tub compared with Kirstie.'

Her simile was not only honest, it was also apt. Her own comeliness was domestic. To say that was not to belittle it, for, whatever female emancipators might say, a woman looked her best when busy in her house, making it into a home.

Kirstie, on the other hand, with her long, lovely, melancholy face, and her unhousewifely habits, was like one of those creatures in woman's shape that, according to Hebridean legend, now and then came from their other world to live among people, nearly always, alas, bringing doom.

Those cups of tea, however, were as companionable as any ever drunk. Dugald tried slyly to speir about my past and my plans for the future, but his wife shut him up. I was in East Gerinish, she said, because I had a right to be there, and this was a little party to welcome me. There would be plenty of time afterwards for questions to be asked and answered, or not answered, on both sides.

There was no doubt that the shrewdest questions would come from her. She seemed to think, judging from smiles I caught her giving me, that I was as much to be pitied as Kirstie, or at any rate to be sympathised with. Her husband lacked the insight to see that. All he could think of was that I was using my advantages as a gentleman to seduce a simple strong-backed woman who, if corrupted by me and my fancy ways, would no longer be useful to him as a lifter of stones.

After we had finished our tea he wanted Kirstie to go with him to the jetty and get some work done while the sun shone. His wife had a jollier idea. If I didn't mind, why shouldn't we all go along to have a look at old Angus's house and see what it needed done to it to make it habitable. While we were there we could have a look for the money that he was supposed to have hidden away. Of course if any was found it would belong to me, but it would be fun helping me to look.

After yesterday's storm I had expected to find the landscape a desert of sodden heathery bogs and swollen reedy lochans; and so it mostly was, but over all its vast extent the light was so radiant that I felt I could see not just for great distances but into time itself. The ruins of crofts, a mile away, seemed so close in that enchanted air that I saw not only the nettles and ragwort round the doors, but the people coming out for the last time: I could even see the grief on their faces. No wonder, I thought, this was the land of the second sight. If I stayed here I would be seer as well as poet. There were few places in the world where a man of compassion and intelligence might prepare to take up, for a moment or two, without sentimentality or vainglory, the burden of all the multitudinous evils and miseries of humanity, and by showing that they could be borne, even for so short a time, make them less incomprehensible and less terrible; but if it could be done anywhere it could surely be done here.

While the others searched for the money, with the two doors and all the windows wide open, I was more interested in a family photograph of the McGilvrays, taken more than seventy years ago. It was not Angus, my squirrel or miser of a great-uncle who fascinated me—he was an ordinary-looking lad with very short hair and large hands— nor was it my great-grandparents, side by side like Pharaoh and his consort; it was my grandfather, Donald McGilvray, then a child of about six. He sat cross-legged and sailor-suited in the forefront, with a Bible held in his hands in the way that other boys would have held a kitten or a boxful of pet mice.

Because he was the youngest, had he been given the honour of holding the sacred book, or had he demanded it as a right, since he had already shown himself the holiest of the family? Certainly he looked as if he had already learned to put righteousness before love: horrible in one so young. It was easy to see in him the kirk elder who many years later had hardened his heart against his beautiful daughter.

What was much harder to see, though, was the lover who in Glasgow Central Station had pleaded with my grandmother's family, bound for Sydney, to let their daughter

Morag stay behind to marry him. I had heard that he had
gone down on his knees on the hard cement, but that surely
was apocryphal: refusing to kneel before the Lord God,
how could he before Mr and Mrs McKenzie, formerly
from Borinish in Skye? Doubtless they had pointed out
to him, and to her too, that the sunshine of Australia
would be better for her health than the rain of Gantock;
and that, in any case, her fare had been paid for. She must
have added her pleas to his, for her parents, in anguish at
so hard a decision, had unexpectedly given in. When the
train steamed out of the station she was not on it with
them. Instead she had returned with my grandfather to
Gantock where she did not have a single relative. They
had been married in the Auld Kirk, as soon as possible
after the banns were called. Thereafter she had lived long
enough to give birth to my mother.

Had my grandfather, this smug little boy grown up, never
been able to forgive my mother for causing his beloved
wife's death? To the stern Calvinist no one was innocent,
not even a new-born baby.

Like Abraham too had he regarded the birth of a daughter, not as a sign of the Lord's favour, but rather of His
displeasure?

(I could not help remembering that I myself regretted
having so unkind a daughter as Dorcas. But what had that
to do with the Lord, or my deserving?)

Meanwhile the others were enjoying themselves looking
for old Angus's hidden treasure. Under the floorboards
were found some banknotes nibbled to pieces to make a
nest for mice. In all the amount found was two pounds
twelve and sixpence, mostly in half-crowns. I gave it to
Ailie and Hector.

'I thought there'd be more,' said Dugald.

'Maybe Mr McPherson the lawyer in Lochmaddy has the
rest,' suggested Mairi.

Mairi then proposed that we all go to her house for
dinner, meaning lunch. To me she privately whispered
that if I didn't mind she and I might walk a bit behind
the others and have a chat.

'I'm going to call you Fergus,' she said, as we set out,
'and you've to call me Mairi. All we know about you is
that you're Angus's great-nephew, from Edinburgh.'

'From Gantock really. I was born in Gantock.'

'Mr McPherson is as close as a scallop.'

'Rightly so, wouldn't you say?'

'Well no, I wouldn't, not in this case. He knows how dependent we must be on one another here in East Gerinish. We've been anxious to find out if you were likely to stay and work the croft and help with the boat. We badly need another man. Otherwise I'm afraid we'll probably all have to go and leave the place to the gulls and geese.'

'Would Kirstie go?'

'Kirstie was born here. So was Dugald, but he's kent other places since. She's never been further than Lochmaddy in the bus. It's really Kirstie I would like to talk to you about.'

'I thought it might be.'

'You slept with her last night, didn't you?'

She didn't say it as an accusation, but even so I was about to point out, politely, that it was none of her business when I realised that she must see it as her business, as the matriarch of this small and vanishing clan.

'I'm not blaming you. It was a wild night and you couldn't have slept in your own house. Forby, Kirstie likes a man in her bed. I could tell from the shine in her eyes. And why shouldn't she?'

'She mentioned a Mr Caligaskill.'

'Oh him. If he was a Catholic priest that slept alone he might be worth heeding on the subject. But he's got nine weans, and he's been told that if she's ever pregnant again it'll kill his wife. If he wants other folk to abstain let him show an example.'

'Kirstie seems afraid of him.'

'Well, she got pregnant once years ago, before I came here. It seems Caligaskill was after her like a ferret after a rabbit. I wouldn't be surprised if it was him caused her to have a miscarriage.'

These were startling and unsavoury revelations about my last night's bedmate.

'She looks strong and of course she *is* strong, in the back and arms anyway; but she has her weaknesses too. What I'm really trying to say is that she mustn't ever get pregnant again.'

I knew now who had supplied Kirstie with that little packet.

'Unless of course it was by a man willing and able to marry her.'

'Anyway,' she went on, 'though she's very fond of children I doubt if she'd be any good at bringing one up.'

We looked at Kirstie striding along in front of us in cloth cap and Wellingtons, and smoking her pipe. She had told me that the bargain was woman's clothes in the house only. It was certainly not easy to imagine her as a mother.

'I don't know why you've come here, Fergus,' said Mairi, 'and I'm not going to ask. It's up to you whether you want to tell us or not. I will say this, you're a lot different from what I expected. I don't suppose you'll stay here long. Dugald's convinced you won't. Of course you're entitled to leave whenever you want. But please don't just make use of Kirstie. She's the kindest, most loyal, and least complaining person I ever met, and she knows every clump of heather in East Gerinish. To me she *is* East Gerinish, though I don't suppose you'll understand what I mean.'

I understood all right.

This morning I had a visitor, and my hands are still shaking.

For some weeks past I have not been going to the public library regularly, but have stayed at home to work at these memoirs. This has not been because of the librarian's campaign of discouragement—to be fair, it has not been waged relentlessly—or because the sight of the old meek non-inheritors who still timidly frequent it has at last got me down. I have simply felt too unwell to walk the half mile there in wintry weather. Often I feel dizzy and faint. Not long ago I had to be helped into a greengrocer's and given an orange crate to sit on and a glass of water that had a fragment of lettuce in it.

When the knock came I assumed it was Mrs McRorie and paid no heed. Still in my nightshirt, I was having breakfast and thinking how I could condense the East Gerinish section without losing too much flavour and force. The truth is, I am beginning to be afraid that I may not survive long enough to reach the final chapter, which will have to do with my second and final return to Gantock. If this is not written, and written well, then it seems to me that the whole undertaking must fail. So I was reluctant to drag my mind away from those far-off shining solitudes. Then I heard Mrs McRorie opening her door and talking to whoever was knocking on mine. Soon she was knocking herself, urgently.

It must be, I thought, the man come to read the gas or the electric meter. She has a terror about the supply being cut off.

Wrapping my kilt about me, I went and opened the door.

Expecting to see, as well as Mrs McRorie, the cheerful gasman with his book in one hand and his torch in the other, I was taken aback to find instead, on our dull landing, at its dullest that dreich March morning, a creature of not immediately determinable sex, who looked dressed up for Hallowe'en.

His hat, with a brim wide enough for at least four pigeons to land on it, was purple. His cape, which might have served to mesmerise bulls but not to keep out Glasgow cold and rain, was purple too. It came well below his knees but didn't quite hide his trousers of yellow and black checks. Along with this flamboyant outfit went a pointed beard, long hair, lilac-coloured gloves, a perfumed smell, an upper-class simpering accent, and a cultivated lisp.

If this character read meters, I thought, with a chuckle, they must be those of high-class brothels.

He astonished me by crying, with a strange eagerness: 'Mr William McTavish?'

'This gentleman says he has come all the way from Paris to see you,' whispered Mrs McRorie, much impressed. 'So I thought it would be a pity if he went away disappointed.'

As soon as she said Paris I knew who he was: my son Torquil. Samuel Lamont had told me he lived in Paris, and was a painter of some reputation.

My immediate impulse was to shut the door on him. This effeminate aesthete was a stranger: he had nothing to do with me. As a small boy, when I had tried to interest him in playing with a girr he had made it clear that he considered me an uncultured oaf. Being not so hard-hearted as his sister, he had done it as inoffensively as he could; but I had been offended all the same.

I thought that Samuel Lamont had betrayed me, and I almost betrayed myself by weeping.

'Pleath,' he said, in an agitation that seemed genuine. 'Pleath don't clothe the door.'

'It wouldn't be very mannerly,' whispered Mrs McRorie.

I had to let him in. As he stepped past me he drew in his breath sharply, but whether in a sigh of relief that I had not shut him out or in a gasp of dismay at the chilliness and bareness of my living-room, I could not tell.

'It's beastly cold in here,' he said, with a shiver.

I did not ask him to sit down. For one thing, I did not want him to stay long; for another, there wasn't a chair fit for his dandy behind.

He looked at the muddle of manuscripts on the table amongst the dishes, and on the floor.

'I think you've guessed who I am?' he said.

'I have a good idea.'

'I'm sorry if I have invaded your privacy. It is one of the deadliest sins.'

'I'm sorry Samuel Lamont broke his word.'

'No, no, no. Don't blame him. He has nothing to do with my coming here. A friend of mine while in America saw an article in a magazine by a Professor Wienbanger. He brought me a copy because you were mentioned in it. Wienbanger seemed to indicate that you were still alive, and that he had met you. So I flew to America to see him.'

'All that way, to find out about me?'

'Of course. I thought how wonderful if it was true.'

'The man's a fool. I damn near kicked him down the stairs.'

'Oh, I agree. One of those awful Americans who set out to be cleverer than anyone else and end up by being stupider. All the same I feel grateful to him. I can't tell you how excited and pleased I was when he assured me you were still alive, and that he had actually talked to you. Excited yes, and pleased; but ashamed too, deeply ashamed. If he could find you, why couldn't I?'

Though he spoke with apparent sincerity the strangeness between us was growing greater every minute, not less. I had far more in common with the smelly, defeated, semi-illiterate old men in the public library than with this gaudy representative from the world of the arts.

After more than thirty years I could find nothing to say to him.

'You don't look well,' he said.

'I'm well enough.'

'You wish I hadn't come? I can see it in your face. You want me to go away again.'

'You should never have come.'

'You must come away with me. You mustn't stay in this horrid place one more day. It would break my heart. You *must come with me. Now. The taxi is waiting down in the street.'*

'Where to?'

'Paris. That's where I live.'

'What would I do in Paris?'

He smiled, and for the first time I caught a glimpse in him of the small boy who had been scornful of Gantock because it didn't have an art gallery with Botticellis in it.

'Dozens of things, I hope,' *he said.* 'It's a far more significant place for a poet to be than Glasgow.'

Significant was a word I had always distrusted. 'Glasgow suits me,' *I replied.*

'But it is so dreadfully provincial. And so grim. As I came through those horrible streets I couldn't help groaning; and the taxi-driver was so rude.'

'I'm not surprised.'

'Is it their way of showing manly independence?'

I had once thought the same thing.

He tried to take me by the arm, but I wouldn't let him.

'I've got absolutely no right to ask why you turned your back on us all,' *he said,* 'but I would very much like to know.'

'I thought it was you who turned your backs on me. Not that it matters.'

'But it does matter. It matters immensely. May I tell you how much I admire your poems, particularly the Hebridean ones published in the Atlantic Review?'

'I wouldn't have thought their subject matter would have appealed to you.'

Again he smiled, and again was recognisable. 'It depends on the treatment, does it not? If a painter was good enough he could make a masterpiece out of that old kitchen range.'

I was surprised that he knew to call it a range. Would he understand if I called the mantelpiece the brace? 'Hail Mary, full of grace.' *Perhaps he still had an atom of Scottishness left in him.*

'Of course,' *he said,* 'if a writer or artist keeps so far away from the market place as you have done, and never shouts his wares, he will be forgotten; but I assure you I keep meeting people who tell me what a remarkable poet my father was.'

At last the word was out. It did not lessen the strangeness between us: on the contrary, it greatly increased it.

'*I keep telling everyone my father was Fergus Lamont, the poet.*'

He pronounced Lamont with the accent on the second syllable. It was a measure of the distance between us.

It had become too much for me. If he didn't go I would be too confused and might start weeping in self-pity.

'I'm sorry,' I said, 'but I want you to go. I've been alone too long.'

'But I would like to help. I came here to help, if I could.'

'Well, you can't.'

'Money? I hate to mention it, but it is awfully important, isn't it?'

'I have enough.'

'You don't seem very luxurious here. And it's beastly cold.'

'I don't need luxuries, and one gets used to cold.'

'You never were one for possessions, were you? Even my mother admitted that.'

He spoke of her with some bitterness. I felt I ought to have rebuked him, but I didn't. I ought also to have asked him if he knew how she was, but I didn't.

'There are a hundred things I want to ask you,' he said, 'and here you are pushing me out before I've asked any. For instance, am I to tell her you're alive and I've spoken to you?'

'I doubt if she cares one way or the other.'

I hoped, and dreaded, that he would mention Dorcas who, if she had loved me, would have been my favourite. As Lady Arnisdale she would move in aristocratic circles where he would be as much out of place as I, though for different reasons. Still, she was his sister and perhaps they kept in touch.

'I've made an awful mess of this, haven't I?' he cried. 'You weren't prepared. But I was afraid that if I let you know I was coming you would have gone away again.'

By this time I had begun pushing him towards the door.

'It's not right you should be living in a hovel like this,' he said, 'and the rest of us so comfortable.'

He made it sound like an accusation, and perhaps that was how he partly intended it. If he had despised possessions and prestige and reputation as I had he might have been a better painter.

'After Pennvalla, this must be purgatory.'

'Pennvalla was a long time ago.'

'*I never knew you.*' *Again he made it sound like an accusation, but this time perhaps both of us were being accused.*

'*Nor I you,*' *I said.*

'*Surely it can't be too late?*'

But of course it could. As my grandfather and my mother had found out.

After I had shut the door on him I stood behind it knowing that I had been wrong to reject him, as my grandfather had been wrong to reject my mother; but like my grandfather I did not open the door and shout the forgiving words.

There must have been many moments, with his face against a closed door, as mine was now, when my grandfather had seen himself, not as one of the elect, but as one of those cast into outer darkness.

NINE

How happy those ten years in East Gerinish were, how sad their ending; and how meritorious our labours, though unavailing.

It would take too long, and involve too great an expense of feeling, to describe those thousands of often weary, monotonous, comfortless, frustrating, rain-sodden, and tempest-tossed days, which nevertheless were so inspiring and fulfilling.

There was the Saturday five years after my arrival in East Gerinish when Kirstie came home with a telegram in her pocket.

Though in August with the sky blue it was again a day of strong wind. It came louping off the sea and dealt mighty blows. Heather, grass, bog myrtle, and our hard-won corn flew like legions of terrified creatures towards the hills and away from those mad giants out in the Minch, whose spits flew faster and further than seagulls.

Against my advice Kirstie set out to Cullipool for tobacco. We kept bicycles in a hut at the road-end, but she had to walk two miles to get there, and besides, even on calm days, she was the shakiest of cyclists.

I could have forbidden her to go and she would have obeyed. After all, not being able to obtain good cigars, I had myself given up smoking. But she would have been woe-begone and restless, and would have smoked dried

nettle leaves with an abominable smell. At that time too
our cow was pregnant, and Kirstie was moodily jealous. I
would come upon her in the byre with her brow against its
swollen side, murmuring to it in Gaelic. I had to be more
patient than usual in explaining how a child would not add
to our happiness, but would destroy it.

I might have gone with her if I hadn't sprained my leg
the day before digging peats. I rather liked appearing with
her in the public bar of the Cullipool Inn, cudgelling with
my eye anyone who dared to snigger at her. To be fair to
the locals, though, they all showed her respect, though they
never really took to me.

She had promised to be home by seven. So at six I set
off at a slow hirple, leaning on a stick, to meet her. Laddie,
our collie that had taken the place of Djilas long deceased,
accompanied me. The sight of her in the distance walking
sturdily towards me in that vast solitude was always a joy
and comfort.

She had offered to bring me a newspaper. Sometimes
I felt guilty because I didn't know or care about what
was happening in the outside world. But I didn't think
there would be any newspapers in the islands that day.
The 'Lochinvar' wouldn't have left the mainland.

I was approaching the posting-box on the stob, very
quietly, so as not to disturb the hawk perched on it, when
I caught sight of her still a long way off, walking slowly,
and carrying something on her back.

She had said once that she could think better when she
was carrying something heavy, but not too heavy, as her
body was steadier then and her mind clearer. Whatever
those brighter thoughts of her were I was never told. Only
to Ailie and Hector did she tell them, in Gaelic. With
me, and with Mairi and Dugald too, she was as shy as a
five-year-old child which has drawn pictures at school and
is afraid to show them at home lest they be misunderstood
and laughed at.

She was staggering a bit, because of the wind buffeting
her bicycle, for it was this she was carrying.

I was glad to sit on a bank under the hovering hawk and
wait for her to come up to me. Laddie raced to meet her.

'Why on earth are you carrying your bicycle, my dear?'
I cried.

As she set it down she stared at it in puzzlement, as if she hadn't been aware that she was carrying it. She set it down too with absurd carefulness, as if it was a boxful of eggs, or a baby. I had seldom seen her look so mournful.

'It's got a puncture,' she said.

'But it could have been mended at the road-end.'

She took from her jacket pocket the buff envelope of a telegram. It looked as if it had had bloodstains which had been wiped off. This was nothing unusual. The post-office at Cullipool was also a general store that sold butcher-meat.

As she waited for me to read the telegram she picked up Laddie and, somewhat to his alarm, hugged and kissed him.

The telegram was from Sammy Lamont. It said that his father had died on Friday morning at 10.30. It must have arrived yesterday at the post-office, but Mr McFarlane, the postmaster there, would have thought that there was no point in putting the living to unnecessary trouble for the sake of the dead.

Kirstie did not ask what the telegram was about. She might hours or weeks later, or she might never ask at all.

Grief and shame caused me to be a little sharp with her. When she made to lift the bicycle again, like an ant replacing its load, I told her not to be foolish and to leave it lying in the heather; no one would steal it.

'I want to carry it,' she said.

There was no use arguing with her in that mood.

'Please yourself, my dear.'

To feel self-pity in her presence was always difficult: she herself endured so nobly.

'If we had a child,' she said, after we had gone about quarter of a mile in silence, 'I would not wear trousers.'

She often made remarks like that. Reply was impossible. But thinking of John Lamont dead I sighed.

She thought that I was in pain with my leg, and offered to carry me instead of the bicycle. She meant it too. I declined.

'If we had a child,' she said, after another quarter of a mile, 'I would throw away my pipe.'

The funeral would be held in Gantock. I could not go

back there, not for a long time yet. In any case the telegram had contained no invitation.

'If I had a child,' said Kirstie, when we were within sight of our house, 'I would feel like a woman.'

'He would grow up and break your heart, Kirstie.'

'It would be a little girl, like Ailie, but with red hair like yours.'

'She would be ashamed of you.'

'When I was an old woman she would look after me.'

'She would go away and leave you to starve.'

As a conversation it was futile: she in her innocence expected from a child love and lifelong loyalty, I in my guilt only dislike and betrayal.

She knew that I was married. I had asked her never to speir about my wife and children. Unique among women, she had never speired.

I did not attend John Lamont's funeral. Nor did I send any black-edged note of condolence.

TEN

One of the few letters I received in East Gerinish was from Mary Holmscroft. It came from Barcelona, where she had gone to lend support to the Republicans.

It was brought to me by Hector and Ailie on their way home from school. Every weekday morning the school bus picked them up at the road-end at half-past eight, and set them down again there at half-past four. In winter therefore their long walks to and from the road-end had to be done in thickening darkness. Sometimes one of us adults accompanied them in the morning, and went part of the way to meet them in the afternoon. After Hector was nine he decided that they did not need an escort. He lit and carried his own hurricane lamp. His mother, with daily apprehensions, had to let him have his way. The alternative would have been to board them out during the week with some crofter near the school at Cullipool, but this neither she nor they wanted. The education authorities were not sympathetic. In their view East Gerinish was no longer a fit place in which to bring up children.

These then were the weary, indomitable, and rosy-faced bringers of Mary's letter. Hector proudly pointed out the

foreign stamp. I recognised the handwriting, but I did not
open the envelope until they were gone with Kirstie. Either
she or I always went with them that last half mile to their
house on the sea's edge. Poor Ailie was always glad of a
carry then.

I mused about Mary for a minute or two. In its early days
I had tried to keep myself informed about her Parliamentary
career. It had been, alas, too predictable. She had made
a name for herself as the most rabid of the Clydeside
revolutionaries. The theme of her every speech was always
the same: the immorality of a society in which the rich had
more than they needed and the poor less. Since that was
the criticism that wounded them most the Christians among
her Conservative opponents, and they all called themselves
Christians, abused and derided her at every opportunity.
When she claimed that there could be no honest laws of
property in a society where a few owned a great deal and
many owned very little, she was yelled at as an instigator to
theft and pillage. Once in the House of Commons she had
read out, with all the wrong inflections, parts of my poem
'The Stairhead Lavatory', to shrieks of sarcastic merriment.
Cartoonists had taken to depicting her with a comically
humourless face and bandy legs that steadily grew bandier.
She quickly became far better known than I ever was.

Nevertheless it was fondness and not envy that I felt
as I began to read her letter. I still thought of her as a
sister.

Dear Fergus,
    You'll be wondering why I should want to write
to you of all people, in your skulking-place in the
Hebrides. It occurred to me the other day that the
war here represents the kind of conflict that has gone
on in your mind since you came under the delusion
that your grandfather was an earl. On one side are the
Republicans dedicated to do away with stairhead lavatories or their Spanish equivalents, and on the other the
Royalists determined to preserve those refinements of
body and mind which generations of ease and privilege
have brought about, and which of course the material-
istic multitudes wish to destroy out of envy and spite.
Am I being fair to you, Fergus? If I am, and these

two loyalties really have been in opposition in your
mind, and you haven't just been striking attitudes,
which side would you fight for, if you were here in
Spain?

Yesterday I watched a church being burned down
and two priests being stoned. Of course I was horrified,
but do you know what I imagined? I imagined it was
the Auld Kirk of Gantock, and whom did I see first
up the steps with the matches and the can of paraffin?
Yes, Fergus, you. 'The murderers of your mother'
you used to call the pious hypocrites who worship
there. Do you remember your own poem 'McSnob on
the Kirk Steps'? No one has ever put it better, John
Calderwood said. But we know, don't we, that our own
home-grown capitalists and exploiters have never been
as flagrantly cruel as their Spanish counterparts? Our
Cargills and Kirkhopes and Kelsos in their big villas
have been known, haven't they, to murmur a word or
two of regret that squalid places like the Vennel, and
Lomond Street, happened to exist? If you ask me if I
would like to see them run squealing like rats down
the steps of the Auld Kirk the answer is Yes, yes I
would.

Nothing in my life has given me more pleasure than
being in this great and beautiful city, and knowing
that it is at long last in the hands of those who built
it, the workers. It is the first time in history that
this has happened and my fists clench with joy to
see it.

Do not remind me that on the other side are many
workers. Do not remind me that in this war, as in
all wars, workers are killing workers. I have seen
Fascist corpses, with their hands rougher with toil
than either yours or mine. I know they should have
been my brothers, not my enemies. Yet I was glad
that they were dead, and I hope that many more of
them will be killed, for in this war there *is* a side
whose cause is good, and that side must win at all
costs.

I have met a very interesting man here, Enrique
Carbonell, a professor at the university. I was surprised, I must say, to see among his books a copy of

your Lomond Street poems. He said something that I am having a hard job trying to believe, though John Calderwood has said it too. He said that in those poems you give the poor their victory, that you celebrate their refusal to be cowed by centuries of poverty and degradation. I read some of them several times, and I think I saw what he meant, but all the same, Fergus, I wonder what would happen if they were read out to the sort of people they deal with, at a closemouth say in Lomond Street? You should try it some day. After all, you do call their young 'wolves', without any irony that I can see.

I shall be returning to London soon. I can best help there. Letters from you are as rare as butterflies in winter, but if you were to write me, and miscall me as I have been miscalling you, I would be very pleased. I still remember, you see, those penny pea-brees in Pacitti's in Morton Street.

When Kirstie returned I read this letter out to her while she was preparing our supper. In her place other women would have been jealous and aggressively inquisitive. All she said was: 'I saw a butterfly in the winter-time once.'

As we supped our broth, ate our salty beef, potatoes and turnips, and drank our sour milk, all of it home-produced, I held forth on a subject that I had brooded over often out on the Minch fishing or on the hill digging or in the byre milking cows or on the moor cutting peats, to the disgust of Dugald who liked his workmates to think only of fish, drains, milk, or peats.

It seemed to me that since Scotland was small, proud, poor, and intelligent, with a long history, she, better than any country I could think of, certainly better than backward Spain or class-ridden England, had an opportunity to create a society in which poverty and all its humiliations had been abolished, without refinement and spirituality being sacrificed. It would be a help that the Scots had never regarded themselves as particularly refined or spiritual.

'Would you like more soup?' was all that Kirstie said.

In the Scotland of my dreams her kind would be needed too. In the past the Scots had lost too many battles because, while waiting for the fighting to begin, they had been given prayers instead of second helpings.

I did not reply to Mary's letter: not even after the war was ended, with victory going to the Fascists.

ELEVEN

One warm sunny afternoon in September we were working at the hay, in the high field at the edge of the sea. Mown hay made Hector, then aged ten, sneeze incontrollably, so it was his job to fetch us water from a spring and sprinkle oatmeal in it. In his sister's opinion he ought also to have been guarding her against clegs, but he preferred to scan the sea like Columbus, through his toy telescope. Following my example, he wore a kilt.

It was he who first saw the big white yacht coming round the headland.

He let out a whoop and waved his pirate's cutlass, a flag leaf.

We all stopped to look, except Dugald who, with a scythe in his hands, went non-stop like Father Time.

To our surprise, instead of steaming on past, making for Lochboisdale or Castlebay, the yacht turned into our bay and anchored, still well out, for the shore was rocky, but close enough for us to make out on the deck people gazing through binoculars in our direction.

Because of our efforts to keep East Gerinish alive we had attracted some attention. One or two pessimistic agriculturists had come to inspect what we were up to. In summer a few tourists or holiday-makers not afraid of a long walk had ventured in to have a look.

It was hardly likely we had ever been heard of by the owners of so princely a yacht.

Even Dugald turned to look when Hector shouted that a boat was being lowered and two men and two women were climbing down into it. In the clear air we could hear their laughter, mixed with the singing of larks and piping of oyster-catchers.

Mairi tucked her blouse inside her skirt, and adjusted the white hankie over her hair. The least vain of women, she was still not going to look too much like a peasant.

Kirstie wore a man's singlet that revealed her fine breasts but also the sweaty hair under her oxters. Her trousers were held up by galluses, and her hair was covered by the usual cap.

'Friends of yours, do you think, Fergus?' asked Mairi, coming up to me.

She knew I was of aristocratic origin. She knew that I had been an officer in the War and had won the MC. She knew who my wife was. I had told her because I had needed someone to help me keep my secrets.

'They might be, Mairi,' I replied.

Perhaps Grizel Mutt-Simpson had given up being a conquistador and was now a buccaneer. More likely, this grand yacht belonged to Betty's latest and richest paramour. If so, she would be one of the ladies now being ferried ashore.

'Kirstie,' I cried. 'Go home and wash and put on a dress. Would you go and help her, Mairi?'

Like every other woman I had ever met, Mairi was an admirer of Betty's. She was convinced that I must have been the cause of our estrangement. A quietly fanatical believer in marriage as a necessary and sensible institution, she would have rejoiced if Betty and I had been reconciled, even if it meant poor Kirstie's heart being broken, and the end of East Gerinish.

'Come on, Kirstie,' she said, rather tartly. 'Let's go and make ourselves presentable.'

With his green sword at the ready Hector had gone down to the jetty, as if to defend it against these invaders. Ailie, fascinated by this opportunity to see richly dressed ladies, raced after him, slapping her legs to knock off clegs. Fair-skinned, she was their favourite victim.

Dugald wiped his face with a towel. He reeked of sweat. So did I. Luckily, the scent of hay and meadow-sweet was stronger.

I felt tempted to make for the hill and hide there till our visitors, whoever they were, had gone.

The boat reached the jetty. Hector stood his ground, but Ailie hid behind a rock.

The ladies were helped out. They laughed gaily. They put up white parasols. They spoke to Hector. One would have patted his head if he hadn't stepped back. We heard the refined voices but could not make out the words.

None of them was Betty, thank God. Nor Dorcas. Nor Grizel.

Dugald's thoughts were simpler. 'Now where would any man get the money to buy a boat like that?' he murmured.

He was not envious, but he couldn't help being struck by the contrast between the paltry rewards his own Herculean efforts had brought him, and the great wealth of the man who owned that splendid yacht, without having so much as hammered a nail into it. Dugald and his kind have always been the despair of revolutionaries. They are well aware of the enormous injustices of society, but these, they believe, are caused by a combination of luck and base human nature, and so are irremediable.

Hector came puffing up to us, red-faced and excited.

'They're looking for you, Fergus,' he shouted. 'They asked me if this was where you lived. I said it was. They gave Ailie a brooch.'

'Did they say who they are?' I asked.

'One of the men said his name was Donaldson. He said you knew him.'

They were now out of sight on the path below that led up from the shore. I could not therefore see yet the knock-knee'd gait, or the shine of the domed bald head. Nor could I hear the deep self-satisfied voice showing off his knowledge of the sea-shore flora and fauna. Much of it would be spurious.

Though I had made no effort to keep in touch with what was happening in the literary world I knew that year after year, like a cow calving, he had been turning out best-selling novels, two or three of which had been made into popular films. As a consequence he was well-known and well-off.

Long ago, in a pub in Edinburgh, after the literary success and financial failure of his two earliest novels, he had declared, with passion, that if the great British public, and the greater American public, wanted trash dressed up in pretty ribbons and were prepared to pay for it, then by God that was what he was going to give them. Campbell Aird had pointed out that lucrative trash could only be produced if the producer was convinced that it was not trash at all but powerful and exciting stuff, as good as Shakespeare's, better even, for it lacked the dull and contorted bits that made *Hamlet* and *Lear* such hard going. Trash, if it was going to be bought and enjoyed by trash-lovers, had to be genuine and not artfully synthetic. Its author had to have his whole heart and soul in it.

(There was only one exception, Campbell had added: this was Betty T. Shields. She knew that the honey she was purveying was really kach, but then her powers of transmutation were unique.)

It had been by demonstrating how essentially commonplace and shallow his heart and soul really were that Alisdair had won his reputation and fortune. He had also been awarded a CBE for his services to literature.

'This Donaldson,' asked Dugald, 'does he really know you?'

'He used to.'

'Is the yacht his?'

That wasn't likely. Alisdair had married the youngest daughter of Lord Fountainbridge, the Edinburgh beer baron. Remunerative though literary trash was, beer was much more so.

They were in sight again. A stile in a drystone dyke presented an obstacle that caused laughter. Dugald looked away when one of the ladies lifted her skirts and climbed over, waving away help offered by the two men.

The other woman, who seemed older, would not have got over at all without help. Nor, indeed, would the other man, who, even from a distance, looked fat and unathletic. Donaldson, in his characteristic way, tried to show off by vaulting over nimbly, and banged his leg against the sharp stone. Or so I deduced from the way he crouched in pain, holding his knee.

His companions were more amused than concerned. I suspected they had all wined copiously at lunch.

Inhospitably I felt sorry that there had been two weeks of sunshine, with the result that the track along which they were now ambling (in Donaldson's case limping) was not muddy. Still, there were hard ruts, likely to be sore on feet elegantly shod.

A long way behind came two members of the crew carrying picnic baskets.

The lady who had lifted her skirts was now chasing butterflies. Her playfulness made all the more noticeable the somewhat assertive dignity of her companions. Donaldson himself, in spite of his sore knee, was the most pompous of the lot. Look at me, his every limping step said, I am the famous and wealthy novelist about to greet the obscure and penniless poet.

Our two dogs had scampered to fawn on the visitors, who patted their heads.

In the distance, across the vista of purple heather, Mairi and Kirstie could be seen returning. Kirstie seemed to have on a white dress.

'Bless my soul, Fergus,' cried Donaldson, when he was still some thirty yards away, 'I would never have recognised you. You look so magnificently rustic.'

Usually a man wearing a kilt is at an advantage over any other man wearing trousers, but, alas, the one I was wearing I had worked in for years and its original tartan was overlaid by another that consisted of the stains of peat, sharn, dung, ink, fish, tar, kelp, blaeberry juice, and several other local substances.

'How do you do, Alisdair?' I said, calmly.

'In Lochmaddy, Fergus, we were bombarded with tales of how you and your intrepid companions have so doughtily reclaimed the wilderness. So we thought it would be unforgivable if we didn't drop in and offer our congratulations. I would like you to meet Lady Margaret Whitehope, her sister Lady Cynthia, my wife, and Sir James Whitehope, my brother-in-law.'

His wife was the skirt-lifter and butterfly chaser. She looked at least twenty years younger than he.

She came up to me, softly clapping her hands. 'Mr Corse-Lamont,' she cried cheerfully, 'we were told that your helpmeet—is that a suitable term?—is a most remarkable woman called Kirstie McDonald.'

Her sister and Sir James were indulgently amused by her amusement.

Donaldson was proud of his young wife's high spirits. 'Indeed yes, Fergus, we have heard tales of this extraordinary Kirstie of yours. Where is she? I hope you are not going to hide her away from us.'

'Didn't we see her from the yacht,' cried his wife, 'her and another woman?'

'That other woman, the one without the cap,' said Dugald, 'was my wife, Mairi. She and Kirstie went off to make themselves presentable. It is a way women have, you know.'

They all found that grave remark of his: 'It is a way women have, you know' very funny.

Evidently they had discussed Kirstie, my freak of a mistress, as they thought. No doubt they had discussed me too. Being insiders, they knew that as the husband of Betty T. Shields I had the distinction of having been cuckolded by a woman whose advocacy of chastity and virtue had made her famous and rich. They knew too that I had children who had rejected me. They knew that I claimed to be a Corse of Darndaff. Their view of me must be that I was a clown, for whom a fit mate was a half-witted woman who wore men's clothes and smoked a pipe.

Seen at close quarters, Lady Cynthia looked immature. She had a childish habit, whenever she thought she had said something witty, or whenever she made a comic face, of looking round to make sure that everyone was appreciating it. If she had been born in Lomond Street, she would have been told at any closemouth: 'For Christ's sake, Cynthie, grow up.' As it was, born in Fountainbridge House, the youngest of the family, she had been encouraged to remain a pampered child far too long. The result was this immaturity which would last all her life. She was not really pretty, either; her hair particularly, compared with Kirstie's, was short, drab, and lustreless.

'Let's have our picnic,' she cried, and instructed the two sailors how to spread out the cloth and set out the eatables. There were bottles of wine.

'You and your friend will join us, won't you, Mr Corse-Lamont?' she said.

'I'm not one for picnics in the middle of my work,' said Dugald, gravely.

They thought that remark, too, very funny.

Lady Cynthia handed Hector a sandwich so thin that he couldn't hold it in his fingers as he usually did with a piece; he had to let it lie in his palm. When he sniffed it, politely, he couldn't help making a face. Whatever expensive pâté was spread on it wasn't to his liking. He would have preferred his mother's home-made bramble jelly any day.

Ailie, though, was determined to be as well-bred and dainty as these perfumed and richly-dressed ladies from the big yacht. She nibbled at her sandwich as a vole might at a stalk of corn.

She was wearing the brooch they had given her. It was really a white button with the yacht's name, 'Alexandra', on it in gold letters.

'We must wait, Cynthia,' said Lady Margaret, 'for the ladies.'

Mairi and Kirstie were at the moment out of sight. No doubt they were taking their time so as not to arrive flushed and sweaty again. Mairi too would be giving Kirstie advice on how to conduct herself.

'Been writing any more poetry?' asked Donaldson, not really interested.

'Some.'

'I've just had word that my latest, *Sweet Smell of Clover*, has been bought by the film people. The money will come in handy. Cynthia and I are in the process of buying a house in the South of France. Both of us like sunshine.'

'What's happened to your Scottish Nationalism?'

'An aberration of enthusiastic youth, Fergus. Let's whisper it: we Scots need the English, bless them, a lot more than they need us.'

Those last few words were stuttered out slowly, as if he'd suddenly been paralysed. So he had been, by astonishment.

I turned my head. Kirstie and Mairi had appeared. He was staring at Kirstie. So were they all, and they were all astonished. So was I.

I had stupidly forgotten. I had been like a careless whist-player who has not noticed he had the ace of trumps in his hand.

In a loose white dress, with a white rose in her flowing hair, and with sandals on her bronzed feet, Kirstie could hardly have been more simply dressed, or more beautiful. Dark with the sun, her face, which I had sometimes thought too long and melancholy, was like that of a Celtic princess of legend, with eyes milk-wort blue and lips red as rose hips. Even I who had seen her naked many times gasped at the loveliness of her strong bronzed

arms and feet. In her speech, and in her every move-
ment, there was a strong simple grace that had us all
enchanted.

Hector and Ailie were uneasy too. They had seen this
Celtic princess before. They were afraid that one day she
would replace for ever the Kirstie of the cloth cap and
Wellingtons whom they knew so much better and loved.

The two ladies tried at first to look on her as a peasant
woman who had turned out to be rather handsomer than
they had been led to believe; but their amused amazement
soon gave way, in Lady Cynthia's case, to dismayed admiration, and in Lady Margaret's to grim-faced determination
not to admire too much.

The look of delight on Sir James's big purple face took
me back to my boyhood ploy of fishing for treasure with
lumps of clay. Thus might one of us have looked if he had
brought up a penny and found it was half-a-crown.

Donaldson himself reminded me of a cow with its horns
fankled in a gate. He must have been exercising his wit on
the subject of Kirstie, wearer of men's clothes and smoker
of a pipe. Now on the subject of Kirstie, sister of Deirdre,
he wanted to be gallant and parade his florid prose in her
praise, but he could not, jealousy had a stranglehold on
him. His titled wife, the success of his books, his money
in the bank, his house in the South of France, and his
CBE, all were outshone by my being loved by so superb
a woman.

It was no good his trying, an hour or so later, as he
was about to step into the boat, to spoil my triumph
by mentioning my daughter Dorcas, then eighteen years
of age.

'I suppose you know she got engaged recently to young
Jack Pilrig, Lord Arnisdale's heir?'

'Yes,' I lied.

His wife peevishly called to him to hurry. She had a
headache, she said.

At no time would she give him the lusty connubial
joy that he was so fond of describing, with polysyllabic
vagueness, in his novels. Tonight all he would get would be
sniffles of complaint for having exposed her to comparison
with the most beautiful woman both of them had ever
seen.

As the boat headed for the yacht I stood on top of the cliff, like a Viking chief, hand-in-hand with my Celtic princess.

TWELVE

It would be foolishly immodest of me to pretend that the letter from Mr Paul Levanne of New York which found its way to me, and the subsequent printing of twenty of my Hebridean poems in his magazine, *Atlantic Review*, were not events of note; but they happened at a time when something of greater importance was affecting our little community. Mairi, hitherto staunchest of us all, was passing through a crisis of lost confidence and weakened will. One of her sulkiest gibes then was that our struggles seemed to have only one purpose so far as I was concerned. Bitterly she would protest that neither she nor her children were going to waste their lives in a useless wilderness so that I could write sad poems or that Dugald her husband could grow warty potatoes.

Yet it was those poems of mine that helped to lift her out of her depression. She admitted it herself.

In our lonely lives there was a consoling beauty that made the harshnesses and inadequacies worthwhile; and it was in my poems.

All the same there were times, particularly in winter, when I felt despondent myself. The persistent damp made me rheumaticky. Often I could not lift a peat off the stack, far less hold a pen, so stiff and sore were my fingers. But there were many more times, even in winter, when, in spite of pain and weariness, I felt happy.

Coming home, day after day, with Kirstie, to our house where the peat fire needed only blowing to come to life again, was a joy that never turned stale. We came home from the sea, from the hill, from the moor, from the fields, from rare visits to Cullipool and rarer visits to Lochmaddy; and always, whether in the sweet clear air of summer evenings or in the chilly damp dusk of winter, the sight of our house lifted the weariness from our shoulders and the doubts from our hearts.

It was not simply a coming home: it was a renewal of faith in our love for each other, and in our hearth as the place where that love was most joyfully expressed.

On Sundays I would go with Kirstie, whatever the weather, to the kirk and stand there by her side, often with the rain pouring down on us through the broken roof, while she prayed or sang a hymn in Gaelic. Those pilgrimages to the deserted church meant a great deal to her, but for me it was always the return home that was the holier journey.

THIRTEEN

One Saturday afternoon, in the first June of the Second World War, I was seated in the small walled garden that Kirstie and I had made, working at a poem in the rose-scented sunshine, when I heard, some way off, Ailie, then ten, shouting tragically to her brother, who was thirteen: 'Wait for me, Hector, oh wait for me.'

About two hours earlier they had gone off with Kirstie to take a look at some cattle we had grazing in a green field near the Seal Rocks.

Unexpectedly here was Hector back, panting, and unwilling to come into the garden although he knew he had as much right to be in it as the bees. He stood looking at me over the dyke.

'Why, what's the matter?' I asked. 'Have the Germans landed?'

Since the British Army's retreat from Dunkirk some weeks before he had been on the look-out for spies and invaders.

He scowled and shook his head. I understood that I was not to joke about the War.

Then Ailie arrived, her face as red as her skirt. She was panting too, but where her brother looked huffish and angry she looked tragic and frightened.

She came right into the garden and stood beside me, getting her breath back.

'You said you'd stay,' muttered Hector.

'I couldn't, Hector. I couldn't. I was frightened.' Suddenly she was weeping.

'Don't cry,' he shouted. 'What's the good of crying?'

He threw a stone at some finches marauding in our blackcurrants. I was astonished. Usually he was the first to argue that the birds deserved their share.

'What's the matter?' I asked.

Like most brothers and sisters they sometimes fell out.

'It's Kirstie,' sobbed Ailie.

'She's ill or something,' shouted Hector, unnecessarily loud.

I smiled. When she had gone off with them Kirstie had been as rosy-cheeked and vigorous as ever.

'Kirstie's never ill,' I said.

They both stared at me, Ailie sadly and Hector, it seemed, impatiently.

'Sometimes she is, Fergus,' whispered Ailie. 'Sometimes she's in pain. She always said she didn't want you to know.'

'But this is worse,' muttered Hector. 'She couldn't get up.'

Even then I was not alarmed. Living so much alone, these children had become over-imaginative. I had seen them not only speaking to stones but also hearing the stones' answers.

'Where is she?' I asked.

'On a rock down by the shore,' said Ailie.

'Near Seal Rocks,' added Hector.

'She wouldn't speak to us, Fergus,' whispered Ailie. 'I think you should go and see.'

'But Kirstie's like that, isn't she?' I said. 'She doesn't have to speak to keep you company. You two know that.'

Ailie put her mouth close to my ear: 'Hector doesn't want to say it, but he thinks she's dead.'

Hector heard. 'Well, she's very funny anyway.'

Still I was not alarmed. Of course Kirstie was funny, in many different ways. It was what made her so delectable.

'She can't be dead,' whispered Ailie. 'Can she?'

'Why wouldn't you go near her then?' cried her brother. 'I did. I went so near I could have touched her. She wasn't breathing.'

'But you said her eyes were open.'

'Yes, but they weren't seeing anything.'

'Well,' I said, 'I suppose I'd better go and see what it is you're talking about.'

'Good,' sighed Ailie.

Hector was still scowling. He shook his head.

'He thinks you should take a cart or something to carry her in,' whispered Ailie, 'but he doesn't like to say it.'

'I wouldn't think there's any need for that,' I said. 'She's just fallen asleep. Sometimes she sleeps with her eyes open.'

So sure was I that Kirstie, immortal Kirstie, was just sleeping that as I led the way along the path over the moor towards the sea I wasn't thinking only of her but also of the disaster that had so recently befallen my old regiment, the Perthshires, a whole battalion of whom had had to surrender to the Germans.

I was thinking too of my own moral stance in relation to the War. It seemed to me that my duty as a poet was not to take part in the destruction and defeat of the present enemy, but rather by exerting all my imagination and compassion to see hope for humanity, when the War was over and the slaughter of millions was ended.

I would catch another glimpse of that difficult hope when I came to the shore and saw Kirstie safely asleep.

The children were unusually silent. They did not race on ahead as scouts and explorers. Hector kept well back. He plucked a blade of grass and holding it between his thumbs made of it a mournful whistle. Nearly forty years ago in McSherry's Wood I had cut my lip doing that.

Ailie kept close behind me. Whenever I turned she gave me a quick anxious smile.

The path down to the shore was steep and rough. I offered to help Ailie but she shook her head. It was as if it was very important to her to be independent then.

The shore was a jumble of rocks as smooth as seals. Real seals were basking on other rocks not far off-shore. There was a strong smell of seaweed rotting. A few weeks ago it had been washed up by a storm. The morbid would have thought of a battlefield of corpses, the hopeful of fertilised fields.

Ailie squeezed her nose with her fingers.

We walked over sea turf and clumps of thrift and wild irises. Some oyster-catchers rose, uttering their shrill cries.

Suddenly yonder was Kirstie, with her back to us. There was something odd about her posture. It would have been odd if she was just asleep. It would not be odd, though, if she was dead.

She *was* dead. I knew it before we reached her. She was

slumped sideways, with her head resting on her left arm. Her cap had fallen off and her beautiful black hair was loose. Her feet were bare.

Though I was sure that she was dead I called to her quietly as people do to wake someone sleeping whom they love.

Ailie was holding on to my kilt. Hector had come down on to the shore but had halted a good way off.

I sat down on the stone beside Kirstie and held her upright in my arms. Her face turned towards me with a jerk. Never had she looked more droll or lovable. Her eyes were open. I thought of milkwort, shyest of flowers.

Flies from the rotting seaweed visited our faces. Ailie and I chased them away. Kirstie did not.

'Is she really dead?' whispered Ailie.

'Yes, Ailie, I think she is.'

'How do you know? Are you sure? I haven't got a mirror. Have you?'

'No.'

'Will this do?' She handed me a small, smooth, flat, oval stone, the kind used to skiff a long the top of the sea.

I held it to Kirstie's mouth. It stayed dry. I gazed at it more intensely than I had ever looked at a stone before. It was beautiful. The sea's tongue, delicate for all its power, had given it its shape and smoothness. God knew how, millions of years ago, it had got its subtle mixture of colours.

In spite of this terrible thing that had happened I did not feel surrounded by malignant presences.

Ailie, though, was not so sure. She took the stone from me, and softly, very softly, breathed on it. It became moist. She looked awed, as if she had just performed a miracle. Then she looked round in search of other living things. As she gazed at the seals, and at some terns skimming past, and even at the flies, her expression was one of wonder, relief, kinship, and love.

I looked for Hector. He was gone.

'I told him to go and get Mum and Dad,' she said.

'I didn't hear you.'

'No. I waved.'

So far she had not dared to touch Kirstie. Now she stepped forward boldly and took her hand.

'Oh Kirstie,' she sighed, weeping quietly.

If I closed my eyes I might have imagined that it was just another of the sea's many noises. There was no resentment against anyone or anything in her weeping. She suffered but she accepted. So had Kirstie. What secrets had they told each other in Gaelic?

Further along the shore a flock of curlews waded in the water. They uttered their haunting melancholy cries. Kirstie had often gone walking in the rain. 'To hear the curlews,' she had said, though she had used their Gaelic name, Guilbneachan.

More and more I was realising what I had lost.

Minutes passed. Neither Ailie nor I spoke. We were as quiet as Kirstie herself. We heard seals grunting.

'Mum said,' whispered Ailie, 'that if one of you went away the rest would have to go too.'

Each one of us being a pillar supporting the house.

'Well, Kirstie's gone away, hasn't she?'

'She has, Ailie.'

'So will you go away yourself, Fergus?'

'I don't know, Ailie.'

'I think we'll go to my grandfather's farm at Inverness. Dad doesn't want to, but he'll have to now, I think.'

'Will you be glad to go, Ailie?'

She took time before answering. She was determined to give as honest an answer as she could.

'Well, I'd like other girls to play with sometimes. Hector's all right. I suppose he does his best, but he's a boy. Besides, he's got to go to secondary school after the holidays. That means he can't stay at home. So will I, in two years. Yes, I think I'll be glad to go, Fergus.'

'But you'll be sorry too?'

'Oh goodness, terribly sorry. I'll be sorry all my life. Will you, Fergus?'

'Yes, Ailie, I will.'

She was beginning to get agitated. With every minute that passed Kirstie went further and further away from us.

'Are we going to wait till Mum and Dad come?' whispered Ailie. 'Shouldn't we go and meet them?'

'Would you like us to go and meet them?'

'Oh yes.'

'All right, we'll go.'

'Will we just leave Kirstie here?'

'No. We'll take her with us.'

She looked puzzled and worried. Was I going to perform a miracle more disturbing than her moist breath on the stone?

'How can we do that, Fergus?'

'I'll carry her.'

She almost smiled. You are, her kind and truthful eyes said, too thin, too old, you limp, there is grey in your hair.

'I'll not be able to help much,' she said.

'I'll take lots of rests.'

Like the widow in the ballad whiles I would gae and whiles I would sit.

'Shouldn't we put on her socks and boots?'

'Could you do that, Ailie?'

'I'll try.'

She did try too, bravely, on her knees; but the task was too much for her. I had to help.

I would have liked to carry Kirstie in my arms, like a bride over a threshold, but, in spite of all those years of digging, they were not strong enough. I had to take her on my back, with Ailie's timorous help.

I remembered that there was a kind of star so compressed that one thimbleful of it would weigh a million tons. Surely it was a similar compression, of unimaginable goodness, that caused Kirstie to be so crushingly heavy?

FOURTEEN

We did not deliberately plan, Mairi, Dugald, and I, a small private funeral: we just took it for granted that in this, as in everything else for the past ten years, we would be left to get on with it ourselves. With us independence had long since passed from a principle into a habit.

To satisfy the law, a doctor was needed to certify death. One was summoned with great difficulty. He came next day, Sunday, grumbling at having had to walk for miles in pouring rain. He asked for a dram before he as much as glanced at Kirstie in the bed.

That Sunday was a long wet dreich sad day.

The doctor was a cheerful, white-haired old man, semi-retired. 'Must have been her heart,' he said, as he signed.

'Famous for her strength, wasn't she? Often happens. Knew a caber-tosser once. Legs like cabers. One day there he was tossing away among the best down at the Cowal Games, and two days later he was gone. Went out like that.' He snapped his fingers. 'Bonny woman too,' he added, with a last look at Kirstie. 'I didn't know that. Well, I'll let Donald McVicar the undertaker know and he'll either come out himself or more likely send somebody for like me he's a bit shaky on the pins for a brute of a walk like that.'

'There will be no need for Mr McVicar's services,' I said. 'We shall manage.'

He had been giving me some odd looks. I was dressed in my best kilt and jacket, and was wearing my MC ribbon and medal. I felt that Kirstie would have wanted me to.

'Suit yourselves,' he said, giving me the oddest look yet. 'Like everybody else Donald's always on the look-out for business, but he might not be sorry to miss this one, on the edge of the civilised world. Were you thinking of making a coffin out of driftwood?'

'Why not?' I said. 'She gathered a lot of it in her life-time.'

Mairi took me aside. 'I should have told you this before, Fergus,' she whispered. 'Kirstie mentioned once that she would like a nice coffin. I doubt if you and Dugald could make one out of driftwood that would have pleased her.'

John Lamont, expert carpenter, could have, I almost said. What I did say, humbly, was: 'I'd like her to have what she wanted.'

'She also wanted a minister to take the service at the graveside.'

'That,' interposed the doctor, cheerfully, 'might not be so easy. I doubt if there is a man of God throughout the islands willing to stand up in public and send her off into eternity with his and the Lord's blessing. I mean, she wasn't married to you, was she? I understand you've got a wife living somewhere. No business of mine, but then I'm not a man of God.'

'I've been a bit worried about that,' said Mairi.

I had forgotten that, since Kirstie had been living with me in what the ministers would call a state of adultery they would hardly think her death an occasion for forgiveness.

'Bastards,' I said, bitterly.

'Well no,' said the doctor, reasonably. 'You really can't blame them. You broke their rules. So did she. If one of them was to let a fit of pure Christianity get the better of him the Lord might be pleased, but I'm damned sure his congregation and colleagues wouldn't.'

'You'd have thought,' said Mairi, with a sigh, 'that the War would have made us all a bit more tolerant.'

The doctor poured himself another dram. 'Ah, you're presupposing, Mrs McLeod, that tolerance is in itself a good thing. Not many people really believe that. Most of us are prepared to tolerate only what we understand and approve of.'

I walked with him most of the way to the road-end where his motor-car was waiting. There was little wind, but the rain was steady. We did not speak much. Every stone on that track reminded me of Kirstie, and the doctor kept damning them for bruising his feet and making him stumble.

So Kirstie had her nice coffin, made by craftsmen in Glasgow, and delivered to us by two of McVicar's henchmen. It was of polished oak, lined with white satin, and adorned with golden-coloured tassels. In it Kirstie looked like the abbess of some great convent. She should have been lying in state in a vaulted hall, with nuns praying round her.

Young Hector refused to look at her. He would not even go into the back room where the coffin lay on our kitchen table. Nor would Laddie, our collie, which raised its head and howled at intervals of half an hour.

No one sympathised with Hector more than I, who had refused to look into my mother's coffin.

Ailie was bolder. She gazed so long that her mother had to tell her to come away.

'*Is* it Kirstie?' asked Ailie, hours afterwards.

We knew what she meant. It was hard for us who had seen her spread dung and gut fish and scratch her oxters to believe that this woman with the noble, austere face had once been our Kirstie. It was hardest for me, who had slept with her.

We had loved her, but we had not valued her as much as we should.

'Don't blame yourself, Fergus,' said Mairi, weeping in my arms.

I was weeping too. 'But we laughed at her sometimes.'

'Well, why shouldn't we? She didn't mind. I think we loved her most when we were laughing at her. Well, I did, anyway. I don't know about you and Dugald and Hector. I do know about Ailie, though.'

I left it to Dugald to try and find a willing clergyman. He did not succeed. Perhaps he might have if he had had months, but he had only three days, and they included Sunday, a day when in those parts it was not possible to buy a loaf of bread far less persuade Calvinist ministers to put pity before dogma. In any case, Dugald, his own morality Deuteronomical, could not have been a very persuasive envoy.

If nobody minded, he said, and if nobody expected too much, he would himself read a passage out of the Bible at the graveside. After all, there would only be ourselves present.

Hector offered to play on his bagpipe some of the tunes Kirstie had taught him. He wasn't a very good player yet, he admitted, but Kirstie hadn't minded his mistakes.

There was the grave to dig in the old kirkyard, where the ground was stony. Dugald and I found it hard work in the rain, requiring more skill than we had thought. He kept forgetting, and remarked more than once that if we had had Kirstie to help we'd have got it done a good deal quicker.

Hector walked up and down over the old flat gravestones, practising. He tried hard but he did make many mistakes.

Mairi and Ailie brought tea and pieces. We sat in the broken church and had a sad picnic. Still forgetful, Dugald chucked away a crust— since he was five, he muttered, he'd hated black crusts; but before we had time to rebuke him for his sacrilege an attendant gull pounced on it.

We kept assuring one another that though it would not be the most expert of funerals Kirstie wouldn't have minded.

FIFTEEN

Tuesday at three was the time fixed. The morning was damp but with gleams of sunshine. The whole countryside was fresh and sweet. There would be a lot of larksong that day.

It was the kind of morning when Kirstie, driven by some instinct, had used to play truant from work, and go walking, as far as twenty miles there and back, into the hills or along the coast, to secret places dear to her. When she had come back in the gloaming her mood had always been strange and distant. It had seemed to me that she was still trying to recover human thoughts and feelings, after having been for hours, God knew what, a seal perhaps or a curlew or a hare or a dragonfly. As a poet seeking new experience, I had myself tried often to taste life as wild creatures did, and to enjoy, even for a few seconds, a holiday from being human, but I had never got anywhere near. Kirstie, I felt sure, had passed over that boundary many times.

We had indeed not valued her as we should.

I spent the morning of the funeral at the McLeods'. We would leave for my house where the coffin lay at half-past two. It was curious how, with only ourselves to consider, we were so concerned about not being too early or too late. Keeping to a time-table, we seemed to hope, would help us to discipline our grief for a little while longer. With so few of us to attend to so much we could not afford any breakdowns just yet.

Ailie and Hector had been kept off school. They went off to gather flowers, Dugald to look at a pregnant cow. There was no urgent need for her to be looked at but Mairi urged him to go. Work, she said, was the only way by which Dugald could express his feelings. Anyone watching him examine the cow would see how much he missed Kirstie.

Sitting in the sunshine, Mairi and I talked, as she peeled the potatoes for lunch.

'I think I ought to tell you, Fergus,' she said, 'that we've made up our minds to leave East Gerinish and go to Inverness.'

'I understood Dugald was still thinking it over.'

'He thinks he is, but it's really been decided. We'll go some time before the winter. It wouldn't be fair to the children to ask them to stay here any longer, cut off from the rest of the world.'

'They've always seemed to me very happy here.'

'We've all been very happy here, Fergus. It'll break our

hearts to leave. But I've got to admit I've been feeling restless and discontented myself. I suppose the War has something to do with it. And now Kirstie's death. Anyway, my father's getting old. He'd like Dugald to help him run the farm. Dugald will have more scope there than he's ever had here. Look how hard he's worked, how hard we've all worked, and what have we got to show for it? Look at yourself. You had more money when you came here than you've got now.'

'I'm not complaining. I have your friendship and my poetry to show for it. I have memories of Kirstie.'

'When we leave what will you do? You can't stay here all by yourself.'

'I really haven't thought about it, Mairi.'

'Tell me I'm a nosy besom if you like, Fergus, but there's something I'd like to say to you.'

'Say away.'

'Is there any chance of you going back to your wife? I know you've been living with Kirstie as man and wife, and I expect a woman like Betty T. Shields would be shocked by that kind of thing, but I read a story of hers once, years and years ago, in the *People's Companion*, about a woman forgiving and taking back her man after twenty years of separation, and after he'd done lots of things far worse than anything you've done I should think. Mind you, I was never very sure just what the wicked things were that he'd done, for she didn't make them clear, being too ladylike I suppose, but they were terrible anyway, in India and other places in the Far East. I remember it brought tears to my eyes reading how she forgave him and took him back. It was so beautifully written. I was about eighteen at the time.'

I was searching in my mind for words which, without being spiteful, would indicate what a monstrous hypocrite Betty was, when we were interrupted by shouts from Hector and Ailie.

They came running towards the house, carrying armfuls of flowers.

'There are men come for the funeral,' shouted Hector. 'Lots of them.'

'They're all gathered at Fergus's house,' cried Ailie.

'Going in and out all the time,' panted Hector.

We never locked doors in East Gerinish.

'All right,' said Mairi to her children. 'Get your breath back. What do you mean by "lots"? Five? Ten?'

'Oh, more than that, Mum,' cried Ailie. 'Thirty at least.'

'Thirty? Don't be daft.'

'We counted them,' said Hector.

'Well. Did you notice any women among them?'

'No. All men. Dressed in black, and wearing hats.'

Mairi stared at me. 'Well, she *was* well-known,' she said, weakly.

I wasn't sure myself whether to be angry at the presumption of gatecrashers or moved by the decency of simple folk who had not needed an invitation to come and honour a dead isleswoman.

'I hope they don't expect us to feed them,' said Mairi.

'I don't think they'll be interested in food.'

'There's that.'

In those parts it was the custom to bring a bottle of whisky, or rum if you were odd enough to prefer rum, to a funeral. I had seen in a corner of the graveyard at Cullipool lots of empty bottles lying in the long grass like exhausted hares.

'Goodness,' said Mairi again, even more weakly.

I knew what she meant. Our quiet little funeral looked as if it might turn out to be a bacchanalian ceremony, and she didn't know whether to be pleased or horrified.

I didn't know myself.

SIXTEEN

They had come from townships up and down the island, some as far away as twenty miles. Their coming had not been organised. They had heard that Kirstie McDonald, strongest woman in the island, and daughter of the late Malcolm McDonald, had died suddenly and was to be buried on Tuesday at three in the afternoon in the old kirkyard at East Gerinish. So that Tuesday morning, leaving their wives at home, they had put on their Sabbath blacks, thrust into their pockets bottles of whisky flat-shaped like Bibles, and then, by hired bus or decrepit car or rusty bicycle, headed for the East Gerinish road-end. There, seeing the state of the track, they had dismounted and taken to their feet. One car-load, however, who had made the mistake of broaching their bottles too soon, saw no reason why they should not motor all the way. They quickly came to a halt, with a shattered radiator. Their vehicle, abandoned as not worth the expense of retrieval, was still there couped into the heather when some months later I left East Gerinish for good.

Though no coherent discussion could have taken place on the subject, it had been agreed that in spite of my not having been married to Kirstie and therefore not being entitled to the role of grieving husband, they would nevertheless honour me as such. Therefore, when I appeared, every man there, except the one or two already incapable, took off his hat and at the door of the house shook my hand, murmuring the traditional Gaelic condolences.

To Mairi's indignation, one white-haired patriarchal old man with the reek of whisky off his breath took her aside and informed her that since she was a woman and Ailie a female child they must not take part in the procession to the kirkyard. It had been the custom for hundreds of years for females to stay at home at funerals. It made no difference at all that the dead person was herself a female. If Kirstie could have been consulted, he said, he was sure she would have wanted the old custom to be observed. There was in his opinion no need to know the reason for a custom, but his own father had once told him that females were barred because it was not in their nature to give the Lord his due at a graveside.

Dugald quickly let me know that he had changed his mind about reading from the Bible. All these men had been to dozens of funerals. They were expert judges as to a minister's performance. They would be scornful of his.

There was no question either of young Hector playing his bagpipe. Not only was he too bashful, it would also have been denounced as sacrilegious. At Hebridean funerals in those days if any man needed help to stir up the appropriate emotion in himself, either joy if he believed that the departed's soul had gone to the Lord, or sorrow if to the Devil, he was expected to use the time-honoured method of frequent swigs of usquebaugh, which after all was the water of life.

Still not sure whether to be angry at or moved by all this usurpation, I was pushed into pride of place at the head of the procession, immediately behind the coffin. So were Dugald and Hector.

The coffin was carried by relays of mourners. From the house to the kirkyard was a little under a mile. There must have been at least a dozen halts, for rests, changes of carriers, and refreshments. Hector whispered, with scorn, that Kirstie could have carried it herself without stopping once.

By the side of the track not far from the kirkyard the laird, Major Pert-Thompson was waiting, dressed in a dark suit. He had come to take part in the funeral.

He was not an ancestral laird: the estate had been bought by his father, who had made a fortune in Malaysian tin.

I had met him only three times during my ten years in East Gerinish, and each time only briefly. He was fat, with a big loose face that almost had dewlaps. He had talked to me as to an equal, though once I had had a peat-spade in my hands. Wounded in the War, he walked with a limp. Though our conversation had lasted only two or three minutes he had been several times on the point of inviting me to his mansion-house on the other side of the island.

He had mentioned that he had seen me years before at the Victory Ball in Edinburgh Castle. He knew people I knew. He hinted that I had had the reputation of being a bit eccentric. From his floppy grins it had been obvious that he thought my eccentricity had since progressed, like a disease, which was why I had given up my home Pennvalla and my famous wife, to come and live in a wet wilderness with a woman regarded locally as eccentric too.

Talking about Kirstie he turned wistful. Perhaps the story that when eighteen they had been lovers was true.

I felt no animosity towards him on that account.

The procession halted not far from where he waited. This was not in deference to him, it was simply felt that another halt was due. Some of the mourners whose crofts were on his land lifted their hats to him, those independent of him raised their bottles. All were as respectful to him as a tribe in Africa might be to a representative of another, which had bigger huts, more cattle, and more ornamental women.

He came limping along towards me.

'I say,' he said, shyly, 'do you mind if I join in? I've

known Miss McDonald, you know, since we were both ten years old.'

Dugald by this time had had many bottles pushed into his mouth along the way. He had therefore been shedding some uncharacteristically noisy tears for Kirstie, and uttering some uncharacteristically bellicose complaints about his having to leave his ancestral shore. He was in no mood to welcome a laird.

'It would have fitted you better, Mr Pert-Thompson,' he cried, 'if you had done your duty by her while she was alive. For years her thatch was falling in, many times you and your factor were told, and not a damn thing was ever done about it.'

By general agreement a funeral was no place to debate a landlord's responsibilities towards his crofting tenants. Still, there was plenty of time, the sun was shining and larks singing, no one there loved a laird and this one anyway was an incomer, the whisky was flowing, and Kirstie had never been one for demanding attention, so none bothered to chide Dugald or apologise on his behalf. Indeed, some of the most boldly inebriated congratulated him in Gaelic, a language the laird did not know. Hector, though, whispered to him to be quiet.

Simultaneously like ants, the mourners decided to move on. The coffin was picked up, empty bottles were tossed into the heather, and those with whisky still in them stowed in pockets.

Pert-Thompson walked beside me. 'Sorry about that, Corse-Lamont,' he muttered. 'I know the poor chap's badly upset. He and Kirstie were neighbours for a long time.'

'Now that Kirstie is gone,' I said, 'he is faced with the reality that East Gerinish is an economic impossibility.'

It must be remembered that, as chief mourner, I was constantly having bottles pressed on me. Those offers I could not refuse.

'It always was, you know.'

'He thinks that you, as landlord, could have helped more than you did.'

'I'm afraid the place is just a bog, a beautiful bog perhaps, but a bog just the same. By the way, I met a chap a few weeks back who was in the Perthshires with you during our War. He thought you'd gone to Australia.'

We had now followed the coffin into the kirkyard.

I noticed that the grave had been made to look more like a grave. A couple of the mourners with mud on their best boots and trousers were leaning on spades, which I did not recognise as mine: they must have brought them with them. They had a way of spitting on their hands that showed them to be professional gravediggers.

All at once the whole concourse of mourners became aware that there was no minister to take the service. So far as I could see there were no consultations. Yet a solution emerged.

Two old men approached me. The younger, who must have been at least seventy-five, I remembered as one of the passengers in Big Ian's bus the day I had come to East Gerinish. Big Ian himself was dead. This leathery old man looked as if he would outlast another two bus-drivers at least. He introduced himself as Daniel McIsaac.

'There is no minister,' he said.

'Four were asked,' I replied. 'All refused.'

Pert-Thompson was shocked. 'Did they, by Jove?' he murmured.

Old McIsaac gave him a scornful look. 'It was proper for them to refuse,' he said. 'Kirstie McDonald when all is said and done did not live in the way a Christian woman should. Also, she dressed in men's clothing, which Scriptures tell us is an abomination.'

'As a young girl,' sighed Pert-Thompson, 'she was the most beautiful I have ever seen.'

McIsaac was too old to be knocked down for his abuse of Kirstie; in any case, he had not really said it abusively. And Pert-Thompson's praise of her more than compensated.

'Hamish here has agreed to do what is necessary,' said McIsaac, introducing his companion as Hamish McKinnon. 'He used to do a lot of lay-preaching before old age weakened his wits. He'll manage fine, if somebody keeps a hold of him. He's tumbled into a grave before now.'

Mr McKinnon gave us a whisky-scented, donnered, blissful smile.

There were bound to be comic elements in a funeral service conducted by a tipsy old man of eighty who had to be held on either side, and who several times fell asleep on his feet. The singing too, led by a retired precentor, with his tuning-fork that he struck against the handle of a spade, was all in Gaelic, and excessively lugubrious. Also it consisted of not just one hymn, which would have been quite enough, but half a dozen, one of which, judging by the tune, was 'By cool Siloam's shady hills', which had for me poignant connotations. Several of the mourners, feeling drowsy, wanted to lie down in the sunshine and enjoy a snooze, but they were not allowed to, being kept upright and awake by digs in the ribs, admonitory coughs, and, in the worst cases, knees in their behinds. Pert-Thompson spent most of the time knocking off clegs that feasted on his fat neck. He was the only man there that the grey-winged bloodsuckers tormented. The accessible skin of everyone else, including me, was too tough.

I was aware of these, and other, comic aspects. Yet, at the finish, when every man there, including the laird, was taking his turn to throw a valedictory spadeful of earth on to the grave, I was in tears.

I thanked McIsaac as spokesman for the rest.

'It wasn't for you,' he replied, frankly. 'It was for Kirstie. And not just for her either. It was for her old father whom everybody liked. As for yourself, you'll be going back now to wherever it was you came from. That is what we all recommend.'

I said nothing.

An hour after the coffin had been covered they were all gone. None was left behind. Those unable to walk were cleeked by others not too steady on their own legs. Pert-Thompson, after shaking hands with me and again nearly inviting me to his house, took his leave. Dugald and Hector went too: Mairi and Ailie would be waiting for them in my house, with tea ready. I was left alone with larks and empty bottles and memories of Kirstie.

SEVENTEEN

The McLeods left East Gerinish early in October. Mairi and the children had wanted to go earlier. They saw no sense in waiting for corn to ripen if it was never going to be harvested. But they had patience with Dugald, who still on wet or dull days would go and stand in the midst of his corn, as if to comfort it, and on sunny days as if to praise it.

It was no good reminding him that there was taller, more golden corn waiting for him on the farm near Inverness. We knew that East Gerinish meant more to him than it did to the rest of us. There had always been a religious quality in his devotion to those sour acres. Whether ploughing a piece of soggy ground or mending a dyke, he had really been building his temple.

I have tried to do justice to his attitude in my unpublished poem 'Clearing a field of stones'.

Their flitting involved carrying their belongings to the road-end where a van waited to take them to Lochmaddy. About a dozen men from Cullipool walked over to help, without being asked. They were soberer and more thoughtful than at the funeral. The Gaels' songs about leaving home are sadder than those about death. They talked quietly among themselves about the likelihood of other townships falling derelict, and even about the possibility that the whole island one day would be given over to gulls, geese, and lairds.

I refrained from pointing out that East Gerinish was not yet quite derelict, since I remained. They did not take seriously my intention to stay. I overheard them agreeing among themselves that a winter on my own would either kill me or drive me away. They talked about an old man in another abandoned township who had lived by himself for over twenty years, but he was a native of the place and could subsist on whelks and dulse.

On their last journey to the road-end the McLeods stopped at my house to say goodbye. There were only three of them, Hector being already at Inverness. It was a sunny afternoon, and we talked outside.

They had only a few minutes, Dugald said, looking at his watch. A car would be waiting for them at the road-end. They would spend the night in the hotel at Lochmaddy. Tomorrow they sailed for the mainland. He would never come back.

They were dressed in their Sunday clothes. Mairi seemed more anxious about their not getting mud on their shoes than about their leaving me on my own. But I was not deceived.

We talked about the weather. Dugald, looking again at his watch, remarked that if I didn't do something about the stack of peats I had built it would let in the rain, right down to the ground. He also reminded me to be sure to milk my cow Maise regularly. He had no high opinion of me as a milker; neither had she.

Ailie promised to send me a postcard from Inverness. She was the only one crying.

Mairi looked as if she was about to say something affectionate, in acknowledgment of our friendship of over ten years; but she could not think of anything in the four minutes exactly that Dugald allowed.

Ailie kissed me on the cheek. Mairi and Dugald shook my hand. Mairi murmured that if I ever was in Inverness I was to be sure to look them up. It was obvious she didn't think I would: these inadequate farewells were forever. Dugald said something that he had said several times before during the past few weeks. With my record in the last war, and with so many high-class friends I should not find it hard during the present one to land some easy well-paid job: there were always plenty going. My hands would get soft again in no time.

Ailie whispered that when I was putting flowers on Kirstie's grave I was to put one on for her.

Then they were gone. Several times while they were still in sight Ailie and her mother turned and waved. They must have thought I looked forlorn at the door of my house, with all round me the solitudes of East Gerinish. It seemed to me they were more forlorn. They were the last true exiles. I did not count. This had never really been my home, no more than Pennvalla or Siloam Cottage or 437 Lomond Street.

Mrs McRorie is right this time. It seems I am dying. I have had a slight stroke. I should be in hospital. At least I should see a doctor. It is all this writing that has done it, she says, more truthfully than she knows. The strain of writing with necessary restraint about Kirstie's death has been too exhausting.

I will not be buried in East Gerinish. Here in Glasgow will do just as well. Kirstie will be with me until my last flicker of life; after that both of us will be nobody's business.

It may be that this manuscript will never be read by anyone but myself. If that is the case, it does not matter that in these last pages the handwriting has become well-nigh indecipherable. If I am very patient, and take six times as long as I used to, I can form clear enough sentences in my mind, provided I attempt neither passion nor subtlety, but however I strive the pen in my fingers has little force and produces only squiggles that, an hour afterwards, I can scarcely understand myself.

Part Six

ONE

When my own turn came to go, at the beginning of March,
on a dull blustery morning, there was no one, not so much
as a cow or dog or hen (all sold or given away) to say
goodbye. Carrying a smaller suitcase than the one with which
I had arrived, I set off at as steady a pace as I could,
considering how at my heels howled the demons of self-
insufficiency that had been my companions all winter.

I had already the day before said farewell to Kirstie in her
grave, but as I passed the kirkyard I had to pause, even at
the risk of letting those demons race on ahead.

As a last gesture, shaking my fist at the sky would have
been foolish. So too would have been kneeling on the stony
track, for I had only a dead woman of no conceivable
influence to pray to. In desperation therefore, I saluted,
as I had done at the Gantock War Memorial; and while
I was doing it I heard curlews advising me to go back to
Gantock, and help it endure not only the dreadful nightly
expectation but perhaps also the more dreadful reality, of
air-raids.

Then I picked up my case and went on my way.

On the red posting-box the old hawk perched. It did
not rise until I was close. I had seen it there many times.
I liked to think that we knew and respected each other.
'Goodbye,' I shouted up as it hovered over me. 'Goodbye,' it mewed down. I could see its eyes. They were not
contemptuous. It felt no goodwill towards me but it felt
no enmity either. It had its own secret life to lead, my
presence or absence made no difference. I wished it
well.

The car I had arranged to meet me at the road-end was
late. I waited stoically in the small wooden hut I had
helped to build, with small spiders falling on to my neck.
After being so long out of the world, I must on no

313

account show impatience with its inefficient, inconsiderate, and selfish ways.

The car turned up over an hour late. Instead of apologising, the elderly ill-looking driver grumbled surlily because I was not carrying a gas-mask: his own was slung round his neck in a cardboard carton. He muttered that his taxi was a public conveyance, and his boss's rule was that passengers must have their gas-masks with them.

Patiently I explained that I did not have a gas-mask. Also I pointed out that nothing was less likely than that gas bombs would be dropped on us on our way to Lochmaddy.

My courtesy and reasonableness seemed to offend him more than my gasmasklessness.

Perhaps, I thought compassionately, the poor fellow had a son serving at sea or was afraid he had cancer. The ruder he or anyone else was the more gracious I must be. This tactic, I soon discovered, when tried out on him gave me much satisfaction and strengthened my self-confidence, but somehow increased his surliness.

I quickly had it confirmed that to be calmly tolerant of the nervous ill-temper of worldlings not only gave me satisfaction and confidence, it even exhilarated me. In effect and taste it outdid the finest whisky. Was it, in humbler degree, how saints and martyrs felt?

The handyman at the hotel, who boorishly told me that it was not part of his duties to clean the shoes of those merely lunching and not staying overnight; the waitress who attended to other people before me though they had come into the dining-room at least five minutes after me; the fat greedy bore in green plus-fours in the lounge complaining about the frequency of spam for lunch and the scarcity of whisky; the three idle fellows (it amazed me how in a country at war there could be so many of them) hanging about the door of the public bar, who ignored my politest of requests that one of them might be so good as to carry my suitcase down to the pier for me; the agent there who told me with unnecessary brusqueness that there was no cabin available; and the porter, a man of sixty or so, who muttered in Gaelic (thinking I would not understand) that I was big and conceited enough to carry my own case on board, and didn't I know there was a war on, and people were supposed to carry their own luggage? all these, and others, who either paid me no heed at all or else churlishly turned their backs (in so small a place, in so short a time, there seemed an astonishing number of them) I not only forgave, if not quite instantaneously, but also sympathised with, for they had not had my opportunity to scour their souls of the inspissated moral grime that, alas, inevitably accumulates during human intercourse.

Is this forbearance of mine genuine, I kept asking myself, is this philanthropic graciousness sincere? Will they be permanent or will they soon wear off?

I examined the possibility that I was not really interested in these other people; that I was still, as in the past, interested mainly in myself. I recalled how, when I was turning the other cheek, as it were, to the fellow who had refused to clean my shoes, I had not bothered to study the effect on him of my purged and vital humanity, I had preferred to study its effect on me. I, not he, had been exhilarated.

Perhaps, though, I was being unfair to myself. It could well be that my experiences in East Gerinish, taken all together, but particularly my love for Kirstie. and hers for me, had made me, unknown to myself, a good man. During the past ten years life had not been easy. There had been very little free-wheeling. On the contrary, there had been nothing but braes. This past winter had been one of Himalayan steepness.

Surely I was entitled to accept, as a possibility at least, that I was returning to Gantock, not as the saviour I had in my magnanimous and extravagant youth dreamed I might be one day, but as a giver of courage and hope.

TWO

In the crowded, stuffy, and smelly third-class compartment—there was no other kind on that too democratic train—on the way from Glasgow to Gantock, a grey-haired, tidily dressed middle-aged woman, after eyeing me for some time, leant forward and whispered hoarsely: 'Excuse me, mister, but I'm thinking you never got that tan in this country.'

The others in the compartment, all whey-faced like her, waited sullenly for this toff in the cape, kilt, and balmoral, this brigadier in mufti, to snub her for her inquisitiveness, which they knew was well-disposed and indeed complimentary, but which I, member of an alien tribe, would consider vulgar.

'You are right, madam,' I said. 'Not in this country.'

I used the accent that I had evolved in East Gerinish: not quite landed gentry, not quite officer-and-gentleman, but not mere school-teacherishly superior either; in short, it was an attempt to make an authentic Scottish accent sound refined without at the same time sounding artificial or effeminate.

On the whole I was encouraged by its reception. Eyes blinked, eyebrows crept up like mice, noses whitened with strain, and groans were suppressed. It amounted to a judgment not immediately unfavourable. If these people, mostly from Paisley, a town with an abbey, were inclined to pay tribute, so too would be Gantockians.

'You've been in Africa or India, that's whaur,' said the grey-haired woman. 'You talk like somebody that's been a long time among blacks.'

Some of the others nodded, as if they too had been thinking the same thing.

I let it pass. I had not been lying when I had said that my tan, which was really a weather-beaten ruddiness, had not been acquired in Scotland. My companions, abhorring fresh air and calling it draughts, would have preferred the Belgian Congo, where it was as hot as in this compartment, to windy East Gerinish.

On the platform at Gantock Central I stood looking at scenes still familiar though dismal. The glass roof was painted black, and the people all looked sulky and suspicious (as notices on the walls exhorted them to be.)

The grey-haired woman approached me.

'Excuse me again,' she said, 'but do you ken whaur you're gaun? You look loast.'

'Thank you, madam,' I replied, with a smile. 'I am not lost. I was born in Gantock.'

'Aye, in the West End nae doot. That's whit I was thinking. They're a' generals that come frae there. Weel, you'll hae to walk or tak a bus. A number 9 would do. There never were ony taxis to be had here, but there are even less noo. It's the war, you see. Maybe if you were to phone Ferguson the undertaker he micht send a caur, but

I wouldnae coont on it. They say he's saving his petrol for
the hundreds o' funerals when the bombing starts.'

She hurried away, to her room and kitchen, or, if she
was one of the better-off ones, her two rooms and kitchen,
which, more likely than not, would be clean and, considering how low in the social scale she was, trimly furnished.

I was home at last.

I went into a telephone kiosk and rang up, not Ferguson the
undertaker, but John Calderwood. I did not know whether
he was alive or dead. If alive, he would be an old man of
seventy.

'Gantock 4545. John Calderwood speaking.'

I recognised his voice at once. Though he had not taught
for many years, it still had a trace of pedagogical irritable-
ness in it.

'Who is this?' he asked, sharply. 'Have you got the wrong
number?'

'It's Fergus Lamont,' I said.

'Fergus Lamont? Fergus Lamont the poet?'

Whatever he had become, I would love him. He could
have said Fergus Lamont the failed aristocrat, Fergus
Lamont the rejected husband and despised father, Fergus
Lamont the unlucky lover, Fergus Lamont the fool. But
he had said Fergus Lamont the poet.

'Yes, John, the same.'

'But I thought you were in the Hebrides. In fact, that
you had died there, some months ago. I saw something in
the newspaper about it.'

Had Betty, informed by her spies of Kirstie's death, been
sowing hints that it was I who had died?

'I assure you I'm still alive, and back in Gantock.'

'Yes, I think I recognise your voice, in spite of the accent.
How long have you been here?'

'About ten minutes. I've just come off the train.'

'I suppose you'll be staying with your relatives, the
Lamonts?'

'I don't think so. John Lamont's dead.'

'Yes, I heard. Look, why not come and stay with me?
You used to look on Ravenscraig as another home.'

Not because of him, though: because of Cathie.

'I wouldn't want to inconvenience you, or anyone else.'

'There's no one else. I live here on my own. A 9 bus will take you to the gate.'

'Thank you. I would like to pay someone a visit first.'

He appeared to laugh. 'May I ask who?'

'Someone I treated very badly.'

I did not have anyone in particular in mind. There were so many to choose from.

'What about your luggage?'

'I have only one suitcase.'

'It's raining. You'll get wet.'

'I'm used to rain. I'd like to have a look at the town, too.'

'You'll find it as much in want of grace as ever before.'

He hung up then, after that strange remark for a lifelong atheist. Had he, in his old age, undergone some bitter conversion? The Christ of the sheep and goats would suit him well.

I walked along towards Auchmountain Square. There, at the heart of the town, where once flower-beds had been, were air-raid shelters of brick, ugly as tumours. Above in the grey sky, like gigantic kidneys, floated barrage balloons, protecting the shipyards and docks. Shop windows were boarded up; so, it seemed to me, were the faces of most passers-by, with resignation. One old man, carrying his gas-mask like a schoolchild its satchel, saw me looking at him with friendly interest, and scowled. I did not blame him. At his age he deserved ease among flowers, not terror in brick tumours.

There were still one or two benches in the Square. In spite of the rain two old men were seated on one. They were talking to pigeons. One of these came and pecked at my shoe, in the myopic hope that it was a lump of bread. It reminded me of Uncle Tam, who had gone blind and was now probably dead. He was one of those I had behaved badly towards.

Still carrying my case, I went up the steps of the Auld Kirk. They did not seem so spacious now, nor were the pillars so imposing. I tried the massive door, knowing it would be locked. It *was* locked. Vandals and desecrators must be kept out, as well as those wishing to pray for private peace or public victory. These would have to wait till Sunday.

I noticed that I was being watched from the pavement by the two old men who had been seated on the bench. Evidently I was more interesting than pigeons.

'Are you selling Bibles, mister?' cried the one wearing the blue scarf.

They both wheezed with laughter at the joke.

They were as old as Uncle Tam would have been had he lived.

I descended to them.

'Tell me, gentlemen,' I said, 'did you ever know a citizen of this town called Thomas Pringle? He used to keep pigeons. I believe he went blind some years before he died.'

'If Tam Pringle's deid,' said the one wearing a green scarf, 'it must hae happened damn sudden. We were talking to him no' less than a week ago. Isn't that right, Bert?'

'We telt him he'd better get a lick o' fresh paint on his stick,' said Bert. 'Because o' the blackoot, you ken.'

This was the best of news.

'Does he still live in Kirn Street?' I asked.

'He's lived naewhere else that we can mind o'. His first wife died there.'

'Has he married again then?'

'Aboot a couple o' years back. A flat-chested woman this time.'

That was another joke. They laughed again. Tears were in their eyes. Life was bloody awful, but it was funny too.

'But she looks efter him weel.'

Suddenly they had to hurry off, towards the nearest public lavatory. The need came on, grumbled Bert, like the stab of a bayonet.

I headed for Kirn Street.

Girrs had once bounded down those steep braes like gazelles. Burdened with my suitcase, I trudged up.

At the corner of Murray Street was a little shop I remembered well. It had been the only one in the district that sold a kind of sweet I had a passion for, called Purple Aniseed Balls. Often, with mouth watering and with a penny clutched in my fist, I had opened that door, and thereby rung a bell. The shopkeeper then had been a

wizened old woman called Sadie McParlane. If you said
thanks as if you meant it she sometimes gave you a sweetie
extra.

I opened the door. A bell rang. Was it the same bell of
forty-odd years ago? For a few moments I was seven years
old again. There among the jars on the shelf was the one
containing my purple aniseed balls.

The woman behind the counter was not so old as Sadie,
and she was far from wizened. Chins propped on plump
hands, she was leaning over the counter, chatting to a
customer. She threw me a sedate glance, as if the entry into
her shop of a gentleman in a kilt was a daily occurrence.

Her customer, though, a small woman of about my own
age, gave me a stare that might have been justified had I
been stark naked.

She reminded me of someone I had once known: Alec
Munro, simpleton of Limpy's class in Kidd Street. Surely
no two families in the town could have that combination
of upjutting chin and downjutting nose. In her case the
resultant uncomeliness was exaggerated by her having left
out her false teeth; that was to say, if she had any to leave
out. Her jaws champed as if used to chewing toothlessly.

She must be one of Alec's sisters.

I asked for a quarter pound of purple aniseed balls.

Had they been my own balls, shrunken and dyed purple,
Alec's sister couldn't have gazed at them with greater fas-
cination as they went rattling into the brass pan to be
weighed.

'They mak your tongue purple,' she observed.

How well I knew that. Many times had I studied my
empurpled tongue in a mirror.

'I wonder,' I said, to the shopkeeper, that fat, placid,
and, as I mistakenly thought, humourless lady, 'if you
would be so kind as to allow me to leave my suitcase in
your shop, for an hour or so. I'm visiting some friends
higher up, and as you know it's a sair climb.'

In other places the shopkeeper would have either curtly
refused or consented, and the customer would have minded
her own business. That was never the East End of Gantock
way.

They looked at my suitcase as if it might contain the
proceeds of a bank robbery or a dismembered body.

'Whit's in it?' asked the shopkeeper. 'I'm asking, just in case you never come back to claim it. They're wild folk higher up. Aren't they, Mrs Paterson?'

Had Archie Paterson, my classmate in Kidd Street school, managed to avoid the embraces of Elsie Tweedie, only to fall into those of one of Alec Munro's sisters?

'You can see it's been a very guid case in its day,' said Mrs Paterson. 'Real leather. Wha is it you're visiting, mister? Maybe Mrs Livingstone and me can show you a short-cut.'

'The only ither time I've been asked to look efter somebody's case,' said Mrs Livingstone, 'was when an auld Indian peddler came into the shop. He was desperate to run and find a public lavatory. He looked green through his black. I would hae offered to let him use mine, but he's forbidden by his religion, isn't he, to be beholden to women, especially foreigners?'

'That hot food they eat must be bad for their insides,' said Mrs Paterson.

'Will it be all right if I leave it here in the corner?' I asked.

'I close at eight sharp, mind. But haven't you forgotten something?'

I couldn't think what she meant. I was sure it wasn't payment for the service.

'Coupons. You need sweetie coupons for sweeties.'

'Oh. I'm afraid I haven't any.'

'Noo where d'you think, Mrs Paterson, he must hae come frae no' to ken that coupons are needed?'

'Across the seas shairly.'

'Do I have to hand the sweets back then?' I asked.

'Oh, keep them. Even if it gets me the jail.'

'Thank you. Good afternoon, ladies.'

As I went out I heard Mrs Livingstone say, in her staid voice: 'I think, Mrs Paterson, we're safe in thinking nae German spy would hae the nerve to come in wearing a kilt and ask for purple aniseed balls.'

'Without coupons tae.'

How much of their laughter was satirical, at the expense of the toff in the kilt who used a body's shop as if it was the left-luggage at the station, who'd asked for sweeties without coupons, and who had tried to make them think he was Scottish because he'd said 'sair' instead of 'sore', and how much was plain and straightforward at an amusing little interlude, would have been hard to say. It always was in the East End.

More than thirty years had passed since I was last in Kirn Street. Mary Holmscroft, whose chief fault was trying to make complex things simple, had said I had given up the Pringles because I had become a snob. That was true, but there had been other reasons: aesthetic repugnance, for instance; moral anguish at seeing people I liked having to endure conditions that grew more squalid every year; and (though this was a secret Mary could not have known about) fear of Aunt Bella's celebrated breasts.

I entered by the bottom of the street, which meant I had a good hundred yards to walk to reach Uncle Tam's close. Since it was now after four the schools had skailed. Some little boys, none older than nine, caught sight of me. 'Jesus Christ,' yelled one, 'look at the fuckin' big kiltie!' In their young faces was not a trace of humour or amiability. One lifted a stone.

Some women at a closemouth were shocked. They shrieked to the boys to stop it. One, whose son was among the young savages, threatened to 'skite the erse aff him' when she got him home.

In spite of their uncivilised surroundings these women had with unconscionable effort achieved some idea of civilised conduct; but they had not yet been able to communicate it to their offspring.

Children in the West End never threw stones at strangers.

Did Mary still think that redemption was simple? Replace these dreary crowded tenements with spacious villas in streets with trees, and lo, the savagery would vanish. Challenged as to the cost and effort needed, she could point, fairly enough, to the stupendous cost and effort of this present war, so willingly and resolutely borne.

As I approached the women they gaped in amazement, but also with appreciation. They were pleased that so braw a gentleman should be walking along their street. They expected a show of fine manners.

I did not let them down.

'Thank you, ladies,' I said, doffing my balmoral and giving a little bow. 'Good afternoon.'

What could I have added that would have honoured them for their determination to be decent and civilised, however coarse their way of showing it, and however degrading the conditions they lived in? I would have had to recite to them my poem 'Wolves in the Vennel', written twenty years ago but more than ever relevant. Unfortunately, they might have misunderstood it, and instead of feeling grateful would have felt insulted.

'Good afternoon,' they chorused.

Always when Gantock women were gathered together, particularly at a closemouth, one at least was an insuppressible humorist. It was so here. She was a small woman with a grey coat and a ferrety quickness. Out of the corner of my eye I noticed her dropping a curtsey and whispering something. Her companions laughed, but in moderation. One shrieked, but the others hushed her. This street was their home: any stranger, however comic his dress, gait, or face, must be allowed to walk along it without molestation or affront. If they had known me though, how boisterous their mirth, how bawdy their proposals, and how warm their affection.

THREE

As I entered Uncle Tam's close I felt surrounded by danger. My enemies were all within me. If I did not now show more courage and less selfishness than ever in my life before I might do great harm to a blind old man who had once loved me.

On the door was the same brass name-plate, polished as bright as in Aunt Bella's day. 'Thos Pringle' it said, in the plainest of letters. Uncle Tam had whispered to me once that he would have preferred something a wee bit fancier, but Bella had reminded him that it was a room-and-kitchen he lived in, not a mansion. One of her favourite sayings had been: 'Be whit you are, and naebody can ever put you up or doon.'

She would never have approved of the doormat. Oval in shape, it was of green coir with little white and yellow daisies woven into it. Evidently the second Mrs Pringle for all her flat chest had romantic ideas. I did not think she would have the same implacable pride as her predecessor, who would have promptly told me that after staying away for more than thirty years I had forfeited any right I might once have had to be sorry for her husband.

The door opened. A surprisingly small, white-haired, sweet-faced, clean-looking, and flat-chested woman, in a blue dress and white apron, blinked at me through steel-rimmed spectacles. She had an orange cat clasped in her arms. Before I had opened my mouth she put a finger to her lips.

I could not recall any girl of my acquaintance who might have grown up into this diminutive, pleasantly dotty housewife. She must have played her peaver in some street outwith my territory.

Even with spectacles her own sight seemed weak. She stooped to peer at my sporran. Her cat was beginning to take an interest in the badger's head when she straightened up again. It miaowed, and she patted it on the nose with her finger.

'Hush, Marmalade,' she whispered. 'Maister's sleeping.'

I wondered if I had come to the right door. It was hard to think of Uncle Tam as Master. I had never heard him bossing anyone in my life. Nor had I ever known him to take a siesta.

'Is Mr Pringle all right?' I asked. 'I mean, is he keeping well?'

'He's fine. A bit lost at times, but you would expect that, wouldn't you? He and Marmalade spend maist o' their lives sleeping.'

She spoke as if she'd known me all her life. It would have been the same with Jack the Ripper. Her friendliness was instant, absolute, and universal. It was the nicest kind of daftness I had ever seen.

'I wouldn't want to disturb him,' I said.

'He's just sitting in front of the fire, you ken: no' in bed. He'll wake up when he smells the sausages frying. It's sausages we're having for tea. Drummond's sausages. I always think Drummond's are the best. Mind you, you've to queue up for them.'

'I'll come back tomorrow,' I said. 'What would be a suitable time?'

'Weel, he rises early. Up wi' the lark at six every morning, Sundays and a'. He sits and looks oot o' the windae at the river. He cannae see it, but he can mind it.'

'If I came about mid-day would that be convenient?'

'Every morning, rain or sun, he taks a walk. That's at ten.'

'Perhaps if I came then I could accompany him?'

'No, he wouldnae like that. He likes to walk by his lane.'

'What time does he usually get back from his walk?'

'Aboot eleven. He brings in a paper, you see. I read bits oot to him. Aboot the War. He likes hearing about the War.'

'I'll come about eleven then. Would you please tell him that Fergus Lamont called and will be back tomorrow at eleven?'

My name meant nothing to her. 'If I mind I'll tell him.'

'Thank you, Mrs Pringle.'

'Thank you yourself. Say goodbye to the gentleman, Marmalade.' She lifted the cat's paw and waved it.

It was far from her intention to indicate to me that my visit did not deserve to be taken seriously, but that certainly was the effect of her waving the cat's paw at me.

I felt most condignly rebuked.

Going down the stairs, I remembered that of all the creatures in the world Uncle Tam had disliked only cats. He always imagined them with their mouths full of pigeons' feathers.

That he slept so much and yet got up so early did not necessarily mean that he found life tedious or unbearable. It could be a delayed consequence of the damage to his brain. He had always been easily interested.

I could not help smiling as I pictured her reading out to him news of the War. Her thoughts would never be on the sinking of ships or the burning of cities, however sensationally these were described. She would be thinking about her cat washing its face, or about standing in a queue for Drummond's sausages.

FOUR

I had been hurrying along, thinking of Uncle Tam and his fey little wife, and not paying much attention to where I was going, when some instinct told me I had wandered into Lomond Street itself. I stopped, afraid. Alarm bells rang in my mind. I wanted to turn and flee. Then I thought to walk along it would be a test. If I felt humiliated and defeated all over again, and hated everyone I saw, it would mean that the years in East Gerinish and Kirstie's love had been wasted.

I set off on that momentous traverse. Because the rain was heavier now there were few people about. Two boys were playing with gas-masks on. A dog was barking mournfully. I had never realised before how narrow and dismal the street really was, subterranean almost, with the high stone tenements closing it in like cliffs.

The closemouths were deserted. There was too strong and chilly a wind blowing straight through them.

Old landmarks were gone. The window-sill where the Kennies had lived, a family as fanatically Orange as the Jeffries, had always been painted red, white, and blue. Now it was indistinguishable from all the other grey, sooty, undefiant window-sills.

I could see no sign of air-raid shelters. If bombs fell most people would probably congregate in their closes, with blankets and hot-water bottles; others would stay in their houses and sleep under beds or tables; others again might take to the hills above the town.

Near my own close I passed two little girls of eight or nine. They were neatly dressed, one in a red raincoat, the other in a blue, with hats to match. They spoke to each other primly and properly, as if to their schoolteacher, saying 'not' instead of 'no'. Their kind were always to be found in the meanest streets. They had mothers resolved to save them from being coarsened by the squalor in which they were obliged to live. Those women would perform prodigies of economy in order to be able to afford their daughters every chance to become better than the daughters of women not so self-sacrificing and indomitable.

A middle-aged woman, burdened with a heavy shopping-bag, and muttering to herself, approached me. If I offered to carry her bag or relieve whatever anxiety she had, she would no doubt regard me with hostility, convinced that my purpose must be either to steal her purse and ration-books, or to rape and murder her. What if, though, she smiled, thanked me, and let me carry her bag to her door, where I would take leave of her with a bow or, why not, a kiss of her hand?

In the event she didn't even notice me as we passed.

Another woman approached, also middle-aged, under an umbrella. Dressed in a blue coat with white buttons, she would have been more in place in a street of red sandstone tenements with tiled closes and inside lavatories. Perhaps she was the mother of one of the little girls.

It was ungentlemanly to stare, so I passed with a quick glance at her face. This was pale, and her mouth had an ugly twist that looked permanent, possibly the result of a stroke.

The stare she gave me was longer and more curious. This was only to be expected. It did not necessarily mean that she was bad-mannered.

I had passed, and was about to dismiss her from my mind with a measure of pity, when she called what sounded like my name, although her twisted mouth blurred her speech, reminding me a little of Mrs Sneuch-Sneuch, long since dead.

I had once been well known in that part of the street. So it was perhaps no cause for wonder that I was now being recognised, even thirty-odd years later.

She had stopped and was staring at me. The wind tugged at her umbrella.

'Excuse me if I'm wrong,' she said, 'but weren't you once Fergus Lamont, that lived in this street?'

In spite of its distortion, I recognised her voice, and also the hint of good-natured, bantering laughter in it. Thus had she once, in McSherry's Wood, when we were both seventeen, asked me if I didn't think that my hand, wandering up inside her skirt, wasn't being just a bit too common for an earl's grandson's.

For she was my old sweetheart Meg Jeffries, who had so rashly become Meg McHaffie.

As I walked back to her, slowly, my legs felt weak. After Kirstie, and Cathie Calderwood, this was the woman I had loved most. If I had married her I might not have become an officer and gentleman, and I would not have lived in a fine big house like Pennvalla, and I would never have gone to East Gerinish and met Kirstie, and perhaps I would not have written such good poetry, but I would have been happy, my children would have been fond of me, and I would not have been faced with the prospect now before me, of lifelong homelessness.

'Meg Jeffries,' I said, holding out my hand.

She gave me hers. 'Not for a long time,' she said. 'Margaret McHaffie.'

But still, marvellously, without a trace of pity for herself. Her husband had been killed, her family had disowned her, and she had been left to bring up her children alone. She must have had some serious illness, the aftermath of which was this twisted mouth and these pale cheeks. Things at present could not be all that well with her, or surely she would not have come to live here in Lomond Street, in its decrepitude. Yet she looked and sounded as unembittered as on that other rainy evening long ago when she had left Siloam Cottage, perplexed and worried, but in love.

Her presence was like a benediction. My own self-pity slunk off in shame.

'So you never married again?' I said.

I was still holding her hand.

'I had my weans to bring up.'

'How many, Meg? I hope you don't mind me calling you Meg?'

'I wouldn't expect you to call me anything else. Three. All girls.'

'Are they here with you?'

'Just Margaret. She's my youngest. The two others are married.'

For a few moments her voice trembled a little, and she tried to take back her hand. I held on to it.

'But what are you doing here, Fergus, in Lomond Street of all places?'

'I was visiting Mr Pringle in Kirn Street.'

'He went blind, didn't he? How is he?'

'I didn't see him. He was asleep. I'm coming back tomorrow.'

'Are you on leave or something? You look as if you're just back from Africa or some place anyway where there's a lot more sun. Are you a colonel by this time? I saw a picture of your wife in the paper a week or two ago: wearing some kind of uniform, and visiting soldiers in hospital. Very handsome she looked. Just the kind of woman you always said you would marry. Good for you. I noticed too that you've become a grandfather.'

So Dorcas had given birth. My suffering then was tragic, not merely querimonious, as I thought of Dorcas's child whom I would probably never see.

'Your two other girls, Meg, where are they?'

'Bridie, she's my eldest, lives in Liverpool. Her husband has a good job in a paint works there. Well, he had. He's in the Air Force now. And Eileen's in Glasgow. She married a schoolteacher. He's in the Army.'

'Good luck to them all, Meg. I hope that you and your family here in Gantock are friends again.'

'I'm afraid not, Fergus. You see, I let Bridie and Eileen marry Catholics too.'

Grandson of Donald McGilvray, I almost asked her, in indignation, why in Christ's name she had done any such thing.

The rain was still heavy. We could hear it stotting on her umbrella.

But why, if she and her family were still estranged, had she come to Gantock where she must run the risk of meeting some of them, in the street or in shops? Did she hope that out of one of those stony-faced encounters reconciliation might flower?

'It's silly standing here getting wet,' I said.

'We could go up to my house, if you liked. Margaret doesn't get home till six. For a cup of tea. It's on the top storey, though.'

But I did not want to see her in those surroundings. Also, to be truthful, I was beginning to find the paleness of her face, the wryness of her mouth, the whiteness of her hair, and the impossibility of ever being able to help her, too much to bear.

So I lied. 'I'm sorry, Meg, I can't, not right now. I tell you what, though, couldn't we meet tomorrow, say, for lunch? There must be some place left in Gantock where one can buy a decent lunch, war or no war.'

'I'm working, Fergus. Part-time. I finish at four.'

'What time do you have off for lunch?'

'Half an hour. We stay in and eat pieces.'

'Well, we'll certainly have to meet again and have a long chat.'

'I'd like that, Fergus.'

'It's a promise then?'

'It's a promise.'

'Good. I'm staying at Ravenscraig with John Calderwood. His telephone number is 4545. That's easy to remember.'

'I'll remember it. Goodbye, Fergus, and good luck.'

'Good luck to you, Meg.'

I had to let go her hand at last.

FIVE

By the time I had collected my suitcase from the sweetie-shop—with much relief, for it contained some irreplaceable manuscripts—and found a 9 bus to take me to Ravenscraig, it was six o'clock. Luckily the rain was not so heavy and the sky looked brighter. Because of the blackout no lights could be seen in houses or shops. In Pennvalla there would have been still an hour to go before going upstairs to dress for dinner. Here, in Gantock, even in most of the villas, it was already tea-time, with people sitting down, in the same clothes that they had worn to work, to eat high teas that, in these restricted days, would not be quite so high; but there would still be potfuls of sociable tea. The meal would be eaten in a room where there was a fire, in most cases the kitchen. The warmest place would be occupied by father, who deserved it after working all day in poorly heated office or shipyard: though the children might think that the schools hadn't been too well heated either. Few graces would be said, even by families that still went to church on Sundays. But if the Lord was not thanked for food which was not as appetising as the eaters would have wished, neither would He be begged to keep the German bombers away: it being stoically understood that He had nothing to do with where Field Marshal Goering sent his murderous aeroplanes.

Such were my thoughts as I sat in the bus, in the company of other Gantockians sober-faced with similar reflections.

John Calderwood must have been watching from a

window because he had the door open before I had time
to ring the bell.

Never having known him to be an impatient watcher
or eager opener I felt for a few seconds touched and grateful.

Then dismay took over.

The man in front of me, crouched sideways, leaning on a
stick, had a face so screwed up and shrunken from habitual
malevolence as to suggest that he had lost not only the desire
to look happy and hopeful but the physical ability. He gave
me a snarl that, I saw, was his best approximation to a smile
of welcome.

Yet any of his pupils in Kidd Street school nearly thirty
years ago would have recognised him at once. Even the least
sensitive of us then had been aware that though he wanted
to love us he could not: not because of our academic shortcomings or because some of us stank through not washing
often enough, but because he had seen us developing into
eager conformists, indolent and cowardly acquiescers in the
iniquities and inequalities of society. That was why he had
been provoked into hurtful sarcasms.

As if to emphasise how grimy and threadbare his humanity was become, he was more smartly dressed than I had
ever seen him before, and not in the old semi-bohemian
intellectual's way either, but in an ultra conventional suit
of black jacket and grey-striped trousers, with a stiff collar
very loose round his shrivelled neck.

He was by no means drunk, though. Indeed, he did not
get drunk all that fateful evening, though he consumed
more than a bottleful. His misanthropic rejoicings did not
have that excuse.

He kept giving me grimaces which I had to accept as
cordial.

As I found a peg for my wet cape on the hall-stand where
Cathie's bright hats and coats had once hung I could not get
rid of a suspicion that in spite of his miserable faces he was
happier than he had ever been in his life before.

Thanking him as civilly as I could, for it was a form of
reproof, I went upstairs to the bathroom, past the window
of the landing where Ceres or Naomi still stood up to her
breasts in yellow corn. The crack that my penknife had
widened in the door was still there as I found by stooping

and peering through it, but Cathie of the French songs and dainty bottom was not there, and never would be again.

The towel I had to use to dry my hands was not fresh and it had a hole in it. The lavatory seat had a hinge loose. The whole house, I soon discovered, was shabby and dirty.

My host called to me from the lounge. When I went there I was pleased, though surprised, to find a fire roaring in the grate, and, on the same small table where once the goldfish bowl had stood, a tray with two glasses, a jugful of water, and a bottle of Chivas Regal whisky. This last particularly was a surprise. Even in Oronsay, where it was considered more necessary than food, whisky had become very scarce, and funerals therefore very gloomy.

'You'll have a dram, Fergus?' asked my host.

'With pleasure, John.'

He poured two very generous ones. 'Help yourself to water if you want any. I prefer it neat.'

As I poured the water into my glass I remembered the goldfish, and Cathie and me sprawling on the carpet. My hand shook. Some water was spilt on the table.

Behind my back my host chuckled. He was enjoying my agitation. Perhaps he was mad: fifty years of castigating the lunacies of mankind had turned his brain. Or perhaps insanity was in the Calderwood family. In him it was taking the peculiarly evil form of enjoying other people's unhappiness.

'Well, Fergus,' he said, 'after so long an absence, what would you like us to drink to?'

'To the people of Gantock,' I said, remembering that he had said they were more in need of grace than ever.

He lifted his glass and then drank.

'The best thing that could happen to our beloved native town, Fergus, is for a few bombs to fall on it.'

I was shocked. 'Rather an extraordinary thing for a past member of the Independent Labour Party to say.'

'But, Fergus, I simply want them to have an opportunity to find out the truth about themselves. Words will not do it. Words deceive. Bombs, I should think, are much more forthright. A few weeks ago, Fergus, an old woman from the East End, your part of the town, was given three months' imprisonment for using implements to procure an abortion. The other woman in the case had already got seven children, and was terrified at the thought of having another, especially in war-time. Well, his Lordship the Sheriff chose the occasion to deliver an impassioned harangue about the sanctity of human life, and this in the midst of a war which he thoroughly approves of and in which, before it is over, millions of fully-fledged lives may well have been brutally destroyed.'

I might have had some sympathy with what he had said if he had not said it so gloatingly.

'No one in Gantock seemed to be shocked by his hypocrisy,' he went on. 'No one pointed out to him that war is the greatest abortionist of all.'

'Perhaps, John, they did not think it was hypocrisy. Perhaps they believe that the war is being fought for something more important than life itself.'

'In which case, why send the old woman to jail? Evidently she considered compassion more important.'

I was beginning to suspect that he had invented this altruistic old abortionist.

The more he was enjoying himself the more malign he looked. 'I put it to you, Fergus, as a man of some insight, that it is the taking of life that is sanctified, not life itself. Is not war blessed by bishops, moderators, rabbis, mullahs, and bonzes, not to mention witch doctors?'

It amazed me that at seventy he should still have the same half-baked ideas that he had had at forty. He had said these very things to me about the 1914–18 war, only he had said them then as if they were scorching his heart; now he was saying them as if they gave him as much pleasure as the whisky did.

Did all old men wish to revenge themselves on a world that had not listened to them?

I tried a little raillery. 'Surely, John, as a once dedicated teacher you must admit that humanity is not all stupid and vile. In the innocence of children is there not hope?'

In my face he read Dorcas's rejection of me.

'I can see, Fergus, that you're still the same sanguine simpleton as ever. How you used to infuriate Mary, if you remember. Still, it has had its advantages. You could never have written such good poetry if you had been able to think things out to their nihilistic conclusion. Then you would have had to remain silent. Like me.'

I could have retorted that if ever there had been sanguine simpletons they were himself and Mary, who had believed that poverty and war could be abolished by books and speeches. But I refused to be provoked.

I tried to introduce a less contentious subject.

'I hope you're not depleting your stores of coal and whisky for my sake,' I said.

'My cellars are full, Fergus.'

'I understood coal was rationed and whisky in very short supply.'

'Not if you have plenty of money. You did not imagine, did you, in your simplicity, that the rich, those that have not yet fled to the fleshpots of America, restrict themselves to one egg a week, one bag of coal, and one dram?'

'I suppose not. But I would not call anyone patriotic that used money to get more than his fair share.'

'But, Fergus, in the end, is not every man his own country? Therefore who is most selfish is most patriotic.'

He had always been able to beat me in debate, even when, as now, he had been defending outrageous propositions. I had used to think that the reason was his better education. Now I saw that what made him unbeatable in argument was that he had long ago given up and let go, thus giving himself leisure to develop his pessimism; whereas those of us who still clung by our finger-nails to the debris of hope had neither breath nor thought for anything but holding on.

I tried another subject.

'Do you see Mary often?' I asked.

'Not since she went over to the enemy.'

I was confused. For a few moments I wondered if he meant the Germans. People with principles, I knew, were expert at vaulting from one extreme position to its opposite.

'Didn't you know she's now a member of the Government? Minister of State at the Scottish Office. One of Churchill's crew. She was speaking in the town hall here two or three weeks ago, exhorting us all to pull our weight in defeating the wicked Nazis.'

'They *are* wicked, John.'

All the same, I could not help recalling Sir Jock Dunsyre's remark that he had never known a socialist whom high office and fraternising with the upper-class had not corrupted.

My host rose. 'If you don't mind, Fergus, we'll eat in the kitchen. It's warmer there than in the dining-room, and it saves the trouble of carrying dishes.'

We had as high a tea as I had ever seen: real eggs, bacon, liver, sausages (so good they must have been Drummond's) onions, and mushrooms; bread with plenty of butter; two kinds of jam, strawberry and blackcurrant; pancakes and potato scones; and apple tarts. My host ate, I thought, with more relish and greed than a cynic should. I felt obliged to eat frugally myself, in some kind of rebuke; but to my chagrin he did not seem to notice.

He asked questions about East Gerinish. Expecting, if not praise, at any rate respect for our efforts to be as independent as possible of the world which he despised so much I was hurt when he dismissed our endeavours as stupid and misguided. He had often thought of writing a book, he said, on how sheer lack of intelligence stultified most human activities. My experiences in East Gerinish would provide a very relevant chapter.

This, from a man who'd never had a blister on his hand, was hard to tolerate.

'What I mean is,' he went on, pleased with himself, 'why break your backs struggling with the wilderness when there were fertile acres not far away, those from which your ancestors were driven, and to which therefore you had a right?'

At that point the air-raid sirens went. It was a sound I had not heard before, and it startled me. Calderwood said not to worry, it was no doubt another false alarm. There had been several lately. The authorities were nervous.

He thought I was afraid for myself. It amused him that he, the pacifist, remained cool and cheerful while I, the hero, was fidgety and apprehensive.

We heard whistles being blown on the street.

'Zealous fellows, our air-raid wardens,' remarked Calderwood.

Then we heard, unmistakably, the noise of approaching aeroplanes.

'Heading for Glasgow,' said Calderwood.

Suddenly guns began to fire. Our window rattled. Then came explosions. They sounded near. The window rattled more frenziedly, like an animal in danger. Gun-fire and explosions mingled in a terrifying racket that took me back for a few seconds to the trenches, where, according to Betty, I had been happier than in her bed.

Something metallic crashed on the roof.

'Shrapnel,' I said.

'They've got a battery up in McSherry's Wood,' said Calderwood.

He stood up. 'We'll be more comfortable in the lounge. In any case, that's where the whisky is.'

'But the town's being bombed.'

'It sounds like it.' He tried to hide his glee, by speaking softly.

'Can't we do anything to help?'

'We can keep out of the way.'

'Excuse me.' I hurried through the dimly lit house to the back door. I opened it, cautiously. The sky was red with fire over the town. More bombs exploded.

'The bastards,' I cried.

'Explain,' murmured Calderwood at my back, 'why our airmen are heroes that drop bombs on German towns, and yet German airmen that drop bombs on our town are bastards. And of course vice-versa.'

Again I might have had some little sympathy if he had spoken with his heart breaking.

'Would you say, Fergus, judging from the fact that the fires seem to be in the East End, that they are trying for the shipyards, legitimate targets? In that case ought you not, as a patriotic citizen desiring victory, hope and pray that they miss, even if it means that they hit instead tenements crowded with women and children, some of them known to you?'

I did not want to listen to him. He was not mad; he was too sane, which at such a time was far worse. Nor did I want to stay in his house, though I had none of my own to go to. He was right, though: I could be of help to no one.

We could smell the burning now as well as see it.

Though more shrapnel was falling, into trees this time, I rushed out into the garden, where I stood shaking my fist. I did not know at whom or what. I felt no hatred of the young German airmen doing their loathsome duty, and for the people of Gantock, at that moment suffering terror and pain and death, I felt only pity and love.

FOOTNOTE

My father, Fergus Lamont, died on 10 October 1963, twenty-two years after the events described in the last pages of his book, and within hours of his writing the word love. He was cremated two days later. Mr Hector McSpeug, undertaker, took charge of the arrangements. Using funds left by my father for the purpose, he chose eight old men from the public library clientele and carried them to the crematorium in his two newest Rolls-Royces. They were the only mourners. Afterwards they were taken to a public house in the vicinity, given some beer and whisky to drink, and then delivered to their respective homes.

My father's suitcase, full of manuscripts, came to me through Samuel Lamont. They included that of the present book which would be best described as a self-portrait.

The only liberty I have taken has been to remove from the text the many poems scattered throughout, some in their entirety. Their most effective place is elsewhere.

In that first air-raid on Gantock over one hundred people were killed, and many more injured. Two streets that suffered heavily were Lomond Street and Kirn Street. Among those killed were Mr and Mrs Thomas Pringle. Among those severely injured was Mrs Margaret McHaffie.

T. C-L.